RIVER OF LIFE

RIVER

OF

LIFE

robert f. edwards

Order this book online at www.trafford.com
or email orders@trafford.com

Most Trafford titles are also available at major online book retailers.

Note for Librarians: A cataloguing record for this book is
available from Library and Archives Canada at
www.collections.canada.ca/amicus/index-e.html.

Printed in the United States of America.

ISBN: 978-1-4269-5675-1 (sc)

Trafford rev. 02/14/2011

 www.trafford.com

North America & international
toll-free: 1 888 232 4444 (USA & Canada)
phone: 250 383 6864 ♦ fax: 812 355 4082

TABLE OF CONTENTS

FORETHOUGHT

Every story has a beginning, middle and an end. And this story is no different than any other that has been written before, or in the future. However to enlighten the readers of how it came to pass, I would like to share the beginning of when this story was written. I had just completed the life long dream of reaching the peak of Kilimanjaro, totally exhausted and wanting to remain sharp of mind. I started the descent and thought of this story; to keep my mind from hallucinating in the thin air, at the great altitude I was at. On this particular journey, I experienced not only the fulfillment of climbing Kilimanjaro, but another boyhood dream of crossing the Sahara and experiencing the sea sands of this remarkable landscape, and seeing with my own eyes El' Alamein and the great battlefields of the North African campaign fought by Field Marshal Rommel and General Montgomery. I have always loved history, and when I first entered the city of Alexandria and saw the great port, I stared in wonderment, to think back when Alexander the Great first saw this also, and rewarded it by calling it his own. To travel up the Nile, to Luxor and Aswan, to visit Abu Simbel is to re-live the moments of the 'River of Life' itself. To know that this is one of the cradles of civilization, and one of the great cultures of ancient times, yet in many ways it has not changed from the first days of the pharaohs .

I had been away from my beloved wife for the better part of two months. These are the days where the internet was out of my reach, and there were only a few moments of reassurance we had with each other, when I was able to reach strategic areas of this journey to send a fax. The keepsake that my wife gave me before I left on this long journey was a lock of her hair. More than any other possession I had packed, I treasured this memento, and even more today.

When I was in Poland, I visited Auschwitz. I will never be the same. It is a place that has recorded horror, unthinkable to the average mind. I was mesmerized by a display of what appeared to be a huge pile of steel wool, with a braid of golden hair penetrating from it. When I asked what I was seeing, the guide told me, that when the victims went into the gas chambers, their hair turned to that color of steel wool. These were the remnants from the shaved heads, of thousands that perished in the gas chambers. The unusual golden braid of hair played on my imagination.

Another inspiration for this story came from a woman I met in Krakow and the events that happened to her family under the occupation of Nazi Germany during the Second World War. I asked her if I was ever going to write a story, could I share her experiences, and she kindly granted me this request.

It is my wish to acknowledge the many souls that perished in the holocaust. The Polish intellectuals, teachers, doctors, aristocrats, the very heart of the culture of Poland. To the priests, the nuns and those of strong Catholic belief that were systematically taken to this death camp and annihilated. To the peasant that got in the way or the Russian soldier on the Eastern front.

My life has changed over the years it has taken me to write this story. Yet today, as I did in the days crossing the great Sahara and spending my time in Egypt, I wear the galabya, and enjoy the feel of freedom and movement in this garment of the true Egyptian.

I hope, in some small way, that this reflection of some of my experiences, my love of Egypt and its culture, and the history that I have witnessed in this world will provide a measure of enjoyment in the readers' mind.

Artist Paints From Bulletin Picture

—By Bulletin Staff Cameraman.

When Phyllis Humphries, of 6 Rosslyn Court, young Edmonton artist and singer of more than usual ability, saw a recent war picture in The Bulletin titled "Man Made Misery," it made such an impression that she immediately got out her brushes and palette, and using The Bulletin picture as a model, painted a touching picture of the Polish woman who, standing in the ruins of her bomb-demolished home, with all the members of her family killed by the air raid, sought solace in prayer. The picture, an outstanding example of the painter's art, is today on exhibition in a Hudson's Bay Company window where it is drawing considerable attention. Miss Humphries, who is the daughter of Mr. and Mrs. H. Humphries, is a keen artist when she can spare the time from her duties as cashier at the Dreamland theatre. She studies with Mrs. Percy Mortimer, and Major Norbury, well-known art critic, considers her a "born artist." At the Edmonton Exhibition, this year she took three specials, two firsts, and a third prize, and her work in general was highly commended. Miss Humphries is also a talented singer who has been heard in Edmonton concerts on many occasions. But her first love is painting, and her work is already receiving the recognition of the experts.

TRIBUTE

This is a special tribute to a remarkable person, Phyllis Verdine Humphries. Born January 5, 1908, and deceased December 13, 1996.This is a tribute to her accomplishments, in a period that this book was dedicated to. An extraordinary woman, she was born to English parents, Ada Alberta James and Harold Humphries. They emigrated from England and settled in the general vicinity of Edmonton, Alberta. Her parents were in every sense of the word, 'homesteaders' that challenged the hurdles of owning land in part of the British Commonwealth, at that time. After her primary years, her mother and herself spent a greater part of her teenage years and early twenties in Edmonton, Alberta.

At this time, the development of her amazing talents was undertaken. She was not only an accomplished pianist, but she could play any string instrument, and also the five-tier pipe organ. Along with her musical talents, she was blessed with a "god-given voice", according to her mentor, Lawrence Tibbet, who at that time was the sensation at Carnegie Hall as a baritone. He commented to this gifted opera singer, that with her "god-given voice", she could join him in Carnegie Hall singing operas.

However, there is more, and that is where this book enters into the tribute bestowed upon this outstanding woman. And that was her further artistic abilities. She was able to paint in three mediums, oil, watercolor and pastel. She not only exceeded the expectations of her teachers and fellow art students, but when her works where entered into exhibits in Edmonton, they received nothing less than First Class honors.

Now brings this notable woman's life into focus and its relationship to this book. Though she never traveled to these places, and all her paintings were inspired by postcards, or small black and white photographs, her works clearly reflected life, as depicted in this story. This first illustration by Phyllis Verdine Humphries was completed in 1939. This work was based on a photograph, taken by a journalist of a peasant woman in Poland after her village, her home; her life had been destroyed by the invasion of Nazi Germany. Phyllis Verdine Humphries rose to the moment with passion and painted this image from a newspaper clipping. When she was encouraged to make this work known, immediately The Edmonton Journal captured a photo of her holding the painting and the information regarding her effort on the front page of the newspaper. It went one step further, and the painting then sat on display in the most prominent window of the Hudson Bay Company window, on Jasper Avenue in Edmonton, for over a week, so the residents of that city could see this accomplishment of a young artist. This painting reflects the horror of what a civilian experiences in a war.

The other paintings were on a subject that was very dear to Phyllis Verdine Humphries's heart, and that was Egypt. She had a great admiration and respect for the culture of Egypt, and its past. Not only did she have a great passion for Egypt, but she was haunted by a nightmare that reoccurred through most of her life. It was always the same, starting with King Farouk and their tour through the pyramids, ending with a chase by a mummy, before she woke in terror.

Much of her artwork depicts this area of the world, and it goes without saying that the pictures speak for themselves. However, for the reader to fully appreciate the depth in her achievements, I need to elaborate on the painting known to her, and anyone that asked, as ' The Holy Carpet'. So the story goes that this young artist was inspired by a small faded print of this pilgrimage. This event took place every 10 years, and the caravan moved endlessly through the wilderness of the Great Sea Sands to complete the trek to its destination, and pay homage to what is being carried on the back of the camel. Many years later, Phyllis Verdine Humphries met a man that had accompanied such a caravan. He was amazed and speechless that this artist had captured the colors of the great Sahara, and the sands of the endless desert that it commands.

By the beginning of World War II, Phyllis Verdine Humphries had married a young soldier, only to be left as a war widow by 1944 with two young children, a son and a daughter. In the years that followed, the family lived on a small War Widow's pension. This was subsidized by earnings made with her talent as a music teacher, instructing students both from her home and at the Royal Conservatory of Music in Calgary, Alberta. Many years later, once the children had grown, the family moved to Vancouver, British Columbia. She retired from her teaching and enjoyed her remaining years in the company of her children and grandchildren. Just shy of her 90th year, she left this world, a much better place than when she had entered. This concludes my tribute to this remarkable person, Phyllis Verdine Humphries, my mother.

Poem to Ra

Let Man believe in Ra,
For without his return

Each day to the skies,
Life would be in darkness

And all things of this earth
Would be no more.

Ra is the light of the world,
He is the life that we all share

For we are nothing without
The power of Ra .

Let each day remind us
Who we are, and who Ra is.

We are the children of Ra
Let us worship Ra

From the day we are born
To the last breathe that we take.

April 26/2006

List of Illustrations

CHAPTER 1

 The old man put on his shawl and looked around the room before he headed to the door, which would lead him down the narrow stairs to the street. It was his room, it held his things, and oh yes, it held many of the memories of his past. The past, yes the past that was what he had left behind, just the past, but what a life it had been. He was talking or thinking to himself again. No, he wasn't dead yet. The door was in front of him now and his thin right hand reached for the handle. Once the door gave way to his wishes, he went through, like so many times before. The long stone stairway which was older than time, stretched before him. As he walked down, the narrow walls on each side gave him support and reminded him of so long ago. The light ahead on the street was waiting for him. It was late afternoon and the sun was giving up its place in the sky.

The old man now entered the street he knew so well from his boyhood years. Through- out his life, this street had been with him at one time or another. His mind moved back again to that one part of his life where he lived now and stopped living. She had seen this street with him. He moved out into the movement of traffic. It was always the same, from little children playing to trucks bringing in goods to sell. The small shops that lined the street were reopening for the afternoon and evening trade. The people moved with or against the buses and cars, both seem to know which way to move to give quarter to the other, with the help of a horn now and then. The shops were the same, as when he was a boy, small one-owner shops, where each man knew the other. Better than most husbands and wives, thought the old man, as he looked around before moving out into the main stream of things.

robert f. edwards

He moved out of the way of the horse drawn carriage that was passing, a donkey with a man of his age, going the same way. Looking up and around for his next move, his eyes saw what had always made him feel at home. It was the people that had lived there for thousands of years, from one life to the next, from childhood to his age and then some. Doing the same things as their father and his father before him, it was timeless and at this moment he was a part of it. The street was lined with shops, with everything from fresh vegetables to hand made jewelry. The repair shop for bicycles and the meat that had been killed that day for market. So it went, on and on, shop after shop, each looking after another family.

Always the world was changing and Egypt was not only a part of it but in the middle of a foreign war. The Europeans had started another war but this time it was moving around the world. So, like other places, the money-hungry people from the north had moved death and destruction to the shores of Egypt. This was in part due to the shipping lanes from the Mediterranean and the Red Sea and the Suez Canal. Though, the old man thought, the British had never promoted the canal and more over, didn't take part in the building. It was their bankers and financial people that had bought up the shares in the canal when Egypt couldn't keep up it payments. He saw the irony, for people that didn't want any part of opening up the waterways, despite thousands of years the leaders of this part of the world had wanted it; now the British owned the controlling interest in the canal.

By the time the next person entered into his family, the British had set up a military base in Cairo and along the canal. It was said to protect their interests, but to many of the Egyptians, it was just another foreign army on Egyptian land. The father of his family's new member was one of their rank. This was why this new son of the family was born in the old city of Luxor, far away from the danger of the great cities of Cairo and Alexandria. Though his father was there for the birth, his father had to return to where the power and changes were happening. This great capital of once what was

River of Life

the known world, Cairo, and now one of the great cities of the world.

Before the father was to leave, this first son of his must be given a name, but what was the name to be? The name for this person that some day would be the head of the family and all it stood for. A name to indicate that today was going to be better that the past. The same hope that the small shopkeepers always held, waiting and hoping for the next item to be sold. The endless people looking, shopping for what they needed, or were willing to give up their money for, in exchange. The locals bought food and clothing, but it was the tourists that were changing this old city forever. They were now everywhere, day and night, all year around, and they were now the live blood that kept the small shopkeepers hoping, dreaming of tomorrow and the day beyond.

The old man had now reached one of the large circles, designed for traffic to move from one direction to another without holding up anything that was in motion. He looked around in all directions before his next move. His eyes saw the line-up of horses and carriages waiting for a fare. The tourist's fare was what every driver hoped for, and then the basheis in addition, if he had pleased them. These were long hours for the driver, which would start in the early part of the morning. He would have his horses here at 4:00 a.m., even before first prayer, making their way to be first in line. Long after the darkness of night had closed up the streets to the locals, these men would wait hoping and bartering with tourists for that last ride, before returning home with their share of the days take. Oh yes, and for most of them the dream of owning the horse and carriage some day or maybe his son, the dream of tomorrow.

The old man was now across the circle and looked back at what he had done once, so many times before, when his eyes saw some thing that made him stare. He was looking at a local coffee shop, where the men were drinking coffee or tea, while many of them were enjoying the water pipe. Yes, life was good, but these men were not, for it was Ramadan and the

3

sun had not set. He looked away, as with other good Muslims, his fast had not yet past until after sunset and prayers. Moving onward, one of the many mosques came into his view. He passed people coming through the open doors; the light spilling over was greater that what the sun was leaving behind. Was this what it would be like, when he would take that final journey over to the other side, going into the light, the great light of Allah.

He removed his sandals and went in for prayer. He was early tonight, but he wished to see the sun set on the Nile. After his prayer to Allah, he got up and continued on his way. The night was giving back the heat of the day, as the sun was saying its last farewell to this day he had shared with all living things. He walked ever closer to his and all Egyptian's beloved Nile. He eventually came to the main street that ran parallel to the river of life, the river of peace, the river of food, the river of the beginning. He watched as the waters flowed in the river, this great part of his life. As always, he was seeing it for the first time. Since he could remember, his eyes would fill with tears as his heart remembered what the Nile had given him, and what he had now, and forever more had lost. His one true love, then, now, and always. He moved along the main street on the Nile past the great Temples of Karnak. These overwhelming monuments of Paranoiac legacy, the Egyptian past, his people. He stood and looked onto the temples and his mind's eye moved from one row of pillars to the other, reading the once colorful cartouches. Oh yes, it was his past, like each and every Egyptian before him, now and in the future, this would always be the beginning of the human race and his race. These Temples and all the others throughout Egypt were the record of his people and what they had given and done for the human race. This was why thousands of years later, and tens of thousands of kilometers away, people came from all around the world to look at what nature had left of this great time in the history of man.

Once more, like so many times before, he looked on, but it was the feeling in his soul that told him what had been re-

River of Life

corded and why. With one last look, he forced his head away, so his eyes would move from their trance. At last his feet moved again, and were on their way to his goal, to see the sun set. He must push on, with all his mind and heart, if he was to get there before night and the darkness ruled again. The next place to stop him was the Old Winter Palace. It had changed his life so long ago, first a joy when one is full of happiness, only to be followed by disbelief and then hopelessness. It was more than a hotel for the tourists back then, and he would always think of it as one of his temples. He did not look for the signs of the past, like he did at the great Temple of Karnak. The people dressed differently in this grand hotel, but they were of the same breed, just rich and foreign. He turned his eyes away as they filled with tears.

The sun was nearing its end as he moved closer to his destination. The wide stairs brought him down closer to the water's edge and lead him through to the open-air restaurant. He was here at last, and looked around for a table that was away from the others. He spotted one that was just perfect, outside, close to the water, and like so long ago by itself. He pulled out the chair facing the water, and sat down. The long wait for this moment had come. Before too long, the cannon sounded the end to fasting for one more day. The sun had set and all that remained was the beautiful color it was leaving. His eyes never left the West Bank as the waiter asked for his order. In a slow voice, just above a whisper, he said a water pipe with apple tobacco, and mint tea. The waiter stood there for a moment until he realized this was the entire order.

The old man's thoughts returned to his journey from home. For a moment, he reflected on the people he had seen along the way, and the ones who had seen him. He had walked among them as if he hadn't been part of their lives. The Egyptians hadn't noticed him, even though he had put on his galabya, which was of the finest Egyptian cotton. His dark brown robe, with its high collar signified wealth, not the open neck with strips that the working class wore. The two pockets were well hidden on the sides, only he known where to touch.

robert f. edwards

As an added precaution, they slanted backwards, a challenge for the pick- pocket, if he was able to get that far. This was where the old man kept his most valuable possession, which he had with him at all times. It was part of his life, a part of his soul, and had been since his early twenties. Now as always, he could feel it in his pocket. This greatest of all gifts, he wore each day. His beloved had given the watch to him on his twentieth birthday. The pure silver casing held a Swiss movement timepiece. The face of the watch was decorated with artistic work from Morocco. The hieroglyphics relayed events before his birth and included his name and his family tree. Oh yes, the old man thought, the past is all he has now, the past and the moment that had changed his life forever.

The weight of the pocket reminded him of the watch again. It had a double cover that held what was so dear to his heart and soul. Even now, after all these years, just the thought of it made his eyes fill, and his heart grow weak. The very knowledge of that small but priceless compartment, gave him such joy and sadness all at the same time. Over the years he had wondered how one person could stand such moments in their life. Tonight was no different than any other time before, the days, the nights, the months, and oh yes, the long years, and so many of them.

Just then the waiter returned with the water pipe and mint tea. The old man was still looking out to the West Bank, but his mind thanked the waiter silently, for bringing him back to the moment. He nodded to the waiter that all was right and nothing more was needed .The coals were burning and the apple tobacco was lit as he held off pouring the tea. It was not Egyptian tea, but Moroccan, and needed to sit in the hot water with the sugar. Both the mint and the sugar had to steep together to get the true flavor. As the tea worked its magic under the cover of the pot, the old man picked up the pipe and took a long breath from it. The water jumped to attention and now mixed with air bubbles, happy in its bottle, eventually to let the sweet smoke enter the old man's mouth.

River of Life

He drew deep into his lungs the mild flavor of the sweet smoke.

It was not often that he smoked the water pipe, but tonight was one of those times. It was a night to remember the past, and his life before he met her, and his life afterward. Oh, how long it had been afterward, more than a dozen lifetimes. The smoke drifted around him as he exhaled. It took him back to the first time he smoked the water pipe in her present. She had waited for a moment when no one was watching and asked if she could try .He was so Egyptian and she was so foreign. At first he thought he heard her wrong and had asked her to repeat it. Yes, she had asked if she could try smoking the water pipe. She was so very different than any woman he had ever met. In his country, no women would consider smoking the water pipe, especially not by asking a man to show her.

But that was her, and so like a boy caught doing something he shouldn't, and a father being asked to explain something he was embarrassed to, he reluctantly agreed to show her. He had done it slowly, and let the little bubbles start slowly, and when the bottle filled with sweet smoke, he handed the pipe to her. She struggled so hard to bring the sweet apple smoke down in her lungs and to share what he was enjoying. It was not to be, for her lungs were not used to this way of smoking. She was not only foreign; she was also the new woman of the century. They tried things, to say the least. She smoked those little cigars that foreign women did, believing them more equal with men and independent.

Everything was so new and different when he was around her. Now for just a few moments, they were alone. She tried again, and again, and wouldn't give up; she just wasn't that kind of person. Her face was red for more reasons that one. He took the pipe from her and again he mastered the little bottle to fill with sweet smoke, and run the over flow through his nose. She looked at him and said, "I want to taste it." Without thinking, he leaned over towards her, and as he did, she opened her mouth. Before he knew what was happening, the smoke came out of his mouth and into hers. It was as if the smoke was sharing their bodies. He pulled back just before their lips touched, but the smoke continued on. It had done what they had not, to touch each other's bodies. The smoke entered her lungs, and as she let go of it, her voice returned. She smiled and looked into his eyes, and said "it makes me a little dizzy". He was ashamed of his thoughts, jealous of the smoke that had been inside him, and then her.

He stared ahead, unseeing, as he was back in that moment. The old man pulled hard on the pipe and his mind slowly turned back to the present, for the love of Allah, please come back to the present, the voice inside him cried out. As a distant traveler returning, he gradually became aware of the sound of his own heart beating. He was once more looking at the West Bank, with his eyes in the present. Ah, to look at the Nile now, the sun was giving off its last light of the day. The long rays of color lying on the water, to form dark and light blues. These were mixed with red and yellows lines, rippling from the mighty current. It was always here, beside the small homes that claimed their right to live on this river of all rivers.

As his eyes still moved in the same direction, he saw the neon lights of the restaurant and a few other buildings that claimed to be a village. This was where tourists should be, to enjoy the true feeling of the area. The great works of the tombs of the Pharaoh were just ahead. The one-man boats that moved people back and forth were on both sides, waiting and hoping for a fare. The old man looked down for the first time at the teapot before him. With both hands he moved to the glass and the teapot. One hand lifted the pot and the other held the glass a ritual he had done many times. His eyes glanced away to the south, to the Valley of the Kings. He then returned to his tea, the brewing had started. First it was pouring the mint tea into the glass, then the tea from the glass back into the pot. This had to be done three times to mix the mint and the sugar together in the hottest of water. After the old man had completed this, he then poured the tea into the glass for the fourth time. His eyes looked at the glass and yes

River of Life

"The great works of the tombs of the Pharaoh were just ahead."

Original photograph   Robert F. Edwards
Egypt November, 1999

9

robert f. edwards

it was ready. He saw the 'Turks head' a term describing the one to two centimeters of foam formed at the top of the glass. The old man looked once more at the glass, holding it with two fingers around the top of the glass where the foam was. He lifted the glass to his lips. The hot sweet mint did not disappoint him. It was all he had wanted to break the fast. As the hot sweetness moved in his mouth and ever downward, his whole body took on the warmth and strength.

He put the glass back on the table and his eyes moved once more back to the hill across the water. By now darkness had moved well into place and the night sky was just a lighter shade of darkness than the hills. It appeared as though a painter had given an extra coat of black to the hills. Still the old man looked as if there were a spot on this canvas of nature with a hole or mark in it. To him it was there, and all his life he had gone there to be alone. There was only one person that had seen it after he found it, and oh, no, he was going back again to the time when his life had meaning and the world belonged to the future. As he let the pipe fill his lungs, his mind was filled with the past, his past. He would not fight it this time, but remember the time before and what had happened after the great moment in his life.

River of Life

CHAPTER 2

His time to come into this world had been 1914, to an Egyptian family in Luxor. He was the firstborn of their children. The man and his wife were from a rich and noble family. This was one of their many residences, for none could be called home. All were large and even when they were not there, the houses ruled with out them, as the servants not only cared for, and did their duties, but also had rooms of their own. A few valued servants had small apartments inside some of the houses, or separate dwellings on the grounds. So it was, families that had lived together under one ruling family for years, maybe hundreds of years. It was to be the house in Luxor that was the place the newest member would be born. The family went back in the history of Egypt itself to the time of the pharaohs. From that time so far in the past, to the moment this new gift had come into the family.

Alone, the father went into the great study and sat behind his large desk. The name he chose was important, for this future ruler of his wealth would use from this day forth. So, the father sat and contemplated the room around him. The first thing that came into view were the two doors across the room. They were large and made from the great woods of Africa. The carving was done in the days of the Mameluke dynasty, a time when the slave-soldiers reigned under the power of Salah ad-Din. They looked small in the wall, which swept from floor to ceiling at just under 8 meters. Though the room was large by any standards, it felt small and intimate with the multitude of objects accumulated over the years. This room was a museum for all the men that had ruled in this family. This was the seat of power. Now it was his turn, and today he was to pick a name for the one that would also sit here in this room and rule the family.

robert f. edwards

As he sat there, his mind thought of how very old this family, his family really was, and of those that had come before him. There were no pictures of these men of old, the leaders of his family. Eventually, his eyes came to the old papyrus works, and further to the left the parchment; his family history of the rulers of this house and their involvement with the kings and rulers of their times. He closed his eyes and put his head into his hands and rested his elbows on the top of the desk. As his eyes adjusted to the new darkness, his inner eyes opened up to the past. The old ones would tell him the name of their new member, his son.

Time moved around the room, but the man was not part of his surroundings. He was now in the past, looking for the name of the future. Then, from out of the darkness in his mind, the name came to him. It was Horus and Salah. So, now he knew what his first son's name was to be: Horus-Salah. A radiant glow filled his heart, and for the first time since he had entered this room, a smile came across his face. Yes, this was it. It represented all the greatness of the past and of what Egypt stood for. Without looking around, he pushed the chair back, and stood up. He walked through the great door in front of him.

He must tell his son of his name. As he moved through the large hall to see his wife and first born, all he could think of was the name. He must tell his son first before he said a word to anyone else. He opened the door to his wife's bedroom and saw her resting. He quietly moved to the small bundle of cloth beside her. The servant said nothing, and looked down at the floor as soon as he had entered. His wife had her eyes closed and his son was also sleeping. He had been only hours into this new world and new life. The father looked down once more, and with unsure hands, moved towards this small little person, his son, his first-born. With both hands, he picked up his son for the first time. The baby's eyes opened, though still saw only darkness. It was good enough for the father, and he brought this little bundle up to face level, looked into the small red face, and said in a low voice," I want you to be the

12

River of Life

first person to hear your name." With that, the father whispered in the baby's tiny ear, 'Horus-Salah'.

It was done. The person who would wear this name had heard it first from the man who had give it to him and the world. Just then his wife looked up, saw the two men in her life together, and closed her eyes again. All was well in this family tonight. The man placed the little bundle back beside the woman that had only hours before had given Horus-Salah his entrance into this world. The man looked down at both of them once more and then left the room.

Within days, this father of Horus-Salah would be taking his leave of this house and returning to the one in Cairo. This was one of the seats of power that his family owned. He began the trip back to Cairo without delay, and within days, his personal servant and he were saying their good-byes to one and all. They made their farewells to the newest member of the family and added wishes of good will. The leader of this family made all haste back to Cairo, the seat of power for his family and Egypt.

Egypt was fighting for its freedom from a war of debt. The country was broke, trying to pay its share for the Suez Canal. This massive undertaking had left a burden too great to bear for his country alone. Great Britain stepped in, and now owned the larger share of the canal. She was demanding to put her people and army on Egypt's soil to protect her interests. Egypt was at war; a war of debt, and Britain was collecting. This was under the pretext that she was at war with Germany, and must keep the Suez Canal open, and out of the Germany's hands. So, the ruler of this family needed to get to Cairo to assist his country to remain in good standing with the rest of the world.

For Horus-Salah, and the family in Luxor, things continued much the same from one day to the next. As one day followed the next, the weeks quickly added up into months. The baby was fast growing into a little boy. The household watched in marvel as each day he changed. It came in small steps, each one as important as the other. One was saying his

robert f. edwards

first word, next was his first steps, and so it went. In these first months, his father came and went without knowing him much. The first year had come, and now as going. Time had a way of moving all that was in it path.

It was 1915 and the great wars were still going on. The problems of the world weighed heavy. Some were saying it could be the end of the world, and for all the people dying, it was. For the family in Luxor, the world revolved around little Horus-Salah. He was a happy little person, and made those around him the same. One year leaves and a new one enters. The years, both inside this haven, and out, didn't change much. Before one could tell themselves, let alone someone else, it was 1918 and Horus-Salah was four years old.

The war had just ended and was known as the World War. This was a year for Horus-Salah that had started just the same as all the others in his short live, but was not to end the same. Late in the year his father returned to Luxor, like he had done throughout Horus-Salah's life. It was always a happy time for Horus-Salah and his mother. As a matter of fact, it was a happy time for everyone in the household. This time it was different, for after a few days, the word came down to Horus-Salah that he and his mother were moving to Cairo with his father. Hearing this from the grapevine, Horus-Salah asked his mother if this was true. The answer was yes. They were moving to another one of their homes, the one in Cairo. At first he couldn't believe what he was hearing, and then 'why', was the next unanswered question. Oh yes, his mother gave him one answer, and his father another, and so it went. Each person had a new answer to the question. But to him, no one told him why.

So, like many times before, he went for a walk in the hills. It was more like a run at first, then a walk, and again more running. He always ran towards the valley of the tombs, and this time it was no different. But yes, it was different, for he now had gone farther than ever before. No, he wasn't lost, so he told himself, but he was a far way from home. Then for the first time he took a good look around him. He was a long way

14

River of Life

up the hill, over looking the great temple. He just stood there for the longest time, looking down. It was so far down; it made his small legs feel weak in the knees. That was when he sat down on the hill. Yes, this did make things look better for him. Now what to do was the new question in his small mind. As his breathing became normal, he sat up straight, and looked completely around him. There was a hole just below him. It may be a small cave, or something like it. He looked at it for the longest time, just thinking, what it was and what might be inside, if anything. Like all boys coming up five, going on fifteen, he would have to go down and see for himself. With all that running out of the way, and the reasons for it behind him, now all he could think of was the hole below.

Down he went, slowly, for just below him the cliffs dropped off to the valley below. As he reached his goal, the opening was much larger than it had appeared from above. Now that he was in front of it, the entrance was taller than he was, maybe four to six meters high. The big question in his mind was how far in did it go? This question was not to be answered today, or for a long time afterwards. He just kept looking into the cave. Then, into his mind came another idea, it could be a tomb. Yes, now he had made up his mind for today, it would be a tomb. This was not that farfetched an idea, as it was on the West Bank and just above the Valley of the Kings. Many people were buried here, as far back to when the Pharaohs were building their great tombs below.

As he turned to look out, the sun was still moving in an upward movement to the sky. However, the sun would never get the right angle to light more than a few meters into the cave. So this was all he could see and his attention moved to the opening. The walls were smooth, and had been made by tools. The opening was at a small angle, so it would be very difficult to see from above and below. Horus-Salah sat inside the dirt opening, and for the first time looked out towards the hills beyond. The Nile was no more than a ribbon of blue between the small green lines on each side of it. Then, the endless sand that covered most of Egypt and its neighbors. As he

15

sat and looked from one side to the other, his eyes came to a stop. For almost directly across from this opening was the city of Luxor. He kept looking to see if there was any thing he could recognize.

As time moved, he didn't, for it was like being on top of the world and looking down on the city he was forced to leave. This was the only place he had ever been, and now it was going to be taken, no, he was going to been taken away from it. The tears came to his eyes, and then followed each other down his face. One after another until the wetness was felt on the dry earth below his feet. He had lost track of time, his eyes were red, and the little sobbing that was deep inside kept coming out. He eventually cried himself out, and could look again without tears. It was still there, Luxor, the city he was born in, the city of great Pharaohs and their Queens that had reigned the people of Egypt.

He was Egyptian, and he was part of the past, just like he would be part of the future. So, from that moment on, this would be his place. He had a right, for it was he that had found this place, this cave, this tomb. Then, it came to him, like a voice inside the tomb, or inside his body. The rulers of long ago had started their tombs when they first came to power, and kept building the tomb until the end of their reign. So be it. This was going to be his tomb, and he alone would build it, a step at a time, from this day on, until his time was finished. After all that had happened today, he looked around one last time, and for the first time since he had heard the news of moving to Cairo, he felt better.

With that, he got up and looked down, boy, was it a long way to the bottom. Then he saw the small path that he had used to catch his breath not so many hours ago. This was the way down, so he set off to retrace his steps. Once back in the house, his nanny asked where he had been, admonishing him for being away so long. For the next week there was great activity in the house. Everyone packing by day and farewell parties at night. Each night, as Horus-Salah lay in bed, he would

River of Life

think of his secret place, his new home, which would be never a house, but a home for all times.

The day quickly came for the family to leave for Cairo. The servants that were staying behind, which were most of them, were crying. So were the ones leaving. Young Horus-Salah could understand all this crying, for he too had cried, until there was nothing left to make tears. That was how much he had cried, thinking of leaving here. His father and his servant had already left. His mother's servant and the others were just about to start. So with his hand in the tutor's hand, and his nanny just behind, they to left for Cairo.

The journey held nothing for him. It was one more kilometer away from his home, and each day was going in the wrong direction. So it went, day after day until they arrived in Cairo. Compared to Luxor, Cairo was endless, and maybe it was, to those that never left. The house was also so much bigger than the one he had lived in all his life. It was all so different. The living room and dining room was for lots of people, and later he would know why. There were so many servants, that at first he thought maybe every servant had one servant also. Oh yes, it was different, and nothing was the same as the home he knew.

The days moved into a routine, and soon he fell in with this new way of life. His father was one of the big differences in his life, for now he saw him at least once a day and sometimes a lot more. This was one of the good things that was happening. The guests and parties kept coming and going. To his young mind, it was more like a hotel, than a house where a family lived. The days moved on, with the months, and then the years came and went. There were changes, the biggest of them all happened just after the family arrived in Cairo. His mother had taken him into her study and told Horus-Salah that he was going to have a brother or sister. It would be nice to have one or the other, but to his knowledge, he didn't have anything to do with it. He hadn't even thought about having one or the other. However, he was told it was going to happen, and yes, it did.

robert f. edwards

Less than a year later, his family had their first girl and he had his first sister. His mother was very happy and his father was also proud. Her name was Mabia. Each year, his mother and little sister, and of course himself, made their way back to Luxor to visit and rest from the hectic schedule in Cairo. His father continued to come and go just like the old days. It was a bit of heaven to Horus-Salah and he said nothing about the visits he made alone to his secret place high up in the hills. Oh yes, the cave, the tomb, his real home. He was no longer the little boy who had first found it. For now it was 1922, and he was 8 years old. Almost a man, well, at least he was going in that direction, he knew this and others told him so. In the last years, whenever he came to his cave, it felt like home of the present, and the future.

Today, he noticed a group of people below him, cleaning up one of the tombs, or so he thought. He would discover later that the area was being worked on by a man named Howard Carter, an archaeologist. This man and his group were excavating one of the tombs in the Valley of the King. The tomb of Tutankhamun, the boy King, had been discovered intact after all these years. All of Luxor, no, all of Egypt, and much of the world had this discovery on their minds, and there was talk everywhere. His father made his was back to Luxor as soon as the word reached Cairo. Lord Carnarvon was on route also, to join his daughter and Howard Carter for the opening of the tomb.

Father was at home, or at least in Luxor, and the house was full of important people. To Horus-Salah, it just meant that the household from Cairo was moving into Luxor, just on a smaller base. Luxor itself felt the world moving in from all parts. During the next months, more and more burial treasure was seen by the eyes of the world, for the first time in centuries. His Luxor was once again a center of world attention. To Horus-Salah, the discovery held more significance than mere artifacts. Horus-Salah remembered the day that he had found his cave and claimed it for his tomb. This young king must have started his tomb at about the same age as Horus-

18

River of Life

Salah. Tutankhamun was a young man, or just a teenage, the reports were saying.

So Horus-Salah spent more and more time in his secret place, just above all the movement of the young king's tomb. It was one of the best years of his life; no, it was the best year by far. As the workers moved carrying one load of dirt to another, so the world moved its attention to this great find. Horus-Salah's father decided to move his family back to Luxor. When Horus-Salah heard this news, his heart stopped beating for a moment, he was so very happy. Things would be never the same, but at least he was back in the place he loved and belonged. The days moved with his heart, and both were in tempo with each other. The way of live for him had improved, and so did his studies. He could read and write in four languages. Speaking proved to be more difficult. The rest of the subjects he fared well in. Another birthday came and went. There were always lots happening around the city, and the Valley of the Kings, especially with all the people coming and going in his own house.

The years followed from one to another much the same, but the date on the calendar kept changing. This, and his height, made Horus-Salah realize that he and all living things were getting older. Each week he would spend time at his secret place. From listening to the visitors to his house, he was learning what to do when discovering a tomb and this encouraged him to go deeper in his cave. Moving the dirt and rocks quietly, he slowly inched further back. With each year he came closer to the past, just like below.

One day he was filling his excavating buckets as he had always done, and then it happened. The small rock he removed opened up into a room. If only I had more light, yes, more light, he thought to himself. The answer was to bring more candles next time. It was always next time, he thought, as once more he returned home. It was a big day in his life, but more was to come, oh yes, a lot more was to come this day.

robert f. edwards

CHAPTER 3

The old man pulled himself up from the chair and came back to the present. It was along way back as he looked out in front of him. The night was in full progress and the Nile was only visible from the moon's dancing reflections skipping across. He looked skyward, mesmerized by the sparkling stars set in their jet-black pool. He turned his head over his shoulder and then he saw it. The true Arabic moon. There it was, that quarter-slice looking down at the world that he knew, and said 'this is our place and I am part of it'. The patient waiter stood there motionless, as the old man gazed up at the moon. After an eternity, the old man glanced back and finally their eyes met. The old man gestured to the waiter, to take him to his table. Once again, the waiter stood patiently waiting for his order. The old man pointed to the teapot and said, in a low voice,' more tea', and with that, the waiter left with the pot.

The old man's eyes returned to the hills beyond, looking for just one spot. His eyes peered through the darkness, scanning for that deeper shadow. The waiter promptly returned with a teapot in hand. The old man eyes never left the other bank, and with one hand motioned for the pot to stay and the waiter to leave. A lengthy time past before the old man's eyes returned to the table. He commenced his ritual, both hands moving the tea back and forth to develop the Turk's head in the glass. Ah just right, his mind told him, as he lifted the glass to his lips. Yes, the tea was perfect. He didn't care what time it was. Time for him was man-made, and tonight, he wanted to be with his thoughts and his god, Allah. Again, his eyes when back to that west bank, the valley of the dead and looked for that spot. He knew where the spot was only to well, even if his eyes couldn't see it. It had been his place most of his life. This was his true home, then and now.

20

River of Life

He looked hard into the night and the darkness, but it was not holding him, he was going back to another time. His mind was there, and now his middle eye had returned; he was back as the young man.

Horus-Salah moved along the hill that would lead him to his little tomb, but today he had remembered to bring more candles. He arrived at the entrance to the tomb, oh yes; it was a tomb, not just a cave. He just knew it had to be a tomb. Back in the area where the little hole was, he placed the candle. By moving still more dirt and rocks, it was finally large enough to put his arm and head in. He cautiously put the candle in first with his hand, and then peered in. It was a small area, it wasn't a room. But was it a tomb, or was it a cave? His eyes searched, penetrating the darkness, just to see anything. The walls were smooth, and man-made. Oh Allah, it was tombs, oh yes, what had he found! His eyes then saw it, the coffin, and the burial mound. But it was too small for a person's body. Not even a baby's body, for theirs were put in jars. This was a coffin and there was something in it. He was only a teenager, and this was his only excavation, but he knew this tomb had not been opened for a long time. He could very well be the first to do so. As he pulled his head back from the small opening, and his hand followed, his mind was racing. What to do now? Tell the world, or keep this holy place and its owner to himself?

It was time to get back home. He reluctantly left his great find and returned to the civilization of his daily life. As he approached the house, he noticed the yard was full of wagons and men. Horus-Salah entered his yard, and asked what was happening. The answer was 'They are coming'. This left him no wiser than before he had asked the question. Moving into the house, he searched out his nanny, she would know. After he located her, he was right; she did know all that was going on in this house.

robert f. edwards

The Count and his wife were coming to stay with them. But who was the Count, and why were they staying with them, to say nothing about how many people were they bringing with them. His nanny told him they had a daughter about his age, and she would have her own nanny and tutor, and personal servant. The next question that came out of him was 'How important were these people?' Again the nanny had the answer. The Count was none other than Count Van Shoaerman from Poland and his wife, descendants of the royal family of that land.

Of course, he had to know 'Why are they coming?' They are leading up a group of archaeologists for Poland's interest in the Tutankhamun tomb. In his mind came the thought, 'and who's other tombs would there be?' but that was where that question ended. One whole wing of the house was being turned over for their stay. It was to look more European that Eastern to make their stay feel more like at home. His father was always looking at the wishes of the government but this time he was going to the limit. As the household got most of the jobs done in the weeks ahead, soon came the word that they were two to three days away.

The days moved even faster that before. The day came when the first rider arrived to say that they would be at the house before dark. The last finishing touches were done, and the family was sitting around as if nothing was going on, now or before. 'They have arrived' came the announcement from the servants to the family. His father went to greet them at the door, and wish the Count and Countess well, and also greeted their daughter, Anastasia. After the welcoming at the entrance, his father had the servants show them to the wing they would be staying in.

More and more wagons came, and carriages of servants. Now Horus- Salah understood why these people needed a whole wing of the house for themselves. The last count from the servant's report was twenty-two or twenty-four. It was good for all that darkness had just fallen. The servants were putting the last things on the dining room table for the meal

River of Life

that was to follow. Dinner was to be at eight, and it would be just the families and their personal servants. The guests were dressed in formal European eveningwear for dinner. The Count was in a tuxedo and his wife and daughter were in long formal gowns. Anastasia's tutor and nanny were dressed in their uniforms. Horus-Salah's family was dressed in the finest Egyptian clothing. So too were his tutor and nanny. Each person sat across for the other of his class, except for Horus-Salah, for his sister and Anastasia were sitting opposite of each other. Even at the small angle that Horus-Salah and Anastasia were at, their eyes met and it was the beginning.

Once more, the old man looked out of his normal eyes, at what was there, and not through his middle eyes at what was in the past. The night air was getting cold. The old man reached around himself and pulled the blanket closer to his body. With this, he looked around to see if any one was left. Ah yes, a few people, all foreign. His hands went to the tea, and then his lips tasted the sweet liquid. His eyes returned to that spot over there, yes, over there where he wanted to be now and for ever more. On the opposite side, on that dark hill, was his home, his tomb. The cave that all his life he had visited, and like the great ones, he had over his lifetime made it a part of every thing he was, and had been. Unlike the great ones, he had done all the changes to his liking, and also, only one other person had been there in his lifetime. Though his eyes focused on the hill, it was his middle eye that saw the place he called home. Yes, the thought came, tonight, maybe tonight. Then his mind went back, just like there was a switch inside his head. He was back, once again looking at Anastasia.

robert f. edwards

The dinner was over, and through out it, the only people to say anything were the servants serving the food. His father and the Count had exchanged a few words in English. It was the first time Horus-Salah had heard his father speak in this language. As he listened to both men talk in the same language, it sounded so different when each spoke the same word, how strange it was to his ear. Not long after the servants stood waiting at each end of the long table, did his father push back his chair and the small group moved away from the table. His father and the Count moved to the library. His mother and the Countess retired to the sitting room. This left the nannies and tutors with the children. Soon after the tutors left for their rooms and the nanny took control of duties. Horus-Salah and his sister went one way, and Anastasia and her nanny went the other. Yes, there were the well wishes, and the goodnights now said in English. It was the first time he had said these words outside of learning them in classes. So it went, the first meeting.

When he got to back to his room, which was not fast enough for him, all he could think about was that girl, that wonderful person called Anastasia. As he got into bed and lay there staring at the ceiling, all thoughts were about this girl. He had never seen a more beautiful person in all his life. Her skin was white like the most pure cotton, and her hair it was the color of gold. Her eyes were blue, like the shallow banks of the Nile. The rest of her was so different looking, her clothes foreign to those of his mother. The two females had long dress, but that was where the similarity ended. The Countess's dress was low cut in the front, showing her well-formed breasts. The same cut on Anastasia's dress hinted that womanhood was coming but hadn't arrived yet. Sleep came to remove his thoughts, only for them to return on the days that followed.

The next morning came, and so for all the mornings that would follow, Horus-Salah would get up and rush out of his room. Then he would wait, and wait, until the others would show up for the morning meal. It was, and would be the same

River of Life

from now on, with him always first, to be waiting but saying nothing. Even when the moment came, and Anastasia would show up, and oh, yes, her parents and the others, it was her he only had eyes for.

In the following days, at first the tutors would teach their students alone, but this changed after a few days. The main reason was that the children and even the tutor needed more practice in English. In the afternoon, the tutor would give the children a rest from their studies, and help his mother and the Countess with their English. It was a wonder to Horus-Salah that each family spoke four different languages, but English not French, was the common language that was being chosen.

The first days were difficult, for changes were made on a moment-by-moment basis. At times, Horus-Salah wondered which one was his nanny and tutor, and which one was Anastasia's. It was hard for him to do both people's wishes at the same time, or to listen to them at the same time. It didn't matter to him as long as Anastasia was present, to him that was all that counted. He had it bad, from the start; it was love at first sight. His sister and Anastasia played together after their studies were done, which gave him time to go to his home, the tomb, to think of Anastasia.

It was some time later before all things that have changed became the order of the day, and settled into a routine. The two families moved about their days together, or in harmony with each other. The Count and his father would go down to the site, as it was known, but to Horus-Salah it would always be the boy king's tomb. The Countess and his mother were always working together, as other guests joined them for dinner or outings. There was always a lot going on.

This gave Horus-Salah more time to go to his home, overlooking the Valley of the Kings. Many long hours he sat and watched the valley below and sometimes looked for his father or the Count. It was impossible from the height he was at, for all the men below looked like little toy soldiers. Some were Egyptian workers, and other's supervisors, to say nothing of

25

robert f. edwards

"Many long hours he sat and watched the valley below ..."

Original photograph Robert F. Edwards
Egypt   November, 1999

River of Life

foreign men standing around. It was a beehive of workers, moving from one place to another, always moving. Day after day, month after month, it never stopped, and Horus-Salah never stopped watching what was going on.

For his own tomb, he had brought extra candles and had moved more of the dirt from around the entrance, far back from the opening where he now sat. During one of his hard working days, he had made his way into the small room beyond the wall. There was a burial chamber and sarcophagus, still where so long ago it had been placed. Horus-Salah knew he was the first to see it in many centuries. It was so small; it wouldn't be a man or women's mummiform coffin. He told himself he wouldn't open the coffin, for respect, but that was only half the reason. The other half was fear, which not even to himself he had not admitted to.

So it went; sometimes when he came up, like today, he would not even go inside. It was often enough just to be here, looking at the village below and the Nile. He also enjoyed looking over at the other side to Luxor. From this distance it looked so peaceful and clean. Today, his mind returned to what it always did, when he had free time for himself. Anastasia, how he would like to be with her, and know all about her. She was the one person he wanted to be around all the time. Although they studied together, and sometimes played games in the courtyard, he never had any time to be alone with her. She was much more outgoing than his sister and himself. She wanted to see things and go places that her nanny would be saying 'no' in her mother language. Then, the nanny and Anastasia would exchange words back and forth, and their voices would get louder. If Anastasia didn't get her way, she would walk out, getting the last word in, which Horus-Salah didn't understand and never asked her about.

Most of the time, things went well and as the months exchanged with each other, he did get to spend, little by little, more time with Anastasia. These were the best time of his live, he was thinking. They would talk and he could never get enough of the way she would speak English in her Polish accent. The days were happy days for everyone. He told Anastasia about his live before she came into it, and his dreams for when he grew up. She also shared her dreams with him.

He once more looked down at the valley below; this was a place he had never told anyone about. No, he wasn't ready to share this, not even with Anastasia, not just yet. She was different from him in many ways. She was a take-charge person, where he was a look-on person. She always looked like she knew where she was, and where she was going. Oh, how he wished he, the man, was more like her, yes, he did admire her so much. Her head was always up and she looked right into your eyes when she asked you something. It was as if she knew what she wanted, and was going to get, sooner or later. Her way of doing things was more direct than his and so much more what he wanted to be like. She had become his ideal. Sometimes he felt that she liked him more than she given others to believe, but then, he would think it was all in his mind. He enjoyed being with her more and more, and couldn't imagine not having her and her family at the house.

Once again, Horus-Salah was feeling like the old days, when he was so young, and Luxor was the only place in the world. He looked down again at the valley below. His mind thought of the young king and his child-bride, was this what it was like to be in love? Then, with this thought in his mind, he quickly pushed it out as fast as it had come in. However, it took hold somewhere in that gray area of his brain. Slowly he got up, as he had done so many times before, and started his way down the hill to the house.

It was a greeting he had heard many times before. The servants, then his nanny, told him that all of the family would be going back to Cairo. What was this, he asked himself? The servants have no answer for his next question. He ran into the house to find his mother, and prayed she would be alone. To his surprise both of these wishes came true. As he entered his mother's room, he asked if he might speak with her. "Of course, "came the answer from his mother, and so he asked if

River of Life

it was true and why. She knew what the question was, even though he had not asked it.

"So, for the first part of your question, yes, both families will be returning to Cairo. Our family will be going back to the house there, and the Count and his family will be returning to Poland". She had hesitated to add the answer to his next question, but the look on his face gave her a long moment to do so. His face drained white, then red, before returning to normal. What a few hours can do to one's whole life, he was thinking, as he heard the last part of this horror story.

It was true that all of them, both families, were moving back to Cairo, but now Anastasia was going to leave for Poland. His mind asked himself, 'where is Poland anyway?' After what seemed a lifetime to him, but was only a few minutes, his mother asked, "Are you alright?"

He managed to look at her, and in a small weak voice, replied, "Yes".

"Well," his mother said, "You see the Count's work is done here, and his government wants him to return to Poland." He nodded and the voice inside said, 'Poland, again that name'. It took forever, or so he thought, to get the next word out, and it was 'when', just 'when' that was all he could get out for now. His mother replied," we should all be in our new places by next month, if all goes well."

"Goes well!!? " his inner voice screamed, how much worse could the news be? He just stood there, like something had changed him to stone. Once again, his mother asked, "Are you alright?"

He answered yes and asked if he could be excused. Outside the room, he let out the first moans and the tears were forming in his eyes. Quickly he rushed back to his private sanctuary, his room, the one he had grown up in. He was leaving it again, but what was so much worse, was Anastasia was leaving him. Oh Allah, not that. He had never thought this would happen. He had so much he wanted to say to her. Now the tears filled his eyes and overflowed down his face on to the bed.

robert f. edwards

How long it was he would never know, but it had been the afternoon when he ran into his room, and now the morning sun looked in to tell him a new day had come. He had made it through the night alone in a blanket of tears.' Allah' was his first thought, 'what has happened', and then the tears from yesterday returned. Somehow he pulled himself together and went down for breakfast .He wasn't hungry, but wanted to see Anastasia. No, he had to see her. As he came into the room everyone said 'good morning' to him, which only made things worse for him, but then his red eyes saw the only person he wanted to see. She looked the same as the last time he saw her. With the strongest voice he could muster, he returned the greetings and sat down. Between playing with his food, and stealing looks at Anastasia, he got through the first part of the day. He had to get control of himself, and then he must talk to Anastasia alone. Oh yes, alone, he must tell her, once and for all, how much she meant to him.

When the day approached afternoon, when it was rest time, he entered the garden to sit under one of the trees, and there she was. Oh Allah, it was now, his time had come. He walked up to her, as man in a teenager's body and child's heart." May I sit with you," he asked? She moved over, and that had to be the answer, until he looked at her and saw tears running down her face. To ask what was wrong was to ask a sick man if he was scared of dying. So, with a place to sit, he did so, and both of them were together. The tears that were hers now were shared by him for once more he was crying. Both of them just sat together in silence and cried. What may have been an hour was a lifetime to these two people on a bench in a garden. It could have been Adam and Eve just told they had to leave the Garden of Happiness.

After some time, the two pairs of eyes red with tears looked at each other. Her voice came through first and said," I don't want to leave..." He was waiting for that, then the last word came from her mouth, and it was "you". His ears heard it, his mind understood it, but his face showed it most of all. The tears were running down, but his face was smiling. She

30

River of Life

"... he entered the garden to sit under one of the trees..."

Original artwork, watercolour   Phyllis Verdine Humphries
Circa 1930's

looked up at him and then said, "You are a funny person, my little Horus, the Egyptian". He just kept crying and smiling. He couldn't speak, the waves of happiness and sorrow moved back and forth, as if his whole body was at sea.

After what seemed longer to them than anyone else, time moved on. His red face, wet from the tears, looked at her and said, "Thank you for being you." With that, her hand reached out to his and held it for the first time since they met. This, to both of them, had been all their lives.

She then asked, in her Polish accent, "What are you going to do with your life?"

He just looked at her and said, "It is all planned for me. I will follow in my father's footsteps. He will tell what to do, and when he wants me to take over, when he wants to retire." In turn, he asked her the same question.

She said without hesitation," I will do what I want when I am finished my schooling."

"And what will that be?" was his reply to her answer."

"I will be important and famous".

He said, "I know you will, "with all the sincerity of someone that could see into the future. So it continued; one question after another, their hands always together.

It had been only a few hours that they had together, when her tutor came into the garden and told Anastasia that she shouldn't be alone with Horus-Salah. They both looked at the tutor as if she had woken them from a dream. Anastasia replied to the tutor that this was a private matter, and that the tutor had no right to intervene in this matter. Anastasia also said, "I will return to the house when I am finished speaking to Horus-Salah."

A look came over the tutor's face, and she said, "We shall see about that".

Once the tutor had left, the two looked at each other as if nothing had interrupted this moment. It was the beginning, and one meeting that they both wanted to prolong together. For now, they have each other, and before both got up they

River of Life

looked into each other's eyes, and said at the same time, "I need you". Reluctantly, they walked back into the house to be joined by others.

The days moved faster for both of them now, and each moment together was a treasure unto itself. What little they have known of each other, from all the months before was now moving together. Every moment they could was spent with each other, alone or with others around, but always together. The servants would look up from what they were doing, when the two would enter and smile with that look of knowing something that was not to be said. A week had passed, and then another. The two of them were in their own world of dreams and happiness.

During one of these days, Horus-Salah said to Anastasia, "I would like to tell you something very special in my life".

She looked at him and said, "Well, go ahead". He could never get used to her strange forwardness.

With all his confidence and courage he said," I have a special place, my very own home. Well, it is more than a home; it is my place in this life and the next."

"What are you telling me, Horus-Salah?" she asked.

"I am trying to say I have found a place that overlooks the Valley of the Kings, and, for a better word, a tomb".

"A tomb?" was the reply from her lips, unsure of what she had heard.

His answer was, "Yes, it is mine, and you are the only other soul on this earth that knows about it".

"What do you do with it... and when do you go there?" was the next question.

"Well, to answer the first one, I have keepsakes in it for myself ... and the ageless one".

She interrupted, " You said one not ones."

He looked into her eyes and said; "I should have explained better, the one that is still there is the ageless one".

"Ah", she jumped in, "Someone does know about it, as well as you".

robert f. edwards

"Well, yes and no, you see, it is a tomb built long ago, for a special person, or thing, and they are still there".

"How do you know they are still there?" was the quick question.

"I have been working at the tomb for many years". Boy, did he sound old and wise at the same time, he thought.

With a tilt of her head, she coyly asked," Oh, in this live or another?" This was what he liked about her, she was so different from any other person he had every meet.

"No, "came his reply, "I was very young when I discovered it, I just found it by accident." He felt her teasing nature, and now wished he had never started. She looked at him and knew she was going to lose his confidence if she kept interrupting him.

With this thought, she said, " I will keep quiet until you finish, please share this with me".

His confidence returned and so he shared it with her. "It was a tomb, with a small coffin, which I have never opened, in a room towards the back ". He admitted to start going there so long ago, when his parents told him the family was moving to Cairo. He needed to have a place to be his home forever. He looked into her eyes and repeated, "Forever ". When he wanted to be with his thoughts, or when he was unhappy, or just wanted to be there, it was his home. She had a hard time not to say, 'what kind of a home is a tomb', but only talked with her body language and not her voice. "I am Egyptian," he heard himself saying," I think as one". He hesitated as he looked into her eyes and said, "I think in the old ways of this land. I think in the ways of the people that lived under the pharaohs. My real home must be for this world, and the next, and this place is mine".

For the first time, she understood the things she liked about this young man that stood before her. He was different that anyone she had ever met. He was wise for his years, and strong, yes, very deep and strong. She now wanted to listen to this young man with an old mind. In a soft voice, she said, "Please go on". He was about to start again, only to hear an-

34

River of Life

other voice from the house calling to them both. The nannies had been looking all over, to tell them the latest news.

When all four were together, the nannies said, "You first", and "No, you".

Anastasia snapped at both of them, "Well, what?" and with this her nanny said, "We all leave next week". The two young people looked at the nannies first, then each other, in despair.

Anastasia put her thoughts back together first, and said, "If that is all, please leave us now". The two nannies took their leave without another word. The young couple looked at each other, and the tears were slipping down the faces that had been so happy just moments before.

robert f. edwards

CHAPTER 4

 The old man leaned back in the chair while the soft winds from the river touched his face. He removed his mind from the past. Oh, Allah, yes it had to rest, and so did he. The stars were out as he looked up to the heavens and let his mind drift here and there, anywhere but back to those times. 'Rest' it cried unto him and he let the smallest of sounds come out to say, 'stay to the real world'. 'The real world, he repeated,' is this what the real world is?' he screamed out in a voiceless mouth.

Oh yes, the moment is here and now, in Luxor, where he had spent his life, on and off. To come back here where in the summer months are so hot, the air burns the lungs and you search for even the smallest tree to give you shade from the god Ra, the sun. Water, that life force, you must have. The autumn, like life itself, can be the time of reward or failure. But now, it was for him and the land, the winter months and the end of the season of life was at hand, for both him and the land. He was a part of this, his home. Nothing matters now but the winds and the clear skies. This was what was now, and what he had now. If only he could keep it, and not return to the past. But, what was in the present for him was another day just as yesterday, or maybe last week, the same as tomorrow, or the day after? He looked again across the water, and his eyes move hopelessly to the spot

Oh Allah, here I go again, to the past, yes, to the past that is all that I want, and all that is real to me now.

The next day was closer to the trip, and while most of the household was getting ready and exhilarated, there were two that didn't share in it. Once more in the garden, this had be-

River of Life

come their meeting place. The two long faces looked out into the openness, and sat like some of the statues around them. On this day, however, Anastasia asked in a soft pleading voice, "Would you show me the tomb before we both leave Luxor?"

Horus-Salah looked up, somewhat surprised, but said "Yes I will." So, both of them planned a way in which they could be missing from the house, but not look like they were together. Soon, it was set. Tomorrow would be the day; someone other than himself would see his secret, in this century. Anastasia admitted she would have a hard time sleeping and couldn't wait. The rest of the day continued with the others directing them on what had to be done. Night came at last, now the end the day.

The next day came, with Ra, the sun god letting all know that the skies belonged to him, from the beginning in the east, to his farewell in the west. Ra told one and all that he was just starting his way to the apex. This would be a day when all living things would know, and feel his presents. By mid-day, his warmth would be more than warm-blooded beings would wish to feel.

This was the time Horus-Salah and Anastasia were going to meet and start the journey to the home of Horus-Salah, and the tomb of the other one. For the remainder of the people of Luxor and Egypt, it would be their rest time, trying to find shade from the ruler of the skies and the fullness of his strength. The hours followed each other, one by one and the time was quickly approaching. As if an air raid had sounded on the streets, the lanes were emptied of all that was living. The fields saw animals under trees, or in the weeds of the banks of the great river. So it was as Ra, the ruler of life made his was to the top of the sky.

The two wound their way along the bank of the Nile, then through the small village and up the road towards the Valley of the Kings. Even now, Anastasia's face was red, and the first signs of perspiration were on it. The long road lay ahead. Horus-Salah was a fast walker, he tried his best to slow down, and Anastasia tried her best to keep up.

So it went, for the first hour, with rest periods on the way. By the second hour they were high above the Valley of the Kings. The view and the light breezes helped keep Anastasia's mind off how high she was, and how hot also. Now Anastasia's clothing was showing large patches of wetness. Horus-Salah tried not to notice, but would stop more often to rest than he did when he was alone. Just when Anastasia was questioning herself for doing this climb, and how much more she could take, Horus-Salah stopped. Oh, another rest, thank God, came to Anastasia's mind, as she climbed up to where Horus-Salah was standing.

The view took their breath away, for it was as if they could see the entire length and breadth of the Nile. The city of Luxor lay at their feet. She stood mesmerized, looking out as far as her eyes could see. For the first time she didn't feel the heat. Horus-Salah said in a quiet voice, "We are here."

She turned her head away from the view, but saw nothing of a tomb. In a breathless gasp, she managed to get out, "Where is the tomb?"

"Oh," Horus-Salah said, "It's down there," his finger pointing the direction.

Anastasia looked down on the slope where she stood, still puzzled," Down there ... where?"

Horus-Salah seemed to look at his feet, and said once more, "Right down here." It was directly below, straight down.

"How do you get down there?" was the question from her lips, almost to herself. Horus-Salah was the one to give the answer.

"This way "came the response as he moved to the edge. Slowly he moved, winding his way down the cliff. As she watched, it was one of the few times in her life that she could remember feeling scared. She looked down and her feet didn't move. Horus-Salah looked up, and saw what was happening. "Just look at my footprints, and nothing else," he told her. "Follow me, it is not far."

River of Life

Tentatively, she took the first step, and then another, until she was right behind him. He offered her his hand, and she grasped it before her mind asked any question. They moved slowly downwards, then from nowhere, there appeared a big hole, or so she thought at first. Before she could say anything, both of them were in the opening to the tomb.' Oh God, we made it came', to her mind, as she still grasped Horus-Salah's hand.

For the first time, they looked into each other's eyes and smiled." We made it," Anastasia proudly exclaimed, and his off-hand reply, "Yes, we did." Now both of them knew what was unsaid, in thought-words. This was the only time Horus-Salah had been here, in his life, with another person. And what a person she was, he looked up at the sky, and thanked Ra the sun god, and Allah, the almighty god. She looked out to the lands that lay before her, and didn't want to every go back.

After what seemed a long time, both of them sat at the opening looking at the world. The world of the past and the present was before them. It had been the river that had brought people here, and today was no different. As the two pairs of eyes moved across the landscape, they saw the long wide blue ribbon. On each side of this great waterway was green plant life of all kinds. This was the reason that people came so long ago, and now why they stayed. This long stretch of life gave all that was needed to be here, then and now. No wonder the Egyptians were always thought of as the 'people of the Nile.' For just beyond this line were the great deserts.

The two young people looked at what was Horus-Salah's beginning and would be his end. It was where he belonged; now he had someone to share it with. But did she, he wondered, and then she looked at him and said, "You do belong here." It was as if she was reading his mind and maybe she was. The heat of the day had reached its greatest point and the two still sat at the opening, as if they were a pharaoh and his queen.

robert f. edwards

She was the first to get up, and when she did, she asked, "Can we go back into the tomb?" It was more of a command than a request.

Horus-Salah was up now, and replied," If you wish". She looked eagerly at him and said, "Well, then let's go". Happily, he took a few steps into the entrance, and returned with candles. "It is dark back there," he said, and lit the candles. The two, with candles firmly in hand, entered the tomb.

It was just a short distance, but once away from the opening, it was another world. This world was in darkness and cool. She was a bold person, but still glad that Horus-Salah was in front. This was not her land, and the unexplained she had not learnt. The gossip buzzed around Luxor and maybe the world by now, about the curse of Tutankhamun on opening his tomb. Lord Carnarvon's death, and others that had taken objects from the tomb of Tutankhamun to say nothing of the unexplained happenings, such as the lights going out in the city of Cairo at the moment of Lord Carnarvon's death. These and many more things were going through her mind, as she took one step after another.

Horus-Salah, on the other hand, moved confidently forward, for it was a part of him. Now and forever more, it was going to be his place, his resting place in this world and the next. He knew this. It was already there in his heart and soul. Yes, he would always share it with the one that came before him. It was built by others, but they were letting Horus-Salah share it. Anastasia and he were now as far as they could go. In front of them was the small opening that Horus-Salah had made into the final resting place of its rightful owner. He moved up to the hole and then looked back," Are you all right?" came the whisper from his mouth.

She answered with a nod, and said in a small voice, "Is this the end?"

"No," he said, "but this is as far as I have gone." He moved aside from the opening to let her have a look inside. As they changed places, she put her candle inside the little opening with her hand.

River of Life

Peering inside, she said, "Oh, yes, I see the coffin."

"I told you it was small, didn't I," Horus-Salah said, as if he had to defend himself. She stepped back and looked at him.

Their eyes met and she said," Let us remove the rest of this wall, so we can go inside together. "

He looked at her and said, "But it is their resting place."

"I agree," came the reply, "but we came here to look and show our respect, didn't we?" He hadn't thought of it in that way. He had only wanted to share this most important place in his life with her. Now, to enter the final resting place of owner of the tomb was something else, in his mind.

She looked at him and said, "If you are afraid, or don't want to, that is fine with me." He knew this was to edge him on, and now it was his call.

"Well, with the two of us we may be able to move enough of the wall to enter," he said out loud, but his mind added,' should we?' So, it came to pass, that the two of them worked side-by-side, moving dirt and rocks until the once sealed opening felt the air of the present. With each rock removed the hole, the workers moved faster, to bring more light into the past and the resting place of the one who lay there.

It was late in the afternoon, the people back at the house would be up from their rest and the two new archaeologists would be missed. Horus-Salah said to Anastasia, "We must return to the house now." She looked at him with both surprise and amazement. She said nothing, but her expression said so much more. "Yes," he said, "We must go now, for it is getting late and we will be missed."

"We are so close," she implored, passing another rock to Horus-Salah.

"I feel the same way, Anastasia, but we must go now."

For the first time since they had been together, he was in charge. At first, she couldn't believe it or accept it, but a moment later she found what she had always wanted, a leader. So, with a look of disappointment she started to move towards the opening with Horus-Salah in the lead. On the way back to the house, little was said. Both had agreed never to mention anything about where they had been this day to anyone, no matter what. Once back in the house, and a change of clothes, things were back to normal. They were back to normal for all but two people, preoccupied with thinking, 'what is next?'

River of Life

CHAPTER 5

The old man remembered only too well those moments in his life. He smiled at the darkness. Looking around for the waiter, his tea was cold. He had no idea what time it was, for to have a watch meant to be ruled by it. Now in his later years, he had returned to when time was ruled by the light of the sun. Also, he had to admit to himself, by another light, also but not his time. He once more looked to the heavens to see the stars. They were out in their fullness. His mind ran back and forth. All that was left were the memories of the past, and the mysteries of the present.

The stars were one of those mysteries. He looked for the few constellations that he knew. Yes, over there he found Aries, then the Big Dipper. His mind jumped back to the time he was crossing the Great Sahara Desert. It had been the desert people that showed him how to read the stars, for they were the ones that could move across this terrain by only looking up at night. Ah, the Blue Men, and the mesmerizing dances their women would perform. The drumbeats, he could still hear in his inner ear.

The long beautiful night on the sea sands, with the light winds always moving the sand, swirling about. Always light from the stars, until the next day gave notice to return. He loved the desert and the peace it gave to the soul. With that thought, he moved his hand to the pocket. The watch and the treasure inside gave him the same rush of pain it always did. He wanted to take the watch out, and open the back, to feel the treasure that lay inside, but no, not yet. He told himself, ' later, then you can hold what is so dear to your heart'.

He looked up and saw the North Star, then went back with his eyes to that hole in the darkness, on the other side of the river. He couldn't see it; however his inner eye kept look-

robert f. edwards

" ... back to the time he was crossing the Great Sahara Desert."

Original artwork, pastel   Phyllis Verdine Humphries
Circa 1930's

River of Life

ing, knowing where it was. It was his home, his place of rest from this world, his crossover to the next. Yes, his middle eye knew where to look. His eyes held to the spot.

The next day came and both Horus-Salah and Anastasia were called together by the two nannies. As all four of them stood facing each other, the nannies told them that tomorrow would be their last day in Luxor. The two younger members just looked at the floor, as if for answers. Both of the nannies realized how sad these two were, and said that they could have this day together. The nannies would cover for both of them, if anyone were looking for them. The two young people looked up, as if they had been woken from a sleep. The nannies then added that they must know where, and what the two would be doing, if they were to cover these two adventurers.

Both replied with the same answer, "Back to the digging."

"Where is that?" asked the nannies.

Horus-Salah answered this question with, "High above the Valley of the Kings." He surprised Anastasia with that answer, for she was sworn to secrecy. Horus-Salah would explain to her later, by telling her that the hills were full of paths in all directions. Even if one were following, they would not find his place, his home, and the tomb.

The nannies looked at one another, and nodded that the two would have their support, but to be back no later than yesterday's time. All agreed and the two archaeologists got up to leave, only to be called back. "You two may need these things," smiled the nannies. They handed over a packed lunch, and smocks to keep their clothes clean. The two nannies said, "Have a happy day together, and be careful on all things you do."

The young couple looked at each other, and said, "Thank you both for this day, and your understanding." Out of the room, the two looked into each other's eyes and broke into laughter. This was going to be a great day, even if it was to be their last. They were going back up to the tomb to find out what was there. What a great way to share their last day together. So, off the two went on their journey into the hills and into history as well. The sun had moved half way in its daily path. They had made good time today, and the day's heat was still to come. At the opening they set out their candles, as if they had been working on this site for many years.

The old man pulled his eyes away from the shoreline. He moved his head upwards and stopped. "The stars, oh the stars," his mind said and then his lips. The heaven was full, with the brightest stars in the Milky Way and its dusting of light. What a sight, what a beautiful thing. He thought of how little he knew from the past, and how much the future was an unexplained mystery. He remembered a time in his life when he was with men that crossed the desert, with only the star as their maps. His eyes looked for that group of stars, the Little Dipper and the Big Dipper. More, he heard himself say, as he scanned the heavens. Concentrating, he was able to add a few more constellations to his list. Still, it was a poor showing for a man that had spent so many years in the great Sahara. Thanks to Allah, he was here tonight, and the Blue Men, for their knowledge of the night sky. What a time it was, in the desert that had seen so much of his life. His eyes roamed from one side of the sky to the other. His mind moved back to a time when the stars danced, and he had shared their happiness with another. This was the time to remember tonight. For it was this memory he had come down to the water to call back. And so he let go, and went back to the tomb and Anastasia.

River of Life

The two of them looked at each other with the candles lit. Horus-Salah was the first to move to the back of the tomb. He was ready to get into the inner burial chamber and Anastasia was right behind him. Once inside the small chamber, behind the partial wall that they had removed, the small coffin dominated the room. They judged the room to be 3 to 4 meters in width, and the same in length. The walls were covered with hieroglyphics. Some told of the gods and their instructions and others of events that had taken place in that time period. Horus-Salah could only understand small parts and he knew that the cartouches were for gods. .

He was trying his best to explain this and what he was reading on the cartouches to Anastasia. She in turn was lighting more candles, placing them so the light would give more guidance to his work. The writing told of the goddess Isis, and one of her temples. It also told of a high priestess and her oracles, with the help of her cat. As Horus-Salah was trying to translate, suddenly Anastasia repeated "Cat". He stopped to look at her as she pointed to the character of the cartouche. More than one of them had the same symbol, which he was sure meant 'cat'. The burial chamber was now full of the smoke from the candles. It had a heavenly glow about it, with the soft light flickering. The small room took on a holy aura to both of them.

Anastasia was the first to break the silence with." I have to go outside to get some fresh air," she said. It was Horus-Salah this time that followed. The fresh air was welcomed by both of them as they felt the heat of the day. Though they were at the opening, the bright light of the sun made them look back into the semi-darkness.

Once their eyes adjusted, Anastasia looked up at Horus-Salah and asked, "What do we do now?" For the first time he was sharing this important part of his life. It was also the first time he had ever heard Anastasia asking, rather than telling. This was so different, he was disconcerted for a moment before he replied, "I am not sure."

robert f. edwards

"What do you mean, you are not sure?" She was back to being her regular self, thank Allah for that.

Then he said in a low voice, "We do not have much time left today."

The sun was past its half waypoint in the sky. She looked back at the opening and asked, "How much time do we have?"

"Maybe 3 to 4 hours, that's all," came the answer. He was thinking of the burial chamber and said, "I would like to spend more time looking at the drawings on the walls," as he pointed in that direction.

"Fine," agreed Anastasia, as she turned and moved quickly past him into the chamber. They were soon back in the inner chamber, a place without natural light. Their surroundings were from another time, if not from another world.

What had this cat been able to do, and how did it do it? These questions were left unspoken, but were in both of the discoverer's minds. With both hands carrying candles, the two, side by side, searched the walls slowly. Horus-Salah gained a little more information but Anastasia's patience was growing shorter every minute. After scanning the walls completely from top to bottom, Horus-Salah looked at Anastasia and said, "I can't read the calligraphy". They turned their attention to the small items that lay on the floor. One by one, they sorted through the objects, some were dishes for eating out of, and others were jewelry. There may have been food in the small jars. They found many combs and toys that made this final resting place a comfortable home for this remarkable cat.

Now both of them were looking over the coffin itself. "Are we going to open it?" came the question from Anastasia.

With a fast reply the answer was "no."

"You always surprise me," said Anastasia, then she added, "that is what makes you so special to me".

He looked up and said, "I feel the same way about you." It was time to move to the outer part of the tomb, which they both did together. Back at the opening, looking at Luxor in the distance, he said, "this is the most important day of my

River of Life

life". She didn't say a word but reached out and took his hand.

Then she said, "Mine too, my Horus," and nothing more. His mind thought, "Horus-Salah is my name, but just Horus is the god's name". Then like a bolt of lightning, he understood what she had really meant.

He looked into her eyes and was about to say thank you, but before the words formed in his mouth, she put her lips to them. It was the first time he had been kissed on the mouth. They kissed again, and again, until they both knew that they had done it right or at least to their satisfaction. She was the first to break the silence;" you are a fast learner". His eyes told her everything she wanted to know, and maybe a little more. She put her arms around him and whispered in to his ear, "my little Horus," just that, nothing more.

He held her, and whispered back, "I will be yours for evermore!"

The old man almost jumped out of the chair with these thoughts. As his mind came back to the present, it was only then that he became aware that his right hand was back in the pocket of his galabya. Oh yes, the right hand held the silver watch. Now his mind was back with the hand, holding, feeling the watch. It had never been the watch itself, but what was inside that could bring tears to his eyes. Now was no exception. The eyes that had looked for so long at the hills were filled with tears. It was his mind and not his hand this time that would bring the watch out of the pocket. If this watch with its priceless treasure was to leave the pocket, he knew his hands would open the back. Oh Allah, he heard from another part of his mind, 'please, please just for one moment'. He told himself, 'No forget it, the time is not now, but later'. So it went, back and forth, for how long he was unable to tell. When rest came from this mental debate, the watch was still in his pocket, so much the better. He knew in his heart that

49

he would not be in control if the other side won. Looking up and seeing the stars brought him the peace he needed. Ah, the stars with their changing light, from bright to invisible. He lost himself in this peace that was so welcome for now. As the stars danced and the light clouds moved their curtain across the endless darkness, his control returned to him. Not peace, but control, the only thing that was left.

His eyes returned to where they had been most of the night, to the hills across the Nile. His middle eye knew where to look, even if his outer eyes couldn't see the tomb, his home, and his place. It was there that he had kissed for the very first time. His lips could feel that kiss, and that moment was as alive as if it had just happened. His body had to feel the galabya to know it wasn't true. What was time, if not just like the stars that you could see one time, and not the other? That you are here, now, in one-way and body, then another, some-where else. It is so real. Back at the opening to the tomb with...he stopped. It was so hard to say her name, in his mind, or on his lips, without the tears coming. He must stop now, or the great rain would return, and his face would have the rivers of sorrow running down. He looked harder into the darkness.

Anastasia and Horus-Salah both looked up at the blue sky. The sun was being pulled back to earth. Ra the true god of light and warmth sat on the back part of this day, looking down on the two young lovers. As their witness to the unspo-ken vow that were taken before him, Ra was the true ruler, before, now, and forever of Egypt and its living things. They both felt the warm assurance of the ruler above; that what had been done today was good and honorable for them both. What was only a moment in time, but a short lifetime for the two lovers; they looked at each other again. Horus-Salah was the first to break the silence. He said in a low voice, more to himself than Anastasia, "we must leave now".

River of Life

Still holding hands, they turned to look one last time at the inner part of the tomb. Slowly they made their way back up to the trail. She stopped and turned to look back down to where the tomb was but now couldn't be seen. She said in a voice so quietly that he thought it might have been for her alone, "this place for us three".

He repeated, "Three?"

She turned to him and said in a hesitant voice, "Yes. Just the three of us, the Cat, you, and now me. I know you said no one has been here before but you and now me, since the building of the tomb". She was back to more herself.

"That is right," he replied.

"What I am asking is, please let it be just our place, which you share with the cat and me. No one else, now, or in the future."

"Of course," he said, "I wouldn't have it any other way."

She pleaded, "For now and ever more, please?" It was one of the few times he had ever heard the word please come from her, to anyone.

He added, "Yes, forever more". So, with one long last look she moved toward the trail that was to take them back to the house. The trail closed faster than their minds wanted it to, and before their hands parted, they were back in the garden.

Both of the nannies were waiting, looking grateful to see them. They tried to pretend to be cross, since the pair had been gone for most of the day. After a few questions from the nannies that they were all right, they were told that there was just enough time to get change and get ready for the guests arriving. As the four of them walked through the garden towards the house, the flowers sent up their fragrance, that Egypt was famous for in its perfume. The nannies had been enjoying their wait in the garden, and commented on the delightful scent. For the young couple, their minds were still back at the tomb, in their own world that was so different. The only flowers there were dried, and from another time.

Once in the house, both nannies and their charges said their good byes for now, and went their separate ways. This abrupt change brought the young people back to reality quickly. The long look that they gave each other did not go unnoticed by their guardians. They moved to their separate wings of the house in. Horus-Salah washed and put on his evening galabya. In another part of the house Anastasia was finishing up with jewelry, which would accent her simple long white dress. Throughout the house, people were preparing for the last dinner before leaving for Cairo.

The guests were arriving and being escorted into the great hall next to the dining room. Both the parents stood in the receiving line, as each guest was introduced. So it went from the beginning and for the next three hours. The head of the servants moved around like a general looking over the battle line. Events moved smoothly. They always had, and always would under his stewardship. The evening wore on while the two young adventurers sat at opposite ends of the great table, with a nanny on one side, and a tutor on the other side. To everyone else, things looked normal and in their right form. To these two, it was as if they were under house arrest. The latter may have been closer to the truth. For by now, the nannies knew that there was more than just a fondness between these two. As employees to both parents, and having good positions that were hard to replace, neither Egyptian nor Polish nanny was prepared to lose this for puppy love.

To Horus-Salah and Anastasia, there was no happy ending to this evening, for it would be lost time not being together. The evening grew later, and by ten p.m. the dinner was over, and most of the guests moved into groups. The men were enjoying brandy and cigars in the library, talking about the things men talked about. They all expressed their regrets to the host and his friend the Count, on how much the area would be at a loss without their help and guidance. Both men welcomed this praise, but as they were in separate groups, were not aware of how much admiration from their peers was being expressed. The message was the same to both of them. This night was just the occasion for such sentiments, so both men expected this from one and all that night.

River of Life

In another part of the great house, the women were doing somewhat the same. However, the discussions centered on the family, questions about the children, and the changes that would be facing both women. All the quests offered their admiration and support for these brave women. The children, as they were referred to, had been excused with their nannies and tutor. The six of them said their good night's in the formal way of the time, and retired to their quarters. All things had a beginning and an end, and so was this day. This day had been the beginning for Horus-Salah and Anastasia, not the end.

The sun was up and pushed the darkness from the sky. The servants went about their chores as if the ruler were giving instructions, as well as being invisible. For the heads of the ruling family, the sun had been no incentive to leave their beds or discontinue their rest. The evening had been late as the last guests said their good byes, and the families were able to settle in their quarters for a long over-due rest. The servants were putting the last things in readiness for the trip to Cairo. It was midday before the ruling class took their places, and were informed on what was ready and what still needed to be done. The family would leave on the boat before dusk to start their journey down the Nile. One by one, the hours ticked away as preparations were being finalized.

At the chosen time, the two family and all the servants that were required were on board. The cabins on the first deck were allotted for the families, and down below were the servants. The ones that had the least contact with the families, on a one-to-one basis, were below the water line and furthest away. The evening meal was served and the table seemed small, compared to the one at the house. It brought the two families closer at least, thought Horus-Salah and Anastasia. It did not feel like they were going to Cairo to say good-bye, but were on a holiday down the River of Life. This was a quiet time for the parents, this time before the final good-byes, which would be less than a week away. The many months that the

53

two families had been under one roof had made them one. Now the family was breaking up.

For Horus-Salah and Anastasia, they felt their lifeblood was flowing into the Nile with the current, always bringing them closer to the end. To Cairo, where it would be much more than farewell, it would be the end of their lives, at least to them. As dusk approached, the little lights made their presence known on the shoreline, dancing on each side of the river. The Nile had been always a part of the journey for the people of this land, of Egypt. It had moved the Great Ramses, and the Pharaohs before him, and after. It moved the kings and rulers of today as it had in the past. It was for one and all that made Upper and Lower Egypt one. One river, one way, one people, one Egypt, it had been in the past and now would be in the future. It was the water that was in the veins of all that were born here, and lived here. It was the River of Life.

To the young people, it was the river of despair, always moving towards the end, and their end of being together. Oh god of the Nile, is it the end? The night gave the stars a chance to replace the little lights along the way. All about them was total darkness, with the exception of the sky above. The stars, large and small appeared in the night sky. Horus-Salah stood at the rail, looking up for what seemed forever, asking questions that his mind had no answers for. As the wind turned cooler and the night longer, he eventually moved back to his quarters, no wiser or happier. The day had come to an end, in more ways than one.

The ship was of a considerable size and well appointed for the comfort of its guests. For Horus-Salah and Anastasia, it could have been a rowboat, for the lack of privacy it provided them. If it wasn't the nannies or tutors, it was a crewmember, always someone near them or close by. The days were hot and long, and the families moved from one side to another, looking for shade and to hide from the ever-present sun. No so hiding place could Horus-Salah or Anastasia find, for a private word to be spoken for each other, away from others to hear.

River of Life

The days continued, from morning counting down the hours of the day, lunchtime, rest time, and on to evening meals. To both of them the first full day on the water wasn't a happy one. As for the rest that were on board, events were moving along very well. The men spent most of their time with the captain. The women sat talking about all the things that meant a great deal to them, and no one else. For the servants, it was almost a holiday, for the crew did many of their tasks. In general, all but two people were enjoying the river Nile's journey down to the sea.

The River of Life moved ever forward, sometimes opening up and slowing, to show its great width. Then without any warning, it narrowed and the current was felt by all that moved along on its back. So it went from one hour to the next, as the sun god Ra watched from above. This day ended just like the one before, and may well be like the ones to come.

Anastasia moved about the upper deck trying to enjoy the sun and read a book along side her mother. She had wondered what it would be like to return to her homeland with its four seasons. All would be so different than what she had become accustomed to. Oh, what would it be like, not to be near her little Horus, her Egyptian, her man? With that thought in her mind, yes, he was just what she had always thought she wanted in a man, in all of her twelve years. Her mind argued with itself, you are just a girl, a child. On the other hand, what is a person and when does one know what they want in life, and with whom?

She went back and forth until her mother interrupted asking, "How is the book?"

She looked down at the words and said, "it will do for now." She realized she had been on the same page for more than an hour. Anastasia glanced at her mother and asked in a soft voice, "what is real love?"

The Countess turned and replied, "What a question to ask, what are you reading?"

robert f. edwards

Anastasia closed the book and said, "Just a poor story in a poor book." She got up and said, "I am going to my quarters, I will see you at dinner."

The Countess nodded and thought, ' what a time to have a teenage daughter', for next month Anastasia would be thirteen and back in Poland. The Countess's thoughts changed from her daughter, to the idea of being back in Poland. The place she was born in, had grown up in, and above all, loved as her home, her country. Oh, to be back home with her people, and her home. She had been home sick from the moment she was told they were going to Egypt. Now she was going back to where things were normal, and the world moved forward in an order that she knew and understood. To be back home, thank God and all the saints.

Anastasia had reached her quarters, only to turn and go up the stairs to the inner lounge. With her book in hand, she sat alone. Oh, to be alone, it was a feeling that moved her into despair. "Please God," she asked out loud, "never leave me alone, and please let me have Horus-Salah." Horus-Salah was in his quarters, studying language and Greek philosophy. The language other than his native language he used the most was English. Since Anastasia and her family had been staying with his family, the words spoken by the learned ones was English. Now, for over a year it was not only his second language, but also the one he used the most. With this thought in mind, his eyes filled with tears. In a matter of a few days, he wouldn't be using this language other than to study.

He couldn't continue with his studies on any language, so he turned his attention to philosophy. The Greeks were the world's greatest philosophers of their time, and still studied. He often thought of Cleopatra VII and other Greeks, and of course, the one who named the second largest city of Egypt after himself. Alexander the Great and all his followers, did they all want to become Egyptian like Cleopatra? Ah, the question had no answer, he thought. The study of this subject would never have an end, was that not philosophy in its true form? His mind continued down this path, if the teacher

River of Life

started a subject, he could convince others that this was the correct way of thinking. Then, as new information came forward, their arguments would not be as valued as originally thought.

The one philosopher that came into mind was none other than the great Aristotle and his principles. Oh my, he, Horus-Salah was questioning the works of the great ones. Was he the new philosopher of his time, or more likely a member of the school Zeno? Was he a Stoic in his thoughts, when it came to pleasure and pain? Who was he, the boy of his father's house, or the man who had found his love? Was it the will of Allah, or was it the gods of the past that played this game he was a part of? Was it the test of manhood or the divine mind that no reality mattered other than the submission to its divine will? He looked up from the pages that he had not read. The night was upon him and all around this place. He closed the book and prepared himself for dinner. It would be the last time aboard this ship on the Nile.

The old man had been looking at the waters of the Nile all this time. They were high and the flooding would begin by next week. The life of the Nile would save its people once more. The once calm waters now rippled with the strong current flowing in the center. Every day, its strength would grow and widen, until the banks could not hold it back. Then let the flooding begin. "Oh yes, my young Horus-Salah, my young philosopher, my young self, " the old man said out loud. Only the wind from the water heard and carried the words. The old man glanced down at his brown galabya. His left hand closed over the watch in his pocket. Yes, his mind returned to the watch and what was in the back partition. His left hand was unconsciously drawing forward the watch. He shook himself back into control, not now, but later, came the command.

His left hand stopped at the opening. He looked down and thought of his life as a Muslim, being left-handed. Life, for young Horus-Salah the philosopher of fourteen was hard. I am eighty-four now, and can still say this. Do you remember the days and nights that this left hand was tied to your back, as a reminder to only use it to remove the waste from your body? Do you remember the nanny saying,' you will learn what this hand is for, and nothing else.' But no, then and now, and always will be, this is the hand you use the most. 'I am, and have always been left-handed,' came the words again from his lips. How could I have thought of being a philosopher, when all I knew about the subject was what I had read?

His mind now was back unto itself and his lips were closed to the secret of the mind. What is philosophy, anyway? It is one person's view of life that others care not to question, but accept. For him, life was the day and nothing more. It was the light of day from the darkness of the night. It was knowing when you come away from the small death of sleep, that your eyes see another day. A new beginning and the end of the rest forever, for its time had not come. The days to start anew and all the yesterdays but a memory. The tomorrow that may never come. Yes, this is what life was, and is to all living things. They were at the call of the moment of this terra firma, air and water. Mother Earth and her rules, life and death, nothing more.

The old man moved his eyes back to the waters, then onto the hill, before they rested once more on that spot. His life had been there, at that spot, and now it was time once more to make the hajji to his ruler, the sun, and the giver of life, the god Ra. He was made up of the sands and water of Egypt, and nothing more. His mind jumped back to the boat, and the times of yesterday.

Horus-Salah put his books down and dressed for the evening meal. The last one on this boat of despair, he thought to himself as he entered the dining room. He sat himself in his usual spot between his nanny and tutor. Anastasia was

River of Life

seated in the same manner, however at the other end of the table. Their guardians were not going to let the young lovers have any time together, alone, or in the eyes of other. Just another day and all would be over, the guardians said to themselves. For within the next day or two, one family would be on the boat back to Poland, and the other to the big house in Cairo. Things would be back to normal, or would they? The meal progressed with one dish after another, and then to Horus-Salah and Anastasia's relief, finally the end. The men moved as they always did, to themselves with brandy and cigars. The women did like-wise to another part of the boat, with tea and the talking that never had a beginning or end. It was only useful for the soul to let time move on.

For the young couple, it was now or never for their goodbye. Would the goddess of love come to their aid? Would the gods hear the call of the beginning of love, and not the end? Both Horus-Salah and Anastasia, in opposite corners of the room, were saying their prayers to different gods. It may have been the god Isis, or the goddess Venus. The four guards and their two prisoners of love were the only ones left at the table. The Egyptian nanny asked if the other three caretakers would like to join her for tea before retiring for the evening. So with the gods hearing the call of love, the two pairs of eyes sought each other. Not alone, but nothing is perfect. The four women talked about the changes that were happening. The return to Poland and their homeland, two of them shared with the others and how much they had missed it. The Egyptian women told of all the things had they were looking forward to once back in Cairo.

The two young people sat looking at each other, not taking part in the conversation, but struggling to keep their moist eyes from overflowing. It was the nanny of Horus-Salah that saw the two brave faces, and the first trickle of tears escaping. She said in a low voice, "Horus-Salah, would you please go up top and see how the winds are, and give us a report on what you find?" He bent his head low to hide his wet face, and nodded as he got up from his chair.

59

robert f. edwards

The Polish nanny looked at Anastasia, and said, "You can go also but bring back the report in Polish." The four of them chuckled to themselves, and as the young people freed themselves and quickly raced from the room.

The young couple welcomed the light breezes that cooled and dried their tear-stained faces. Horus-Salah spoke first, "It is going to be hard not to be with you, or to even see you," he said.

"I know, for I feel the same way, my little Horus", she never used the other part of his name. It was as though he was her little god. Maybe he was, he thought, for his feelings for her and her welfare was all he wanted in life. She told him, "This can't be the end, we must keep writing to each other".

He added, "And when we are adults, what then?"

"First things first, "she came back with, then added, "you are named after a god, it should be easy for you." They both laughed and laughed. It was the first time in days, maybe weeks, for both of them.

They discussed what Horus-Salah would do about the tomb. He promised that once a year, he would return to the tomb and check that all was well. They both agree that if he was to write on this subject, it must be in code. They considered what would be appropriate for the cat's tomb, but meaningful only to them. The decision was made, and they chose the name Felix, for both households had cats and wouldn't create any curiousity to either household.

This diversion helped, as neither one wanted to talk about the future, for it was not in their control, and it was the past that was theirs. The light winds were on their backs as they moved forward. It was only when they both stopped, that they felt the wind still pushing. Yes, it was like life, always pushing you forward until you stop, and are pushed over to the end. Maybe both of them were thinking this, for at the same time they turned to face the wind. Without a word, they held each other against all that was there, now, and forever. It was an unspoken vow that they had taken and given to each other. This vow was sealed with a kiss from young trembling

60

River of Life

lips. Before anything could be repeated, a voice was heard by both of them.

A crewmember approached them and said to Horus-Salah in Egyptian that they were to return to the sitting room now. The three of them slowly walked back to join their guardians. The Egyptian nanny spoke first, "well?" The two young people hesitated, and then felt their faces grow warm under this scrutiny. All the women laughed, and the nanny commented, "The wind is strong, for you both have red faces, maybe a wind burn, yes?" The two young people took their seats silently, with heads bowed. After a few moments of silence, the Polish tutor said, "It is time to retire for the night." One by one, each rose from their chair and exchanged the pleasantries of 'good-night' to each other. It was the 'good-night' of Horus-Salah and Anastasia that the others were waiting to hear, watching from the corner of their eyes. The two quietly whispered ' good-night'. Some thought they heard 'my love' added softly, the others saw the look, which was enough for them. As Horus-Salah lay in his cabin, before sleep overtook him, his thoughts were of Anastasia and their vow. In another part of the boat the same thoughts were being shared.

The sun was soon up busy, and the crew with it. The morning reached the half waypoint as the first view of Cairo was seen. The great pyramids of Giza welcomed their return from Upper Egypt as they have done for hundreds of years. They were nearing the end of a long journey from Luxor. It was as if the boat itself knew the end of this voyage was at hand. Quickly it moved down the river, and the first buildings of the great city could be seen. All the crew were topside and activity was hurried as they prepared to dock. Voices shouted out commands, as they slowed to slide into their appointed slip at the pier. Once settled in it, and securely tied down, the crew put in place the gangplank for the guests to depart.

It was happening so fast, with the two families bustling around each other. The carriages were waiting, and as one filled, the next came to take its place. What looked like total confusion was moving very well. Soon the families were well

robert f. edwards

"The great pyramids of Giza welcomed their return... "

Original photograph   Robert F. Edwards
Egypt   November, 1999

62

River of Life

on their way to the house in Cairo, and their servants were following a short distance behind. The entire luggage was being sorted; some would be going on to the house, and the rest to the train, before another ship and the long voyage on to Poland. As Horus-Salah and his family arrived, the servants of the great house stood outside to greet them back.

So it went for the rest of the day, people moving here and there. All the rooms had been prepared days before, but the personal belongings from the boat had to be placed in order. What a day, and a full one at that. All were tired and welcomed the end, which was in sight. Dinner was served in the small dining room. The meal was one of Cairo's best, but only the two families shared it. A lot of small talk moved round the table, much like when they had all met for the first time. To each one of them, in their own hearts, it was a way of saying good-bye, and a lot more. During the coming week, the days were for resting and meetings. The evenings were filled with one party after another, for welcoming one family back to Cairo, and saying farewell to the other. Horus-Salah and Anastasia had never met so many important people, all from different fields of life. From high-ranking government officials, to professors of archeology, many lawyers and bankers, the list was endless. It seemed each person in Cairo wanted to welcome back or say good-bye to the two families. It was during one of these moments that both Horus-Salah and Anastasia realized how important their families were, and how powerful their father had become.

Each night, the families stood on opposite sides of the great hall, in their receiving lines. The guests' name and rank was called out as they approached each family to pay their respects. A knowledgeable servant stood behind each father, whispering in his ear any private information about the guest as they came forward. So it went for hours each night. The same procedure, and the same entertainment, with only different names and faces. Even Horus-Salah and Anastasia were exhausted as each evening came to a close. The rule at hand for them was to be seen but not heard. The tutors were close by to enforce this rule, but went one step further so the two of them were not to be seen together. This came from the ruler of the families, their fathers, the law. It was their station in live now, and would be for the rest of time, for all that knew about the future of things.

By the end of the week, all were glad to welcome the end. Some were wishing to be back in Luxor, mostly the two young lovers. Soon the time came for the next move. For now, the two families must say their good- byes. The next day, the Count and his family would leave for Alexandria, and board the ship back to Poland. During their last supper together, the mood was somber. Each word spoken from one to another held more than what was actually said. At moments, one heard a man's voice break during conversation, or a discreet hanky move to the women's eyes. For the last night together, it was a sad time for one and all. When the evening closed, each on felt like an actor that had finished his part in a sad play. As each said goodnight to the other, it was more than a final good bye. The evening ended, and so each went to their own room to bed.

The next day was one of getting to the train station, and on board the train. It was moving so fast now; no one had time to think what was really taking place. One family on the outside of the window, and the other on the inside. Then the whistle, the smoke, and the closing of the window. The last moment of the hands at the window from inside, as those out- side watched. Before Horus-Salah realized the gravity of events, the train was only a thin line, with smoke following it. It was over she was gone and a part of him also.

River of Life

CHAPTER 6

The train pushed and pulled its way to the station waiting in Alexandria. For the travelers in first class, the motion in the large chairs helped them sleep or rest through the endless miles. As one or more would look out the window, it looked back with desert landscape. Only now and then would one side see a moment of the coastline. It was a short distance, but not an enjoyable one. For the Europeans the train did not meet their standards, and for all the others, it was over-populated. The air was hot and when the windows were open the smoke replaced the air. So it went and as people moved about when the train stopped here and there along the way. Each time the conductor asked for tickets, he in turn was asked, 'how much longer to this stop or that'.

By late afternoon, the train stopped at the Alexandria station. The Count and his family, and the entourage of servants wound their way through the crowd and were met by the carriage driver to take them to the ship. As the small caravan moved through the streets towards the harbour, it was still part of Egypt, Anastasia thought to herself. 'No, I have not left Horus-Salah.' The great ocean liner waited at the dock. It was to set sail at first light. To the latecomers the ship was a welcomed sight, and the stateroom met their standards, at least for the Count and his family. The servants didn't fare as well but 2nd class was better than with the poor and homeless in stowage. As the last people and supplies moved aboard, the ship made its final farewell to the port. All that was going aboard was loaded, and the rest had said their good-byes long before the horn gave its farewell. The lines were cast off, and the great ship moved out to the open waters.

By the time breakfast was finished the next day, the ship had made its way into the sea-lanes and was up to cruising

robert f. edwards

speed. The first days were always interesting, if only to explore the ship, and to meet the other passengers, and this day was no different. All the passengers were curiously wandering about to orientate themselves to their new environment. As new acquaintances were struck up, the day changed into night. The dancing and entertainment was arranged to please one and all. According to the captain's report on the matter, it was a success. The night was warm as the ship moved along the coastline of Africa. Small glowing lights were still visible from the shore.

By day, the sun grew stronger and the sea emitted a turquoise glow. Anastasia knew it was the Nile flooding its banks, and that was why it was so large. The Mediterranean was known for its turquoise water and today was no different. As sail boats and other small craft vessels passed by the ocean liner, the passengers would wave down to the smaller boats. It was an enjoyable time for most aboard and the time passed quickly. It was only yesterday, no, the day before, people were saying; though they had been only on the ship a few days, the easy living made them forget time itself. For at noon the next day, the ship would be leaving the gentle waters of this turquoise sea and entering into the cold waves of the Atlantic. Soon the ship changed from west to north along another coastline.

For Anastasia, it was the end of the land that she could see, that was part of Horus-Salah's world. It was the end of any hope that the ship would have to turn around and go back to Egypt and her little Horus, her man, her love. This didn't happen, in her dreams, or in the real world. The ship was making good time. In fact, it was better than half a day ahead of the E.T.A., so the word came down from the captain. The rest of the trip continued much the same; only that heavier clothing was needed for out on deck. The ship was within land sighting of England, if the fog broke.

Then by midday, land, yes land, it was England. The ship never stopped or reduced its speed as the coast moved parallel along side the mighty ship. The day moved as fast as the

River of Life

ship and the tip of England was approaching. The open sea laid ahead, then Sweden, and for the Count, Poland and home at last. The ship had gained a half a day by the time it slipped into the harbor. The next day the passengers left the ship to its crew and it captain.

The Count and his family, tired of traveling still made their way to the train station. The sound of tracks under their feet was a reassuring sound. They were back on land and near their home. Home at last, after a long time away, oh how long it had been, they thought. It was only Anastasia that had other thoughts, which she shared with no one.

As the sea had taken up Anastasia's time, getting his life set up in Cairo had done the same for Horus-Salah. He was preoccupied with getting back to school, and catching up on what had happened with his friends. He was glad he had so much to do, for it took his mind from what was always there. He would be in his room studying and look up only to think of her, his Anastasia, and tears would form. Sometimes, he would think of running away. He dreamt of returning to his real home up in the hills, across from Luxor.

Oh, to sit and look down at the Valley of the Kings. To see the Nile, and the people sailing their little feluccas. The boat people moving up and down the Nile, as their fathers did, and their fathers before them. To see the white sails moving across the backdrop of land, with their masts pointing to the blue sky. "Oh," Horus-Salah said out loud," I must go back home". He was so homesick, not just for his place high above the Valley of the Kings, but everything it looked over. The city of Luxor, the river, the land and the hills. Oh yes, this was where he and his beloved Anastasia should be forever, he thought. The tears ran down his face wetting his galabya or the marble floor below. He must stop this line of thinking; his mind was fighting within itself. At last he made his way to bed, to end another day in his own hell.

For the Polish train that ran across borders and hills, from one country to another, the cargo didn't matter. It was tracks below its carriages and the mighty engine at the head

67

robert f. edwards

"To see the Nile, and the people sailing their little feluccas."

Original artwork, pastel   Phyllis Verdine Humphries
Circa 1930's

River of Life

that counted. The kilometers clicked off like the second hand on a watch. As people aboard looked out the windows, the country was at peace with itself. The sky as blue with white clouds making it picture perfect. Anastasia was one of those people with her face towards the window. The countryside was so very different from the land of Egypt, she thought. Everything is so green, and the hills are lower, but all green as far as the eyes could see. The trees were large and of many different kinds and shapes. The little buildings, homes, and barns, all appeared as a classic work of art from the masters. Her mind was enjoying what her eyes saw and was at rest.

The train pushed it way through the border into the station, and customhouse. At long last they could see their country, their homeland Poland. In less than an hour, the papers and customs checks were over. Now the train and its travelers were headed to Warsaw. They were on Polish soil, they were home. Even Anastasia looked happy as her eyes stared out at the land before her. The little farms gave way to small villages as the train raced onward to Warsaw. It was getting dark during the last hundred kilometers to the large city, where the Count and his family would stay the night. They were to board the train the next morning to Krakow, and their home at last. The train pulled its wagons into the Warsaw station on time, and in the dark.

The Count and his family were taken to the best hotel, which was expecting the travelers, weary and tired. After cleaning up, and consuming a simple quiet dinner, the family retired for the night. Much was already done by the time Anastasia and her family got up for breakfast. The Count was informed that all was ready for him and his family, to go to the train station, and on to Krakow. The Count acted on this knowledge and the last part of the journey was about to being.

Once the train started to move out of the station, it quickly gained the speed, which it would continue with until they arrived in Krakow. The day was warm, and the view from the windows added to the happiness of being back. The train rocked from one side to the other, always moving closer to

robert f. edwards

home. It left behind a cloud of smoke that resembled a dragon running backwards, twisting and turning. The trail of smoke moved higher and higher, until the white clouds finally took it in. By mid-day, the engine had done its work, and the passengers were at the final stop Krakow, and for the Count and his family home.

The servants left to look after the mansion were as anxious as those on the train. It had been a long time since the Count and his family had been home. Would every thing be in order, and to the Count's satisfaction? They could only wait, and hope. It was their jobs and way of life that they were anxious about.

For the others on the train, it was good to be home, seeing old friends and associates. They were anxious to share what had happened through the many years away from Poland and their home. Soon they would be joined together. The Count and his family's limousine made its' way up the long drive to the great doors of the mansion. All the staff was waiting, lined up on the steps to the front entrance. The runner had done his job for each servant was in line by importance, to welcome the owners back to their home. So the long return came to a happy end, as the Count stepped out of the limousine before his servants. Each person knew that from this moment on, his or her life was to change. Some would be back to the old days; other would have to be learning what changes had to be made. But to day was theirs, the owner and his people.

The days that followed were the same as the ones in Egypt for the Count and his family, one party or gathering after another. The month was over and the next one well in hand before the household settled into a routine. One by one, things got to where they were meant to be, in the order of things. The reign of the household and its procedures was back in the hands of the Countess. The comings and goings were organized, and the house was being run in an orderly manner, as the owner wanted. The Count still had to journey back and forth to Warsaw weekly, but the servants only no-

River of Life

ticed his presence when another party took place in the evenings. It was only for his manservant that accompanied him everywhere that knew of his activities.

For Anastasia, getting back into the life style of Poland was different, but with her old friends and schoolmates, she was able to settle into the routine quickly. It was the nights in her room, where it was darkness that she moved back to Luxor and her little Horus. Her mind would ask a thousand questions with no answers coming. Sleep would give her mind a rest until the next day. So it went day in, day out.

The summer greens turned to the rusts of fall, changing to the whites of winter, and then back to the hopes of green again. Time past, with the two young lovers writing each other, from letters received to letters sent. Sometimes once a month, and other times longer, they both had to wait for each other. The two always hoped and waited, anxiously anticipating another letter to arrive. The days and weeks changed into months, but their love remained the same throughout.

One year had past, then another, and so it went. The world moved on and the two lovers continued on, but not with each other. Horus-Salah went every year to his home, his tomb. He would always spend time back in Luxor with his family, and as he got older, would be sent there on the train. These were the happiest times of his life without Anastasia. When he was once more alone in the cave over-looking the valley below, he some-times missed Anastasia so much, he had to look around not to believe she wasn't there with him. Then, tears would form, and the valley would be blurred, as if a painter had spilled water on the landscape he was painting.

So nothing changed, and yet everything was different, in the worlds of Horus-Salah and his beloved Anastasia. They both lived in different parts of the world, and their life styles were so different. Yet, in all this, it was much the same, for they were ruled by their class in life. The freedom was only granted by their parents' wishes, and they followed a similar life. They both lived in an all-same sex world. Anastasia was in an all girls' college ruled by a teaching order of nuns. The only man, or male presence in the area, was the old gardener, and the good father that came for confessions and mass. At home, it was much the same for her; void of men or at least young men her own age group. The world was for her, one class of people and one kind of sex. Female only, morning, noon and night in this world she lived in. If the nuns had known that she was writing Horus-Salah, it would have been a great sin. The sin would have been greater; especially if they found out he was not even a Christian. The world was changing, but not that much. So, it was when she came home for Holy Days or national holidays that the letters would be there, waiting and hoping for a reply. Each year, the words changed, but not the meaning.

For Horus-Salah it was much the same, he was in an all man's world. Women were mostly behind closed doors, with their mother, or under the protection of other women. Most of the day, women were not even seen. It was also his faith that kept the opposite sex away from each other at all cost. Both Anastasia and Horus-Salah never questioned this aspect in their life, for it was the way it was, and had been. Neither questioned whether their relationship was different or unnatural. Some things did not bear thinking about all together, and this was one of them. The seasons came, each in their allotted turn, letting the world know that the earth was still rotated around the sun.

Anastasia's body was letting her know that she had gone from a young girl of twelve, to now a young woman of seventeen. Though her height was a few inches more, it was the rest of her body that told the story. Her waist was just as small, but her hips had move out into full womanhood. Not to mention the full bush of hair that was now covering her mound of love. Her small breasts with their little points had grown to full size that women dreamt of, and men wanted to see. Her long hair blonde was her crowning glory, to frame a beautiful face and body.

She was now a woman, in both mind and body. She felt the better part of grown up. Next year she would be finished

River of Life

the grade schools and enter university. On to finishing school, and then the world her mother lived in. To her, this was a question of past. She wanted to be in the man's world, and do things that men were doing. One came to mind at once, to return to Egypt and work in the Valley of the Kings. She had enjoyed those times, and the most importantly, she would be back with her little Horus. She must stop calling him 'little' Horus, for he was now nineteen years of age.

For Horus-Salah, life to had now moved him from his boyhood, into the new age of manhood. He too had grown taller, but not as much as he wanted. His face showed the world that he was a man, by having a light beard. His body was strong and fully developed in all ways. Between his legs was the dark hair of manhood and in the morning his manhood told him it was ready. He was a very good-looking young man.

He had finished his grades and had done well in them. He was learning more about his father's business. He had done some traveling to Kenya and Tanzania with his father. It was the first time in his life that the two men spent any time together. He had always loved his father, but now respected him even more. He was also very proud that his father had done so many things with his life. He now understood what his father had done to look after the family and what a great responsibility it was to be the head of the clan. His father encouraged him to go to England to finish his schooling. To both of them this was an order to be done.

At first, Horus-Salah didn't put to much thought into the positive or negative of the request- like order. However, when he was once more alone, he gave it more thought. To be away from Egypt, and moreover, to be away from his home, and all that life meant to him, was more than he could handle in his mind. Then, to be close to Anastasia, and maybe to see her, was the other side, which made him feel warm inside. Back and forth his mind worked, over and over, but in the end he knew he would do what he was told to do. This was in the past, and the present. There would be no changes in the future.

The heat of the summer was upon all of Egypt, and so once more Horus-Salah had a chance to visit Luxor. It would always be his first place in the world; he thought that he would always want to be here. Just to sit in the tomb, and look down upon this area of the world, was all he wanted out of life. Then his mind added just as quickly 'with Anastasia by his side'. "Oh, Allah will this ever happen?" he asked out loud to the heavens above. There was no answer, only the might rays of Ra overhead. In both Anastasia's and Horus-Salah's lives, the long days of summer were coming to an end. They were being replaced by the shorter days of fall just ahead. For both of them, it was not only the change of a season but also a change of their lives.

River of Life

CHAPTER 7

When Horus-Salah returned to Cairo, things looked the same as always. Horus-Salah was called into his father's study. Horus-Salah had been in the study only three times before in his life. He was always told of a great change in his life when it happened. So this time he didn't expect any different. His father was seated at the great desk that dominated the room, and sat behind it as a ruler would.

Horus-Salah entered the room more as a servant than a member of the family, to say nothing of being his father's first born and a son. The father acknowledged the boy's presence by looking up, and with one hand, gestured in the direction of a chair near the desk. Horus-Salah moved towards the chair, and then sat up-right, waiting. It seemed to Horus-Salah an eternity, as his father worked on the papers before him.

Then without warning, his father said, "I have news from England on your studies". Then it came, the news and the order, all at the same time. Horus-Salah now knew why he had been sent for, and what was yet to happen to him. His father, without looking up from the papers on his desk continued, "You have been accepted at Cambridge University." His father stopped, and then added, "The dean will have you take the entrance test at the college for your subject in university. You will major in sciences, law, and economics. The next term is in October. I have registered you for it. Also, you will be lodging at the college."

Horus-Salah waited for more, but the room remained silent. After what seemed forever to Horus-Salah, his father once more raised his hand and pointed to the door. With this dismissal, Horus-Salah got up from the chair and said, "I won't let you or this house down, Father."

robert f. edwards

The face behind the desk still didn't look up, but said, "I wouldn't expect anything less from you." As Horus-Salah turned towards the great doors, his father turned the page on the document before him. He only looked up when he heard the great doors close. Looking at the door his mind flashed, my son the dreamer.

Once outside the room, Horus-Salah went back to his room. He had known that he was going to university, but always thought it would be here in Cairo, or maybe Alexandria. Now, it was to be England, living in groups with hundreds of other men that he had never met. To be alone, in a strange country, and to know no one. He looked around his room as if he would never see it again. The next day, the news was throughout the house. Like all news, it is the people involved that were the last to know. The details came from his manservant, of when and what ship he was leaving on.

In less than two weeks, he would be aboard a ship, moving him away from all he had ever known. 'To be in charge of his life, no' came the answer from within, he was just going to be alone, to do his father's wishes. From being a man yesterday, he had returned to being a boy today.

For the next two weeks, the household was much the same as always. His life didn't change much. It was his manservant and others that got his things ready, and would ask once in a while if he would need this, or that. To him, what would be needed only the English would know. He had been told that there was a dress code, or university colors that were to be worn. His galabyas were one thing that didn't need to go, even the servants knew that.

The days moved fast, a few friends came and said their good-bye, and best wishes. There were no farewell parties, or get-togethers. At times, it was as if they were house cleaning, and he was one of the things that they were getting rid of. The last evening was dinner with a small group of his parents' friends, and all of them wished him well.

The next day, he and his manservant departed for the train station to leave for Alexandria, where the ship lay in the

River of Life

harbour. Once the train reached the station, Horus-Salah continued to make his way to the docks. The ship by now was along side, taking on its' cargo. The manservant went aboard with Horus-Salah to his stateroom. After the manservant helped him unpack and find his way around the ship, they bid their good- byes. Now, in the stateroom by himself, he was really alone.

Some time in the early morning, he heard the horn and movements above, but rolled over for more sleep. By last call for breakfast, Horus-Salah made his way to his place at the large dining room. The ship, by now, was well under way through the channel towards the other end of the Mediterranean Sea.

He ate what was placed before him and went up top. As he looked out to the sea, it went on forever, the green waters. As he changed sides, the shoreline gave him hope that he would be back some day to his land and its people. It was this moment that he recalled one of Anastasia's letters, and how she felt on the ship so long ago, moving her family and herself through these waters. As he leaned on the railing, looking at the dots of buildings on the distance shore, his mind was once again with Anastasia.

If not thinking about her and the times they were together, he was thinking about her letters. How little he had with him, but at least he had her letters. With that thought in his mind, he felt he wasn't so alone. Even better, he would be much closer to her than he had been in years. Yes, there was even hope that he may get to visit her in the years to come. All was not lost, there was still hope.

The ship cut through the waters, making its way into the great North Atlantic. Once though the Gate of Hercules and out into the ocean the ship turned towards its next port. England was a few days away, but to Horus-Salah it had no call to him. The end of this trip would be when he returned to his land, his place, Egypt. The ship was moving him away from where he belonged. For Horus-Salah, the sea was not a place he chose to be. He was definitely a land lover in every way. He had given back to the sea most of the meals, and now could feel the loss of weight around his waist. One more night, and one more day, and the ship would dock at a port on this island that once ruled the seas.

Before the day passed to the half-way point, the ship glided into its' resting- place at the dock. It was well into the afternoon before the passengers were allowed to go ashore. For Horus-Salah and those in the upper class sections, the Customs and Immigration officer came to the stateroom to do the paper work. Horus-Salah also knew that a man would come and escort him to the university.

So as it was planned, so it happened. By late in the afternoon, the man came to his stateroom. Both Horus-Salah and his escort then went to the train station and boarded the train to his new home. Horus-Salah said nothing when the man referred to the college as his new home. Oh, how different life here was going to be. "Oh Allah, please help me," Horus-Salah repeated over and over to himself. It was late when the train pulled into the station.

The man told Horus-Salah that his belongings would come to his room the next day. With that information, both men got a taxi to the college. As the taxi moved though the darkness, the buildings and surroundings looked so very strange to him. When the taxi rolled up the long driveway to the grounds that belonged to the university and college, it was like going into a king's palace.

However, once inside the long hallway, with barren gray stonewalls, he changed his first thought on this matter. During the hours that these two men had spent together, little had been said on either side. The man would have little to report to his superior, and Horus-Salah was no wiser about his new residence. He was escorted to his room, and the 'good-nights' that followed ended the day.

The rules of the college were outlined in a small book that he had been given. The rulebook was signed by the dean of the day. His closing remarks were "Rules are to be obeyed by

River of Life

one and all. All will do well when obeyed, and beware to the ones that don't."

The bell from the church started the day at 6:00 a.m. Horus-Salah's room was more of a cell, for there was no window and when the door was closed there was no light. The small desk lamp was all that broke the total darkness at any time of day or night. The bed was just short of being classified as a cot. The desk was an old wooden table that the previous users had left their names on down the years.

Just as Horus-Salah had finished dressing, there was a knock at the door. A senior student was assigned to show Horus-Salah what was to be done, and where to go, and at what times. To Horus-Salah, these days would always be remembered, and not with happiness. Nor would the days that followed, for that matter, the years. Oh, if he had known about the long years ahead, would this small body be able to endure? It came to his mind what a wise man in Tanzania asked him. "How do you eat an elephant?"

He gave a few responses, with the old man repeatedly saying, "No, that's not the answer."

Giving up, Horus-Salah asked, "What then?" and the old man answer, "One mouthful at a time." Yes, this was what he was going to do one minute, one hour, one day at a time. The other side of his mind asked "How long before the end?" His other side replied, "When you have a degree or your father wishes you back."

He had for all intents and purposes, moved to another planet, with even the people looking different. He had already dressed in the western clothes, and had removed his facial hair. He was trying to blend in as much as possible. He may not have tried so hard, or hoped for so much then, if he had seen what lay ahead of him.

He walked across the grounds to the churchyard to face his first change, to sit in a pew in a church, rather than kneel or sit on the floor in a mosque. There wouldn't be anything of his country or the ways of his land here, today, or any other day. He would always be a stranger in this country, today, and every day thereafter. He would be different, in his color of skin, down to the smallest thought on any subject. He was alone, in a land without friends or hope.

With these thoughts, he looked up upon the sky above. It was like the buildings and the land before it, dark and grey. The cold sky wouldn't allow the sun to warm the earth, and dampness was present everywhere. He was like the sky above, in his feelings this first day, with so many more to follow. To say he was unhappy would only mask how bad he really felt. He pushed hard to get his feet to move to the door of the church. It was his mind that he had the bigger problem with, and it moved much slower. Would he be able to make it through today, let alone the days that would follow?

'Allah', he cried to himself, as his feet moved through the doors of the church, and the beginning of all that was so new to him. For today, and the days ahead, he did what the old man had said about the elephant. As the days moved to months, the only rays of hope came in the way of letters, from his mother and others back in Egypt, in his mother tongue. He knew in his heart that he was Egyptian, and would always be, no matter where on this planet his body was.

It was primarily Anastasia's letters that helped him now, and explained some of the new ways of living in this strange land. She advised him; try not to understand the English or their way, but to live with them. She reminded him of the changes her family had made when in his country. It wasn't her choice to go there; but look what good had come from it. She reminded him also, how much closer they were now in distance to each other. This was, and would be his life support-line while continuing to live here, this place that was so very strange to his way of life.

The months now moved into the winter days, and at times, Horus-Salah wished that hell would come calling for him, if only to be warm just once more. The cold, oh, this frigid cold, would it never give way, both outside the buildings and inside the endless walls of stone. Now the gray sky had support from the winds that drove the rain down, beating on

River of Life

the buildings, and stinging the skin of the residents. The land had a green moss for cover, but the trees and other living things did not fare as well. Horus-Salah felt colder than the tombs of the kings of old. He was so cold that the cells in his bone marrow moved slower and slower. The days came and went, but the cold stayed on. This winter was winning in every way, Horus-Salah thought, even the daylight was shorter. The long nights had more darkness. In this land called England, endless clouds that cloaked it also covered the stars and moon.

Horus-Salah had never seen fog, and did not know what it was the first time. The fog would come down and cover the city, until one was as lost as the bind man with no cane. This white gray mist swirled around his feet, and then would disappear before his eyes. Along with this cover, there was a smell drifting around that Horus-Salah couldn't bear, a coal dust odor. Yes, there was smoke in the air; the little that he could breath. His mind called out to Allah, who would want to live in a place of darkness month after month? The answer was all around him, for now the calendar showed the month of December.

To the locals, this weather made them happy. For this was the time for Christmas, and there was caroling, and reveling and much preparation, all leading up to Christmas Day. Horus-Salah understood what it meant as a religious time, but not the giving of presents and the parties. All that was here was so foreign to him. He was lost both for words and understanding.

Though the days in light were short they were long for him, now that classes were out for what was called 'the season'. There were few students still remaining at the college. The great halls were empty. His room was too cold to stay in and study, so he would spend most of his time by the large fireplace. During these times, there was always a fire in the hearth. This was one of the few places that offered any warmth to him. So there he would be sit, studying, as close as he could get to the fire. He was given the nickname by his

81

classmates, of 'the mummy man' for several reasons. One of the reasons was the layer of sweaters he wore. It was on these lonely days that made him pine for Egypt, and all that was back there. Oh, only if he could study back in Cairo or Alexandria.

This was on his mind constantly, but especially when he had to return to his room, 'the cell' he called it. With the small light on the table, he would get undressed. He would quickly pull back the blankets, five to six of them, turn off the light, and jump into bed. In one fluid motion, he had the blankets up to his chin, and was lying straight. He had soon learnt about losing body heat to the bed covers. It was his experience that just when all the heat from his body had been given up to the bed, then the blankets would return some back to him, to make it through another night. Yes, another night, one less in his life, but also less here in the coldness of this hell. So it went, always one day after the next.

Then, a new year arrived, and the talk of spring. Yes, he thought, if I could make it until then, I may be able to continue. With the help from the letters from Egypt, and well-needed ones from Anastasia, spring came to England, and to Horus-Salah, just in time. Once the trees lost their nakedness, and the flowers appeared in the fields, even Horus-Salah felt better about England. It wasn't just one thing about this country that he didn't like, it was everything. The people were like its climate, cold and distance to him.

He had been here now the better part of a year, and nothing had changed. The life at college was hard, and the lessons long. He had been alone at home, but here, he was alone not by choice. The worse times were when there were class break, which would last for weeks. This was known as study-time or reading time. Most of the time the students would return to their homes for a school holiday. This would only remind Horus-Salah just how far away from Egypt he really was, and there was no way to go home. To ask to return, even for a visit, was out of the question.

River of Life

The summer was warm by his standards and hot for the locals. However, it made life more bearable, especially to Horus-Salah. He could say, to one and all, it was the best time he had spent in this country. He would take long walks on the green grassy hills, and found much to interest him in the little farmlands. He discovered a large tree he enjoyed sitting under, and would read a book, or write a letter. During this time, he thought he could make it here, in this land, but he would never want to stay.

It was during one of these days in the summer that he had got a letter from Anastasia. To fully enjoy the letter, he headed towards one of his favourite trees. By the time he sat under it, mid-day was with him, and he took to the shady side of the tree. Once settled underneath the leave canopy, he opened the letter with great care, like he did all of them. To him, it was opening a treasure, and today the envelope was large, which meant Anastasia's letter would be long, or maybe contain a picture or two. His hand worked slowly, while his mind danced wildly. He gently drew the big bundle out, and the letter started with 'My little Horus'. She almost always started this way. She talked of what it she had been doing, and what her family's plans were, along with the local news.

Then, on the third page, she had some real news and a surprise for him. She told him about what she had been planning for months. The idea first started on a day with her mother, and reminiscing about the times they had spent in Egypt. They remembered the help his family had given to all of them. Yes, this had been the start. Next, she asked her mother if Horus-Salah could come for a visit at Christmas time. This was where it had laid for months. Her mother said that she would bring it up with the Count, and let Anastasia know in due time. Well, the time had come, just last week; her mother called her in for tea, and said 'yes.' The Count had agreed to write a letter to Horus-Salah's father, asking if he could spend the Christmas season with them.

What great news, first to see Anastasia, and to be away from England for Christmas. His heart missed a beat, and he had a hard time finishing the letter. After reading the letter a second time, and then a third time, which he did with all her letters, he knew it would be in his father's response, if he was to go or not. Along with her news, she always added the perfume she was wearing that day. He would hold the pages to his nose, and almost feel she was with him as his eyes closed. These were the moments that gave him the will to keep on with his studies and stay the course. With newfound hope, and a light heart, he went back to the real world that waited his return.

The next few letters were from his mother, which mentioned nothing about Anastasia's invitation. The months now moved into fall, and still nothing from either side, his or hers. He had started the Michelmas term, which brought with it the reminder of fall. The cold winds of October removed the leaves from the trees he loved so much, and the skies returned to the long gray days. This was bad enough, but now the nights were growing into longer periods, and the days gave way, at both ends. With all this, the cold that Horus-Salah had such a hard time handling came too. He was in poor spirits.

When a letter arrived from Egypt for him, he opened it fully expecting it to be from his mother. But it was from his father, the only one he had ever received. His father, in his usual manner, informed him that he had received a request for Horus-Salah's presence at the Count's residence. Horus-Salah was to travel to the Count's estate after the term was finished and return well before the Lent term started. Horus-Salah put the letter down on the table before reading it again, for his hands were shaking so bad that he couldn't read it any other way.

'Anastasia, oh Anastasia', his mind repeated over and over, 'you did it!' Yes, she had done the impossible; she not only got him out of this place, but to be with her as well. 'There was an Allah, and an Anastasia, thank you both', he thought.

The day continued like no other day he had in this place. He was alive again; he had a dream to look forward to. He had

River of Life

hope for tomorrow; he had something to count on in the future. He was happy for the first time in years; he was going to see his Anastasia. This was not only his second year, but also the midyear before getting his first degree. It was the in-between year, when things fit, and so did the students, Horus-Salah was just one of them now. The days moved faster than any other time since he had been in England. His body was still feeling the cold walls of learning, but mind and soul were planning the dreams of being in Poland.

Finally, the term ended. Horus-Salah packed up, and went to the train station once more, but this time heading for to a port and a ship bound for Holland, then on to Anastasia in Poland. Her last letter told him that when the ship docked at Amsterdam, one of their servants would come aboard, and bring him back to the estate. She had added to bring warm clothes. Even now, with all of his sweaters and extra wool pants, he wondered how cold it could be, after living in this place called England.

The crossing was nothing, compared to what he had remembered coming to England had been. Once in the port at Amsterdam the Count's servant came abroad. The two men made their way to the train station, and on to Poland.

CHAPTER 8

 The train was on time. Throughout the night and into the next day the trail of wagons went over rivers and down valleys. They moved from one country through to another, and then across the border to Poland. Each man was in first class, but the servant only joined Horus-Salah for the meals. Horus-Salah wanted to ask a thousand or more questions about Poland, and most of all, how was his Anastasia.

This was out of the question, for two reasons, both being equal. One being the servant could only speak a little English, and the other was it was not done to carry on a conversation with any servant. By the train arrived in Krakow, both men disembarked, not knowing one another much better than the moment of their meeting. The car was waiting to bring them to the estate. To one it was home, to the other it was happiness.

Horus-Salah looked out the window at the snow. It was the first time he had ever seen this, but in his mind's eye he was already looking at Anastasia. The car carried them back to the countryside and suddenly the driveway up to the estate.

They were here. He was here. It was not a dream; he had arrived. The man that had met him at the ship was to be his manservant. This man led him through to the wing that would be his quarters. This was a large suite, and had a sitting room as large as most living rooms, with a small bedroom for his manservant. The large bedroom had attached to it a smaller room, which was the study. To complete their quarters was a large bathroom, and again a smaller toilet room. All this overlooked the grounds and countryside below.

As Horus-Salah looked out of one of the windows, his first thoughts were of paintings he had seen in the art museum. There, before his eyes, was nature's winter landscape. The little fields of snow, with trees covered with their new leaves of

River of Life

frost. The building and all things that were not at ground level, made their presence known, but still were of the common color white. Looking out the window, the scene before was a perfect picture, even with a frame. The warmth of his suite kept out the cold by large fireplaces in each room. What a difference compared to the bleak life back in Cambridge. It was late afternoon, and in this northern part of the world, the sun was giving up its presence.

There was a knock at the door to his suite. When his manservant answered, he came back to inform Horus-Salah that the Countess and Anastasia were in one of the sitting rooms and would like to see him. His heart stopped and his face turned red. It was the moment that he waited for so long. What would she be like, and *would she feel the same*?

He said, "I am ready", and he followed the servant to the sitting room. They knocked, and a voice from the other side said, "Enter". Horus-Salah walked in, followed by the servants in the background. The two women stood up as Horus-Salah came before them. One was in her later years, and the lines of time had left their marks on her face. She showed the class she was from, in her elegant ways, from her dress, to her movement of welcome.

It was the other young woman, he wished he could rub his eyes, for she couldn't be real, let alone be Anastasia. This woman had all the elegance of the other, and was beautiful. He tried to smile as he moved in front of both of them. The two women put their hands out together, and Horus-Salah reached for the senior hand, and then kissed it. The reply came with; "It is nice of you to come, Horus-Salah." He then moved over to the other hand, and did the same. The reply, "It is very good to see you," and with that, her fingers covered Horus-Salah's hand, and squeezed it. He looked up, and saw the most beautiful woman, the most beautiful person in all his life, smiling back at him.

With that, the three of them sat, and were served coffee and cakes. The three talked and asked each other question after question throughout the rest of the afternoon. Horus-

robert f. edwards

Salah learnt that the Count, like his father, spent most of his time in Warsaw versus Cairo. His mind flashed back to those days his father and the Count spent their days together. He wondered if the men missed their friendship as much as he had missed his Anastasia. The answer came back from his mind, 'of course not, they were men and only friends, and his was *love'*.

The three of them were alone now, although the room always had servants moving about. Always waiting to do their job, or an assignment, to these people, servants were a part of life. They were there, but were not seen, only if they didn't do their job were they even noticed. So they talked openly as if it was private, and so it was.

When Horus-Salah returned to his quarters, his evening dress was pressed and didn't have that travel look about it. Once more, he looked around the sitting room in his suite. It was bigger than a classroom at the university. Oh, to be back in the class of style he had grown up in, and had always known, until going to Cambridge University. This was the only time since he left Egypt that he could think of living his life anywhere else. The few short moments of time he had been here in Poland was so different than the grey of England. The sky gave back the sun, no, one did not feel the heat, nor was Ra the sun god giving the same time in the sky, but he was there, and one could feel and see him. For Horus-Salah, the more he saw and learnt, the better he felt. This was nothing to say what joy his heart and mind held, to see the one and only in his life, Anastasia.

Again, there was a knock, and this time it was a male servant to show him to the small dining room for just the family. The two women were already seated. The Countess at the head of the table, and at the other end, the chair was, and would remain empty. Horus-Salah sat opposite Anastasia, which made it hard for him to look anywhere else. The two women had also dressed for dinner in long evening dresses. Both looked and acted the part they were playing in the role of life. The Countess was in a high neck, long-sleeved dress of

River of Life

rich golden embroidery on a blue background. Anastasia was wearing a simple yet elegant green, the color of jade. The low-cut neckline showed her womanhood. The small straps left her shoulders and arms naked. To Horus-Salah, her skin had the whiteness of the landscape outside, with none of the coldness.

The dinner was served, and oh, what a feast it was compared to the food he had forced himself to eat these last two years. It tasted like food, the meat had seasoning in it, and the vegetables had flavors of their own. Oh, to taste real food, he ate like a man that was eating for the first time finally something that was to his liking, and all could tell.

As much as he enjoyed the food, it was a far second to the enjoyment his eyes were having, as he looked up from his meal to see Anastasia across from him. Most of the time he wanted to say,' are you real, or is it another dream I am having?' Then, she would look at him and smile; his life was complete. During one eye contact moment, she whispered, 'I love you'.

His face gave away the message, for he turned red, and the Countess noticed. She asked him if something was wrong? He managed to reply that it was nothing, just some hot seasoning spice. This got a large smile from Anastasia, plus a small giggle. The talk at the dinner table was light, but interesting to one and all. The Countess noticed how happy her daughter was, and how good-looking Horus-Salah was. From the head of the table, she looked at the two young people, and thought that they were so good-looking and happy. Just for a moment, the Countess thought of both of these two people being together, but her mind knew why not; now, or ever. If her face showed anything, the other two didn't notice.

Shortly after the meal was finished, the three went into the parlor. Tea and brandy was served. Horus-Salah enjoyed the tea, but passed on the brandy. It was the taste, more than his faith, which stopped him joining the two women in this drink. As the fire warmed the room, and danced a merry tune in the hearth, the three chairs with their occupants had front row seats. The Countess was in the middle, which helped all to keep the order of conversation flowing back and forth for everyone. They talked about things that happened after the Count and his family moved back to Poland. Horus-Salah told about life in England. Before the information was complete, one of the servants informed the Countess of the hour. All three of them had lost track of time altogether. With this new information, they said their goodnights to each other.

It had been one of the greatest days of Horus-Salah's life. Once back in his rooms, oh yes, his mind said, to have rooms again, and not just an extra long coffin for him, but a real bed. Then his mind stopped him, not now, nor for the rest of his stay here, would he think of Cambridge. His rooms were heated by hot water heating, but there was also a fire going in the fireplace at the far end of the room. He walked towards the window, which was in length taller than he was, with an arch at the top. As he looked through the square leaded panes of glass, the moon was full, and the stars were out. He looked closer through the thick glass, and the world outside had a piece of heaven in its view. With the help of moonbeams, the land, and all that lay on top, was covered in new snow. The world outside this window looked as pure and clean as innocence.

With this, Horus-Salah moved away, and laid on the bed that had been turned down, waiting for him. He lay under the blankets, and thought of all that lay under the snow, and what Anastasia had said to him at dinner. His heart was full of joy, and peace entered into the last moment before sleep took him away.

The morning arrived, and the sun replaced the translucent moonlight through the window. Horus-Salah walked over to the same leaded-glass windows as last night, but this time there was so much more to see. He stood aside as he opened the great windows. As these great protectors from the outside gave way, the cold air rushed into the room. As an unwelcome thief, it removed the warmth from the room, but allowed Horus-Salah the freedom to see what he had wanted.

River of Life

With the cold air moving in, and the warmth leaving, Horus-Salah's face felt both of the changes. He stood before the opening, and saw for the first time what a winter morning in Poland could be. He moved his hand to his eyes, just to make sure it was real and looked again. There, before his eyes, was what last night had shown him, but now there was so much more. The new snow had no marks on it, and was still clean as the robes of the angels in heaven. The little buildings had bigger roofs than walls, for now the snow had covered up some of the walls and added height to the roofs. Out of these tall roofs came white smoke, as if a new pope had been proclaimed. The white smoke moved higher until the bright blue sky took it away. The large trees below had taken on a new life from the day before. Yesterday, when he came, all of them were leafless and had a look of death about them. As he looked at the same trees today, they had three centimeters of what he would learn was hoarfrost. The hoarfrost made everything look like a fairy countryside. To Horus-Salah, this could have been the case, looking out what had been a castle window.

There was so much more to see, but just then his male servant came into the room. The first thing he saw was Horus-Salah at the window. To him Horus-Salah looked like a statue, frozen in time, looking out into eternity. Horus-Salah moved back and with this, closed the view. He turned and said 'good morning' to the servant. Horus-Salah was happy again to day, and oh, what a difference to be speaking in French rather than English. Both last night, and again now, to be speaking in the language which the entire world called the cultural language. After dressing he joined the two women for breakfast. They were busy planning what they would do for the day, and the days ahead.

The Countess, and rightfully so, took the lead. She started with today, which would be going to Krakow. There, they could buy the warm clothing for Horus-Salah, and show him the city, and tell him more about the area that the Count and his family were part of. For the weeks ahead, she informed the young couple of the social events that were part of the up-coming season. This included events such as church pageants, to parties, both at their home and many invitations they had received.

So it went, most of the morning, explaining and listening. The two young people asked questions now and then, about what one event was, or another. The questions were more from Anastasia, for information she thought Horus-Salah would want to know, but was too shy to ask. The main question Horus-Salah asked, "Did the Count and Countess want him to be part of all their social outings she mentioned?"

The answer was always the same, "Why yes, you are part of everything we do, and you are your special guest."

From this meeting, Horus-Salah knew that he would always be in love with Anastasia, as he had been in the years in the past, but now he had support from her mother. His mind flashed back to his family, and wondered if his mother and family would treat his love, Anastasia the same way? After their discussions, the trio moved away from the table and went their separate ways to prepare for the day that awaited them. As Horus-Salah bowed to the women, he looked up and saw Anastasia's face. She was smiling at him, and her lips moved without the sound of her voice. He read again, 'I love you,' on them, and moved his head back down as he turned away. Again, his dark skin felt the glow of red growing on it.

The car came to take the small group to town, down the road with walls bordering each side of the road. The walls were built both by nature and man. One gave the materials, that marvelous ingredient known as snow, as it was removed from the road. Horus-Salah sat facing the two women in the limousine, which gave him a chance to look out the back window when not looking at them. As he looked past them out the window, the road that they were leaving behind was like a large pencil mark across white paper. The more he looked the line moved, changing from one side to the other. Let all that wanted to see the beautiful fairy landscape it crossed. All were

River of Life

happy, but the two lovers were beside themselves, to once more to be together, if not alone.

The car came to Krakow and like many cities in this part of the world; it was the square that all main roads led to. Horus-Salah was given a history of the city and the square by both women. The size of the square, by their information, was the largest, or at least one of the largest, in all of Europe. Then, on to the large church, that was at one end of the square, to all the little shops and cafés that lined the perimeter of this huge area. The day was spent with the trio making one purchase after another. In late afternoon, the sun gave way to the early evening twilight, and the happy shoppers returned to the car and drove back home in darkness.

Once back in his room, Horus-Salah returned to the window and opened it. Yes, it had not changed from the night before. It was still the magic that he had seen last night with the help of the moon and the stars.' Oh, what a place, oh, what a country', his mind keep repeating over, and over again. But it always added 'thank you, Allah, and you, Anastasia.'

That evening was much the same as the night before. The Count would be returning from Warsaw at the end of the week, and would stay home until after the Christmas season. So, this was the last night for a small dinner party of the three of them. Once again, he enjoyed his meal and said his good nights before returning to his rooms. He had never known this much happiness; as he lay in bed dreaming of this new feeling, with his eyes wide open. Sometime during the darkness, sleep replaced these thoughts.

The light of day moved across the windows, and slowly Horus-Salah's eyes opened. As the light of the day grew stronger, and his sleep gave way to being awake, Horus-Salah got out of bed. He went over to the window, which by now was part of his routine. Again, like so many times before, the view had not changed from the night previous. It was the time that had change. The days had moved like the big hand on his watch, only to be followed by the weeks, which had become the smaller hand on the same watch. The end of his stay in

robert f. edwards

Poland, this estate, this room, and oh, no, with his true love, his one and only Anastasia.

Today, as he looked out the window, he saw more than his eyes looked at. It was his inner eye that took charge of his thoughts. It was as though he was looking through the window of a time warp, for as he looked forward into the countryside below, it changed with each thought he had. It moved back to the beginning of his stay, and the first night, and each day after. One by one the day moved past, before his inner-eye, and the view outside.

First came the parties, one after another. This time of year was so important to this part of the world. It was mixed with a religion moment, and a holiday of being free from the normal life-style. The giving of presents and sharing of food, which was the best he had ever known, and the fine wines to celebrate with. The men were home from work, but the study was rarely used. It was a time when most people were in good spirits, and some had too much of the spirits out of the bottles. The women wore new dresses and the men walked tall. The night was livelier than the days. The days were for resting, and getting ready for the night, which would last well into the early hours of the mornings. There was singing everywhere and the people generally were in a giving mood. For Horus-Salah, he had never experienced this holiday celebration before.

He blinked, and then another part of this great time came into his thoughts. The theatre, oh what place to go, that was one of so many things that he personal enjoyed. The plays, the opera, the ballets, all of them. The many stories they told. Each in a different way, but each in his mind, equal to the other. Yes, this was part of the great moment in his life he would always remember. It was part that he would want in his life from now on. The theater had be food for his soul, as the delicious foods on the table were for his body. What a time to be here, and to be a part of the season called Christmas.

Next, came the out-doors and all it's wonderment. The snow that covered everything it touched, and left it clean and

94

River of Life

new. The frost and icicles could paint beauty on all things that were sleeping or dead. The trees changed from bareness with long white leaves. On it went, the days and weeks moving past, like pictures in a photo album. Changing and always different. To Horus-Salah, each was in itself so very precious, but the ones that were the centrepiece always had Anastasia in them. Her presence was all that he needed to be totally happy, and had been each day since he had arrived. The pictures kept coming, and each one was just as prominent as the other was.

He didn't hear his male servant come in, or call out his name. It was only when the man put his hand on his shoulder and called out to him did he feel anything. It was like coming out of a deep sleep when he turned around. The first thing he heard was "Are you all right, sir?" He couldn't speak, but nodded 'yes.' These were the last two full days, for on the third one he would be going to the train station. Back to England, he thought, back there, oh, no, not after being here this long. To be this happy, and to be with the one he loved, then to leave, this was going to be one of the hardest times in his live. It made him remember the time he and his family left Luxor, and the pain he felt.

For now, it was a new day, and one more to enjoy. Anastasia had been planning for this day since he arrived. She had arranged to go on a sleigh-ride through the countryside lanes with some of her friends. The sleigh was one of the authentic old ones as well as its driver. It was one of the sleighs that had been originally used to cross-parts of Siberia, before the railway was built. This sleigh had a small covering for the traveler, which offered some comfort while traveling in cold weather. Both horses and the sleigh itself had large bells, which made a music all of their own, when in motion. There were two large seats across from each other, both soft and comfortable. To add to this, was the large fur blanket, which covered the traveler up to their necks.

As was the custom when on this kind of ride, the supply of vodka was endless. Anastasia had ordered a supply of her

robert f. edwards

favorite vodka,' Zubrovka'. It was by far, in her view, the best vodka in the entire world, for it was made from the bison grass just outside her home. When Horus-Salah joined the others, in planning what the day was to hold, it was talk of this, and putting the final plans together. The food baskets were full of all kind of treats and the last-minute checks of all the small things that may be needed were finalized. Even the fur hat that Horus-Salah was given to wear, plus the warm fur gloves for his hands were thought of. Anastasia had left nothing for chance; this was going to be her going-away present for her Horus, her man, her love.

The time came, with the horses and the sleigh being announced by the bells on both. With the supplies in place, and now the two passengers with their chaperons, the sleigh continued on its way to pick up two more people, to make the group complete. After the last stop and another couple, the list was compete, and off for the ride through this winter wonderland.

The bells gave way to the laughter from within. The food, plus the glasses of Zubrovka were removed from the basket, to find their way into the guests. The sleigh had long ago left the roads, and now was making its own trails along the countryside; while inside the small party was having a great time. It had not been in Anastasia's plans that the chaperons would drink more than they would eat, but this was the case. Under the large fur blankets, the chaperon's eyes grew heavy, before they closed and stayed that way.

The young people kept the party going, as the ride moved from one field to another. Even the sun grew tired and moved towards the end of the day with its first shadows of night. The cold air was present, but only to their laughing faces, for the rest were well protected under a blanket of fur. Horus-Salah had tried some of this new drink, which took his breath away, only to give him a warm feeling that moved throughout his body. Later on, he asked Anastasia in a low voice, about feeling funny and light-headed. She moved closer, and whispered, "That was the way it worked, and too much would do the

96

River of Life

some thing to him as what had happened to the chaperons."
With this information, and little giggle, her hand moved over,
and was on his. He looked at her with a smile that said it all.
This was the happiest moment for both of them since the days
back in Luxor.

The ride moved on into the darkness, and the chaperons
slept in the warmth and peace of their dreams. The two young
couples talked and drank, but it was the movements under
the fur that both couples found new happiness. It was a ride
through a magic moment, the stars were out and the bells
played a tune of making trails for others to follow on this ride
of happiness. Even youth can only last so long, and then it
gives way to rest and sleep, which was what happened inside,
as the sleigh moved across the fairy landscape.

For Horus-Salah, it was better than any dream; even his
soul felt that it moved in and out of his body with gusts of
happiness. For Anastasia, she had perfect contentment, to be
beside Horus-Salah, her love, for now and forever more.
Somewhere between dreams and the real world, the magic
sleigh returned its guests to where they came from. Finally,
the chaperons were woken up as they approached the front
gates. All was well, by one and all, this time marked forever
more.

Anastasia said goodnight to everyone, with that extra
pause and smile for Horus-Salah. Once Anastasia and Horus-
Salah were back in their own rooms, they both separately
prepared for bed. As Anastasia lay in her big bed, somewhere
in the middle her mind went back to the ride in the sleigh,
with Horus-Salah by her side. It was then, as well now, with
these thoughts that her womanhood was wet. In fact, it was
her whole body that had a new feeling about Horus-Salah.
She wanted more than anything to be his one and only forever. As she lay there, in the warmth of her bed, her mind
worked on a plan that just might let this 'dream of dreams'
work for both of them. She knew that Horus-Salah felt the
same, or at least she thought he did. With these ideas, and

more that fit into the same lines of thought, her eyes closed with the sleep of happiness.

At the other end of the great home, Horus-Salah got into his large bed. He too, was thinking of all that had happened this evening and the happiness, both then and now. Laying there, looking up into the darkness, with Anastasia on his mind, he felt his manhood grow to it fullest. His hand moved down over the outside of the blanket, towards that spot. There it was, the pyramid of life, pushing up from under his blankets. His face was red, but the darkness protected him from seeing. He laid there, still thinking of Anastasia, and what a great love he had for her, now and forever. Some time later, his eyes eventually closed, and sleep followed. Last night was one of the few times, if not the only time, Horus-Salah hadn't looked out the window.

As morning arrived, he got up and went to the window, not yet fully awake. There it was, sometime during the night, the small beautiful snowflakes had fallen, and once more covered all that they touched. It was his window into this land that had made him as happy as so long ago, back in Luxor. Oh, what a place, this winter wonderland with its fairy princess, his Anastasia, and her kingdom. He was lost in thought, for this was his last full day here, and then back to England.

It was, and yet could it be, that six weeks had passed by already? It seemed one long dream that he never wanted to be woken up from. The pure joy of each moment, being with Anastasia in her home, in her country, and being a part of her life. Oh, what joy this time had been in his life, as his eyes looked out far beyond the window. He was filled with happiness, and didn't realize that the tears were running down his face, like small lines to form droplets before moving ever downwards. It may have been minute or hours that he was at this window. It was only his body that stood there. His mind and soul were running back and forth over the days gone by. The tears never stopped in all this time, for they were tears filled with happiness.

River of Life

Sometime later, from far away, he felt something pulling on his right arm and a voice, yes, a voice call to him. He returned from his distant place, only to turn and see Anastasia's personal servant, asking if he was all right. He looked as if come back to the living, and said "yes" in a weak voice, which was the best he could do. She looked first at his face, and then at his galabya. He followed her view, only to see two long, damp streaks down the front of the galabya. He had cried for so long that the rivers were halfway down the robe. He turned his head back to the window, not wanting to show that he was still crying.

The young woman than asked again if he was all right and once again he replied "yes", this time stronger. She then told him that Anastasia had arranged a sitting in her suite, for him at two o'clock in the afternoon, and would he be able to come? His red, wet face said it all, as it lit up, and the room became brighter. "Of course, I will be there", came his answer to the question. With that information at hand, the young lady asked for her leave, which Horus-Salah acknowledged.

He then went about his usual routine, and got ready, both for the afternoon, and the long unhappy journey back to Cambridge. Before all that had to be done, it was time to go see Anastasia. He left instructions with his manservant on what was left to be packed for tomorrow, and off he went, with happiness once more.

As he walked to the other end of this large house, he couldn't help but look at everything as a person that was seeing them for the last time. Oh, tomorrow, it was halfway here, and then the good-bye, and back to Cambridge. His face said it all, as he walked from one end of this old palace towards Anastasia. Once outside the door, he looked himself over, or what he could see. His western garments were in fine order, and he was ready to see, and be with his one true love. He knocked on the door.

Her servant answered the door, and he could see Anastasia sitting, patiently waiting. She looked up and smiled, then went over to Horus-Salah with her hands stretched out. He

robert f. edwards

gently grasped them, and slowly raised them to his lips to kiss. As he looked up, both of them were smiling at each other, and one could feel the happiness in the room. Anastasia's servant returned to the far end of the room, and sat at the desk, where she continued to answer letters that had to be done. With this tactful move for privacy, Anastasia and Horus-Salah sat at the table and drank tea.

It wasn't the tea that Anastasia had invited Horus-Salah for, but to ask him about their future with each other. Though she was only two years older than he was, she took charge of things better, and one would have to add, got them done also. It was not that she was a take-charge person, or that Horus-Salah was weak. It was what each was better at, and this was one of hers. She loved Horus-Salah with all her heart, ever since they were children in Luxor. Now that they had spent the better part of a month and a half together, she wanted to plan for the next time together, and more.

As Horus-Salah listened to her talk about the small things that both had shared this last time together, he looked at her with the same love that she had for him. It was not that he was unsure of what to do in their relationship, but that he was the more reticent of the two. It always pleased him the most when Anastasia would take the lead, and get to the main part of the subject. Today was no difference, when she started to ask him how he felt about the future, and mainly theirs. That was when she told him about how she had arranged for him to come for this holiday. She always started with her mother, and then worked her way up to her father, from both sides. After this, it was then up to her father, with the help of follow-up from her mother. She had use this plan to get things she wanted most of her life, and the success had been above average. Now, she was moving on to her next plan, for their future, and wanted his impute.

As he listened, he couldn't help but say 'this sounded more like a plan for battle or war'. She looked at him, and said, "Love is war, when other people don't want you to be with the person you and God want to be with." So, with that

100

River of Life

said, she added, "In your country, people play the game of checkers, in my country we play chess." He knew the difference of the two games, if he could say that chess was a game. He had never played chess, but had watched, and knew that it was more that just a game, but also worked on the mind of the other player. It was not a game of fun, but one of breaking down the opponent's plan to win, and making the winner appear superior to the other.

He looked at her and asked, "Is this going to be a game of checkers or chess?"

He had just got the last word out, when the answer came as, "*Yes, chess*!" The Polish warrior was at her planning stage. She looked at Horus-Salah in a soft loving way, and said in a low voice, more of a whisper, "I love you, and want to be with you for the rest of my life."

His eyes never moved from hers, and in the same soft whisper, he added, "I feel the same way about you, my love." Their eyes spoke for much longer than their words.

It was Anastasia that said something to break their eye's contact. "We must now make plans to bring this happiness to a reality," she said in a firm voice.

"Do you have such a plan, my loved one?" he asked. This was just one of the many things she loved so very much about her little Horus; he was always with her in thoughts and actions. "Yes, these are some of my ideas. First, I know my mother would not be against us following our plan to be together, and would help us. Next, my father always listens to my mother on family matters, and this would be a big family matter, to say the least." She stopped, "This would work on my side of the marriage." She said it now, for the first time out loud.

He looked into her eyes and asked, "Do you really think we could get married to each other?"

She answered, "This is why we are together at this moment, to plan, and see that it can be done."

robert f. edwards

He then replied, "Let the chess game begin." They both giggled like two children in school that had a plan to get the teacher in trouble.

So the planning went on, throughout the rest of the afternoon. At the end, both agreed that it would be Horus-Salah's father that would be the hard part in winning this game of chess, and happiness forever more. He added, on closing this subject, that the only way to eat an elephant was one mouthful at a time. This was another reason why her love was so great for this young man. They had made the first move in this new game of chess, and of the future of their lives. To win happiness together, forever and a day.

So, as the afternoon left, and the evening light grew dim, it was the first time that both of them did not feel only sorrow about leaving each other. Now, both of them had a plan for the future, with each other to be together throughout their lives. Both now had to get ready for the evening events. So, Horus-Salah said his good-bye to Anastasia, with both of their faces showing happiness and looking forward to the beginning, not the end. Horus-Salah made his way back to the other end of the palace, to dress for the evening dinner and events, while Anastasia did like-wise. The last evening for Horus-Salah was not much different than the many ones throughout his stay here, for there were always new people to meet, and a long evening of entertainment.

The hour was late when Horus-Salah returned to his room and bed. As he changed into his bedclothes, he went to the window, and looked out, like he had done from the beginning of his stay here. The night was clear and the stars gave just the right amount of light without the help of the moon. As he looked out into the distance, the shadows of darkness were brightened by the glow from the blanket of snow. He looked up into the starry night, and prayed to Allah for his good fortune and its beginning. Once in bed, his eyes did the rest, for the sleep of peace came quickly.

The next day was well in progress by the time that Horus-Salah joined the others in his farewell, before he started on

River of Life

the first leg of his journey to the train station, for the evening trip to the ship that waited in port. Today was a quiet one, for things were done in preparation for his trip, and now came the waiting. Even Anastasia was quieter than normal, which may have set the mood for Horus-Salah and the others. The day moved hour by hour, to the final good-bye. But, it did come at last, as the large car drove up to the front door, and Horus-Salah's male servant loaded all the luggage in the trunk.

The last person Horus-Salah saved his good-bye for, was none other than Anastasia, so when it was their time, the rest looked the other way, as they all knew the feelings these two people had for each other. The two of them stood beside each other, looking at the car that would be breaking their happiness, for now, but not forever. Then, they faced each other, and quietly whispered, "I love you" to each other. Now, they had said it, for the first time where others could see, if they couldn't hear.

CHAPTER 9

Horus-Salah entered the car, which drove down the road leading to the highway. The first movements of darkness came over the hill and night was right behind. It was not late in the afternoon, but night came early at this time of year, and the clouds were heavy in the sky. Horus-Salah and his manservant didn't have to wait for the train, for it was there sending out smoke and pleading to leave. Horus-Salah was in his private compartment, with the manservant in lower class, as the train pushed its way from the station. The darkness of the night was in full force as the train continued from one station to the next, stopping at some, and not at others. Horus-Salah slept poorly, for the motion and being alone again; all contributed to a fitful night's rest.

The morning came finally, with the male servant helping him get ready for the end of the train ride. At the final stop, a car came for them, and off to the seaport and the ship that would take him back to England and to Cambridge. It may have been the poor night's sleep, or harsh light of day, but now Horus-Salah wanted to run, or cry or both. Oh, how much he wished, in all his heart, he was back in Luxor, back high in the hills, over-looking the Valley of the Kings. To be at home, with Anastasia, in their home, the tomb. To feel the warmth of Ra on their faces, as he moved up, ever on-ward to the top of the sky. He was sick twice, once for his home and homeland, the other was as great, or maybe even greater, and that was for Anastasia. This body took on that of a person old in years, tried of living, as it moved up the gangplank to the ship that would take him away from all that was happiness.

His male servant found the compartment that Horus-Salah would be staying in for the crossing, and after checking it was up to the standard, the servant made his final good-

River of Life

byes. The male servant looked back after his good-bye and added, "I will be in your service, and care for Anastasia while you are away." Horus-Salah thanked him as the man walked away.

Horus-Salah was now truly alone again, but the last words from the servant made him feel that it was just time, before he would return to his beloved Anastasia. This was the end of his fairy Christmas in the land of the snow. The land released the ship, as the mighty engines pushed out to sea.

As the ship moved out to sea, Horus-Salah felt the movement inside his cabin. His body told him to head for the bed, or the bathroom: but not to look at the walls. He moved to the bed and once on it, closed his eyes. The up and down motion kept going on, but at least his dizziness slowed down. His stomach was holding on to what it had been given earlier in the day. Just to rest, and not to be sick was the first thing, and could well be the only thing, he could think of until sleep over-ruled.

It was still early in the morning when he woke, and lay hoping that once back up top, that the ship was the only thing moving. So, up and standing, the day began, then outside for fresh air. On deck, Horus-Salah watched the North Atlantic rolling its high seas, and his stomach joined in. The rail was the first to feel Horus-Salah, and the ocean received what he had to give. Back inside, Horus-Salah made his way down to his cabin. He looked like the sky he had just left, gray and pale. Back on the bed, eyes fixed on a spot, hoping against hope that the movement would stop, or at least the sickness would ease.

So it went, one hour at a time, until the docks of England came into view, and those land lovers were welcomed ashore. This was one of the few times Horus-Salah was actually glad to be in England. "Oh land, thank you Allah" were the first words uttered from his mouth. He sat in the station waiting room, and his mind thought of the horrific experience he had just been through. A lot of things he could be in life, but being a sailor wasn't going to be one of them. Some day, when he and Anastasia were back in Egypt, he swore to himself, he would only travel by water if it were his gentle Nile. Oh, the Nile, and the little feluccas with their sails that catch the light winds, these were so different than those great waters out there in the oceans of the world. He remembered how as a boy he thought he was one of the great sailors of the world. Now he knew it was due to the giving waters of the Nile, to say nothing of the shoreline that was always in sight. No, Horus-Salah admitted to himself, he was no sailor, and would never be.

Now that the land had given him back his stomach and an appetite, he headed towards an eating area in the building. After collecting his luggage, he made his way on to the train station. The day was the same as he remembered England, cold and raining. The wind, oh, that cold north wind, that took the wetness of the sea and added a cold numbness and how it made its way into the very bones of all living things. He was back in England. He missed the warmth of the sands, of the desert, or even the whiteness of the snows. This was the place that felt the dampness of a grave, and a watery one at that, he thought. No wonder the people of this land are cold and standoffish, he added in his mind. This was not a place that he would ever feel at ease in. He looked out the window, even the buildings look unhappy, for the dirty black soot of coal dust left streaks by the rain trying to wash it away. To him, it seemed like the buildings, in addition to their sadness, were crying out for help. The people's faces looked gray and wan, and with the dark, drab clothing used to cover skin, all looked unhealthy by his standards.

The hour passed by slowly, as one train came in, only for another to leave. Time moved on, but for Horus-Salah it was the waiting. He was alone, which he didn't mind, it was where he was, and where he was going that disturbed him. As he sat, his mind pondered how one day could be so different from another. It was whom you were with, and where you were, he eventually decided. He thought of Anastasia, and his mood changed even without realizing it, he was smiling. A relation-

River of Life

ship is like life. You don't know where it is going, or where you will end up. Enjoy it for the moment that it brings happiness. With these thoughts, the time moved along with the train taking him back to Cambridge.

The rain banged against the window as the landscape passed by. Horus-Salah looked past it, without seeing, for he was back somewhere riding a train towards his love and her land. The landscape to him was much the same but the snow that had kept it warm had vanished and the sky was crying at the loss. The day was ending, as the train stopped long enough to say good- bye to Horus-Salah. He was back, yes, back here in university, back to his cell that waited his return. He had returned to do what must be done. It was the will of Allah, and his father, the ruler of his life.

He looked around the station, and with resignation thought 'let it be said, let it be done,' and looked for a taxi to take him back to that cell at the university that had been waiting for his return. As the taxi moved up the long road to the gates and past it towards the entrance of the university dorms, Horus-Salah watched the students crossing the grounds. The cab stopped at one of the dorms and Horus-Salah gathered up his luggage. He slowly made his way up the long stairway to his small room at the end of the corridor. What a homecoming, as students past by him, one way or another there was no acknowledgement of him being there, to say nothing of a 'welcome back'. Disheartened, he made his way to his room, or as he thought of it, his cell, as it met both the size and conditions.

The next day felt like he had never left. By the end of the week he was dreaming that he had escaped, and spent his holiday in Poland. By now the routine was boring, that it was a nightmare that one couldn't wake up from.

Time passed eventually, and then months or maybe years, as it was all a dulling blur for him, he finally received that small piece of paper with his name on it. He had his degree, and to add to this, he was now a senior wrangler of Cambridge. At last it was over, and the letter from his father arrived, with permission to return to Cairo. If it had not been for all the letters that he had received from Anastasia, this letter would have been delivered to a dead man.

This period in his life had taken on a lifetime of its own; his only hope of surviving had been Anastasia and her letters. With each one, she had kept their dreams alive. Yes, some day she would accomplish the impossible, and they would be together again. Ah, the end of staying at the university, and more importantly, the end of living in England.

At last, not to be living amongst people that were as cold as their climate. They were the only people he had ever met that could talk to you, and still look down at you, at the same time. It wasn't just one group; it seemed to be the entire country. The ones that perfected their condescension were the ruling classes.

In Egypt, he had seen men dress down others, and even beat them, but these people had a way of getting into one's soul and destroying it. It was as if the dogs had better rights in their eyes that the ones that they were talking too. In fact, he thought, yes, they do treat their dogs better than that. They thought they ruled the world and all others were beneath them.

This may have been an attitude that Germany was trying to change. There was a new leader, Adolph Hitler. Anastasia's letters often mentioned this man and the change's his party where trying to make in Germany. Horus-Salah thought of the British, maybe these cold people, on this cold island, may change some day too. It couldn't be soon enough, as the echoes of their degrading laughter rang in his ears, and the nickname ' Horse Stable', which he failed to see any humor in, but they felt they had the right to do this, for they were English. It was all the small things, and maybe the big ones, it made no difference, for they were the rulers and the world was there to please them.

He would always be sad when he remembered these years, with the people that played a game of life that was to fit their country. To say good-bye to this place, to this land,

River of Life

would be a happy day and a better one for him, he knew. To Horus-Salah, even a watery grave sailing back to Egypt would be better than to spend his life here on this penal island. The days passed slowly as he got his things ready for the journey back to Egypt.

The old man's eyes had not moved for so long that the waiter wondered if he was asleep with his eyes open. Or even worse that this old gentleman had died. Slowly, as if from returning from another world, in another time, the old man moved just enough to put the waiter at ease. He didn't move anything but his head, for the rest of his body was stiff. As he moved his head up to the sky, once again the stars didn't let him down. They were there, even though the moon had found a cloud to hide behind. But it was not the moon of Islam that he was looking for in the sky this time; it was a star. The star had always been the road that travelers used to find their way in this part of the world, and over the years he had many teachers to show him how to read his way. Tonight was easy, for the star was always the brightest in the sky.

It was none other than the North Star itself that he looked for in the darkness. The North Star saw his eyes, and he fixed them on that illuminating glow while his mind went from the present, back to a happier time with his one and only, Anastasia. Somehow this woman, greatest of all women, had returned to this very place, Luxor. To the very tomb that was his home for most of his live. She had done the impossible. She had got the gods to bless their union, and his father to give his consent.

As the old man looked at the North Star, his heart was filled with both happiness and a great sorrow, for this was also the star that led him to be Poland. The land of his one and only love's home. To think of Poland was to think of all that had happened in his life. The good and the bad, the happiness, and the greatest of all sorrows. It was happening again, the sorrow was overruling his thoughts, and tears filled his eyes.

The North Star was blurring before for his eyes. No, he must think of the happy times. The times that came next in his long life. So the tears rolled back, to clear the stars again and let him concentrate on those happy times. Ah, the happiness then, when all he wanted was his, then and forever more.

The day finally came at last, and Horus-Salah was more than ready for it. His bags had long been packed, and only his memories would stay behind in this room, 'the cell', in this prison known to all as Cambridge. He would always have a record there, and a piece of paper saying that he had graduated from there. The taxi came, and Horus-Salah left with it, to the train station, and onward to the port for the ship that would take him back to Egypt, and home. There were no good-byes, or 'we will miss you' from either side, as he made his way back home. The train came and went, with him as part of the human cargo it was taking to the port.

At last, the ship that waited to leave, just as he wanted. Once aboard, the fear of movement, that only a ship on the sea has, returned. But it was the thoughts of getting away from this land, and its people, that put the fears aside, as he went topside and waited with the other passengers for the ship to cast off.

Horus-Salah soon returned to his cabin and the bed. He stayed there, not by choice, but by need, the only movement out of bed was to run for the toilet that knew his needs. So it went, day after day, until dying at sea seemed an option. As his weak body was giving up, the great ship turned out of the Atlantic Ocean, towards the Gates of Hercules. Once through them, they were now into the gentler waters of the Mediterranean Sea. With help, Horus-Salah surfaced from his cabin,

River of Life

which had the odor of a dying room. Once topside, looking out to the south, he saw the first signs of land.

It was his beloved coast of Africa; he was truly headed home at last. The fresh air, and above all, the sight of land, the terra firma, his place in this world, at once raised his spirits. He was almost there, at home, back on the mountain looking over the Valley of the Kings. This was the only place he really belonged. The light winds that carried the drying air from the desert filled him with new dreams and hopes. The day moved forward and followed the ship on it course. By nightfall, Horus-Salah had eaten and walked around for the first time in days. He was back from the brink of death. Each day now brought improvement, both in his heath and his spirits. By the time the ship put into port, Horus-Salah's health was back.

His old man servant was aboard even before Horus-Salah had his belongings packed. After a warm reunion, both men left the ship to wait for the train for Cairo. Oh, to be back on land, and best of all, his homeland, made Horus-Salah remember only too well how homesick he really was, all those years away. Now, with the day light fading, and in the dusk hours, his grateful eyes absorbed the land, the houses, and oh, the people. To hear talk in his language, his native tongue, to taste the food of his child hood. And to breath the air, the dry air, above all, to be warm again, oh, to feel the warm of the mighty Ra, even after he fell below the horizon, to sleep for another day. Thank you, Ra, the mighty sun god, that looked after all of us, but not equally, thought Horus-Salah, as he went to sleep.

The morning came, and so did the train's arrival into Cairo. As Horus-Salah got off, to his surprise, his family and friends were there to meet him. Even his father, that was the biggest surprise of all, yes, he was truly back. With more than one car, the long line of people that had met him at the train station returned as honored guests to his family home in Cairo. There were all the servants, and more friends and family waiting at the entrance door for him. He looked up, so the

robert f. edwards

"... his grateful eyes absorbed the land, the houses, and oh, the people."

Original artwork, watercolour   Phyllis Verdine Humphries
Circa 1930's

112

River of Life

tears in his eyes would roll back, and not down his face. He was happy, oh yes, he was happy, if only Anastasia was by his side now his world would be perfect.

The days that followed were one party and get-together after another. He lost track of the places and the times, let alone the people, and who some of them were. At last, the family said their good-byes, and started to plan for a holiday in his beloved Luxor. To ask him what day they left Cairo, or when they arrived in Luxor, was all part of a living dream .He was here, in Luxor, in the house he had grown up in, near the Nile and the mountains. He looked around, and kept touching himself to feel if he was real, or if only his dying body had let his soul return to this place of a great love, his home.

Eventually, he was able to get away to his real home, the place of his child hood, the cave and tomb, the place that he shared with only the first resident, and Anastasia. As he walked up the long trail through the hills, high above the Valley of the Kings, there was a peace that came over him. He felt the gods that his ancestors had prayed to were welcoming him back. The mightiest of all made his presence known, as the heat and brightness of the day warmed Horus-Salah, as Ra had not all those long years away from this place.

As he moved away from the path, and down where the opening to the tomb was, Horus-Salah stopped before the entrance. He looked into the darkness of the cave, and let his eyes adjust. Then in he went. It was all there, just as he and Anastasia had left it. The candles, everything was in the same place as his mind remembered it. He lit a candle, and then put it into the hole at the far end of the tomb. The burial chamber and its owner were just the same, as all those long years before. He moved around the tomb, letting his eyes take in everything, not checking so much as just recalling what he remembered. When he had finished, he made his way back to the entrance, put the candle out, and sat at the opening, like he had done so many times before. He looked out across the Nile, at Luxor, as the sun moved behind him, yes, he was

really home at last, please Allah; never make me go away
again, he prayed.

His thoughts turned to the person that was always with
him, always on his mind, Anastasia, his only true love. What
was she doing now, and how his life could have so much
more, if only she was sitting beside him now. It was only yesterday, in his mind that she sat there next to him in their
child hood. She was a young girl, and he was a younger boy,
but their love was the same, as it was now and forever more.
She was his and he would always be hers. So as the sun
dipped low, Horus-Salah got up and returned to the large
house, as the others waited for him, and the evening to begin.

It was one of those days that followed another that it happened; his father had him paged to the office. The last time he
was summonsed to this place, he was told that he would be
furthering his studies in England. He walked slowly towards
the great doors, which were at least twice his height, and then
some. With a heavy heart, and a faint touch, he knocked on
the door. He heard the voice within say something like 'enter',
as he opened the door. The large room came into his view, but
it was the desk and the man behind it, that he was looking at.
The man did not look up, but moved his hand towards the
chair in front of the desk.

Horus-Salah sat and waited. Oh, the minutes were long-
lasting moments of horror as each second of life moved away
from him. Then, the man looked up and said, "I have something to ask you." Horus-Salah just looked at him with total
commitment. The man then went on, as if Horus-Salah had
replied. "Son, you know the winds of war are blowing again
from the north," the man said. "Tell me what you know and
have seen on this matter." Horus-Salah's face went from white
to red, and his mouth was dry, but his hands were wet. His
lord master, his grand vizier, the ruler of the clan, his father,
was asking him for his knowledge and his thoughts. Did he
hear right? Before his mind could do all the checks and bal-
ances, the man looked at him and the answer wasn't there.

River of Life

"Where and what do you wish from me," came his reply, in a voice that he had a hard time recognizing.

The man said "Everything."

Horus-Salah started by describing how Europe was changing from a monarchy to different types of ruling classes. He talked about Russia, and how the communist leader, Joseph Stalin, ruled them. In his opinion, he said, 'the world was not big enough for his conquests.' Stalin trusted no one, and no one should trust him. His people were there to serve his means, or die trying. The Russians had always known how to suffer, and they would, and are, under this man. What he gave to his people, he also took from them a hundred fold.

Horus-Salah went on to discuss the man ruling Germany. His name was Adolph Hitler, ruling as the National Socialist Labor Party, better known as the Nazi movement. This man has the right amount of hate and revenge for the whole German people. What was taken away in the last war, he wants back, plus interest. The price he will demand will be high, and paid in blood. This man's word is only honored for the moment, and no longer. The world will remember his rule in years to come. He is giving the German people their place back in the world, but the price has been freedom for all of them.

"Another man is Mussolini of Italy, who would like to relive the past glory of the Roman Empire." Horus-Salah felt he might be the one who put us in a war with Europe. "This man wants all the lands that the Roman Empire had which would be Egypt itself. The Italians are ready to join the dreams of their past, and war is the path. The next man is from England," where Horus-Salah had spent some many years studying. "His name is Chamberlain, and he is a weak man, in his thoughts and judgments." "But," continued Horus-Salah, "he has the mood of his people at heart, and that is not honoring anything of the past to keep the peace of the present. He is not one to have as a friend in these times. England will give up its friends, not to go to war. The next man is from France, his name is Weygand, and his feelings are those of the French people. World War I was the last war for them. Their blood ran until it changed from red to white. The young men were not there to fight for the old men's dreams. Let France look after itself, first and only. The last man does not rule here, but in the U.S.A. Roosevelt is the king on this chessboard. He can afford to sit back, as the game begins. The people in the U.S.A. are just getting out of a depression and are in no mood to fight for what they see as another country's war. Also the Germans are in favor, as much as the English here. Which side will be best for his people, he is asking himself and others."

Horus-Salah stopped and looked at the person on the other side of the desk. The man returned his look, and asked, "Are you finished?"

Horus-Salah added as an afterthought, "I do not know enough about Asia to speak on this subject."

The man spoke again and said, "You have done well, and show some promise in what you have learned. You may be excused," and as an afterthought, he added "our friends from Poland will be coming for a visit later this year."

Horus-Salah wanted to ask it he heard right. To say nothing of all the details, but he moved his chair slowly back and got up. "Thank you, my ruler, my father, for your patience and faith in me." With that, the man nodded his head, and went back to reading the paper on his desk. Horus-Salah's time with his father was over for now, and his heart went back to beating for a person that would live another day.

Once outside the great office, his face could not hold back the news he had been told. Anastasia was coming to Egypt. Oh, what a woman, what a person. How in all the gods' names, can she do the impossible? As he started to walk down the hall, the light shone in from the long row of windows. To Horus-Salah, it looked like a ladder leading to heaven for him; this was the state he was feeling. He reached his mother's suite and asked if she was in, and could he have a visit with her. The servant returned and showed him in. His mother and sister were having tea in the open courtyard as he

River of Life

entered. Both were happy to see him, and soon an extra tea was served and greetings made.

Horus-Salah asked about the Count coming, and contacting Anastasia. His mother took the lead and said that his father had got a letter from the government of Poland, and she had also received a personal letter from the Countess. She didn't know much about the letter from the Polish government, but her personal letter asked if the Count and his family could once again stay with them, while they were in Egypt.

When she finished with that information, he asked if the letter had anything else in it. She added that it would be sometime in the fall, and they would be staying to the end of the year. Some of their time would be in Cairo for the opening of a section of the Egyptian museum. The letter had asked if it was at all possible, that the Countess and Anastasia would like to come to Luxor by boat up the Nile.

During all this time his mother was relaying the news, his sister was laughing. He asked her if something was funny, and both women said at the same time," you."

He then restated it, "Me?"

"Yes," his mother replied, "You have a look that says it all, my son."

He once more jumped in, "What kind of look?" and both women laughed again, even louder.

His mother stopped long enough to add, "In love, my son, in love." Again, the women laughed and laughed, until he joined in, for his happiness was so great.

He returned to his suite and changed for the outdoors and then left the house. He just had to get back to his home, Anastasia's and his special place. He walked so fast, that it was close to running up the hill, towards the tomb. Somewhat out of breath, he entered the opening of the tomb and turned around to sit. Oh yes, he was home, looking over the valley, the Nile, and the city with his thoughts, and the mighty Ra shining down on him. He thanked all the gods, and the one and only Allah, for the news that brought so much happiness to his heart and soul.

robert f. edwards

The days moved once again into weeks and then past into months as he waited. The whole family got letters from each member of the Count's family, but it was the ones from Anastasia that Horus-Salah wouldn't share with anyone. Anastasia's letters were personal in every way. From her great love for him, to her having the support from her mother, to the consent of her father for them to be together. She wrote about her plans for the trip, and that her father would be asking for permission, on Horus-Salah's and her behalf, to be together for the rest of their lives. As Horus-Salah got one letter after another, the great plan of Anastasia's was not only working, but also each piece was fitting together. Oh, what a woman, what a great plan she had put together. He waited throughout the endless nights, until that day came, the one he had been waiting for. Anastasia's last letter came, with the sailing time and her arrival date in Alexandria.

For Anastasia and her family, the preparations for the journey were much the same as the first one, so many years before. It had all started that day that Horus-Salah and she had talked about being together for the rest of their lives. After he had left for England, and the festivities finished for the season, Anastasia got started on her mother. One afternoon, when both of them were alone together, Anastasia brought up the subject of Horus-Salah and his family, and developing a closer relationship with their family. Before the afternoon came to an end, the Countess had become one of their supporters. The Countess had always liked Horus-Salah, and was fond of his mother, remembering her kindness all those years before. Both families had always stayed in touch with each other throughout the years.

The Countess had never thought of Horus-Salah as anything but a childhood friend of Anastasia's, until his last stay with them. It was then that she had noticed a change, the way they were together, and the deep understanding that they had for each other. She had wondered how this could have developed, as both of them had only being together for so short a time.

River of Life

This was explained when Anastasia told her how Horus-Salah and she had been writing to each other for years. They both had remained steadfast in their feelings for each other, from those days long ago in Luxor. Now, the Countess saw a much clearer picture of the relationship. As the two women talked on a one-to-one basis, the Countess understood much more. When the two women finished talking that afternoon, both were working on the plan that Anastasia had in mind. This had been the first big step, to get her mother on board. Now there were two of them, to work on the plan and the Count. "Ah, the Count," the Countess had said, "leave it to me in this department." So, the plan now took on a forward motion. The next step was to get the Count to understand, and accept, if not to agree to the plan of Anastasia's.

The weeks moved forward and nothing changed, but patience was paying off. The Countess kept Anastasia informed on what she was doing on this subject. 'It was a woman's thing, to support love and marriage,' the Countess thought, 'it was her duty to all women in the world, to say nothing about her own daughter.' The plan moved to the next step, her father, and what his thoughts were on this most important part of her life.

It happened one night when just of the three of them were dining at home. Anastasia's father asked if she had heard from Horus-Salah lately. It was his way of saying he knew all that was going on in his household. He always wanted to think it was so, and now he would exercise this in his own family. Yes, he had done it, the surprise move, one of the characteristics that Anastasia inherited from him.

Now, it was her turn to be taken off guard. She had a look of shock on her face, and before she could answer, she looked at her mother. Her mother was all smiles, and that was all that Anastasia needed to know. Her mother had moved their plan to the next step.

It was now her turn to make it happen or not. She looked at her father and said, ever so casually, "Not this week."

robert f. edwards

He returned the look with a smile, and said, "How is the big plan going?" Then she knew her mother had done her assignment well, and her father was in agreement. Step two was here and now it was up to her to proceed.

She was smiling too, and added, "Do you have any thoughts on this subject?"

One and all had a good laugh. "Subject, is it?" her father added, still smiling, "I would have thought getting married was more of a vocation." Once again, all of them laughed, and Anastasia now had her family's acceptance.

All three of them talked as one, and the plan became theirs, and not just Anastasia's. Her father asked, "What is next?" Anastasia's mother looked at her, as well as her father; she was in charge. Just for one moment, she held this new power, and said, "To get to Egypt". Before the night came to a close, the team of three discussed how to get the Polish government to send them on the next part of the plan. They hoped to get the Egyptian government to recognize the Polish government's contribution of the time and money it had spent, under the Count's supervision all those years before. It was agreed upon, that when the Count returned to his duties in Warsaw, he would ask about this subject.

The weeks past into months, and letters from Horus-Salah and Anastasia crossed, from one part of the world to another. The weekends when her father was home were the same as they had always been from her childhood. 'She must wait; she must wait', she told herself, over and over again. This was when she needed Horus-Salah most of all, for he had a calming effect on her.

Just when she was going to ask her father if anything was going to happen, he gave her the answer. It was better than she had hoped for, the government agreed to send the Count and his family to Egypt. Also, the Egyptian government was going to ask for Horus-Salah's father to be the host for their visit. Anastasia jumped to her feet, and before both her father and she realized what was happening, she was in his arms. It was one of the few times she had shown her feelings

River of Life

so openly. Once more, standing back from each other, there was a new feeling of closeness both of them had for each other.

Anastasia was anxious to write Horus-Salah of the news, but her father said that it was up to the governments in both countries. The very best she could say to Horus-Salah in her letter, was that the plan was going forward. So, this was what she had to do, and so, this was what she had done. Oh, the rules of the game, one must play by the rules. She didn't like the rules but what could be better, she was winning, and so the game must continue. The trip was now being planned from both countries, and by both families. It was much the same as that happened over a decade before. The going-away parties, and farewell visits from friends while the servants were preparing for the long journey ahead.

Before one could count the days that Anastasia and Horus-Salah had been waiting for, it was here. The Count and his family were to leave the next day. All of the servants and their families came to say their good byes. Most of these servants had been with the Count's family for many generations. It was more like their leader was going away, than their employer. Also, they wanted in their own way, to wish Anastasia all the happiness and success on this trip, for her and Horus-Salah. Gifts came, from the poor to the rich, the food, the flowers and all the other gifts, large and small, would have to stay behind.

But, the one gift that would go with each of them was the love for this family. The Count and his wife, to say nothing of Anastasia, were well thought of, and loved by these people that his family had governed for centuries. The last day at home came, and with all the good-byes behind them, all that was left was for the next morning to come. The motorcade came up the long driveway with the largest car leading the way. As the Count and his family got into this car, the servants by rank got in the cars that followed. With tears and waving from inside the cars to the large group outside, the cars started back down the long road.

robert f. edwards

CHAPTER 10

The waiting was at an end, and the start of the long journey to her Horus-Salah had begun. For the Count and his family, it was déjà vu. The train pushed its way out of the station, and traveled down the trail of tracks that it knew so well. As the day left, and the night came, so did one country after another. The next morning, the traveling group had taken up residence in a hotel at the port city. The servants reported back to the Count that the luggage which had come by truck the week before was now in a cargo hold aboard the ship. A report came from other servants that the family could board the next evening. The ship was to leave at first light the following day.

As the schedule tightened, the Count made any last minute changes needed for his family. The Countess and Anastasia used the stopover to shop for last minute items and gifts that were totally European. This day went faster then any of them wanted, as there was a lot to do. With the hours marching always onward, one by one, the long list was completed. By evening, the family and servants were looking forward to bed and rest. The next day was spent doing those last little things that always show up, then on board the ship and their new quarters for the week that lay ahead.

Much the same thing was happening in the cities of Egypt, well at least two of them, Cairo and Luxor. Horus-Salah was still in Luxor, and watched as the servants moved things around, to make ready the suite for the Count and his family. It was the same suite that they had had all those years before. The orders had come down from his father, that all was to be just the same as when the Count and his family had left it, all those years before. It was to look and feel as if they had never been away. The servants were to be the same, wherever possible. The rest of the house was also to be put in

River of Life

readiness for the visit. This meant that a large party and entertainment was in order.

For all the preparations, Horus-Salah was in charge. He made sure that everything was done, right down to the smallest detail. He wanted his father to be proud of him and the Count and Countess to be impressed. It was Anastasia that he wanted to please the most, for he was hoping she would feel this was her second home. As Horus-Salah's long list was getting completed, the same things were being done in the house in Cairo, but it was his mother that was the overseer.

The days were still hot, and evenings were the most enjoyable part of the day in both cities. All that had gone through the heat of summer welcomed the coming of fall. Horus-Salah called his personal servants together the morning before he was to leave for Cairo, and put his oldest and most trusted one in charge of any unfinished jobs still to be done. With his other servants, together they left for Cairo, and then on to Alexandria, and his Anastasia. There was only that night and a day to spend in Cairo and Horus-Salah gave his reports, and was brought up to date on the events planned in Cairo and Alexandria.

The waiting was nearing an end as Horus-Salah made his way by train once again to Alexandria. This time, his heart and spirits were high and he had not felt this way for a long time. In fact, he thought, it was when he was on another train, moving towards Poland, on his way to see his beloved, his true love, Anastasia. For him, some things never changed, only came back with more, and in this case, it was full of joy and true happiness.

He and his servant checked into the hotel two days before Anastasia's ship was to arrive. He liked Alexandria as a city, and enjoyed the horseshoe-shaped harbor that the city surrounded. His room in the hotel looked out over the sea, and his mind wandered back to the past of this great city, and its founder.

As a state of peace came over him, he thought of his country's past, and it's present, but his mind kept returning

123

to thoughts of Anastasia and her plan. She had done so much, and had come so far with their plan. It would soon be the final test, if his father would let the plan happen. Just for a moment, sadness swept over him, for the task was so great, the odds, oh, the odds were.... His mind stopped, and he quickly changed his thoughts. They returned to Anastasia, and what he could give her, in some way to share his love, by way of a gift. Yes, a gift, and what better place than Alexandria, to find one.

He knew right away, his old friend, and one of the family, would have the answer, and the gift. This wonderful man and his family were very rich and powerful in Alexandria. They knew all that was going on in the trades. That afternoon, he went by himself to the office and was greeted personally by Luckman. Horus-Salah told him of his wishes, after they had a long visit catching up on the news with their respective families. Luckman was, in some ways, closer than his father, and a good friend. Horus-Salah could confide in him, and ask his advice more comfortably than his own real father. It may have been that Luckman was more real to him, as a person, than the ruler of his house and his life. For Horus-Salah, it was easy to tell this wonderful man how much he loved this woman that was to join him in the next few days.

After all the news was shared, it was time for lunch. Luckman took him to a favorite restaurant, overlooking the inner-harbor. As both men enjoyed each other's company, they looked out over the city and the spot where the ancient fortress had once stood. Both men loved the history of their land, and this was one of monuments of its past greatness. Now, where this fortress had once stood, was Pharo's Lighthouse, one of the Seven Wonders of the World. With both of them talking about everything, and nothing, the meal was served.

After the main dishes were eaten, and coffee was ordered, Luckman said, "I know what I would give, if she were mine, to show your love."

River of Life

Horus-Salah sat up straight in his chair, and replied with one word, "Yes?"

Luckman looked around, and in a low voice, said "a cartouche with her name, and yours on it."

"Why had I not thought of that!" exclaimed Horus-Salah, as his mind grasped the idea as if it was his own. Luckman only smiled and waited. "When could it be ready?" Horus-Salah asked.

"Tomorrow afternoon", came the answer. Both men got up from the table and made their way to the door. After the good byes, and until tomorrow was said, Luckman took a taxi, while Horus-Salah started to walk down the street.

The light winds from the open harbor only made him wish he could see the ship that his lovely Anastasia was on. The boats and ships moved on this water highway with the grace of ballerinas before his eyes. He was back in his country, his land, and there was a peace that came over him. The streets were a mixture of old and new. The people dressed in the old traditional galabyas, which he loved to wear so much, while others were in the most up-to-date fashions from Europe. Ah, Egypt, it had it all, and more. He strolled along the wall of the harbor; watching people in all their daily activities, from babies and young children being fed, to men in a hurry to get catch a taxi.

What a great day to be alive, and what a great place to be, came across his mind, as he returned to the hotel. That evening, he again walked the streets of the inner city, past the many stores and street vendors amongst the crowd. It was the time when most people went shopping, for their necessities, and their dreams. He loved the lights, the noise, and the large crowded streets that dwindled into narrow lanes. Cars couldn't move as fast as the people walking by, and streetcars past by him on either side.

The order of life, and what made this a great city in the past, was still present today. He was a happy man, and what he saw gave him joy to be here. The next day came at first light, and started with the calling to prayer. Horus-Salah

robert f. edwards

"He strolled along the wall of the harbour, watching people in all their daily activities,..."

Original artwork, pastel   Phyllis Verdine Humphries
Circa 1930's

River of Life

checked with his servant, that all was done and ready for to-morrow, and the arrival of Anastasia. The morning past, somewhat of a waste, as he sat by the window, looking out, as if he was a spy on the city below.

By afternoon, he had made his way to Luckman's office, and was greeted warmly by the staff and then Luckman himself. Once in Luckman's huge office, which looked like a compact-size world museum, he sat down in a chair that enveloped him in comfort. Luckman joined him in another chair that was its twin. The both men talked about the day before, and then Luckman smiled that wonderful smile again, and added, "Come take a look." With that, his hand moved in and out of his pocket. It returned with a small package that he handed to Horus-Salah. Horus-Salah's hands were shaking as he took it. Luckman said in a soft voice, "Open and see for yourself."

Horus-Salah did what he was told, and oh, what he saw made him speechless. There, in this small box of beauty, was the cartouche. It was of pure gold, but it was the artisan's work that made it priceless. Each hieroglyph had so much detail, and what made it remarkable was the way both sides locked together, to become one. Each side had one name on it. One with his name, the other with Anastasia's. Also, what was just as remarkable was the size. It was small and delicate. It could be worn in many ways, for the assortment of attachments was many. Anything from the placement of a pin brooch, to a necklace, and even an earring.

Horus-Salah looked back and forth between this piece of art and Luckman. He didn't need to say anything for his face told Luckman all he needed to know. After what seemed a long time to both men, Horus-Salah added, "you are a true romantic." The older man again smiled that knowing smile.

The ship was making good time in these calm waters, but it wasn't fast enough for Anastasia, as she had her servants continuously check on when the ship would arrive in Alexandria. She was restless, and very anxious to see her little kind Horus-Salah, her love forever. From the porthole she could

127

robert f. edwards

see the shape of the land as the ship moved in slow motion along it coastline. Each mile brought her closer to the next step in her plan, to be with Horus-Salah forever.

With these thoughts in her mind she went over to the drawer where she kept the gift she had for him. She had to have something that was close to him, or would be, after she gave it to him. She went into the drawer, and removed the small box. Then, with one hand, she opened the gift box to look at her gift, to the one and only man that would be in her life.

Slowly, she removed the silver watch from the box. Yes, it was what she had been looking for; the craftsmanship was up to her standards. It was one of the finest works of it period, and the Swiss movement met the workmanship of the artist's work on the outside. Both the inside and the outside were commissioned for a great Polish leader and poet. She had worked hard to find this rare piece of art that was meant for a man and had a purpose. She held it in both her hands, as she turned it over and over, from the back to the front, and back again. With her one hand, she moved to its side, and with a click, it opened like magic, for the viewer to see the fine hands telling the time in roman numerals. She gazed at the watch face a long time, and at the same time listened to the music that came to her ears. 'Ah yes, the song of love, and of the spring of life, it was just right,' she once more thought. But it was the back that had the gift that was hers alone. This would be her part and her part only, for her beloved little Horus.

She was just about to check it, when there was a knock at the door. With one word "enter", and at the same time re-placing the watch in the box, she moved it back to the drawer. The door opened, and her servant entered with the news that the next day, in the late afternoon or early evening, the ship would be docking in Alexandria. "Thank you," came her reply, "is there anything else?" she added. The servant then told her there would be a going-away party tonight, and the family would be at the Captain's table. Anastasia looked at her and said, "What, you didn't think I knew of this before now?" The

River of Life

young servant knew she was far too late with the news, and asked if she was needed for anything. The answer was fast, "no, you may go," came from Anastasia.

Once again alone in her suite, she put her thoughts back to Horus-Salah, but this time it was more about planning to win over his family, and then how they would be married, and live happily for the rest of their lives. She stopped at that thought, and smiled, as if it had already happened. Now, she was coming home, to be with her beloved Horus. She kept thinking of this, even during the last meal aboard at the Captain's table. The meal and the entertainment was all one could ask for, and more, if that was what you wanted. For Anastasia, she would have preferred the Captain to increase speed, and be at the helm.

He kept talking to her and looking at her, as she had noticed from men more and more these days. She was herself, but gave him the cold shoulder, that only a lady of her breeding could do, without attracting everyone's notice. So, the night for her was a boring one, while even on the dance floor, she made the motions to the music, but her heart was in Egypt, with Horus-Salah. At last the hours moved the evening to an end, and she finally returned to her quarters. Once in the privacy of her suite, she prepared for the coming day ahead and to bed. As her eyes found that sleep was upon, her last thoughts were; she would see Horus-Salah tomorrow, oh please, let tomorrow come fast, as she drifted off.

The morning came, as the ship kept moving ahead on course, which never changed through the long hours of the night. Anastasia woke with the knock on the door from her personal servant. She asked, "Who is it?" knowing full well before the answer came. Her servant was the only one who was in the suite, as well as her, and would be the only one to knock on her sleeping room.

The answer, however, was, "Your maid, will you becoming up for your morning meal, or would you like me to send for it?"

robert f. edwards

Now that her eyes were opened, she said, "Enter," and added, "What time is it?" As the door opened, the maid informed her that it was 10:30 a.m. "What!" she said out loud, more to herself, than to the others. She quickly made her way out of bed, as she called out instructions to get her bath ready. 'Why had she slept so long', came to her mind, but no answer was her reward. After the meal was ordered in, and she ate what she liked, she went up top, and looked out to the sea and the shoreline.

It was more the fresh air, than a point on the distance shores that she needed, or was looking for. To her surprise and joy, her mother was beside her. After the usual morning greetings, she asked her mother what was happening, or if there was any news. The Countess replied that the ship was on time, and it should be docking at 6:00 p.m. this evening. Also, there was a telegram from Horus-Salah, that he was in Alexandria, and all was ready. He would be waiting at the exit port for all of them, and the hotel was also ready. Anastasia, in her heart, knew that Horus-Salah would not say or ask about her directly. He was too well mannered and had too much breeding to do anything like that, but deep down, she wished that he had, just the same.

She returned to her room and walked over to the desk, to look at the present she had got Horus-Salah. Once at the desk, she opened the little box once more, and there it was; the watch with all its fine art work. She put the small box back on the desk, and with one hand held the priceless watch. She didn't spend more than a moment looking at the outside, for she had examined it many times before. As she opened the front cover, what looked back was the fine workmanship of Roman numerals, with three hands, each moving to the correct time. It was the back of the cover that she had an artisan work with pure silver, the words "time is our only loss in this world, my dearest Horus-Salah, yours forever, Anastasia." She looked for a long time at the words and smiled, with one thought, and one thought only.

River of Life

Horus-Salah was the romantic one, but she was getting more like him, her one and only love. With that out of her mind, she turned the watch over and opened the other side. She looked at the picture of the two faces that smiled back at her. It was from the last Christmas that Horus-Salah had spent with her family in Poland. Now that she put some thought to the time, it was at the New Year's Eve party that the picture had been taken. She had them enlarged with his on one side, and hers on the other. When you opened the back, both pictures were looking at you and smiling. She had done this many times, but always for the same reason, and without thinking, she bent down and kissed Horus-Salah's picture. This time was no different.

However, this time she added something of her that was personal for Horus-Salah, and only for him. Now, with one long last look, she closed the back and returned the watch to its little box. This time, she put it in her carrying bag. She would not have it separated from her, until the right moment came for her to give it to Horus-Salah. It was done, and just when she was thinking on what next to get ready, the ship's horn blasted out three, maybe four, she wasn't counting.

Then came a knock on the cabin door. With a strong reply from her, with the words, "Enter," the maid came through the doorway. "We are entering the harbour ", she exclaimed. Both women shared the moment of arrival, as if they had reached the Promised Land, and one of them had. To every one on board, it seemed longer than the trip itself, to get dockside. One by one, the great ropes pulled the ship to land, and both the people on board, and those waiting below on the platform, were scanning the faces, looking for each other.

robert f. edwards

CHAPTER 11

Horus-Salah and his servant were just one of the many below. Anastasia and her family were doing the same as everyone on board, hanging over the rails. Both sides just waved, at anyone who was waving back. It was a very happy time for all those, on either side. What was in real time, less than an hour, and a lifetime to Anastasia, the gangplank was lowered, and the first class began disembarking. Anastasia tried her best to hold back, but it was finally her mother's hand that did the job.

Once on land, again she looked around, scanning the platform. It worked; she was the first to see Horus-Salah and him, her. They waved and started to move through the masses of people, all doing the same thing. Her family with servants in tow, and his doing the same thing. What seemed impossible a moment ago was real now. The two parties were together. Horus-Salah and Anastasia couldn't hold back, and put their arms around each other. What could have lasted forever for them came to an end, when Anastasia's father asked, "Which way out of this mayhem?"

Horus-Salah released Anastasia, and with a red face, greeted the rest of the family in the formal way. With that done, the servants were told what to do, and where to have the car ready. Horus-Salah and his personal servant showed the family the way through Customs. Once Horus-Salah talked to the Customs officer privately for a few moments, the rest of the party was passed through without examining each and every passport. Anastasia's father had been to many countries, and with high-ranking government postings, but never had he known anyone to receive this kind of clearance before.

The cars were waiting to take them to the hotel and events now moved smoothly, as if this was done all the time,

132

River of Life

or had been worked on until perfected. There were six cars in all, two for Horus-Salah and his main servants, two for Anastasia and her family. The last two were for the runners, or servants that would be just ahead, to make sure everything was in readiness. The motorcade left the docks, and made its way down the main street, alongside the harbor. The small flag on the first car fluttered in the wind, and the congested traffic somehow moved out of the way.

They moved towards the hotel like a long black line, against all other things that lived and were going about their lives. This long black line made all other people and events unimportant. Anastasia wished that in some small way, she were still that little girl again, for then she would be riding with Horus-Salah and their nanny. As it was now, he was in the first car, and she was in the third car. He was their host, and all must be done right the first time. She and her family once more were the guests, and must be shown that measure of respect.

The shoreline moved alongside the road, as the trip came to an end outside of the hotel. The two top floors of the hotel were reserved for their stay, with their servants. The hotel owner and his manager greeted them, and personally showed them to their suites. There were adjoining doors in each suite, and a large living room, with another room for dining in, if one wished too. Next, was the master bedroom, with a bathroom larger than most rooms in the hotel. Off to the other side, was the den, and a small bedroom, with an equally small bathroom for the personal servant. The rooms were designed in a western style, to make Anastasia's family more comfortable.

The ceilings were high, with a fan circulating the air, if not the heat. Each window was a full-length door, opening onto the terrace. Horus-Salah had seen to it that Anastasia's door was opposite his own, and so on down the long hallway, with people matched up to each other's needs. Once the luggage arrived, and the servants were put through their many tasks, it was a long overdue rest-time. This was needed, both by all the activities, and the midday heat.

133

robert f. edwards

Before Anastasia took to her bed for a rest, she went out into the street, and what had been mayhem of people and movement only a few hours ago, was now deserted. She had read somewhere that only mad dogs and Englishmen go out in the midday sun. She thought of this again, only to remember it was India, not Egypt, but the heat of the day told her that the god Ra was at his peak. As she returned to the living room, she looked at the door to the hallway, and knew on the other side of this small walkway, was Horus-Salah's room.

The man she loves, now, and for so many years. In fact it was hard for her not to think of a time that he wasn't part of her life. So close, and yet not together. She smiled, at least she was in Egypt, and her man was in the next room. The plan was working, and she would be Horus-Salah's forever, and he would be hers. With those thoughts in her mind, she lay upon the bed, as the fan above her head danced on and on. In the room across the hall, Horus-Salah looked at the door to the hallway. He had walked over to it more times than he could remember, but never opened it. Nothing had changed, all these years she breathed life into him, just by seeing her.

His face turned red, thinking of his lack of control at the docks. It happened before he knew it. To be in her arms, out there in front of all those people, and oh, Allah, in front of her parents. Thank Allah, it wasn't in front of his father, or their plan would be over before it had a chance. Once more he looked at the door with one thought in his mind; you have done enough damage already. With that thought, he moved away from the door for the last time, and went into the bedroom. Rest came easy, but to sleep was harder, and only for fleeting moments when it did come.

That evening's meal was the first of several in the dining room of the suite. The servings were western dishes, and the wine was of the finest import from France. Horus-Salah and Anastasia sat across from each other, while her parents sat at each end of the table. They all were very happy, and talked about everything, and nothing. Everyone was enjoying both

River of Life

the French wine, and speaking once again in French. Anastasia couldn't take her eyes off Horus-Salah, he was so beautiful, but there was also something different about him from their last time together.' He was older, no... wiser, no... more content, no... What was it?' she asked herself all through the dinner.

It didn't really matter for he was, and always would be, her little Horus, and when he looked at her she had to look down for his face would turn red. Each time it happened, he would say, "This red wine makes my blood boil", and one and all would laugh. Anastasia laughed the hardest, for he fooled no one but himself. My poor dear Horus-Salah, my one and only love, you are my hero. So it went, until midnight called the day to an end, and the goodnights were in order.

The next few days were for resting, and for the women to shop. For the Count, it was a time for him to be briefed on the happenings in Cairo. Then, the trip up the Nile to Luxor, and the opening of the tomb. There was a long list of things to do, and speeches to be given. Much had been done already, but now that the Count was here, he was brought up to date on last minute details. For the Count, his work had started the very next day from his arrival. For Horus-Salah, it was equally as demanding. The train trip on the third day, the departure and arrival in Cairo. The detailing of each step, and once in motion, nothing could go wrong. He must have everything right the first time. If it all went perfect, his father would let him be in charge of the trip up to Luxor.

This might not be the end of his and Anastasia's plan, but it could be put on hold for many years, yes, it could also be the end of their dreams. He must not let anything go wrong. Each detail was gone over, again and again. Each person had at least two back-ups, and on, and on it went. His father was the ruler of the house and his master. He must please this man, more now than in any other time of his life. His happiness, his life, his will to live, was based on this one plan of Anastasia's.

robert f. edwards

She had done more than her part. She had gotten her parents to accept the idea of their marriage. She had even gotten her father to agree to speak to his father, on the subject at the right time. Oh yes, his love, his life-partner, his soul traveler, had more than done her part. She had even got herself and her family here to Egypt. He must not fail. All must, and will go right, or it would be Sete the god of the Underworld that had let him down.

The next day moved like the winds on the sea sands, always there, changing, moving, but not aware until it happened. On the third day, like the winds, it changed, and things were on the move. Long before first prayers, the servants were up with their things-to-do list. Some were down at the station, checking the private cars that the Count and his family would be traveling in. Others were checking the car that would be taking luggage. Still others, the cars and drivers at both ends of the trip. So it went, on and on, each small detail checked and rechecked, again and again. Then, as the Count and his family got up and dressed for the day, it was well into midday for most of the servants and Horus-Salah.

As Horus-Salah joined them for breakfast, he looked calm and relaxed. If only they knew what he had already done, and how he was feeling, they would have put him to bed. But looking at him, he was like the ice on the lake, in the dead of winter, thought the Count. The Countess asked if he had slept well, and with a smile, he said, "As well as I had hoped". Ah, the truth, yes, the truth, if he had slept, it was only for a moment or two.

Anastasia noticed that same look about him, that she had seen the first night. 'What was it,' she asked herself, as she said her good-morning to him? He was dressed in a western suit, cut to the Italian style, but it was made of the finest Egypt cotton. He looked worldly, or was there still something else she was missing. She just couldn't put her finger on it.

There was a light knock at the door, as one of the Count's servants went to answer it. The man in the doorway was one of Horus-Salah's key personnel. The Count made a hand ges-

River of Life

ture to come in, and the man moved without a sound to his master. With a deep bow, and a low voice, he told Horus-Salah that all was waiting. With that, the man disappeared almost before their eyes. Anastasia was the first to see it, and now she knew what it was, that was different about Horus-Salah.

He was a ruler of men in Egypt. His family was far more powerful than even the Count had known about. This was a land that had slaves, long before the Counts' people had came out of the caves. No, there were no slaves by today's standards, but the rules had not changed. There were men who ruled, and others that were ruled. Horus-Salah was a ruler, and under him, no man was to make a mistake. Today, or on this trip, or his life and his family's would not be the same, until their last days. He was not only a ruler of men, he was their leader. Their lives, and their families' lives, were in his hands. Both of them knew the price for this title among men. Horus-Salah would not fail, or any one that he was responsible for.

It was now that Anastasia knew what was different about her little Horus. He was a man of men, and he was hers. Oh, my God, it was happening again, that wetness between her legs. Just looking at him now, did this to her. Oh, did it show, what was happening in her mind, and was her body giving away her thoughts for all to know? Please God, don't let this happen to me now, not here, she was saying so loud to herself, that her lips were moving.

Her mother asked if she had said anything. Anastasia just looked at her mother for the longest time. Then, from a distant part of her mind, she managed to nod 'no' with her head. What seemed to her a lifetime, she was able to pull herself back to the present, without looking down towards her legs. Once more, she gave thanks to God that at least she was still sitting at the table.

Horus-Salah smiled, and looked at her first, then at the others and said, "All is ready. We can leave for the station anytime you wish." He finished looking at the Count, who would be the one with the answer. The Count looked at his wife, and Anastasia, and then at Horus-Salah. "We are ready now." So like the sounding of a call to order, things started to happen. The man left the room with the movement of Horus-Salah's hand. The other servants in the room made way for the Count and his family to leave.

As Horus-Salah was the last to leave the room, he was still the first one to be at the entrance to receive the motor-cade. All six cars were in the same order, and now with the people in the same seats, the car moved away from the hotel. The route to the train station was short and brief. Anastasia was just now getting back in control of her inward self, when they were at the station. The last two wagons were once again made up for Horus-Salah and his companion. The men in the second car moved out first, and cleared the way, as the Count and his family were shown their compartments. It was com-pleted before anyone could remember which car they had got-ten out of, and which wagon their compartment was in. The luggage and personal things were already aboard.

The engine was pouring out black smoke, with a white trail following. The noise of the whistle could be heard above all else. It screamed out that all was ready, and the important people were leaving, and so was it. With that out of the way, the great snake moved from it resting place, and pushed black smoke back from where it came from. The streets moved away, and the open country came rolling in.

It was only then, in the last two wagons, that people started looking around their new surroundings. The Count and Countess were in one compartment, and two compart-ments forward, was Anastasia. Horus-Salah had seen to it that his men and their servants were always in the next car to them. There was going to be safety, and service both, on this short trip to Cairo. The country moved from the coast inland, and the farmers went about their work. Some looked up, as the smoke moved by with a whisper of steam now and then. More often than not, they kept on doing what they had always

River of Life

" ... and the farmers went about their work. "

Original photograph   Robert F. Edwards
Egypt   November 1999

been doing, long before moving bodies of people came and went in their lives.

Anastasia was about to check things out, and see were everyone was, when she overheard Horus-Salah's voice from far away. He was asking the Count and Countess if everything was up to their standards, or did they have any wishes to make. As he made his good-byes, he asked a few questions in the next compartment, and the answer he got must have been what he wanted, for there was another good-bye. Before she was ready, he was at her door, knocking. She didn't say 'who was it', but got out; "Enter", in a soft voice. She said it once more, for her sake, and the door opened. Horus-Salah stood in the doorway, and looked at her. She stood up, but just at that moment, the train rocked.

Unable to keep their balance, both fell into each other's arms. He looked into her eyes with all the love that she had remembered, and returned it with the same. Without a word, their lips locked on to each other. What was a lifetime for them was only a minute or two, at best. As their eyes opened, and their lips parted, they whispered 'I love you', at the same moment. Then, another minute past, before their arms moved back, to give each other some space. Anastasia's eyes widen, as she saw that the door was still open behind Horus-Salah.

With that, she said, "Would you please close the door, and have a seat." Without turning, he closed the door, and started to laugh, and she joined in, even louder. As he sat, they talked about everything, and mostly about the plan. They were still talking when the train came to outskirts of Cairo.

Horus-Salah stopped in the middle of what he was saying, and looked at his watch. He looked at Anastasia in amazement, and asked, more than told, "We are here?"

She looked out the window and saw buildings, which now replaced the fields she had last seen when she had looked out this same window. "We are here," she acknowledged, looking back at Horus-Salah. His face was the one that she had always known, that kind, dreamy face, which was shy and un-

River of Life

sure of himself. The boy she had met so long ago, the only man in her life, her beloved Horus.

As he looked at her, he started to speak. Oh, how he wanted his voice to have a deep, rich, manly sound, but it was high and cracking when the words came out. As he heard them, his voice continued, "I love you, Anastasia, with my whole being, my heart, my soul. You are what I live for; always hoping and waiting for the day we will never be apart. Our lives will be one, forever. My life, my love, will you marry me?"

Her eyes had never left his, all the time he was talking. When he had finished, she never stopped looking, and started to say 'Yes'. It was a start, but not the end to her reply. Once again, she started, "Oh, Yes, my dearest Horus-Salah, I live to be your wife, the mother of your children, to be the other half of your life. I will not be complete, until we are one, and together forever." Their eyes said more than any words, in any language, could be said. As if locked in another time, they stayed looking at each other, with their souls locked in union.

Anastasia was the first to speak, and her voice seemed strange to her, as the words came out "the plan will work, won't it?"

"If it is Allah's wish," Horus-Salah answered, then almost as an afterthought of his own, he said, "and my father's". With both their eyes never changing, she said, "He is the only one left that has not given his consent, and blessing." "I know, and all these years of working on the plan, it is now in his control. He is my father, and the ruler of my house, he has the final word on all things." She was still fixed to Horus-Salah's stare, and seemed to be able to read the thoughts inside his mind. For the first time, she felt fear; the plan may not get the blessing of Horus-Salah's father.

In a voice she did not recognize, her words came out "What if he says no". Their eyes never moved from each other, but had that blank look when both souls are involved. He heard his voice before the words were formed. Then, together they heard "It will be over for us". The words had just hit the air when the deathblow was felt by both of them. Four eyes

141

filled like pools of water. As a lake filled from an inward source, they came to the end of the bank and flowed over. Down, down the river came, running faster as each pair of eyes saw what was happening with the other set. What seemed a lifetime in hell, the rivers ran and ran.

It may have lasted forever, but the train whistle brought them back from another journey, or the stop would have been hell. Their eyes blinked as the tears pushed with more force, down the endless river. As two bodies in unison, both got up and moved towards each other. Their arms moved around the other, and their heads found a shoulder to rest the mind on. They were one, and always would be; but it was now that they wanted to be together, as one forever more.

Without their knowledge, the train had made its way into the station, and was braking hard to stop there. There was a load bang on the door, from the other side. Anastasia was the first to hear it, and acknowledge. By pulling back, and again in a voice that she did not know, said "Yes," then added, "Who is it?"

The reply was her private maid, "We are at the station."

River of Life

CHAPTER 12

 The old man's eyes moved away from the stars. His hands moved to the arms of the chair. His mind changed back to the present, and had all its attention on getting out of the chair. He moved his legs under the table, slowly at first, for they were heavy and had been the longest and furthest part away from him. Each part of him was getting together once more, as being put back together after a long sleep. It was his legs that were having the most trouble moving. The old bones and sinew were trying their best to move. What muscles that were left on those long thin legs didn't have much elastic.

Very slowly, the mind took control and all things started with the request of moving on. He pushed the chair away, and at the same time his once lifeless legs moved upward. With one quick look around him, he moved the chair out of his way. Then, as much younger than a moment before, he started off towards the stairs. The legs that couldn't feel the body only moments before were moving up the stairs faster then ones half their years. Once back on the main wall that protected the land from the Nile, he moved his blanket around his shoulders and was on his way.

He moved by the Winter Palace Hotel, and stopped, turned his head and looked at the front doors. His mind started once more to change to another time. The times he had been on the other side of those doors. The rooms and people, that were inside back in those times. Oh yes, those times, those happy, happy times. The other side of his mind pulled hard, and once again, he was back in the here and now. His mind said 'now, once more,' then the feet were the first to return to the present moment. They started moving on, one step after another, until the hotel was at his back. He walked forward as the cars and buses moved faster in the

robert f. edwards

same direction. People moved both ways, ahead of him and past him, but he just kept moving at his own speed forward.

The darkness was complete, and what needed light had changed over to man's lighting. Still, he moved along the wall until his eyes saw the temple. Oh, the great Temple of Karnack, this time his present mind couldn't keep things moving. All his body came to a complete stop, and made a half turn, so his eyes looked right at the temple. The great Temple of Karnack, the temple of his people, and their gods. The first gods Amun and Re. The world of temples, mazes, sanctuaries, doors and yes, the wall that told of gods and kings. His gods and kings, his people's religion, and pharaohs. His mind remembered the words of Queen Hatshepsut, as clearly as if he was one of them that were instructed to carve Her words into obelisks at this temple of Amun. The words came to him as if she had just spoken them. "I sat in my palace and thought of him who created me (Amun) my heart bade me make for him two obelisks of electrum... then my soul stirred, wondering what men would say who saw this monument after many years and spoke of what I had done."

Then his mind moved to the great Pharaoh Tuthmisis IV, whose greatest religious reformation was the intervention of Ra "the sun god". It was not just these gods, but also all the gods and the pharaohs, and the years of history that stood there. He, a living part of the present, stood before the greatest religious temple of his people's past. He had seen this great works of the masters thousands of times, but it felt like the first time. It was part of his past, and he was part of its present. For in practice, he obeyed the rule of the Moslem faith, as did so many of his fellow Egyptians.

Ah, but the past, and all around them each day, was their true faith. No Egyptian could deny or miss it, each day of their lives. He once more lost time, for what is time, when you are looking at something that is timeless. It was only the cold of the night air that made him aware of the present. He kept his eyes on the beloved temple, until his bones told him that the cold was greater of the two. His mind moved back and forth,

144

River of Life

from his love of faith, and the needs of living flesh. At last, the flesh won the moment, and his feet started on their journey.

His mind left with one thought, of all the greatness that Queens to Pharaohs had placed their own marks of chapels and sanctuaries for the other gods of Egypt. He had never tired of this holy place, where his gods gave ear to his needs. Oh, how he wished he could spend the night in one chapel, or sanctuary, praying to whichever god would listen, but he had to go to the West Bank.

So his mind returned to where his body had made time to, and once more his eyes looked around him. He was at the other end of the great temple. There were a few people walking around, but mostly tourists. He was cold, even with the blanket wrapped around him, and the few other Egyptians were dressed as warmly as they could, while the foreigners were in T-shirts and shorts.

All these years had not changed him. He still felt uncomfortable seeing people not covering their bodies in public. The foreign women, showing off what was only for their husbands to see, made him look the other way. It was not that way when he and his beloved Anastasia were young. Today, people and things were so different, in these far away places. Men had lost their respect, and women gave theirs away, he thought.

He turned his head around once more to look at the temple, and his mind gave a silent prayer to all the gods that he was blessed to live with here. Again, he was heading down the walkway towards the docks. He had gone but a short distance to where he wanted to be, when he saw an old man. When he looked again, no, the man may have been only half his age, but the way he was walking and bent over; life had been hard on him. Now, in his last years, he was poor and maybe homeless. The old man changed his direction, towards this man that was less fortunate than himself. As both men's eyes made contact, he held up his hand and motioned for the man to walk towards him.

robert f. edwards

Without a word, the old man moved his other hand into his pocket, and removed two fifty E. pound notes from his galabya. He moved a few steps towards the poor man, and handed him the notes. Both men smiled at each other, and the poor man was going to say something, but before he could, the old man looked up and said, "Blessed be Allah." With that, the old man started to walk on his way again, leaving the poor one looking at one hundred Egyptian pounds. More than a workingman could make in months of hard labor. He too looked up, and blessed Allah and the ways of Mohammad. Both men were of the Moslem faith, and it was the way of the faith to give alms to the poor; but this was more than a generous amount. As the poor man looked up, the old man was soon lost in the movement of people coming and going.

The old man had gone just a short distance when he came to four policemen, standing and sitting on the wall. One of the policemen called out, and motioned the old man over to them. They all were young, and in their black, coarse uniforms. He had nothing to hide, or to fear from the laws of the land. So, he once more changed his direction, and approached the wall where the four were. As he got closer, he now could see that the four were eating their meal from their canteens. It was somewhat the same as army rations. As he stood before them, the one that had called to him, asked him to share their meals with him. He thanked all of them, and joined in, not that food had been on his mind. It was Ramadan, and the fasting time was over. It was now, throughout the Moslem faith, that friend and stranger shared food. To these policemen, he was the stranger, and so he ate their food and shared their faith; which was his, or at least the one he practiced. With the bread he moved the food from one canteen, only to share some from each ones' dinner. He thanked them, and all gave thanks to Allah.

As he walked away, he again thanked Allah that his live had been conceived in this land, and he had lived here most of it. He looked up at the heavens, and thanked all the gods

River of Life

for the time he had spent on this plant, Earth. Ah, the moon that told all of the start of Ramadan, looked back at him, surround by the stars. He stood still. His mind had returned to the heavens and another time.

Anastasia took the hanky out of Horus-Salah's front pocket, and first dried the tears away from his face, and whispered, "My love, oh, my one and only love." Then, she dried her own with one hand, and moved to open the door to the cabin. Waiting on the other side was her personal servant, and the guard that Horus-Salah had assigned to her. Anastasia's eyes meet the servants, and the maid asked, "Is everything all right?"

`Anastasia replied, "Yes, just fine," but her damp face and red eyes told a story that was different to the servant. She may know later, or it may be one more of the mysteries of her mistress.

The bodyguard looked past the maid, towards Horus-Salah. He said, "It is time, master." Anastasia never heard anyone, let alone Horus-Salah. What was also strange was the way Horus-Salah replied, only with his eyes that met the guards. With that, the guard moved back into the hallway of the train, or maybe off the train, for all that Anastasia could tell. Horus-Salah looked back into Anastasia's eyes, and smiled. All was well for both of them once more. They were together, both in body and soul. In his soft voice, he said in a totally western way, "The show must go on, are you ready, my love?"

Anastasia had only eyes for him, and said, "Yes, I am always ready."

She was back, full of confidence, and was going to win the hand of the only man in her life, now and forever. Horus-Salah moved past the servant and through the door. Things moved quickly now as four men showed up at the doorway, and escorted Anastasia and her servant to the car waiting on the platform. The men moved people aside that had strayed into their path. There was a large circle around the cars waiting for them. Anastasia was joined by her parents in the car that was assigned to them.

Somewhere, in another car, Horus-Salah was being brought up to date on the schedule and preparations. Everything was in order, as the master, now it was his father whom the servants' spoke of, had ordered it. One of Horus-Salah's personal servants adds, "All is well, my little one." Horus-Salah smiled, and said, "Let's begin." With that, the lead car started to move off the platform, and on to the streets that led to the family home in Cairo.

It was not a show of power, but of rank; as the motorcade moved through the streets, and all moved aside in haste. As the lead car moved into the circle, the others followed, like a large black snake working its way around the traffic circle before veering off. Soon, they were crossing the bridge over the Nile. Then, alongside the road that ran parallel to the Nile.

Anastasia looked out the window, and watched the small boats moving in the inner delta. Some were with families on board, while others were men fishing. It was what she had remembered, all those years before. Nothing changed, from what she could remember. It was much the same as it had been for thousands of years, were one of the thoughts that crossed her mind.

One turn followed another, and there was the place. The house was larger, and stood alone, with a great gate in front. The lead car was on it way through, and Anastasia's car was next, then the long black snake brought the rest of the servants and bodyguards. The Master's head servant and staff were at the front door to welcome Horus-Salah and their guests. The head servant remembered Anastasia and her parents, and had a formal but true welcome, for one and all. Horus-Salah's old nanny was also at the door, with the same welcome. Some lesser servants showed this as well, when the family entered the great hall.

River of Life

Horus-Salah and the Count were shown into the great parlor. Horus-Salah's father got up from one of the chairs, and went to greet his old friend, and son. For Anastasia and the Countess, they were shown to one of the many garden patios, where Horus-Salah's mother and sister were waiting for their arrival. As friends, all were happy to be together once more. The servants from both households had their work set out for them. The east wing had been set-aside for the Count and his family.

It was a house within a house. There were three floors, with the Count, his wife, and Anastasia given the entire second floor. Their servants were on the third floor, with stairways to each area. The lower portion was for the resident servants of the house, which were assigned to the guests. It was said that for the Count alone, there were 20 or more servants assigned to his needs. The household was said to say, that women did more, therefore needed more servants. As the two separate groups rekindled their friendship after the long abstinence away from each other, the bees of labor were bringing in the luggage from the trucks. So it went for the balance of the day. As the evening made its way across the sky, the head servants made it known to both parties that the east wing was ready.

With this, both families took leave of each other, and proceeded to their separate wings. The house was like a great bird, with both its wings in full motion. There were a mere three hours before dinner. The personal servants had unpacked most of the luggage and the Count and his family was soon settled in. Formal dress was in order, and all their needs for the evening were laid out. Evening gowns were being selected in the suites of the Countess and Anastasia. On a lesser scale, the same was being done for Anastasia's the office personnel.

The year that had been such a long wait for both families, faded away like the darkness, when the morning light once more enters. For the Count and his family, little had changed in Egypt in their absence and the same had to be said about

robert f. edwards

the east wing. It was a happy moment, to be back with true friends for life. One thing that had changed was their children; Horus-Salah was a young man, and Anastasia wanted to be his women. Both of their children were playing together once more, but a different game.

So, the time came to dine in the great dining room. The room could have seated a hundred, but tonight there was only twenty-five. Each name was called into the room, and then shown where they were to sit. Yes, things were the same, and thank Allah. It was nice to be back. The hours from nine to midnight moved with one dish after another, until the men went into the parlor. The women moved to the sitting room to enjoy the first-hand news of fashion and the art of Europe. The men were also talking about Europe, but about the art of war. Some time before dawn, the last guest bade their farewell, and the families returned to their wing. Rest was in order, for one and all.

The sun was closing in on its apex, before Anastasia moved from her bed. She was not alone, for the heads of the families were not that far into the day themselves. Once everyone made their presence known, together they planned for the day, and those that would follow; both by two different groups, the men and their agenda, and the women with theirs. It was only the evening that the two groups were together. For Anastasia and Horus-Salah, it was unforgivable, but there were no other options. So it went from the first day, to the next, until one week made way for the next. Time was lost to them in this time loop.

It was only the evenings that changed the days. Many of them were held like the first night at the mansion, others were at the great house. Two, oh no, three nights had been at the palace itself. The Count's family sat ten places from the king, with Horus-Salah's own family across from them. Even in the palace, Anastasia noticed a lot more Europeans than Egyptians as guests. The British were in the majority, and the men were more often than not in uniform. Most of them were army, but some navy. Anastasia had a feeling that the Egyptians

150

River of Life

ruled, but the British were in control. The other European men were dressed in formal eveningwear.

However, it did not disguise the German military. Their movements gave them away, noticeable even to this young Countess. The Italians were present, along with a few Americans, and one Canadian. It was the men themselves that told the story of what was happening in the world. Europe was spreading its fear and hate throughout the globe. For all the women, if they were alike in the same thoughts as their men, it was not voiced. The general talk was the same each night, with small changes on the people, but not a change of subject. And so it went, night after night.

One of the subjects with the women that never changed from the first night that Horus-Salah and Anastasia showed up for dinner, was what a handsome couple they made. Each night this subject was renewed and whenever possible, added to with the hopes and dreams of the ladies present. Some of later years would tell stories of their past, being safe to tell with no survivors to confirm or deny. The younger ones, like Anastasia, talked of their dreams that were yet to come. Night after night, stories of the past, and dreams of the future.

The mornings started late for the women in the garden area, with their first meal of the day, which was more of a lunch than the breakfast the men had earlier. The discussions were always the same. What had been said and done last night, and who had the same dress as the evening before. Then, small talk about this and that, which lasted until the real subject came up, what to wear tonight. This continued from one day to the next, as the weeks moved one by one, and a month came and went.

For the men it was different. They were up early and the day started with the running of a country, business, and what was going to be in the plans of the future. For Horus-Salah's father and Anastasia's father, it was only these early morning breakfasts that gave them a chance to catch up on the past, and renew their friendship. For the rest of the day, it was meetings, and plans for the opening in Luxor. Horus-Salah

151

was involved with some of the meetings, and the rest of the time was executing the plans of his elders, either for the evening or to the trip to Luxor.

So little time was given for Horus-Salah and Anastasia to be together, that both looked forward to the evenings, in which they got to see each other, and better still, be with each other. It was better than the daytime; but the eyes of each evening were on them. Even the men of all races marched over to see Anastasia, and would make a comment of her presence, and what an enhancement she made to the evening. So it went, on and on, as this was the beginning and the end, forever. Horus-Salah and Anastasia on display as the main event of the evening, night after night.

For both of them, it was enough to be together, if not alone at least in each other's presence. Between guests coming and going, they would have a few moments of private conversation and share their days spent apart. Anastasia kept asking Horus-Salah if the plan was working, or needed to be changed. Horus-Salah would only ask for her to be patient.

One day started the same as the rest for Anastasia, until her maid brought a letter; well, it was more like a note, from Horus-Salah. It read 'Tonight is the night that my father will announce the departure to Luxor.' When she looked at her mother, and Horus-Salah's, she knew at once she was the only one of the ladies that had this news. It was just one more secret of Horus-Salah's and hers. Many weeks before, seamstresses and tailors had been sewing day and night, for new dresses or renovating old ones, so that something different could be worn each night. But tonight, she would have to have something special. This would be her last chance to add to their plan in front of Horus-Salah's father.

With that in mind, and she added, always on her mind, she asked to be excused. Back in her suite, she asked her maid to take a note to Horus-Salah, only for the servant to return with her message unopened. The maid informed her that Horus-Salah wouldn't be back before the evening. So much for her ideas of going over the plan. So, she started to

River of Life

work on what to wear for the evening, now at the early hour of two in the afternoon. Her servant had every one coming and going, at Anastasia's will and doing her bidding.

Tonight was to be at the mansion, and the guests included the King himself, and all others that were of importance to Egypt and the tomb. The King was at the head of the table and one of his wives was on his right. At the other end, were Horus-Salah's father and his wife on one side, and Anastasia's father on the other side. As the courses ended, and the weight of the food and drink sank down, but just before the eyes of his guests fell into a sitting slumber, Horus-Salah's father raised his glass of fruit juice and said, "An announcement is in order. The ship is ready to leave for Luxor at the end of this week. A toast, to the trip, and it rewards." With that, all raised their glasses and drank to the toast.

It was only a handful of people that didn't look surprised, and Anastasia was the only woman that knew beforehand, that was for sure. The men excused themselves, and moved to the great room to enjoy cigars and brandy, while playing cards or billiards, but all the talk was about the trip, and more importantly, who was going.

This was going to be a very long night, indeed. In the hours that followed, Anastasia received a note from Horus-Salah that he was in the west garden. Anastasia discreetly moved away from the guest she was talking to, and made casual greetings as she made her way out of the room.

Once out of the room, and observing eyes, she went right to the west garden. Horus-Salah was sitting under a tree, looking at the stars when she came upon him. He lowered his head, but not his eyes, and said, "My wish has come true, my star is before me." With that, he got up and looked straight into her eyes. She was once more complete, and reached over to kiss him on the cheek. Like life, it was too short for both of them, but at least it was the moment and the touch. Their faces showed to each other how complete the moment was for both of them. They sat down on the bench, looking in to the garden.

robert f. edwards

She was the first to say, "Well, how is it going?"

Horus-Salah answered, "I don't know, my father hasn't said anything on the subject to me, but that doesn't mean a thing. I would be one of the last to know," he added.

"Well then, who would be the first to know?" came the question from Anastasia.

"Your father," came the answer.

"But, when, and where?" came the next question. Only for the answer to be the same,

"I don't know," but Horus-Salah added, "After the trip to Luxor, would be my guess." The minutes danced away, and an hour passed by, before the lovers knew that time was not waiting for them.

Horus-Salah's servant came first, and mentioned that Horus-Salah was being missed, to say nothing that the women were looking for Anastasia. They both must return now. With that, Horus-Salah got up and looked down at his beloved, and said, "Stay here, and I will return, then I will have your servant return and escort you back, my love."

She returned his words of love, and added, "Forever."

Once back in the great hall, people were making their good-byes and best wishes for one and all that would be going on the trip. The King and his company had long gone, and now anyone that was going, left. Before the clocks could tell it was morning, the dawn had arrived, and the sun gave one and all a new day. The last of the last were helped into their cars that had waited throughout the night.

The next day, or later this day, which would be the right thing to say, instructions came to Horus-Salah, when his father had sent for him to come to the study, which his father referred to his office. Horus-Salah could count on one hand the number of times he had been in the study with his father. Coldness covered his body, not out of fear, but of what was in the summons. As he walked the long way down the hall, he remembered the last time. Oh yes, the last time when he was told he would be going to England for his higher education. His mind was at the door, but his body still hadn't t got to the

River of Life

wing, let alone the door. In due course, his body met his mind, and both knocked on one of the great doors.

His father's voice came through the door as if it was air, and said, "Enter." Horus-Salah stood frozen, but his mind took hold again, and the body opened the door. Yes, just as before, his father sat at the desk and moved his hand to the chair waiting for him. Like last time, he sat on the opposite side of the desk. As Horus-Salah sat, he once more looked into those black eyes that told nothing, but asked for all to know their owner.

His father said, "You and the ship will leave within two days. You will be in complete charge of it guests and their welfare."

Horus-Salah wished to ask so many questions, and one would have been, 'what about his father and Anastasia's father coming to Luxor?' His father's eyes read the question in his son's mind, and answered the one he wished to comment on. "I will be staying behind with Anastasia's father. We will join you there later." With that, his father added, "That is all." Horus-Salah started to get up from the chair, only for the eyes to hold him there. His father look right into Horus-Salah's eyes, but it was like they went through his body, and his father spoke once more. "Have patience, I will give you your answer when you return from Luxor."

It was over, and Horus-Salah started to breathe normally, once out side the great door. He looked around the hallway, both left and right, he was alone. Then, and only then, did he let out a moan. It took him much longer to return to his quarters. However, once back inside, he sat in his favorite chair, and looked out into the garden below. It was an hour or longer, he didn't know when his eyes moved away. His mind was still sitting across from his father.

What was going to happen now, and on the trip, and what was he going to do? But more importantly, what was the answer his father was going to give after Luxor? He felt as if he had been out in the midday sun, and left to die alone. Weak was just one of the words his mind used for this feeling.

Many more came and went, as he grew back his strength. His eyes moved back into the room, and so did his mind, as he heard footsteps outside his room.

At once, he knew it was his personal servant. Before his hand moved from the arm of the chair, there was a knock on door to this room. Horus-Salah said in a weak voice, "Enter." Once inside, the servant looked at his master and asked what was wrong. Horus-Salah knew that he could trust his life with this man, and so shared what his father had said to him. After Horus-Salah was finished, the old man asked what Horus-Salah wanted to do now. Horus-Salah looked at him, more for the answer than the question.

Another hour went by, and most of the plans for the trip were in place. His servant went and got the personal servant of his father, and the two servants went over each step that both masters had wanted. The changes were small, but changes just the same, were made to Horus-Salah's plan from his father's servant. When done, both servants went back to their masters with the changes. Horus-Salah's servant asked if there was anything he was needed for before the evening was to start.

"What about Anastasia, and getting this information to her," Horus-Salah requested.

His servant said, "Would it not be better to tell her yourself this evening, over or after dinner?" Once Horus-Salah heard the suggestion, it made all the sense in the world to him. For in Egypt, and in these very walls, secrets were hard to keep, and information was next to impossible.

This dinner was small be the same compared to some that been at this very table, but the routine as the same. So, after dinner, the men in one room, and the women in another, talking about the same things and doing the same things, more out of habit than pressure.

As the darkness moved deeper into the night, Horus-Salah was the first to find his way into the garden. Anastasia joined him some time later. The two showed their great love to each other, and how much these moments meant to them.

River of Life

Horus-Salah told Anastasia about his meeting with his father and what was said to him. She at once smiled, and looked at him. What had given him a great fear of what was going to happen to them, and their dreams, was just the opposite of Anastasia.

She said, "At last, my father has had a chance to talk to your father." Horus-Salah looked at her, and for the first time since his meeting, saw the message from the positive angle. Right away, Anastasia was in charge. "We must make this trip our show of true leadership and union together," she added.

Horus-Salah just smiled at her, and then said "Just like the days of old, my leader." They both laughed and laughed at their very dying need for each, and the balance both had on each other. Anastasia once more told Horus-Salah that she would talk to her father before she departed on the trip, and get the full information of what the top parent had talked about, and what Horus-Salah's father's outcome was. As always, these moments went far too fast, when a servant showed up, Anastasia was being missed. Horus-Salah said his goodnight to both, and stayed in the garden, while Anastasia went back to the party.

The next morning, Horus-Salah's servant went over all that had to be done before Horus-Salah and his group was to leave in the next two days. Horus-Salah questioned every step, and the servant knew that no mistake, big or small, would be allowed to go unnoticed, or unpunished. After Horus-Salah was satisfied, he excused the servant and went about his own tasks for the day.

Just past the mid-day, he had a meeting with his mother in her private quarters. It was always good to be alone with her, for she was his mother, and one of the few people he could ask questions about personal matters. They talked about what lay ahead for both of them on the trip up the Nile. His mother said, "My dearest son, you have servants to go over all this, and probably have already done so, shall we talk about your real reason to visit my quarters?"

robert f. edwards

"Horus-Salah said his goodnight to both, and stayed in the garden..."

Original artwork, watercolour   Phyllis Verdine Humphries
Circa 1930's

River of Life

They both smiled and with that Horus-Salah asked about his and Anastasia's plan, and what news did his mother have to give on its progress. His mother looked at him, and said, "All has been done as you and Anastasia have asked." She then added, "Both Anastasia's mother and I have been adding here and there, whenever we can, for you both, and your dreams of being together." Once more she looked into the eyes of her son and went on, "Anastasia's father is also for it. He has, by what you have said, had his moment with your father on this subject."

Horus-Salah wanted to ask, 'what did he say', and then left it unfinished, but both he and his mother knew, Horus-Salah was asking what did *his* father say. His mother's eyes moved to look out the window, and said, "The men of the world tell their wives what they want them to know, and nothing else. In this case, I do not know what was said by either."

Horus-Salah's eyes followed her to the window, and asked, "Can you add anything to help?"

Without looking at him, she added, "It is in Allah's hands, and your father's wishes. Have faith in both, my son." He spent another hour talking, but it was of the past, and how both enjoyed being together at these moments.

In closing, he said, "Until this evening, my dearest mother," and left her quarters.

It was the last night before the group, led by Horus-Salah, was to leave by boat up the Nile. Tonight's group of guests was small by the standards set in the days and weeks before. Most of the people, that would in one way or another be taking part in the trip, were having their own good-bye evening, or were busy doing last minute things. For the ones that were here tonight, it was a light and informal evening and ended early.

Horus-Salah had only a few moments with Anastasia, and not in the garden, but in the hallway between goings from the dining room into the parlor. His words were fast and short. "My father will give us the answer on our return."

159

robert f. edwards

Anastasia's reply "It is about time", to the surprise of Horus-Salah. With that, he went his way with the men and hers with the women. So the evening came to a close, and all was ready for the next day.

River of Life

CHAPTER 13

Horus-Salah's servants had checked and rechecked all that was to be done aboard the ship. The luggage and supplies had been on board for the last few days. The Captain had gone over every detail with Horus-Salah's servant and nothing had been missed. Some of the guests for the trip were even on board this very night. As Horus-Salah returned to his quarters, his servant came to him with the final up-date. All was in order. First thing in the morning, Horus-Salah would be given an up-date of the departure time, and any small setbacks. His family and Anastasia's group would leave for the ship in the afternoon. With that last report of the day, Horus-Salah found his way to his bed, and the darkness of the night.

The morning called like the rest, with the sun up before Horus-Salah and the others, from the night before. However, Horus-Salah was not far behind the golden ball, with his first meeting waiting for him. He was to have the meeting in the green room, which was more or less a study or private library. As he went in, and sat down in one of the large leather chairs, his first meeting was with the Captain of the ship. So it went, one by one, the head of one department or another, giving their reports and support. All was well, and going on time.

His servant then told him the next person was the General of the British Army. As the man came in and was announced by the servant, Horus-Salah didn't change his way for him but with a hand, showed which seat to sit in. The General was a take-charge person, and didn't take this kindly, but did sit in the chair that was offered. Once in the chair, and after greetings, the General started to tell Horus-Salah what he and the British government were going to do about this trip, for there would be British guests abroad the ship going up the Nile. He told Horus-Salah that it was his respon-

161

robert f. edwards

sibility to see to their safety, and so would be putting his men in charge, and overseeing the general charge of things. Horus-Salah at once saw the manner or the man, and the problems he was going to have as the commander in chief. Horus-Salah just looked at this man until the General was finished. Then, Horus-Salah said, "I am in charge of this expedition, and you being a military man will understand the chain of command."

The General, who was many years older and a professional soldier, looked at this young man sitting across from him, in a dress, well, in this part of the world, robe. The General was taken back, but didn't show it, as he planned his next move. With that out of the way, the General gave that look of 'you poor young soul', then added, "We," meaning the British, which was himself, "know best what to do in these matters." Before the General had a chance to see the reaction from his opponent, Horus-Salah replied, "Then you will agree with what is being done, and aid its success." The General again was taken back by the command of this young man.

This time, with all the experience of the years he had, and his British breeding, he thought but did not ask, what would that be? The ship is under the Captain's command, and the entire guest list will be his responsibility. The General just looked at Horus-Salah, and knew that even under international law; the Captain was the law at sea. Horus-Salah continued "With the safety of the ship, and all on board, I am asking you for two small gunboats; one to be in front, and the other to be behind." The General couldn't believe he was looking at one so young, but in full control of what had to be done, and the General thought 'his way'. Yes, this would get around, what the home office had told him they wanted the General to do, and still meet with the rules set out by the Egyptians. The General just couldn't bring himself to think of this.

The General looked right into Horus-Salah's eyes, which in turn looked right back. The General said, at last, "It will work," and added "I will need to know the time of departure, and have my boats in position." "My servant will be able to

162

River of Life

give you all that you will need for your part in this expedition."
The General felt for the first time, in front of this young man,
as a junior officer. His face, for the first time, also showed how
he felt, as it changed to a new shade of red.

Horus-Salah knew that he had won, and said, "That will
be all for now."

The General got up and saluted. The rest of the meetings
were just men reporting that all was done right, and on time.
As Horus-Salah was just finishing up and returning to his
quarters, his father had received the first information on the
meeting with the British officer and his son. His dark eyes
look warmer at the servant that gave the up-date. At two in
the afternoon, the long strip of cars came, one by one to the
front door, and the good-byes to the ones going on the trip
started. It had been worked out that Horus-Salah's car would
be last to come, but by taking another route his car would be
there first, and he would be able to greet the guests from the
house as they came abroad.

It was with this plan that he got to see his beloved Anastasia twice. By four o'clock or around that time, the first officer informed him that all was on board and the time to cast
off was for six that night. Yes, the gunboat Captains were advised also. The next few hours, Horus-Salah and the rest of
the guests got to know their way around the ship of the Nile.
It wasn't an overly large boat but with over a hundred guests,
plus the crew, gave it the presence of a much larger vessel as
it moved up the Nile.

As the ship freed itself from the dock, and made its way
to the middle of the mighty Nile, the two small gunboats made
their presence known. This only added to the appearance of
the size of the ship, for now it looked like a whale that was
being surrounded by two dolphins. The trio made a straight
line upstream; the sun gave way to the darkness.

The gentle breezes moved from the land to the open por-
tals, as one and all were enjoying some refreshments or preparing for the meal that awaited them. There would be two
sittings; and at the head table of one of the sittings would be

robert f. edwards

the Captain, at the other sitting would be Horus-Salah. Each night the Captain and Horus-Salah would change times but not the guests.

Tonight, and every night from now on, would be as good as or better than any ocean liner. The food and wine were of the very best, to say nothing of the entertainment that would be talked about for years to come. This was Horus-Salah's moment to prove to his father that he could be a leader of men, and please his father's wishes. Nothing was left to chance.

The Captain was at the first serving of dinner, and though it started at 7 o'clock, it wasn't until well after eight-thirty that Horus-Salah and the rest went for their dinner. Horus-Salah was at one end, with Anastasia at the other end. Both their mothers were in the middle across from each other. In this way, Horus-Salah could keep informed of the guests and by changing every night, would be able to have a general idea of what was going on around him at all times. But it was his servants that would be of the greatest information. The people aboard were from all over the world, but mostly from Europe. The dress and style was of a European flavor. The men, even the Egyptians, were in formal black ties for dinner. That is to say, if not in the uniform of the nation that they represented, and their rank in it.

Horus-Salah looked to Anastasia like an Egyptian god in a European costume. As she looked down the long table at him, her heart moved faster, and the color in her face turned to a brighter pink. She also saw Horus-Salah looking at her whenever someone let up talking to him. He saw his one and only as the most beautiful woman there. And he was right; she looked like a goddess herself, from the north. The long evening dress with its emerald green, gave her a look of purity, and yet worldliness and well breeding, anywhere in this world.

The meal was of meats cooked to the way this class of people demanded, plus all the additional dishes were served to the guests' wishes and desires. Each person had his or her

164

River of Life

own waiter, who stood out of sight, but not out of hand. The dining went well into the hour of ten, before Horus-Salah and the men went up top for brandy and cigars. The women moved into the salon for tea and port.

The small armada moved through the darkness, up the long line of history in these waters. As the people, now some women came topside, each could see the little lights on both sides of the long strip. It was small villages, with the answer to the darkness of the night. Some may be still preparing a meal, or more likely sitting by the light and sharing the day and their lives.

This was the way, before, and is now, and for who knows, maybe forever. It was Egypt. For the Egyptians it had been this way forever, and to Horus-Salah and the others, there was no other way. For the others that were foreign, it looked like large candles dancing on the shore, here and there. The night was warm, and before one knew it, the midnight hour was upon them. One by one returned to their suite, for a last drink, and a game of cards, whichever one wanted. For Horus-Salah, it was his first real test of leadership. As he went to his cabin, all was well.

The dawn broke across the bow, but Horus-Salah was already up. His servant had his things ready for the day, and most importantly, for the morning. One by one, the men in charge of each area of the trip came and went, after giving Horus-Salah their report. All was on time, with no changes to the master plan. As the morning came to its full view, the rest of the guests started their day. First order of the day was always the morning meal, which was open seating. They went up top for the sun, or games to be starting for their enjoyment. Anastasia's servant came to Horus-Salah's cabin, and asked if Horus-Salah would be joining Anastasia for the morning meal. Yes, Horus-Salah would be joining her for breakfast.

With that, the loved ones showed up at a table for two. It was the first time the two had been able to sit in public, with just the two of them. Horus-Salah was feeling his new power.

robert f. edwards

He looked at Anastasia, and said, "How am I doing so far, my love?"

With one big smile, she looked at just the two of them together, and said, "Just fine, my leader." The meal for both of them was one of the best they could remember. Both agreed it was the company.

After this moment, the two became one in pubic. For they were everywhere together, as both of them saw to the other guests' needs and enjoyment. But it was them that brought the most excitement to those they came upon. For the women, all they could talk about was the two beautiful young people. Oh yes, and how much they were in love, and were perfect for each other.

When the women had exhausted this subject, they would seek either Horus-Salah's or Anastasia's mothers, for any news that one or both of these young people had said or done. When the group was not blessed by one of their presence, the women would add what their thoughts were on the two. This only added to the ever-growing story, of two that were meant for each other. Some of the women that had known both families for a long time, told how as children they had promised each other that they would be together for life. Others that were newer to the group would talk about how they felt the two loved ones would be the happiest couple on board. Yes, they all talked about marriage, and when the two families would announce the wedding.

So, like the party back in Cairo, the subject was the same, but now continued day and night. As for the men, it took up less of their conversation, until Horus-Salah and Anastasia came upon a group of men. The men, at any age or nationality, became like schoolboys around the most popular girl. Once the two left, the men also would be talking about the two. But, in the end, it would be that Horus-Salah was one lucky man. For the single men, there was still hope, and for the others it was something they had missed in the past. They would add that they too had a good wife, as if it was the right thing to say, when finishing their dreams.

River of Life

The Captain informed Horus-Salah that the ship would be in Luxor late the next day, and would stay docked overnight as planned. He asked Horus-Salah of any changes in the plans of any of the guests. He then invited both Horus-Salah and Anastasia to the bridge. The couple accepted the offer and followed the Captain to the command center. As the Captain showed both of them around the bridge, and answered their questions, he asked if Horus-Salah would like to take the wheel. Horus-Salah looked at the Captain and then at Anastasia. Before the Captain could reply, Anastasia said, "Go ahead Commander-In-Chief".

So, with that, Horus-Salah took up the post at the wheel and kept the course. Horus-Salah steered the ship up the river, and Anastasia wished in her heart that she could do it also. She looked on with all the pride of making the right choice in a man, a leader of men. For Horus-Salah, it was a new experience, and when he was about turn the post back to the first mate, the Captain assured him he was doing fine, and to continue. Little did the people on board notice the change at the helm. Horus-Salah moved the ship up river and he was aware of how strong the current was, as it made its presence known to the ship's hull.

His thoughts went to a time of his ancestors and the ships that they used, and the manpower that it must have taken to move up river. The over- powering of men, both in mind and body, to go against the river. As the ship moved ever forward, with the small gunboats off its starboard side, Horus-Salah took his eyes off the bow, and looked at Anastasia. She smiled back and added, "Will you be wanting a boat this size for your own use?"

He laughed and said, "I am going to be returning this one to the good Captain right now." With that said, he looked at the Captain, and gave back the wheel to the first officer, who had the watch. Both of the young lovers thanked the Captain, and left the bridge.

robert f. edwards

Once outside, Anastasia reached over and took Horus-Salah's hand. Holding it, she said, "I am very impressed that you could handle a boat of this size."

He added, "So am I, for that matter," as they walked back to the lower deck.

The afternoon saw the people doing much the same on board as was done in the morning. The midday meal was served in the same way as the morning, and people found what was to please them, or at least amuse them. By early evening, the guests' one and all had a full day, in their minds. So, the evening meal was being dressed for, and the night was to begin. At both settings, the Captain and Horus-Salah made the announcement of arriving in Luxor the next day. The daily social activities were posted through out the ship, but this was the formal announcement. The evening was much the same as the one before it, with one big difference.

After leaving the table, both Horus-Salah and Anastasia did not go their separate ways, but stayed together, as the rest moved around them. As it was the custom of the time, both the men and women went their separate ways, to be joined by others of their same sex. This was not for Horus-Salah or Anastasia, who went together up top, to enjoy the cool night air, the stars and each other. Once up top, it was only the servants and the ship staff that were present. They were, for what counted to them, alone with each other. It was the first time to be together alone since the train. Oh yes, those short moments out in the garden, if one wanted to count them too. Both sat in the great soft chairs on deck, pointing out the shoreline. Anastasia looked at Horus-Salah, and he looked at her, and then added, "at last." It was the same thought that both were thinking. What may have seemed along time to any looking on the two, just sat looking at the shoreline, saying nothing. It was the pure enjoyment of being together that the lovers were enjoying.

In due time, Anastasia told Horus-Salah that she thought he was doing a good job, but asked did he need her help. His reply was, "I always need you, and your aid when I was

168

River of Life

young, now and forever, my dearest one." That started both of them talking about the past, the times when they had the freedom of children, and when both of them would spend time up at their special place. The times they shared looking down at the Valley of the Kings, and across at Luxor. Both sat back in the chairs and kept talking, but it was more like they were traveling back together in that time with each other. Sharing, that was what they had done all their lives, from those times so long ago.

As the soft winds moved across the deck, and the little lights on the shore past by, they too moved on to the days when Horus-Salah had spent time in Poland with her family. The hours had come and gone as the two lovers talked about their short lives together. It was midnight before one of the servants came up, and mentioned how late it was, and that tomorrow would be a full day coming into Luxor.

After the servant left and once more it was just the stars, the water, and the night, the two lovers got up and Horus-Salah put his arms around his beloved. Anastasia followed his example with her arms. The winds were the only thing that came between them. Then Horus-Salah looked into her eyes, and her lips found his. What both wished in their hearts would last their lifetime, their lips told the rest of their bodies. Horus-Salah's manhood let his mind know that he was ready to be her husband, in all worldly ways, and the wetness Anastasia was feeling confirmed that she was also ready for the union of marriage.

Afterwards, both didn't want to part, but they did, and with their noses touching, they opened their eyes and looked once more at each other. Again, their lips gave way, and their bodies moved even closer than before. The heat of the night was light compared to the heat in both of their veins. Once more, their lips broke apart and their lungs reached for air, as their eyes opened again to see each other. Anastasia's hand moved from Horus-Salah's shoulder, down his back, and up again and down. It as if she was trying to find the spot that would push him inside her. At the same time, Horus-Salah

169

was doing like-wise, to find the magic opening into her. Both were wet from their own body's moisture. It was a need that was experienced by both men and women, which the lovers needed to fulfill *now*. Just as their bodies had taken over their minds, and the next move was to take place, a voice from far away yet close by was heard.

It was Horus-Salah's servant. He was standing just a few feet away from the couple, and once more said, "Master," louder than before. This time, Anastasia put her hands down to her sides, and took her eyes away from Horus-Salah, to look in the direction of the voice. When she saw the servant, her face changed and she looked into the servant's face now. With this, Horus-Salah followed, and now too was looking at his servant's face. The servant's eyes were looking at the deck and did not change. It was his voice that made his presence known to the two. Then, he once more said, "Master, the Captain wishes to see you now." With those words, the servant, not waiting for a reply, moved back into the darkness.

Horus-Salah's face was red, and so was his lover's, for more than one reason. What were a few moments, but to both of them seem much longer, Horus-Salah said in a voice he didn't recognize, "I must go to the Captain." Anastasia heard the words, but just stood there frozen, and still needing the air her lungs were looking for. Her eyes had moved back to Horus-Salah, and once more, the two felt the peace come over them. In a small weak voice, she acknowledged what had to be done by a smile, and a simple, "yes."

Horus-Salah walked her back below to her apartment, and both didn't dare to hold each, other let alone kiss, for both knew that her bed was much closer than the Captain's quarters. As Anastasia's hand turned the doorknob, she smiled again, and said, "good- night, my love."

Horus-Salah smiled and said, "good- night, my love," but added "until tomorrow."

She went inside, and Horus-Salah moved back down the hall. The servant was waiting at the end. As Horus-Salah came to be in front of the servant, he asked, "where is the

River of Life

Captain, and what does he wish to see me about?" The servant replied that the Captain was in his cabin. For what the Captain wished to see Horus-Salah about, the servant could add nothing to the question. So it was that Horus-Salah made his way to the Captain's door and knocked. "Enter," came a voice from the other side, and Horus-Salah followed the request. Once inside, the Captain, on seeing who came in, started to get up from his desk, only for Horus-Salah's right hand guiding him back down to the chair. Then, the Captain showed another chair for Horus-Salah to be seated, and both started with some small talk before getting to their purpose.

The Captain then told Horus-Salah the exact time the ship would be arriving in Luxor. However, the main reason for the Captain to ask for the visit was about some of the passengers, who wished to stay in Luxor. Horus-Salah asked how many, and what was their reason. The Captain's reply was most were British, and a few French, the total would be seven to eight couples. "What is their reason?" again asked Horus-Salah.

The Captain was at a loss, but added, "They don't like being on water, or on a ship." With that information, Horus-Salah told the Captain to call a general meeting for 10:00 a.m., and tell one and all of the time of arrival at Luxor, and also the time of departure for Aswan. With that out of the way, both men returned to small talk before Horus-Salah said his goodnight.

Once outside the Captain's cabin, Horus-Salah made his way back to his suite, where the servant was waiting for him. His bed was turned down and his night cloths were lying on the bed. The servant stood and waited for more instructions from Horus-Salah. "Before you retire for the night," Horus-Salah said to his servant, "contact my mother's maid, and have a meeting arranged for 9:00 a.m. for Mother and me." With this last order, the servant took his leave. Again, Horus-Salah was alone with his thoughts. He made his way to the bedroom, and gave up the day for the rest he needed for tomorrow.

robert f. edwards

The dawn had reached the skies, but Horus-Salah was there to see it. He was still asleep when the servant knocked on the bedroom door. The servant entered with mint tea, and fresh bread, plus the morning greeting. Horus-Salah's first words were, "What time is it?" before his eyes opened. His eyes were still closed when his ears heard, "Eight a.m., my master." With that news, now Horus-Salah's eyes joined his ears, and were opened. Sitting up in bed, with tea in one hand, his voice joined the rest of his body. He asked, "Has the meeting with my mother been arranged?"

The servant looked somewhat surprised, and replied weakly, "Yes, just as you asked."

Horus-Salah then got out of bed to get dressed. As he finished getting ready, he sent his servant to ask if his mother was ready to see him. Upon the return, the servant's reply was, "she is waiting." With that Horus-Salah made his way to her suite and knocked. Her maid came to the door, and showed him in to the sitting room, where his mother acknowledged him. After they shared morning greetings, Horus-Salah started to ask for her advice on the matter of the guests that wanted to stay at Luxor. With this news, she then asked the first question, and many more followed. When she shared the news with him, both started to think of what had to be done.

First, it was not thinkable to have some of the guests left on their own in Luxor, and to change the plans for the rest was just as unacceptable. Time was not on their side, for at 10:00 a.m. the Captain was going to have a general meeting, and would be asking about the guests that wished to stay behind in Luxor. His mother and Horus-Salah had less than an hour to work out the problem. No one could refuse the guests the right to stay at Luxor, but one of them *must* stay behind and look after them.

His mother came up with the idea first, and with a little work on it from both of them, it was agreed upon. So this was what would be taking place once in Luxor. The ones that wished to stay there would be put up at the Winter Palace. From there, his mother's servant would stay at the hotel at all

172

River of Life

times. His mother would stay behind also, but at the beloved home, and start to get ready for his father and the Count to come from Cairo. The outings for the guests that would be staying behind could be organized so none of them would have time to go to the Valley of the Kings, until his father and the rest were ready to go. As the plan received its final touches, time ran out, and both of them had to join the others for the meeting with the Captain.

Now that all the guests were together, waiting for the Captain, Horus-Salah sent his servant to tell the Captain what had been discussed, and decided on for the guests that wished to remain. With that out of the way, Horus-Salah was trying to give Anastasia and her mother the latest up-date, before they heard it from the Captain. Both ladies received most of the information just as the Captain came into the room. After the good mornings and pleasantries were exchanged, he started to give the information to the guests. The first was that at 4:00 p.m. that day, the ship would be docking at Luxor. It would be docked over-night, and then first thing in the morning, the ship would start its way up the Nile to Aswan. He told the guests that they all must be back on board no later than midnight.

Then, one of the English guests asked about staying behind. With that question, the Captain replied, "For the people that requested this, I will inform you, once the others have had their questions answered." There were some small questions, about where to go, if anywhere, this short time in Luxor, for everyone on board knew that they would be coming back, for the event that was in the Valley of the Kings. As most of the guests were staying on the ship for the rest of the trip up the Nile, the Captain excused them. One by one, they went back to what they were doing, or on to the next things that they had plans for. However, the ones that wished to stay at Luxor until the ship returned were told by the Captain to stay.

He informed them that they were booked in at the Winter Palace. When they left the ship, he would no longer be responsible for their welfare. He also told them that Horus-Salah's mother would be in charge of the events and arrangements that they wished to take part in, until the rest of them returned. There were a few questions from this small group, however, everyone in the group knew, once they were on land, that their whereabouts at all time, had to be known and cleared by Horus-Salah's mother in advance. That also included the servants that these people had with them. There was some talking going on after the Captain left, but there would be no changes to what he had told the group.

Horus-Salah, Anastasia and their mothers went over to the open sitting area. Anastasia was the first to ask, "Why were these people allowed to stay in Luxor in the first place, and break away from the rest of them?" Horus-Salah told her that most of them were British, and lived by their rules, and not any one else's. Horus-Salah's mother added that they, meaning the British army, were really in charge of Egypt now.

It was the Countess that asked the next question, more to the group than to any one individual. She asked if she too could stay behind, to be with Horus-Salah's mother. Horus-Salah's mother was her very best friend, and she may be of some help, but most of all, she would like to spend as much time with her friend before returning to Poland. The other three looked at her, and it was Horus-Salah that spoke first. "I understand your wish, and for my answer, it is yes, please stay with my mother, and be by her side in all matters with these people."

It was Horus-Salah's mother that spoke next, with a big smile on her face, that said it all, "thank you my friend," looking at the Countess.

The last one to say anything was Anastasia, who looked at her mother and laughed, "You both trust Horus-Salah and me to look after all the rest do you?"

Then, all four laughed, with the Countess adding, "It is you two we have to put all our trust in." The four of them knew only too well, what she meant.

River of Life

Yes, the plan that all of them had been working on so hard must come first. Anastasia replied, looking at her mother, "Have you talked to Father, about what was said to Horus-Salah's father?"

"No," came the reply, "and it is not your father that has the answer, but Horus-Salah's." The four of them looked at each other, knowing full well that Horus-Salah's father was the only one with an answer, and he had told no one.

As the ship moved ever closer to Luxor, the four sat and talked about the past and the present. For Horus-Salah and his mother, it was coming to their first home, or the one that they thought of as home, and not just another house. For Anastasia and her mother, it was the first time being back after all those years away. This was Egypt to them, and all the good moments that they shared, came and went like one long and beautiful time in their lives. It was well past noon, and lunch had come and gone. The heat of the day came down, so everyone was looking for shade somewhere on the ship. By late afternoon, the four of them were still on deck, enjoying the mighty Nile, and the shoreline it passed.

It was Anastasia that saw the first buildings in the distance of Luxor. She pointed with her hand, as the others followed her eyes direction. It was the village of Karnak that the four of them were now viewing. As the ship moved ever closer to the waiting dock, the village became clear to all of them. What grandeur of monumental architecture came into view, as Luxor and its spectacular Temples of Karnak made their appearance. For Horus-Salah and his mother, it was home at last. For Anastasia and her mother, it was a long overdue return to a happy time in their lives.

The ship came alive, with every moment that the dock came closer. Horus-Salah was looking over the side of the ship, as his mind moved to another time. His mind had gone back thousands of years, when the mighty ship of his ancestors took the Pharaonic, their man of the gods, to this very spot. The great wooden boat that moved up and down these waters, to visit the tomb of the Pharaonic, and the wish of

175

robert f. edwards

" ... the ship moved ever closer to the waiting dock..."

Original   photograph Robert F. Edwards
Egypt   November, 1999

176

River of Life

their final resting places. The peoples' living god; that was the voice of the gods' wishes for the rest of them. The one true messenger. The ruler of all on earth, and the voice of the Sun God. Yes, for over 4000 years, his people had lived here at Luxor and Thebes. And now he was one of them, from the past, returning to their home, and his.

It was Anastasia that brought him back to this time, by asking what he was thinking. He looked at her and smiled, with the reply, "oh, the past."

She then asked "yours?"

He looked into her eyes, and said, "Yes, if you believe in reincarnation." Before she could answer, the first ropes were pulling the ship to land. The docking had begun. It was just moments later that their personal servants were by their side, asking if they were going ashore. The rest of the servants of Horus-Salah were at their stations, and following the orders that had been given. With so many tasks that were at hand, the dock below looked like a beehive that had been over-turned.

The guests that were going on with the trip were asked to stay on board. The small group that was staying in Luxor and their servants were escorted to the Winter Palace. Their suites were waiting for them. As one by one was settled in to their new accommodations, their luggage followed shortly after-ward. Horus-Salah's and Anastasia's mothers left also, but went to the great house that the servants had ready for them. It was of great joy by the faithful, to see their beloved mistress of the house return again. Also, some of the older servants remembered the Countess, and showed the same joy towards her.

The evening was close at hand for those dining at the Winter Palace. There was little time to get ready for the evening feast at the great house, so arrangements had been made for the chefs of the Winter Palace to prepare the meal to be brought in. In one of the great halls, the guests enjoyed a meal that kings and emperors would have been pleased with.

robert f. edwards

The dishes were so many than one couldn't try all of them. The meal lasted well into the night.

As the Captain was one of the first to leave, it was a reminder that those on board would be leaving early the next morning. By midnight, the ones that were going on, were all back on board, and the two ladies were on their way back to the great house. The few people that remained at the Winter Palace continued what they did every night, play cards or billiards, finishing of the evening with port and cigars. The women enjoyed each other's company with conversation and tea.

The new day started, and so did the ship, as it moved away from the dock that had held it. As the large ship made its way to the middle, so did the two small boats, taking up their places at each end of the larger one. The crew had been up for hours, and the ship was underway for sometime, before the guests found their way to breakfast and start the day for what laid ahead.

Anastasia and Horus-Salah were now the center of all that was going on. Each one was asked questions of when and where, to say nothing of what was happening for the rest of the journey. Both the young people replied, "All in good time, and the Captain was in charge of the ship." Not one of the people believed that the Captain, though he might be in charge of the ship, was in charge. From the beginning, all knew that his father had given Horus-Salah, the final and complete say on all matters, small or large. However the two young people stayed to the story and the others accepted it.

The day was much the same as the others, as the ship kept moving towards its next destination. The morning was replaced by the hot afternoon. Only by late in the day, the sun gave way, followed by gentle winds. All were thankful, and welcomed the breeze. After dinner, Horus-Salah announced that tomorrow evening, for those that wished to participate, that they, meaning the guests, would be part of a play. The play would be a make-believe murder mystery on the Nile. The rules were simple; that each guest would be himself or herself,

178

River of Life

but go back to the time the play was written for. Some people that wished to could see Horus-Salah or Anastasia for bigger parts. For most of the guests, it was another night of the same, but for Anastasia and Horus-Salah, it took on a new meaning to their relationship.

For the first time, both were in charge of their lives, and the group that was with them. Yes, they both knew just how important this part of the trip was and their conduct when both their fathers got the news. It would be the final act on their part, for their great plan to be together for the rest of their lives. For this reason, both were always out front and around people, to see where and what they were doing. The night became late, and people were returning to the cabin. Anastasia said goodnight to Horus-Salah in a formal manner, just so all could see. Horus-Salah returned her wish with "until tomorrow my dearest." The two retired with the others, as the ship moved though the darkness.

It was Anastasia that was up first. Horus-Salah greeted her at the breakfast table. It seemed strange, and yet right, for the both of them to be together. Talking together, without their parents or guests sitting with them. After the normal greetings, Anastasia asked Horus-Salah what he thought about the trip so far, and how was it going in his eyes. Horus-Salah replied that in his mind, all was proceeding as his father would have wished, with the one exception of the guests left behind. She asked if any of his father's servants were on board that would report this back to his father.

Horus-Salah's answer was out almost before she was finished with, "My father will know everything, here, and everywhere else in his world." He added, "It is his way."

Anastasia asked, "Is it going to be your way also, when you are at the head of the family?"

"I don't know," came the answer, but then he added, "It has been the way of my family, and others of my kind in Egypt for hundreds of years."

She laughed, and said, "In my part of the world, we call it spying." They both laughed, and went up top to enjoy the day.

179

robert f. edwards

The mighty Nile was like a great serpent, moving inland as it made its way along the shoreline. The little feluccas were going up and down the river, like small birds working the water, forever looking here and there. The gentle winds provided little movement to the sails of the feluccas; so many of them were using the large poles to push themselves along. It looked like some of the feluccas were great cranes, walking down the river. Both Anastasia and Horus-Salah were enjoying the scenery before them, and the farmers working in fields along the shore. At certain points in the river, they could see children playing. It was as it had always been, and to both of them it would always be as such, for this was the real part of Egypt.

One of Horus-Salah's servants came and told him that the Captain wished to see him. Horus-Salah excused himself from Anastasia, and went with the servant to see the Captain. The Captain was on the bridge when Horus-Salah arrived. The Captain asked Horus-Salah to accompany him to his cabin. After both were settled in the cabin, mint tea was served. The Captain told him of the time that they would be arriving at Aswan. The Captain asked if Horus-Salah had any change to the program. The answer came from Horus-Salah as a firm "no." Both men talked about the trip, up to this point, and what might happen later on. Two hours had past, and with both of them feeling that all was in order, Horus-Salah returned to Anastasia to give her the up-dates.

Now he could be in her presence most of the time, for everyone on board looked at both of them as one. They were the host and hostess. As the sun reached its apex in the sky, the host and hostess started to gather round them the people that wished to take part in that night's play. There was a lot more talent than first thought. Before they got started, there was already a team that had both experience in producing and directing. With these people writing the theme of the play on hand, the others took parts that were available, or thought they were best for the part. This lasted all afternoon, and

180

River of Life

started to move into the evening. At long last, one and all had their parts, and knew what the play was all about.

It would start in the dining room with the meal. There would be a murder, the first of three people murdered. Then, the play would move into the parlor, where two of the murders would take place. The last murder would be in one of the cabins. This last person would be the real victim, and would be found by the detective. The detective would be based on the famous character 'Poirot', the Belgian detective in Agatha Christie's novels. The play itself was based on the novel 'Murder on the Nile'. However, by the time the plot had been worked out, it was one play for this ship, and only this one. The play was to involve an American that had stolen treasure from the tomb of King Tut. The first murder was of the person that wanted to buy this ill-gotten treasure. The money was exchanged, but not the treasure. The play continued with the murderer finding the treasure, and killing the person that had stolen it in the first place. The other two people murdered in the play; was one that took part by mistake, and one that witnessed the mistake. So, with all that in mind, the small cast of performers went back to their cabins, to get ready for their night as actors and actresses.

Horus-Salah and Anastasia were pleased with the way people had taken up their parts, and were looking forward to what lay ahead. It was different than most nights the guests had spent doing the same old thing every evening. It was, as one might say, both Horus-Salah's and Anastasia's coming-out party. So, as the minutes moved ever closer to the dinner hour, so did the guests and now the actors. For the two settings at dinner, Horus-Salah and Anastasia were at the first seating, to help the actors and actresses keep to their parts. The next seating with the Captain at the head of the table was the director and the producer, to help the actors and actresses there.

So it went, most of the guests, with a few exceptions, got into the time and place of the play. As the actors and actresses got more into their part and one should add, were do-

robert f. edwards

ing them very well, so did the rest of the guests. There were the ones that took part, and yes, the ones that just wanted to watch. The first murder was in the parlor, done with poison in the wine. The next, was to witness a murder by smoking a water pipe. By now the both groups, the ones that were playing parts, and the ones watching, got involved completely into the time and the place.

One older lady asked another if this was a play, or really happening. The reply was, they didn't know. So the play moved on, with the next report of the American murdered in his cabin. Along with bodies and the murderer in the parlor, was also the great detective. This was where the fun came, with the questions and the answers. Some of the questions were directed at people that were not part of the acting group. These people were complete unprepared, so some of their answers to the great detective were very funny, and the other guests had some good laughs. The play wound up with the explanation for the murders, and the recovery of the stolen treasure from the tomb of King Tut, and the final uncovering of the murderer himself, in true Christie fashion. At the end, the guests formed their own little groups, and were talking about the play as if they had gone to the theater. It was well into the midnight hour before the judging of the play was over.

One after another, the guests went to their cabins to retire after a long day. Horus-Salah and Anastasia exited, but unlike the others, went up top to enjoy the stars, and the light breezes of the night. Gazing at the shoreline on both sides of the boat, Horus-Salah said, "Some people are still up on the land." Far, far away came the sound of music. As the two sat on the deck chairs, both smiled at each other, with Horus-Salah asking, "What do you think the people back home will be saying about tonight's performance?"

Anastasia replied, "The actors or ours?" With that, both of them laughed until their sides hurt. It was now well into midway before the darkness would be replaced with the breaking of a new day.

182

River of Life

Horus-Salah escorted Anastasia back to the door of her cabin. It was hard on both of them to say good-night. What an ending for a great night, at the theater with the first night of their own play. Anastasia and Horus-Salah were of a common mind, when Anastasia said, "it wasn't a romantic play, but does that stop us from changing the ending?" Horus-Salah looked at her, with all the fire of passion in his eyes, with undying love for her. "No" came out of his mouth, before he could stop it. Their hands were already together, and their bodies were next, just when out of nowhere, one of the workers came to clean the hallway.

Horus-Salah looked deep into his beloved's eyes, and once again, they had no secrets from each other. Their hands told it all, with one long and hard squeeze, both of their hands let go. Horus-Salah's face was like the sun, as he looked into Anastasia's eyes, and added, "Not tonight, Josephine."

She replied, "let it be said, let it be done, my little Napoleon." She opened the door to her cabin, and before any more could be said the wooden door separated them. Horus-Salah went to his cabin to retreat with his thoughts.

It was well into the morning before the guests caught up to the servants and workers on board. One by one, they too started their day, the same as it had been all the days before on board. Today, the Captain had informed everyone that the ship would be arriving in Aswan by late afternoon. The expected arrival time was for five o' clock. The ship would dock for the evening, and stay in port for the next day, before going on to Abu Simbel. The servants were getting the outfits ready for that evening's outing, to take place at the Cascades Hotel. This evening was going to be one of the big events of this trip. There was a great feast being prepared by the locals.

As Aswan came in to view, the ship was right on time. For those up top, they got their first look at this garrison town of Egypt's gateway into Africa. The land of the Nubians and their prosperous trade markets were one of the first things that the people on board saw, as the ship made its way ever closer to the dock that was waiting for it. Now the people could see men getting ready on shore for the new arrivals. After what seemed to many as an extremely long time, the ship finally came to rest at the dock. Carriages were waiting to take the guests to the Cascades Hotel and their rooms.

It was when Horus-Salah and Anastasia came into the hotel that the manager came over and asked Horus-Salah if he would come into his office. He told both Horus-Salah and Anastasia that there was news from Cairo. With that information, the manager wished for Horus-Salah to excuse himself from Anastasia, and follow him into the office. Horus-Salah looked at the manager and replied, "We will go with you now". The manager just looked at Horus-Salah and said nothing, and then looked at Anastasia. She was the one who understood first what was happening.

She made a hand motion, and her servant was by her side. She looked at the woman, and asked, "Is my room prepared for me?"

The woman answered with, "yes, Countess."

Anastasia looked at the both men, but said to Horus-Salah, "Until later, for now I will take my leave, and go to my room." Both men acknowledged, as Anastasia and her servant turned towards the stairs. Out of the corner of her eye, she could see the relief on the manager's face. This was Egypt, my dear Horus-Salah; let both of us not make any mistakes, not now, my dearest one, she thought.

The two men watched her walk away with dignity, and then they turned to each other once more. Horus-Salah followed the manger into his office. The mint tea was served, and with the servants out of the room, the manager looked across at Horus-Salah. He then said, "I have news from Cairo," and added as an afterthought, "your father." Horus-Salah looked surprised, but did not show anything else. The manager went on, "the message is that your father and the Count will be two days longer in coming to Luxor, and for you to act according." The manager stopped, and was looking directly into Horus-Salah's eyes. Horus-Salah looked back, and wished to ask if there was anything else, but said nothing. The manager asked

River of Life

if he wished to acknowledge the message. Horus-Salah thought for a moment, and replied, "*Received, and understood*, is all I wish to be sent. We will be spending an extra night here at this hotel. Will you send for the Captain, and have him meet me in my suite."

The manager replied, "It will be looked after at once." His hand pulled a cord at the same time. There was a knock on the door, with the manager's voice saying "enter" and a staff member entered. The manager told him what was to be done, and then turned to Horus-Salah and asked if he or his staff could be of any more service. Horus-Salah thanked him, and asked only to be shown to his suite. Both men got up, just as another staff member came into the room, to show Horus-Salah to his accommodations.

The suite was extra large, with six rooms. Horus-Salah welcomed it at once from the suite he had on the ship. His servant had already been there, and his luggage had been put away in the right places. There were also refreshments on the table in the parlor. Horus-Salah informed his servant that when the Captain arrived, to show him into the study, and then went into the bedroom. It was well over an hour before the Captain was shown into the study. After being settled, the servant went to inform Horus-Salah of the Captain's arrival. When Horus-Salah came into the study, the Captain got up. Horus-Salah walked over and greeted him. Time was short, for the evening's events where coming into play. Horus-Salah came right to the point that he needed to extend the trip for another two days. One of them would be here at the hotel, and the next day would be spent in the surrounding area.

It would be the Captain's duty to inform one and all of the changes. Also, to make all the changes and arrangements. Horus-Salah added, "I would like an update tomorrow morning." The Captain said it would be done, and what time would Horus-Salah wish to see him in the morning. Horus-Salah looked at the Captain, and said, "Nine o'clock." Both men said their good-byes, and Horus-Salah returned to the bedroom. It was time to get dressed for the evening that was soon to begin.

As the people entered into the large dining room, the elegance of the room expressed the requirements of the people that entered. It was all that their class demanded, anywhere in the known world. From the high ceilings to the rich wood, the room itself told all of what to expect in the events that would follow, at such a hotel and in such a room. No one was disappointed. In fact, most said it was better than one could expect back home, where ever that place was. The food was not only of world-class quality, but also consisted of a worldly variety of dishes. As one more came into view, both the tables and the people at them, groaned under the volume. Each person wished to try just one more dish, long after they couldn't enjoy another mouth full.

Long after mid night, people were still sitting at the table, enjoying what was before them, and hoping against hope, that they could find room somewhere to try just one more dish. It was a feast, and the people of this area knew only too well how to please their guests. For their history of serving had been a very long one. The overfed guests moved from the dining area and most of them waddled back to their quarters. The heavy sleep from so much food and wine was all that was waiting them.

It was just the right time for Anastasia and Horus-Salah to spend a little time together. To their surprise, they both started talking about what had to be done with the extra two days. They were becoming the true host and hostess. Horus-Salah also thanked Anastasia for looking after them, and doing the right thing around the manager. They both had a laugh over it, after a moment.

She had acted and thought as an Egyptian, better than her own Egyptian, Horus-Salah. She then added, "Do you think your father will hear of this?"

It was Horus-Salah that looked surprised, and said, "He will know everything we are doing, and I mean everything, down to this moment."

River of Life

It was now Anastasia that looked surprised, with "everything?" coming from her lips.

Horus-Salah said once more, "yes, everything."

"Well then, he better get this one right," and with that she reached over and kissed Horus-Salah on the lips, and said, "You are my only love, for now and forever more."

After the kiss, Horus-Salah added, "And mine." It was as if they had always been together, and moved in live as one, when they were together. Both of them showed it when they were together. As they became more comfortable having the role of host and hostess, they had become one. Even the people around them now looked to see both of them, and took it as natural. This had to be the courtship for one and all to witness.

The two lovers sat and talked about what it would be like, if it was like this all the time. Both knew that it was live itself, for both of them, for now and always. The hour was late, and with a long look into each other's eyes, it was Horus-Salah that said, "We should be getting to bed."

Anastasia's quick mind said, "In one bed, or two."

It was more than a few seconds before Horus-Salah's open mouth got any words out, then it was, "what did you say?"

She started to laugh, and got up from the chair, "come along, my white knight, off to your cabin, but first escort me to mine."

He laughed and said, "As you wish, my lady." So ended one more night of happiness for the two of them.

The next morning, they both awoke to the sun, and the day that waited to start. Long before the guests on board made their way to see the beginning of the day, the workers and staff were looking forward to their morning break. The carriages lined up along the driveway of the hotel, to take the visitors away, first to Temple Philae, dedicated to the goddess, Isis. Then, off to the Mausoleum, of the age of Aga Khan, then up to the Monastery of St Simeon, on a camel. After this, the Coptic Monastery, then the women went to Sharia-as-Souk,

187

robert f. edwards

while the men sat in small open cafes, drinking coffee or tea, trying out the water pipes. The day finished as the last carriages were returning with the sun burnt and exhausted visitors. Guests, upon their return, went to their rooms and were greeted by their beds, for a rest that was surely needed, before the evening was to begin. It was to be the last night before returning to the ship, and moving up the mighty Nile.

Tonight, Anastasia and Horus-Salah had arranged something different. It was to be less formal, and more intimate. The tables were in settings for four or six and each were placed so that one could talk to the other table, if one wished, or to have a private evening, with the ones at their table. All went well, but the group looked, and was exhausted, with the night ending early for most of them. It was barely ten o'clock, and most of them had retired for the night.

Anastasia and Horus-Salah left the main dining area, and went to a small bar, overlooking Elephantine Island. As they sat across from each other, looking down at the water below, the warm evening added to their enjoyment. Small boats returned from fishing, or transporting goods. Even at this late hour, the workers were busy. Anastasia was enjoying a whiskey, while Horus-Salah, like his father, was enjoying a fruit juice. The moon was high and full, to add to the evening for the lovers. The two moved their chairs in such a way that both could see far below, and the activities on the river, while still being able to hold hands.

It was here that history had been made by the great pharaohs, and had not changed for thousands of years. The land and the Nile let people come and go, live and die, but it still did not change its ways. The two lovers had never been here before, so both of them were sharing what the people told of their past, and what it was like in the present.

Anastasia asked,

Would you like to have been a Pharaoh, my dearest one?" Horus-Salah looked at her, and said, "What about you, would you like to have been my queen?"

Her reply came fast, with a smile, "I am yours."

188

River of Life

He smiled and added, "And always will be." They were both at peace with themselves, and the world around them. Horus-Salah spoke next with a question. "Don't you wish tonight could live forever?"

"Yes" came a small voice from Anastasia, but it was her hand that told him more.

It was the right moment for both to confess that they had gotten something special for the other one. Horus-Salah, as hard as he tried, couldn't get Anastasia to share what she had gotten him, and he wasn't going to tell her what he had first. So, has two hearts filled with happiness and joy, the evening came to an end for them, too. With both Anastasia and Horus-Salah back in their own suites, it was their mind's eye that stayed open long, after the other two closed for the night. What peace this night had given them, and what great future it had promised to both of them. Their dreams were of each other, and the future that they would spend with each other, forever and ever more. Even in their dreams, they were together and their great love grew both at day and at night.

The next morning was a busy one, for the servants and staff at the hotel. Horus-Salah and Anastasia and the guests would be returning to the ship, and be on their way. All the packing began to get this party back to the ship. It was still early in the morning, and the ship would not be on its way until late in the afternoon. For the guests, it was going to be a restful day, and started by having brunch in the open gardens. Then, tours of the grounds around the hotel, followed by groups of local dancers and singers, throughout the grounds. There were small sitting areas for those that wished to watch. All this was done to keep the party at the hotel, and still allow time for the servants to prepare the luggage for return to the ship.

All was going well, when the clocks told the time, which had moved into the afternoon. By four o'clock, the carriages were waiting outside the hotel's great entrance, to start the movement of guests back to the ship. And so it went, back and forth, until well into the sixth hour in the afternoon. The

robert f. edwards

Captain had set a sailing time for departure at seven that night, so all would be able to meet his wishes and demands. Once a head count was done to confirm all were there, the Captain informed Horus-Salah that his ship was ready to cast off. Horus-Salah gave his consent, and within moments, everyone on board could feel the movement beneath their feet.

The ship made its way to the middle and then started its course towards its next destination. Once again, people on board were feeling their way back to the routine that they had done before going to the hotel. The dinner was served at the two settings, 8:00 and 10:00. Horus-Salah and Anastasia were the ones at the head table of the second seating. All went well, and the evening ended with one and all looking forward to what was in store for tomorrow.

Yes, they arrived at Abu Simbel. Even for most of the Egyptians on board, they had never been there. But the stories down through the ages were all too well known. This small group of people was going to be some of the first in the world that could say that they were, and saw the Great Temple of Abu. From the men that retired to the parlor, and the rest that moved throughout the ship, that was all they were talking about. Even the lower ship hands were talking among themselves about the next day. It held each and ever one on board, until rest gave way.

For Horus-Salah and Anastasia, in their private moments, the Great Temple made way over everything else. Like the rest, both talked about what they knew and had read about. Not even Horus-Salah's family had been to Abu Simbel. It was a great honor to be the first of his clan to see it. Both of them had wished that their families could have been here to witness the greatness of Ramses II. Even though both their fathers were into the excavations of tombs of the Pharaohs, and unearthing the secrets of the past, both wished that if one of their parents were to see the great work, that it would have been their mothers.

If only Horus-Salah's father had not sent the message of being two days late, then maybe, but it was Anastasia that

190

River of Life

took control of the conversation and said it was not meant to be. So the truth was spoken, and the subject changed. For both of them, these last days were wonderful. It was like looking into the future of their lives together. What both of them knew, so long ago as children, playing together and sharing, was that they were meant to be together, and now more and more people could see. When they were together, it was as if people saw them as one. They worked and thought the same way on things that had to been done. They could jump in and help the other one when it was needed, with just the right thing, at the right moment. It was much more than a team, it was the other half. These were the happy moments.

Again, the night grew late, and robbed the two of more time together. Horus-Salah looked at Anastasia with the words of "until tomorrow, my queen of the Nile, but tonight we must rest." She too looked tired, and moved to get up. The two walked slowly back to her cabin, and after a short goodnight, she went inside, and Horus-Salah made his way to his cabin. He had just entered, when his servant who had been waiting, said, "the Captain wishes to see you."

"When?" came the reply from Horus-Salah.

The answer was just as quick, "when you wish, master."

"Can it wait until morning?" came the next question.

"If you wish it so," came the answer.

"I do" and "have the Captain here at..." Horus-Salah pulled out his watch, and looked at it. "My goodness, it is late, well after two in the morning." He then looked at the servant, and said, "At 9:00 a.m., tomorrow morning." The servant bowed, and asked if Horus-Salah wished anything more this evening. Horus-Salah's hand moved, and it was the answer that the servant was looking for, and left. Horus-Salah went into the bedroom, and fell on to the bed that had been waiting for him. It was only moments, and Horus-Salah was into a deep sleep.

The ship would be at Abu Simbel by midday. As the time approached 9:00 a.m., the Captain was at the main door of Horus-Salah's cabin. The Captain knocked once, and the door opened with the help of the servant's hand. The Captain was shown the same chair that he had sat in before, and the servant went to tell Horus-Salah of the Captain's arrival. Horus-Salah was just getting up, he had slept in, and the servant knew Horus-Salah would need more time before the meeting. After informing Horus-Salah that the Captain was in the other room, the servant asked it he could request the Captain to return later. Horus-Salah looked at his servant with sleep still in his eyes, and said, "Give me ten minutes, or more." With that, the servant went back into the room where the Captain was waiting.

"My master will be ten to fifteen minutes before he can meet with you. May I be of any service to you, in the mean time?"

The Captain looked at the servant, and said, "another cup of tea would be in order," and nothing else.

In due course, Horus-Salah entered the room, and just as before, the Captain started to get up from his chair, only for Horus-Salah's hand to tell him to dismiss the idea. When both men were settled and served tea, the Captain started to share the information that he had. The ship would be at Abu Simbel by noon. There would be guides waiting to take groups of six to eight people from the ship. By six o'clock in the evening, all should be back on the ship, for the Captain would like, with Horus-Salah's permission, to leave and start the journey down the Nile. After some small questions about the day, and the night's sail down the Nile, Horus-Salah and the Captain said their good-byes to each other.

With that out of the way, Horus-Salah told his servant to take a message that he would like to see Anastasia before going to breakfast. The servant was out the door, to do Horus-Salah's wishes just as Horus-Salah finished the order. Horus-Salah was going over some of the last minute items, when the servant returned with the answer. Anastasia's reply was, 'her time is yours, and it would be more convenient if you could have the meeting in her suite.' With that, Horus-Salah got up and thanked the servant, as he went out the door towards

River of Life

Anastasia's suite. Once inside, Anastasia was waiting for him in the sitting room. "Good morning, my leader" came the words, as he sat.

"And a good morning to you, my love," came from his lips. Tea was served, and Horus-Salah told Anastasia of the day's events, and the schedule for returning.

Both she and Horus-Salah, along with the others on board, had never been to Abu Simbel. They both went up for breakfast, and even when seated, they were both still talking about what the day would bring. When the meal was over, and both had gone up top, the chairs were almost full by the others, waiting to see the first spotting of the great works. The temple was in honor of the gods Amun, Ptah, Harakhty, and none other than the god Ramses himself. Just off the starboard side, came the first sighting. Within minutes, the rest were able to see for themselves, the four colossal statues of Ramses II. As the ship grew closer and closer, the statues grew in size. Each was more than twenty meters tall. Now, the watchers could see the smaller ones, of Queen Tuya, and Queen Nefertari.

The total group was ready when the ship came to dock. And as the Captain had foretold, the guides were waiting. Once all had disembarked from the ship, the guides took up their places with the group that would be with them for the rest of the day. Horus-Salah and Anastasia were with two men, one a high commissioner from Italy, and the other was a Doctor of Anthropology from England. The guides would leave at five-minute intervals, as each group they were in charge of, came to the entrance of the Great Temple. Horus-Salah and Anastasia were the first to be at the entrance.

It was then, that the four in the party looked up at the sheer size of the colossal statues. The four statues of Ramses II made one feel that, yes, he was a god then, and still was now. As the stone faces of these gods looked down on those coming to visit Ramses, it made the humans feel like one of the ants of the desert sands. The guide then led them forward to the opening into the temple itself. Once inside, the guests looked at one another, for it was cool, and a welcome from the demanding heat of moments before. As their eyes got used to the new light of twilight in one of the great rooms, the guide started to explain what each was looking at. It was a living history, of the greatest of all Pharaohs, and his closeness with the other gods in his lifetime. As more and more was explained, even for the non-Egyptians, there was mention of the faiths. The recording of Moses, and of wars, and so it went.

Both Horus-Salah and Anastasia, to say nothing of the two others, were speechless as the tour moved deeper into the temple. They felt small, and from another world they knew so little about. It was like a time warp, when at last, they returned to the outside. The heat of the sun reminded them where, and who they were. Just humans, in a world of many living things, now, and in the past. It was the sun, the god Ra that was the greatest of all gods and Ramses II, the greatest of all Pharaohs. What surprised them all was the time they had been in the temple, for three hours, and if asked, one by one would have told of much less. Was it that time, too, was lost in this temple of wonderment? The guide then asked if they would follow him to the smaller temple of Harhor, which like sheep with their shepherd, the four followed, one by one.

It too, had its own command, but their minds were still somewhere in the past, how far back, each could only say to themselves. After wandering through this temple, it was time to think of going back to the ship. The falling sun now replaced the afternoon, and it was into the evening, as the last returned to the ship. It was quiet aboard, as the ship slipped away, back to the middle of the river. People just sat with their thoughts, and what this day had shown them. Horus-Salah and Anastasia were contemplative also, as both sat holding hands, watching the great statues looking back, as the ship made its way back to the present. Night came, and so did dinner, but the people ate little, and retired early. This day would not soon be forgotten.

The crew and the ship moved down river throughout the night, and into the morning dawn. Anastasia was up early for

River of Life

her group. As she dressed, and prepared for the day's events, which she had planned, she called to one of her maids. When the young lady appeared, Anastasia said, "Go to the Captain, and tell him I wish to see him, at his convenience." With that, the maid left to do the errand. She was gone a short time, only to return saying that the Captain would be at Anastasia's service shortly. The maid was just finished with the information when there was a knock at the door. Answering the door, the maid was looking at the Captain. He was shown a chair, and offered tea.

Soon, Anastasia entered the sitting room, and took some tea also. With the greetings out of the way, Anastasia came to the point of her asking for his presence. "When will we be nearing Edfu?"

The Captain looked at her, and thought for a moment, then said, "We will be passing the town some-where around 5 o'clock today."

"Passing?" came the words from Anastasia's mouth, and then she added, "Why are we not stopping there?"

The Captain's answer was short, with "there is no need to."

Just as quickly, Anastasia said, "yes there is. The temple of Horus-Salah is there." The Captain looked surprised at her knowledge of his country and history, but said that he had no instructions to stop at the town, or the temple.

Anastasia looked at the Captain, and said, "You do *now*."

The Captain looked back, and then glanced to the floor, as he said, "I serve but one master at a time." So, once a leader, always a leader, and she wasn't his, not yet.

"So, you are saying that you wouldn't?"

The Captain had been trapped, if he said 'no', he would have to face Horus-Salah's displeasure; and if he said 'yes', what would Horus-Salah do for this disobedience. The Captain's face grew red, as his mind faced the choices. Then, Anastasia could understand what was going through the good Captain's mind, and added, "We could work together."

robert f. edwards

With new hope, the Captain asked, "what do you have in mind?" Anastasia told him that both Horus-Salah and herself, had never seen the temple of his namesake, and tonight, she had a gift for Horus-Salah, which was of the utmost importance. She then added, "Everything must be perfect, for this is going to be a great moment, in both Horus-Salah's and my live."

The Captain's face changed from red to its normal color, and a smile moved across it. "What do you wish, my lady?" he asked,

"You say that the ship will be near the town around 5 o'clock?"

"Yes," came the reply.

"Well then, how long would I have to go to the temple with Horus-Salah, and still be able to keep to the time frame of your master?"

The Captain said, "My master is Horus-Salah, as of now."

She then added, as an afterthought, "He will know of any changes at once." With a smile, Anastasia continued, "yes, for I will be the one to tell him first of my wishes." With that, the Captain was on her side, and the plan was put into place.

The Captain took his leave, only for Anastasia to leave shortly afterward to meet Horus-Salah for their morning meal. She had just sat down, and was talking about the day, when Horus-Salah asked her, "What was the Captain seeing you in your cabin for?"

She looked surprised, and before she had put any thought to her answer, it came out, "how did you know?"

He smiled his loving smile, and said, "It is my responsibility to know, and be told of everything, when I am in charge." She had learnt something more today about her beloved Horus, and his world, and his country. It wasn't just the lifestyle along the river that had not changed for thousands of years but it was also the rules that had not changed.

She smiled back now, and said, "I have a surprise for you tonight, and I wish to honor you, by starting at the temple of the god that give you part of your name, my love."

196

River of Life

He added, "Let your wish be mine, and let them be fulfilled." So, the Captain made the changes to the schedule, and the new stop on the way back to Luxor was to include Edfu. The stop in Edfu would be short, and only Horus-Salah with Anastasia and their servants, would be going ashore.

The day was as any other on board, with people doing things that pleased them, or the staff finding things that would make the guests feel as if it was their right to make others work harder for their happiness. The ship made its way down the mighty river quickly, so it seemed to Horus-Salah, or maybe it was just his wish to get to Edfu. He didn't know what Anastasia had in mind, or planned for this evening, but it must be important, for her to see the Captain and ask for a change of plans. With this in his mind, he too would make it an evening of surprises, for both of them.

As he returned to his cabin, he went to the small safe, and removed his gift for Anastasia. He looked at the cartouche very closely, and yes, it was just what he had wanted and hoped for, in craftsmanship. In his mind's eye, he could see Anastasia wearing it. Tonight, he too, would make it a special night for her. Little did he, or anyone else for that matter, know that Anastasia was in her quarters, doing the same thing with his gift. She now had the watch in her hands, and was looking at the fine workmanship from her part of the world. The hand tooling of the silver workmanship, and the story it told of their lives, up to this point, on the front casing.

Then she turned it over, and the wishes of the future of their lives, was on the back casing. Her face told how she felt, with a look of pleasure. It was when she opened the front casing, and saw the little hands moving ever onward, on the face that had the roman numerals, that she realized that she didn't have much time to get ready with everything she wanted done for this evening. Closing the front case, she was just about to put the watch back, only to look it once more. With love in her heart, and the watch in her hands, she turned the watch over, and opened the case on the back. As she looked into the back compartment, her face, in picture form, was

197

robert f. edwards

looking back at her. Yes, it was the picture that she wished to have in there for her beloved, but it was the other part that kept her eyes glued to the opening. 'Oh yes, my dearest, I will always be yours,' her mind said, over and over to herself.

She finally closed the case, and put the watch back in its safe place for now. She had just returned to the sitting room, when one of her maids asked if she was ready to go ashore. Anastasia looked at her, and told the maid that she was, and did Horus-Salah wish her present now. Before she could answer, there was a knock on the door. One of Horus-Salah's male servants entered, asking for her. As the ship came to a resting place at the small dock, Horus-Salah's servant when ashore. In less than an hour, the arrangements for Horus-Salah and Anastasia were made to see the temple. When the servant returned, it was with the carriages, waiting at the dock for their guests.

There were four in number. One for the guards and guide, followed by the one for Horus-Salah and Anastasia. The next two were for their servants. As the carriages moved away from the dock, and made their way to the temple, the local people stopped and looked at whom the important people were. The distance was short, and before Horus-Salah and Anastasia could talk about what the streets were showing them, they were at the entrance of the Temple of Horus.

The great falcon-headed statue greeted them. The guide told the story of Isis and Osiris, and of their son Horus, and of two hundred years that it took to complete the temple. The guide continued that the Greeks built it, and how it had changed Pharaonic architecture of the past.

It was when Anastasia asked the guide to return with the others to the ship, that she and Horus-Salah had the moment that she had wanted. She looked at Horus-Salah, and said, "Welcome to one of your gods homes, the one you have been named after, my love, my king, my god of Egypt." Horus-Salah's eyes filled, and his throat was dry as the sands of the desert, as he looked at Anastasia, and the temple around them. At last, a voice from far away came, "you honor me too

198

River of Life

" ... they were at the entrance of the Temple of Horus. "

Original photograph   Robert F. Edwards
Egypt   November, 1999

much, my queen." They both were one, and wanted to be such, forever and ever.

Before either could add to the moment, the guide returned and informed them that they must return to the carriage now. With that news, the lovers followed the guide and the trip back to the waiting ship. Once everyone was back on board, the ship cast off, and Horus-Salah and Anastasia were at the rails, when the ship past by the temple of Horus-Salah. Horus-Salah reached over, and took Anastasia's hand in his. They were joined in their minds, as well. The sun was once again saying goodbye to the day, and the coolness of the night was at hand. The sky was clear as a glass ball, changing from a light color to a new dark blue, which would change once more, before the night was over.

It was the last night before the ship would be entering Luxor. The dinner was a special one that Anastasia had arranged, and needless to say, it was Horus-Salah's favorite dishes. Again the two were at the last seating, and it was well into the middle of the tenth hour of the evening, before people were finished. At last, Horus-Salah and Anastasia said their good nights to the last few still at the table.

Both of them went up top. They had found a very private place on deck. It was one of the few times that Horus-Salah had gone back to wearing his Egyptian galabya. The fineness of Egyptian cotton gave the robe freedom of movement, as well as coolness for the wearer. To Anastasia, as he leaned on the handrail, he was the picture of Egypt in all its past, present, and her hope of the future. She stood beside him, as he turned to face her. To him, she too, was all he could ever hope for in this life. In her long evening dress, she looked like a Greek goddess from the past; waiting to grant him any wish a mortal could ask for.

The darkness of the sky gave the backdrop to the millions of lights that the stars were accountable for, but it was the moon. The moon was full, and demanding, for a thousands star did not give the light of this one round globe. Even the lights on the shore looked like candles flashing in the dis-

River of Life

tance. Nature's light sparkled on the waters of the great Nile, and let the lovers see it without the need of man's lights. They stood together, just being together, standing in the moonlight, with their minds as one. It may have been minutes, or hours, for the rest of the world, but for them, it was the moment, forever. Their hands had joined their minds, as their eyes looked out before them, without seeing what lay ahead, both now, and in life.

Anastasia was the first to speak, with the words, "I am yours, and will always be, no matter what lay ahead for us."

Horus-Salah answered, "You know it has, and always will be the same for me. You are the reason that I live, and wish to, my one and only love." With that he moved, from looking at the river of life, to Anastasia's face. With this change, his other hand moved inside the pocket of the galabya. At once, it was around the gift for his most beloved.

She too, was looking now at Horus-Salah. They both knew the time was now, for them to exchange their vows to each other, forever more. It didn't matter what the answer would be, from his father, or the world, for them it was made of two, and it was just them. All the feelings of their childhood, and their togetherness up until now, came in to both of their minds as one. It was more than two people that had found each other. It was two souls that were as one, that needed the other to be complete. Tonight was their commitment, forever to the other soul, no matter what would happen in this world or the next. They would always be one, and together, if not in body, then soul forever more.

As these thoughts were said, in their mind's eye, and some by their voices, Horus-Salah was the first to bring out his gift, and his pledge to Anastasia. As he gave her the gift in its little wooden box, she too reached into her handbag, and removed a little box. The boxes found their new owner. Both couldn't trust their hands. With both hands on the gifts, they looked at each other, and as one, moved back from the rail. As their feet moved, it was their backs that told them that they couldn't go back any further. The ship's cabins were touching their backs.

Anastasia's hands were the first to move, to open the carved wooden box, which she held. As the lid gave way, and she looked inside, her eyes saw the cartouches. At once, she knew what they were, and her eyes ran back to meet Horus-Salah's, which were waiting for the look on her face. Her face and eyes did not let him down, even in the moonlight; he could see what his gift meant to her.

Now, it was her turn, to see what his face would reveal, as he opened his little box. As his hand removed the lid, he was looking at the watch she had made for him. His face changed colors, as she watched his happiness, and surprise become one. Both their hands and feet did not give them the support that they could count on, so with their free hands together, both made their way to the deck chairs. Once seated, they took each gift out of the boxes. Anastasia knew that the earrings had the alphabet of hieroglyphics, but what she didn't know, was what they meant. It was Horus-Salah that said, in a voice so far way, that one had her name, and his was on the other. In her dreams, she couldn't have hoped for anything so complete, to signify Horus-Salah's and her union, together forever.

Her eyes were now having trouble seeing the cartouches, for tears filled her eyes, and started to make a river down her face. Between the wet lines on her face, her eyes never left the view of the cartouches. It was Horus-Salah's voice that brought her back from where her mind had traveled. Pulling her back to now, she could only think from now on, she would wear this gift that would symbolize her thoughts. His name on one side, and hers on the other. These two little cartouches would be as if both of them were together, and she in some small way, was the temple that held them.

Horus-Salah's voice was saying, somewhere with her thoughts, that she was his queen of Egypt, and the goddess of his world. Slowly, her mind came back to being one, and her eyes changed from the cartouches to his face. Through the

River of Life

mist, she looked upon her world, her life, and her man. He was smiling, as if she was as bright as Ra to him. Now that her eyes started to clear, and the rivers of joy were receding, she wanted to see him look at his gift.

He slowly, and very gently, removed the gift from its holding. Now that the watch was in his hands, he at once could see the engraving on the silver casing. Even in the moonlight, the carving told a story of their childhood meeting, and as he turned the watch over, the story told of their union, both in this world, and the next. It was a work of art in itself. He took a moment from the watch, and looked up at Anastasia. She said in a soft voice, "there is more, my dearest."

With that, he sprung the latch, and as the lid opened, his eyes saw three small hands surrounded by Roman numerals. The perfect movement inside gave a soft ticking sound. The craftsmanship surpassed anything he had ever seen. Before he could say anything, Anastasia's voice once more came to him, with the words, "there is more on the other side, my love."

He moved the lid closed, and then changed hands to the other side. It too had a latch, and once again, his fingers opened it. As eyes looked at what was inside, his lungs stopped getting air, for inside was a picture of his most beloved. Before his lungs gave back life to him, the voice of his meaning of life said, "Don't say anything, for this is so you will always have a part of me with you, my one and only."

As his face changed different shades of red, and his breathing returned, the tears fell like rain drops on his galabya. He couldn't take his eyes from the part of her that lay around the picture of his beloved. What seemed like a lifetime of its own, the two looked at each other, and the gifts that were now given. At last, one hand from each found their way to join. And as one, their voices said, "I love you, now and forever more, in this world and all others."

The hours had moved away, and for the first time, the two of them felt the chill of the night. As if from a long sleep, the two got up, and held each other. At first it was the warmth of

robert f. edwards

their bodies that each welcomed, but after being held, and lips touching each other, the warmth changed. They were warm again and complete. Horus-Salah could feel his manhood stand to attention. Anastasia could feel her womanhood, full and wet, for the only man in her life. As the warmth gave way to heat of love, and need for each other, so did the night.

The night watch was changing, and the inspector was making his rounds. The night crewman came upon them, as a ghost out of the night. Just as he was passing, the two came back to where they were, and who they were. It was Horus-Salah's voice that they both heard, as one, that said, "we must wait, the plan." With that, the two lovers moved ever so far apart, but their eyes never left each other's.

The night guard moved past them without acknowledging their presence. But he had been their conscience; to the price they would pay, if the plan failed. The plan, and the one man that held their lives by his word, gave back the chill of night to their very souls. Horus-Salah was the first to break the silence between them and their one fear. "We will know before long, if the plan has worked for our sake," Anastasia's mind forced itself back to the plan. Oh yes, the plan she and Horus-Salah, along with her parents had so long ago worked on. Even in her young life, it seemed many years that she had worked on this plan, to have permission to be together with Horus-Salah for life.

The deck hand was doing his rounds, otherwise she might not have been able to stop herself, and she wanted Horus-Salah right here and now, to fill her young woman's needs. Her mind thought of her poor Horus-Salah and all the rules of his family and this country. 'Why', was the question her mind kept asking, and the answer was the same as always, 'I don't understand'.

She heard Horus-Salah's voice somewhere in the fog of her thoughts. Both of them were seated but still looking at each other, as his voice was speaking," Anastasia". That was all she heard, and replied in a weak "yes?" When she looked

River of Life

into his face, he was still looking for more of answer than 'yes'. "My dearest one," he said again, "are you well?"

Now she was back and with that she answered, "I am fine; my mind was back when we first were working on the plan".

He now understood where she was and had been with her mind's eye. They both knew this was the last night that they would have this freedom, until the answer to all of these years of waiting. Both of them leaned back into the deck chairs and took a deep breath of air. These last few days had given them the feeling of what it would be like to rule and be in charge of others. To have control of their lives and all that was around them. It came natural to both of them, and had not been as challenging as Horus-Salah had first thought.

For Anastasia, it was a way of life; for she had in many ways ruled and guided others, even her parents all her life. She was a natural leader. Horus-Salah would always need her by his side when it came time for him to be the leader of his family and their clan. 'Couldn't his father see this, and know it?' she questioned once again in her mind. 'Of course, Horus-Salah's father did so, why was she and Horus-Salah so full of fear that he wouldn't grant this wish?' Then came hundreds more reasons and a thousand more doubts to the question they had asked each other. The answer was always the same. It was up to Horus-Salah's father, the ruler and leader of the family.

She and Horus-Salah stayed on deck talking hour after hour, when would his father answer the long over-due question and what would his answer be. Nothing had changed but the darkness of the night, for soon the first shades of light were coming though. Both of them had spent the night together but not as Anastasia had planned. The long term plan came first, and would until the question had it answer.

She took a long look at Horus-Salah and both knew it was over due to return to their cabins for some rest, as sleep was out of the question. Within hours they too, would have to join the others for the daily activities and the arrival at Luxor.

robert f. edwards

With a heavy heart and their new treasures they made their way to their own cabins that had been assigned to them. Once inside her own cabin Anastasia looked again at her gift, 'Oh Horus-Salah,' she said to herself , 'I will always be yours and this is the bondage that I will wear, for all the world to know that you hold claim to my body and soul, no matter who says or thinks otherwise.' She put the earrings on and lay on the bed, but in her mind it was Horus-Salah that she was laying beside.

Horus-Salah too, was in his cabin and looking at his gift. He opened the back lid of the watch and saw her picture. His hand was shaking so much he used the other hand in help hold the watch. It was the small part of her that lay around the picture that held his eyes and his mind. He could hear the tick, tick of the watch and the time moving together. But in his mind it was her, and her heart that he heard.

The light came in the porthole but his eyes never changed the view. Only when his servant came into the room, did he look anywhere else.

"Master, do you have any wish for me, at this time?' was the question from the servant. Horus-Salah returned to the present time in his mind and looked at the servant in the light. The night was over and so today he would be in charge again. "Prepare for today," came the command to his mind, but as he looked at the servant's face he realized he had not said anything. Again, his mind said, "Prepare for today and my things as well," his voice carried the message. The servant bowed and went into the other room to do Horus-Salah's bidding.

The day was upon all on board before the guests began the routine of the ship. When Horus-Salah came into the dining area for the morning meal, his eyes saw Anastasia sitting at the table. His mood changed and as the fresh air filled his lungs, his mind became positive again. With a big smile on his face, he moved the chair closer to her and sat down. "Good morning, Horus-Salah," said Anastasia, her smile filled with happiness and added, "Is your new watch not working?"

206

River of Life

He pulled the watch out of his vest pocket, and replied, "Yes, just like my heart, both are working fine, my love". It may be a long time before the two would be able sit and have a meal together, without others joining them.

She looked at him again, and said, "My heart is also fine". The two sat at the table as if they had never stopped talking from the night before.

The time moved far too fast for them, and soon it was midday before they went up top to the deck chairs. Horus-Salah had already been informed that the ship would be arriving in Luxor around six o'clock that evening. Anastasia and Horus-Salah knew that their governing would come to an end this evening. That afternoon, as people came and went they greeted the couple in a very regal way. To all on board, it seemed as if being in the presence of a prince and his princess. As the hours ticked away, so did their reign. Horus-Salah and Anastasia both wondered, would they get to rein like Ramses II and his wife Nefertari, or would they have the unhappy one of Tutankhamen and his young bride?

Anastasia asked Horus-Salah if he thought they could get away to see their secret tomb? Their place, where as children they had spent so much of their time together. Horus-Salah answered, " it is going to be much harder now, than then."

"Yes," she added, "we do have more than just nannies to get out of our way".

They both laughed, and Horus-Salah added, "Well, with all the planning we do, it should be easy for us".

The small feluccas sailed alongside the ship, and continued crossing from side to side behind the great ship of the Nile. They looked to the lovers like great white swans guiding the ship to its port of call. The afternoon sun was hot, but the winds made it a perfect afternoon. Soon, all abroad heard that Luxor was within sight. At once, the starboard side of the ship was filled with guests watching as the city came into view. Horus-Salah and Anastasia joined the others leaning over the rail. It was the same railing that Horus-Salah and Anastasia were at the night before. Today was so different, and yet maybe not? Was this the beginning of a way of life, or the end?

The ship had now moved closer to the shore. Yes, one could see the great Temples of Karnak. Within minutes the ship was making its way to the dock. Horus-Salah could see his father's staff and one of his senior servants waiting below. Horus-Salah looked at Anastasia, and said in a low voice, "our reign is over for now, my Queen of the Nile".

She looked back at him and said, "Only for a short time, dear leader". Both their hands found each other.

They were still holding hands when his father's men came abroad. The servant approached Horus-Salah and Anastasia at once. After the normal greetings, the servant informed them that the small boat was waiting to take them to the mansion on the other side of the river. He also added that the guests would be staying on this side of Luxor at the Winter Palace Hotel. Horus-Salah thanked him. The servant was one the oldest and most trusted of his father's servant.

As he looked at the young couple he thought they looked very young and beautiful, with an air of being regal. He did hope for these young people that their lives would be happy ones, and then his mind added 'together'. One of the younger staff members came aboard to escort them to the small boat that was waiting. The other guests were informed that they would be staying at the Winter Palace Hotel.

Now, with all knowing their new accommodations, the good-byes were made. First it was Anastasia and Horus-Salah, from the captain and crew. Then came the guests, and as Anastasia and Horus-Salah went down the gangplank to shore, people abroad were at the rail waving their farewells. The head servant took note of the people, and their affection for these new leaders. As people left the ship towards the hotel, Anastasia and Horus-Salah were already on the small boat.

It was small compared to the ship but had all the elements of Horus-Salah's status. The boat was used for crossing the Nile from the West Bank to Luxor. As the boat cast off,

River of Life

both Anastasia and Horus-Salah sat outside on the open air deck. They did not hold hands as in the past few days, for now they were in view and sat apart. They were now the children of their parents and must act the part. The boat started its crossing as the two faced the West Bank.

CHAPTER 14

Both Horus-Salah and Anastasia shared the same feeling of returning to their home. For Horus-Salah, it was home, and even though his family spent longer periods of the year in Cairo at the large mansion, this place was the one he remembered to be the happier of the two. He had spent most of his holidays as a boy here, and many times as a young man he would come up here for a rest. As he looked at the small crossing and the other side, he had mixed feelings. He would be under the rule of his father and family now. The freedom he had enjoyed in the last little while would be a thing of the past. His freedom of being with Anastasia was already being taken away. On the other hand, he would be seeing his beloved nanny and the old servants that had been there all the years he had been growing up. These feelings continued to mix themselves inside his mind. He sat and said nothing.

For Anastasia it too, was her home- away- from- home, though she hadn't been here for many years. It was the good times she had growing up and playing in the garden, and living in a new country that she was remembering. But most of all was the freedom she and Horus-Salah had in those days. She would run off into the hills. Yes, the hills, her mind thought, and the day that Horus-Salah shared his tomb. From that day on it was their cave, their tomb. And the owner was theirs to look after.

She turned her head and looked at Horus-Salah. His expression told her that his mind was far away. She turned back to look at the shore which was very close now. Would she be part of the new family that would greet her, came into her mind?

The boat was greeted by servants with four carriages from the great house. The two young people were shown their way

210

River of Life

to the second carriage. Before the other carriages were loaded, Horus-Salah and Anastasia were on their way to the mansion. The distance was not great, but the road was as it had been since the first time, dusty and full of ruts. Already the sun was at its peak and the heat of the day was upon them.

The carriages moved on down the road, and before long both Anastasia and Horus-Salah saw the great mansion. The massive gates came into view, leading to the grounds that surrounded the mansion. Within minutes, their carriages came up to the front of the mansions. The entrance was full of servants and both of their mothers waiting to greet them.

It was great moment and a happy one. After the best wished were done, both Anastasia and Horus-Salah went over to a little old lady, sitting down due to her age and kissed her on the cheek. The three of them had a great love for each other that all others noticed. She was Horus-Salah's beloved nanny and over the years she shared duty with Anastasia's nanny in the growing up of the young girl. For both the young couple, they were children again, at home with a person that they loved and knew that loved them.

As the servants were given their assignments the smaller group moved inside. Anastasia and Horus-Salah followed their parents into one of the great sitting rooms. Mint tea was ordered as the four of them sat down. Both mothers insisted on hearing the news that Horus-Salah and Anastasia had to be shared first. For both of the young people, their wishes were the reverse; however their news was forth coming. Horus-Salah and Anastasia took turns in telling the events of each day that they were in charge of the group going up the Nile. Like the trip, both moved in and out of each other's conversation as if they had rehearsed it. For them, it had become the norm when they moved and spoke around others. In a few words they had become one with each other.

Both mothers were listening to what was being told, but did not give away that a good deal of the information they have already gathered from the servants that kept the family abreast. It was the two young people that the women saw so much had changed in this short time. The mothers couldn't believe their eyes and ears, for both of their children had always been close, but it was different now.

Horus-Salah and Anastasia were acting as if they were already living together and working together. Horus-Salah's mother was the first to start talking after the two had finished their report of events on board. She asked Anastasia about the cartouches that she was wearing. With a fresh color in Anastasia's cheek, she replied, "They were given to me by Horus-Salah". Then, there was silence before she added, "it is my acceptation of his asking me to be his forever". She just couldn't say marrying him, not even to their mothers. For she knew that only one man could, or would give that answer, to all those waiting so long for him to say something. That person would be none other than Horus-Salah's father.

It was Horus-Salah that interrupted the silence of the moment by bringing out the beautiful watch from his pocket, adding, "This is my gift from Anastasia that I will be hers forever". The two mothers saw these young lover eyes were glossed over with happiness, and feared that not all dreams come true.

Now it was both Horus-Salah and Anastasia's turn to ask questions. After Horus-Salah asked about his family, he also inquired if the Count had a good trip coming up here by train? Plus some smaller questions about the events for the evening. It was Anastasia that asked the question that both of them had on their mind. "Did father say anything," she asked," about the plan to Horus-Salah's father?" The two mothers looked at each other, and then at their children.

The Countess spoke first, giving an answer to the question as the two young lover's eyes looked into hers. "Yes, he has spoken more than once about the plan to Horus-Salah's father. The second time, Horus-Salah's father reminded him that it was not his side that did the asking of hands in marriage. Now, the Count dare not bring up the subject again to Horus-Salah's father, for if he does he will do you and Horus-Salah more harm than good."

River of Life

The faces of both Horus-Salah and Anastasia told what was on their minds. They looked like stone statues of so long ago. Sitting and waiting as stopped forever in time. It was Horus-Salah's mother that spoke with her news. She had talked about the two lovers to Horus-Salah's father whenever she could. Her news was more hopeful. She added that her husband would listen and say," If you are right, Allah will have them join, not me." They had to settle for this at the moment

The afternoon had quickly moved into the evening and it was time to get ready for the events at the Winter Palace Hotel ballroom. The four of them got up to depart, and the servants that had been waiting in the wings took each one to their suite to prepare for the evening. For Horus-Salah his feelings was mixed. It was good to be back home, his only real home. He was back in his comfortable bedroom which still contained some of his boyhood things. But at the same time, he and Anastasia had given up their short moment of freedom. He was back to being the child of the man who fathered him.

In another part of the mansion, Anastasia was going over the many dresses and chose just the right one she would be wearing tonight. Her thoughts were looking ahead, at what, if anything she could do to get the answer she and Horus-Salah wanted so much from his father.

For the others it was just another night like all the rest, a feast or banquet depending on which country the guest were coming from. As the darkness informed all that the night was here and they all must begin to be in their right places for the evening. The small group crossed the Nile and joined the other at the hotel. No one knew how many people were there and in some cases it was hard to see who was who. The military men and their aids of high rank were all in their dress uniforms while the other men were in tuxedo. The womens' dresses varied as many as the women themselves in number ,however one could at least tell from what part of the world they called home by the different styles and designs . In their own right, they could have been guests at one of the many tables for royalty.

robert f. edwards

As in the past the night lasted until the early hours of the following morning. The elaborate settings were fitting for the guests in attendance. The gathering of nations and races of people were together under the guidance of one family, and one man that ruled it. Some by choice, other by orders.

For Horus-Salah and Anastasia, there was only one difference, they were back. They were doing what they had done in the past few weeks, being entertained or hosting; it was all the same to them. The only moment of interest came when Horus-Salah joined the men in the smoking room after the dinner ended. He was sitting by himself when the Count came over and put his hand on Horus-Salah's shoulder. Horus-Salah looked up and saw the Count's face smiling at him and then added, "All will work out for the best." Horus-Salah smiled back and thanked him, for both men knew what was on Horus-Salah's mind. The Count removed his hand and added, "Your father will do what is best for you and Anastasia." The Count started to move away, but stopped and added," He will do what's right for both our families."

Horus-Salah was alone again but one of his father's best friends, Anastasia's father, had done his best for both of them. The Count had given him fresh hope that the answer was near. The evening continued, with people returning to their places. It was like a living play with the same actors and actresses playing the same part, night after night. The only difference was the setting. The end of another party and another day had come to a close at last.

The weeks that followed were the same; up late in the morning or early afternoon, then the last minute plans for the day, followed by the evening's events. So it went, day after day, the same old repeat of the one that had just past and the one that would be next. For Horus-Salah and Anastasia they had little or no freedom to be alone. Once in the long week they were able to take their beloved nanny out in the garden as they had done so long ago. She enjoyed talking about the days that they were children and would go off into the hills. She never asked them where they went on these trips in the

214

River of Life

hills. The old nanny would laugh now how both tutors would be sitting waiting with hard words when they returned. All three would laugh about the good old days.

It was on one of these trips to the garden that the old nanny fell asleep and the two lovers looked at each other with the same thought in mind. The tomb, the secret place, their place. They called over the gardener to look after their nanny for a while. Now the two moved like children of old up the hills towards the tomb. As they climbed once more the Valley of the Kings came into view and this time, like before, the Egyptian laborers were busy working.

As Anastasia was looking at them far below, to her they all looked like an ant hill of workers. Horus-Salah was close to their tomb before he turned around to see where Anastasia was. He sat just above the tomb waiting for Anastasia to join him. Once at the spot both made their way down the hill to the entrance of the tomb. After the candles were lit, they both carried the light inside the cave. Nothing had changed, all was the same, and their place and the only resident were just as the last time. They were at their final place, their childhood hiding place. Now it was theirs again, in both the past and the present.

Anastasia took Horus-Salah's hand. In the candle light her eyes were looking at the sarcophagi and thinking of the mummy that it held inside. To both of them it was and had always been a holy place. Their time was short, and so Horus-Salah started to return outside. Once both of them were at the entrance, Anastasia looked at him and said "I wish that when my time comes I too, am placed in here".

Horus-Salah looked into her eyes and said," I will make it so, if I am able." He told her he wished for the same thing for himself.

Now it was time to return to the house, to be more precise, the garden. With that in mind, the two ran down the hills to see what had happened while they had been away. As they entered the garden, the little figure that they had left was still sitting upright, but still sleeping. The two runners sat down beside the sleeping nanny and relaxed. They tried to look as if they had not moved all the time that the nanny had been resting. One eye of the old nanny opened, then the other, and the two over-grown children heard a weak voice say, "Well, was it still there?"

Both Horus-Salah and Anastasia looked at her and smiled with the reply "what??" from both of them. All three looked at each other, as if they didn't know what was being referred to, and no one asked further. The two young people helped their beloved nanny back into the house.

At last, the guests that were staying at the hotel started to return home. The evenings, though the same in nature, were smaller with closer members of Horus-Salah's family and the friends of the Count. The following days were slower, even the mood of the servants was different. It was more like the past when just the two families were the forces of attention.

It was on one of these evenings that a change took place. The families and guests now numbered as small as twenty for the evening. The dining tables were set in a different arrangement. For the first time, the Count and Countess, along with Anastasia were seated at one end of the long table, while Horus-Salah and his family were at the other. The rest of the guests were in the middle. The food itself was the same, but the setting was very different. There was a small glass at each place setting that had never been there before. The very look of these glasses, one could tell they were valuable antiques.

The meal was drawing to an end, when Horus-Salah's father waved his hand directing the servants to leave. Horus-Salah's father was at one end of the great table, with his wife on one side and his son on the other. The same seating was mirrored at the opposite end with the Count at the head and his wife and daughter on each side. An old and trusted servant came in with a large pitcher. Horus-Salah's father moved his hand and the servant went first to the Count and poured the camel milk into the small glass that was waiting, then went over to the Countess and Anastasia and did the same thing. The servant went on to the friends of the Count and

River of Life

guests of Horus-Salah's father, before the servant made his was up to at last to Horus-Salah's father. Horus-Salah's father then took his glass and stood up, toasting with the words that followed. "I ask all to drink this milk in peace, and in three days, I will ask the Count to hear my request" The elder sat down after he finished this announcement. Horus-Salah felt this was the beginning, the asking of the family to be joined or not, to have their children seek a formal relationship.

The evening ended shortly thereafter, and the few guests retired to their quarters. It felt as if had stopped. For Horus-Salah and Anastasia the plan would have an answer within *seventy-two hours*. The long wait was over but the answer was yet to come. Both had spent little time together these last days and did not expect this event tonight. For now, both were in shock that the answer to their wishes, hopes and prays was only days away. The answer; to their lives and the future of their dreams.

As most of the people left the room, Anastasia got up and went over to where Horus-Salah was standing. "Well, now the time has come for 'Mice and Men'," Anastasia said to him.

He looked at her as if she had gone mad, and replied "pardon?" She then realized what she had said had no meaning to him and explained that it was from a book. He still looked puzzled and asked," what has that got to do with us?"

Anastasia said," at another time, if you wish, I will explain the plot of the story, and this saying in it, but for now, what is with the three days of waiting?"

It was Horus-Salah's turn now to do the explaining. "What my father has done is the practice of the desert tribes. When a man from another place comes to the village with a request, the elder of the village drinks milk with him and hears his request. For the next three days, the man is treated like a guest, and then on the third day the man is told what the answer is to his request."

"Oh," were the first words from Anastasia then, "what now should be done?"

217

"Nothing but silence," came the words back." For knowing my father, he will be watching everything we are doing."

"I would have thought he had made up his mind by now," Anastasia said to the answer.

Before Horus-Salah put any thought into the next words he replied, "He has."

"Well, then what's up with these three more days?"

"It is the game of life and the way the desert people think." Then he added, " it is what we will be doing that will make his decision final."

By now the women had come over to be close to the couple. Horus-Salah knew the signs and told Anastasia to be careful what she said and did. She looked at him and said, "It was my plan. Do you think I am going to mess it up now?" and turned to go with the ladies to another room.

Horus-Salah met up with the men in the parlor. It had been a long time since he smoked the water pipe, but tonight he sat alone, thinking and smoking until the Count came over and stood before him. At once Horus-Salah got up to meet the man's eyes. The Count looked into the troubled eyes and said, "Have faith, my son. The long wait is almost over, do what must be done to the end."

Horus-Salah looked back and a small smile appeared, with "Thank you for all you have done and are doing for both Anastasia and myself."

The Count then said , "good-night my son," but this time it sounded as if Horus-Salah was part of the Count's clan, or was it he just wanted to be.

The morning came and midday was fast on its way but for the families of both Horus-Salah and Anastasia, it was just another day. It came and went, and so did the evening, the same way. Nothing happened and so the next day came and followed it in the same way.

The third day started but even the air was dryer and people were up earlier than normal. By mid morning the sun had scorched the earth and any living thing with it. The servants went about their tasks and the family did their daily routine,

River of Life

but all was different. There was an unsettling feeling in the air. All looked forward to the mid day rest and hopefully sleep some of this day away.

At last the evening came with one and all in the small party showing up for dinner early. The group was less than twenty of the closest friends and relatives. They all sat at their places and it was more like the reading of a will than a meal, as one by one looked and waited. The food was of high standards, but this evening most of the guests only picked at the variety that lay before them, so little was eaten.

Once again the small glasses were filled with camel's milk and every one was looking at the head of the table where Horus-Salah's father sat. He was the only one that looked the same as always. Without warning, the tapping of glass and metal informed all that it was time. Horus-Salah's father stood up and the room remained silence. Then his voice filled the four corners of the room, but it was low and soft. As he spoke, he looked at the Count and Countess. "My request, on behalf my son Horus-Salah and our family, is that he be joined in marriage to Anastasia". He stopped and so did the breathing of all that was in the room. Then he continued, "And that both families will become one, and what is mine from this time forward will be yours, and that your wishes are my wishes. I have come to ask Allah to join my son and your daughter, my people and yours, together forever." The Count then stood up as well, "My wish is to accept your wishes, and let God look after our children, and their children's' children."

It had happened. It was over, the plan, the dreams; the long wait was all over. Yes, yes, yes. The two lovers were at opposite ends of the table but now at last they were as one. Horus-Salah was next to his father and when the elder returned to his chair, a thin broken voice spoke the words, "Thank you father, and Allah." Horus-Salah's face told the rest. Long wet lines ran down his face, and then made their way to his galabya. The little rings grew bigger with each added drop, followed by a low moan, deep inside the body and soul of this young man.

219

robert f. edwards

At the other end of the table, Anastasia didn't fair as well. Her tears were like the River Nile in the flood season. They ran uncontrolled down her face and beyond. It was her uncontrolled sobbing that the rest could hear. After what seemed the longest of time, both her servant and her mother helped her from the chair and out of the room. The men sat with their faces looking down, to mask the wetness of their eyes. The women were much more open with hankies to the eyes and noses.

Horus-Salah asked to leave, for he was in much the same condition as Anastasia. He was granted permission by the movement of a hand from his father. Shortly thereafter, the men went to the parlor and the women went their way. All were talking at once about the wedding and the day that would be Horus-Salah's and Anastasia's. The lives they would lead, and the children, and so it went. Both groups of men and women were on the smart topic.

However, for the two lovers they were silent in the garden, with their servants not far away. The two of them sat like statues, looking at each other and holding hands. It was the hands that told the most for each moment one or the other would touch or squeeze the hand of the other just to make sure they both were awake. For them, it was beyond happiness. It was life itself that had been granted to them, to be together for the rest of their lives. Their dreams were one, their happiness one and their love one forever more. They sat complete at last with each other. Some of the servants later would say that the two had a glow about them, as they sat and looked at each other through the hours of the night's darkness. But to them, the light of each other's eyes was all that was needed to be complete. Words would have gotten in the way.

River of Life

CHAPTER 15

 It was the next day as Anastasia was making her way to the garden when Horus-Salah's father appeared as if out of nowhere. Before she knew what was happening, he spoke to her with the following, "Power and wisdom has no gender."

She replied, "You honour me before I have proven myself to you, my lord."

He said nothing, and moved by her so fast that when she turned, he was gone. For the next few moments, she wondered if he had been there at all, and if it had really happened. She turned around again to head for the garden. Her mind was still whirling from the encounter. He was just there, right in front of her, all at once. No, she hadn't been looking at anything, or where she was walking, but just the same, she was sure that she would have seen him. It was the meeting, and when he spoke that held her mind. He was smaller in build than Horus-Salah and lighter in weight. His face was good-looking, but it was his eyes. Oh God, his eyes, she thought. When you looked into them, all you saw was the darkness. The blackness, it was like looking at eternity with no stars. At the same time, his eyes looked into her and read everything she was thinking, both the present and the past. It was as if he knew everything that he wanted to know about what was around him. Then moving like the wind, only to feel, not to be touched. She felt cold even in the heat of the mid-day.

She regained herself and started once more to the garden. Ah, there was her beloved, and their mothers waiting for her at the table. As she sat down, Horus-Salah asked if she was alright, that she looked pale. She laughed and replied, "Not enough sun, my dearest" The conversation went back to the main subject on all of their minds. The wedding day; when and where it would take place, along with the details of how it should be done. This was the only subject people would talk about in the days that would follow. Through-out the day and beyond, the servants would offer their best wishes, and tell both Horus-Salah and Anastasia how they prayed for their wedding and their happiness. Some of them prayed to Allah, others to God.

The days that followed were some of the happiest that both Horus-Salah and Anastasia had since their childhood, in this place that both felt was their true home. The days came and went, just as the weeks did in following. All was well and the plans for the wedding had been set. In the early spring of next year, the wedding would that place in the Count's mansion. All of Anastasia's relatives and friends would be present.

Horus-Salah's mother and his uncle and aunt, plus some close friends would make the journey for the wedding. Then, the newly-weds would spend two months having a honeymoon in Europe. They would work their way down to Egypt by train. There they would be remarrying under the Islam laws of marriage. This would happen in the Great Mansion at Cairo. When all the feasting was over, the new couple would return to Luxor and this is love place that they both would call home.

There was a lot of planning and work to be done before Anastasia and her family returned to Poland later this year. The east wing of the mansion had to redone for their return next year. The mansion with its forty rooms would be redecorated to their liking. Anastasia was in her element, and took part in the smallness of details. Some of the rooms would be left in the traditional Egyptian style. Others would have a European look about them, including the furniture. The planning was endless and the meetings were countless.

A month had past and another was half-over, when the Count announced that his family must return to Poland. Even with so much planning still to be done, and many events that were already in the works, both families knew that the time

River of Life

had come for one family to return to Poland, and the other to Cairo.

No one had sadder faces from this announcement than the two lovers. Their playing house and plans of the future was coming to an end. However, all spirits were upbeat for the change signaled the beginning of the great moment that lay ahead. By the last week of the month, all that could be done was completed and the trip back to Cairo was in order. The ship that would be taking the Count and his family back to Poland was booked to leave from Alexandria.

The end and the beginning were coming together. With many tears and countless best wishes, the day came and the two families made their way back to Cairo. It was a repeat of before but now in reverse, with one exception. The two lovers had won. The plan had worked and the future looked like it was owned by them. Though not married yet, even the family treated them as if the magical day had come and gone. Their presence was seen together most of the time. Anastasia's mother once asked, "What will change when you are on your honeymoon?"

They both replied together, "not much."

Upon the return to Cairo, the subject was all about the upcoming wedding. To Horus-Salah and Anastasia, it seemed strange that just a few months ago, the same people treated them as children, but now they were one of the old married groups. Both men and women asked about their plans, and would they be able to join their upcoming event or party. Anastasia said to Horus-Salah, "we will be on our tenth anniversary before we get through all the invitations".

He added, "Well, we have a life- time to see that we get to everyone." The months that had past were like a fairly tale to both of them and they were the main characters.

Like old age the days came to be counted down for the departure to Alexandria. It would be the same as coming. Horus-Salah would look after the trip and go to Alexandria and see his beloved and her family off to Poland. With the deadline approaching in the next two weeks, the couple called on eve-

robert f. edwards

ryone for their help to arrange the mansion and its improve-ments. What seemed as some fixing up here and there had developed a new look about the mansion. Like its new owners, it would be refurbished with the latest styles with a European look.

It was the room set aside for when the couple returned that both Anastasia and Horus-Salah had the most input. There was to be two master suites side by side, for Horus-Salah and the other for Anastasia. Each suite would be deco-rated in the style of the country that they had been born in. Another four rooms were set aside for Horus-Salah's beloved nanny. She would have her own rooms, plus one for her ser-vant. A sitting room and a small dining room were also set aside.

Her rooms would be across the hall from the children's rooms that both Horus-Salah and Anastasia hoped join them after marriage. It went without saying, that if his nanny was well enough, she would look after their children. The number had be left to Allah, which Anastasia would say' is just an-other name for God.' Horus-Salah would reply, 'as always you are right my beloved'.

The wedding plans were in full schedule was in both countries. But first, the trip back to Cairo. Then, for the Count and his family, on to the city of Alexandria for the ship was to leave by mid August. The packing for both families to leave Luxor had been completed, and only which day of depar-ture was still to be slated. Then, like the wind from the desert, came the day. The long line of cars, the goodbyes and best wishes from the ones that were staying behind, the two fami-lies left the great house.

It was hard on most people but the hardest was by far for both Horus-Salah and Anastasia, for this had been the happi-est time of their lives. It had been even better than the time they had been here as children. For them, they were already as one, and all that was left to do was to write it into law and the custom of the land. With tears and red faces the departure to Cairo got under way.

River of Life

The trip back to Cairo was pleasant. It was a moment for the young couple to sit together and regroup what the last weeks had been and what a change in their lives and the rest of their families had been. For them it was their long, long dream that had come true. At last they would be together as they had talked and dreamed about being married. Now it was just months away. Even the plans had been completed.

Both of them looked out the window of the train at the mountains and desert as they moved past. Their hearts were full of happiness and peace. Their lives were good now and the future looked like it was theirs to hold together forever. The train came at last to the city of Cairo and the first part of the journey was over. At the train station the line of cars was waiting to take the families to the Great Mansion. The servants were ready and waited outside to welcome their master and his family with their friends.

For Anastasia and her family, most of their belongings went on the next train to where the ship was waiting at Alexandria. However, there was still a truck that was needed, just for short stay in Cairo, for themselves and their personal servants' requirements. For in a week they would be on board the ship going back to Poland. Both Horus-Salah and Anastasia wished that Horus-Salah was going back with her, but there was just so much to follow through back at Luxor.

He had to stay and have everything ready for when they returned as 'Mister and Misses', in the late spring of next year. Also, Horus-Salah would be with his mother and his relatives going to Poland for the first wedding. It was a must that he travel with his family on that journey to Poland, for most of them had never been outside their country. For the lovers it was not what they wanted but as others had wished. However both of them reminded each other it was a small price to pay for winning their freedom and to live together.

The days that followed flew by during their stay at Cairo. Meetings and last minute details had to be worked out in the daylight hours. During the nights there was even more to do, with parties to attend or making appearances. Some nights as many as three or four places to go to were in order for that evening. By the time the day came for Horus-Salah and Anastasia with her family to leave for Alexandria. All were exhausted.

The train trip was followed by a night in the hotel in Alexandria and the next morning down to the ship waiting at the dock. Before they knew it, Horus-Salah and Anastasia were looking at her quarters onboard the ship and remembering little of what had happened the last few days. It was the end, or as Anastasia said, 'the beginning of our life time together'.

"This is going to be the last time we will be apart", she added.

Horus-Salah had a great smile on his face and said," You are my leader; make it so, my dearest one".

They both laughed and she added, "Yes, the plan did work and we won each other for life."

They made their way back to the upper deck to join the others. The ship was the same one that had brought Anastasia and her family to Egypt, so they all knew where to go and how to get around onboard. The ship was to disembark late that evening, so Horus-Salah and the other guests were allowed to stay onboard until late that evening. The rest of the day was theirs. The two just talked and held hands, looking at each other, or the things that were going on around them. As if in a blink of an eye, the day was night.

For Horus-Salah and Anastasia, they couldn't believe it was less than a few minutes before Horus-Salah would have to leave the ship. Then, she would be on her way back home to her land, and her part of making things ready for the wedding in Poland. As the two walked the decks hand in hand, Anastasia looked up and saw a star in the night. She said almost to herself, and without thinking, "Star-bright, star-light, make a wish", then added "make a wish, make it right, tonight." They both laughed and kissed each other. She then looked at Horus-Salah and said," You just got your wish, didn't you"?

He laughed again and said, "Almost."

River of Life

The great horn blasted, followed by the announcement for all visitors to disembark. In less than half an hour, Horus-Salah was on the dock looking up at Anastasia on the upper deck. They were apart. Without thinking, Anastasia had her hand clinched around the cartouches she wore. Due to the size, she wore them more often as a necklace rather than earrings. With the other hand, she was waving at Horus-Salah. Like his true love, he too, was waving as his other hand was in his vest pocket feeling the watch. Yes, they were apart, but still very much together. They held a part of each other, both in their heart and soul.

He was still standing on the dock as the great ship freed itself and made its way to the open sea, its rightful place. Anastasia stayed on the deck holding her cartouches tightly in each hand. It was only when the dock couldn't be seen that Anastasia looked down at her hands which were across her chest. Each was holding a cartouche. A cold feeling moved over her and her whole body felt the chill. Her hand moved to the shawl over her shoulders, pulling it closer around her body. She stared into the darkness, towards where a dock was, and the other part of her live was standing. Slowly, as if from an outside force, she moved back inside to join the others. The journey back home had started. She felt for the first time, the fullness of what she had been through all these months. She felt alone, very alone.

Horus-Salah too was standing long after the ship moved into the darkness, and only his mind's eye could see it any longer. The servants patiently waited for their master to show any sign he wished to leave in the coolness of the night. There was no sign that came, as Horus-Salah's hand never moved from his vest and the watch. For the rest of him, he could well have been a statue. His mind was still beside his life, his love, his all. Now, his body was here on the dock, looking into the darkness wishing that he was there, with her, and all that had meaning to his existence.

His personal servant finally came up to him from behind and whispered, "Master, would you like to return to the ho-

227

robert f. edwards

tel?" Horus-Salah came back to the dock in mind and soul, turned and looked at the servant, as a man that sees his life leave him. He didn't say a word but moved towards the servant. With that gesture the servant took Horus-Salah's hand and helped him into the car that had been waiting. The starting of the motor told Horus-Salah, he was going back. Back alone, to his home, his part in live, and he too, felt the coldness of being alone.

The old man looked at the dirt roads. He had walked in the darkness up to the crossroads, past the small village on east side of the Nile. One of the trails led to where his home and the mansion of his family had been. He stopped and looked into the darkness at the over-grown road leading in that direction, and took a deep breath. Oh yes, his mind thought, another time of dreams and hopes, of another tomorrow. He bowed his head as if in prayer, but it was the pain of the past that he was bowing his head to. The past and all it had held for him and his beloved was behind him.

With all the strength of an old man, he lifted his head and looked down the other road that led to the Tomb of Nefertari and on to the Valley of the Kings. His place, and his beloved one's place, the tomb of his and Anastasia. Once more, his feet start moving slowly forward and onward. He had a lot of time before the break of day. Being a man of the desert, he only needed the light of the stars, and tonight the moon added to his needs. His thoughts were of another time, when he and Anastasia would run along the trail and look down on the people below, in the Valley of the Kings. Then, they would be at their secret place and share their thoughts with the true owner of the tomb.

The tears ran down his galabya as his feet moved ever forward towards their goal. His one hand moved inside the pocket and felt his watch, the only thing of value to him in this world. The watch that represented all he had ever wanted

228

River of Life

in life. The dream of being together, today and all the other days of his life with his true love came back to his mind as he held the watch. As his one hand held on to the watch, his mind jumped again to the times she had been beside him.

The bent shoulder moved low following the old tired head. He could almost feel the ticking of the watch, as his feet kept moving. He stopped for a rest and looked back over his shoulder. Far across the Nile, there were still a few lights in Luxor glowing, and now far below in the village someone had a fire burning to keep warm in the coldness of the night.

He looked at the sight before him and his mind returned to the present. Time plays with man's dreams, but the places he dwells in stay the same. All his life and for over four thousand years, men and their dreams came here. They and their dreams were all dead in time, but the desert remained the same. In his youth, he ran up to the tomb, in his manhood he walked up, and now he was old, and he was tottering up slowly, but the tomb had always been there, always the same. It was he that had changed in all these years, not the world he lived in and the dreams he had.

Ah, to be young again, and to see his beloved and hear her, took hold of his mind's eyes while his outer two overflowed with tears. Once more his feet kept him moving and his head was down. His mind jumped back to the dock at Alexandria, watching the ship moving away, into the darkness with his only true love.

CHAPTER 16

 As the mighty cruise ship broke out of the sheltered waters of the Mediterranean into the harsh sea of the Atlantic, it turned its bow once more and headed north. It was a matter of days now before they would reach Amsterdam, their final destination. To Anastasia and her parents, the return voyage was much the same as coming to Egypt. The green turquoise waters made Anastasia feel that little had changed for thousands of years in this part of the world. Near the coastline, she could feel the past, with Roman galley ships moving back and forth from Leptis Magna, or Carthaginian ships sailing in the waters. The waters were like a great pool of knowledge of the past. She loved this sea and always liked being out on deck as much as possible. In today's times, there were always ships and smaller vessels moving past.

Tomorrow by midday, their ship would reach Gibraltar and then on to the Atlantic Ocean. The time came, and most of the guests joined Anastasia and the Countess going thought the pillar of Hercules. As the ship entered the Atlantic waters, all knew that the sea had changed and so did the conditions. The water was dark with white caps, and told all on aboard that the sea was one thing, but an ocean was something different in many ways. By night-fall everyone was now used to the cold and hostile waters that the ship made its way through.

Anastasia moved around in the bed before she had opened her eyes. That sound, that throbbing, all around her, and inside her. 'For the love of God, what and where am I!' her mind called out. Was she inside a whale, or another living thing, and she was hearing the heart beating?

No, came the answer as her eyes opened, only to find that she was in her stateroom, on the ship. Oh, had she slept, and had some of the weirdest of dreams. Now, fully awake she was

230

River of Life

back in control of her thoughts, and where she was, thank goodness. The day was about to begin for her as she got out of bed. After what needed to be done before showing oneself to the rest of the world, she joined the others up on deck. Her mother saw her first, and motioned her to one of the deck chairs she had been saving for Anastasia. As Anastasia settled into the chair, the morning greetings were exchanged. Her mother asked her about the plans for the wedding in Poland, and how the list of things to be done was coming along. The reply from Anastasia was full of details, like asking the bridesmaids, and the people she would need to ask when they had returned home. So the afternoon went, talking about her favorite subject, Horus-Salah and now the wedding plans.

For them, their happiness and plans were all time consuming. Anastasia had written Horus-Salah a letter, telling him how much she missed him but all things were well. She would mail it, or have the ship mail it at the first port of call. The ship was making good time and Anastasia felt she would be back in her own bed before the month of August came to an end.

The Countess confessed that she was looking forward to being home and seeing the old servants and her friends. Anastasia mentioned that she too, was looking forward to seeing her old friends, and telling them all about Horus-Salah, and what a great future they were looking forward to together. As the day made its way to the end, the ships' guests were making their way back to their quarters to prepare for the evening. There was merriment, dancing and a sheer feeling of exuberance. It was one great party of activity that was taking place as this gentle giant made its way to its port of destiny.

It was on the last night, the biggest night of the cruise, the Captain's Ball that everyone felt as if in a wonderful fairy tale, the beginning of tomorrow. The main ballroom was filled with men dressed in their formal uniforms, or black tuxedos with tails. The women were outfitted in every description of gown, full length and flowing, as they danced the waltzes of Strauss and Lanner. Even the orchestra seemed to be filled

robert f. edwards

"... looking forward to being home and seeing the servants..."

Original photograph Robert F. Edwards
Poland   May, 1998

River of Life

with a spirit of celebration that it had not felt on the previous evenings.

The only person who had looked unfazed and completely at ease was the Captain. It was just another port, another arrival, another departure. But for the rest, it would be the end of a delightful voyage. For the passengers in first class, as Anastasia and the Countess were, to even those in the lower extremities of the ship, it was a fine vessel to be on.

As the night-sailing was neither gentle nor rough, Anastasia reminded herself of how Horus-Salah had suffered so greatly in his room with seasickness, and how her seafaring blood enjoyed the salt-spray. Oh, dear Horus-Salah, her dear beloved Horus-Salah, and the man that dreams are made of. Yes, she would care for him, and look after him as no other woman has looked after her man, for he was all that she could have dreamt of. For now, her thoughts were of the future, and not of the past. Poor Horus-Salah, with his weak stomach, and lack of seafaring legs, even to the ships of the desert, he felt no more at ease, and his stomach gave no more quarter when riding the camels. Horus-Salah had so many other strengths that motion should not be one to dwell on, she reminded herself.

She looked at her dance-card, to see who was next to take her back on the floor to waltz the hours away. When the evening ended, there was more than one wet eye in the ballroom. She retired to her quarters for her evening rest when the other women did also. The men, of course, would stay up later and drink the fine cognacs and smoke rich cigars and share the last moments as do.

Anastasia's sleep was unbroken until the sturdy ship shook more than once to remind all that the rest period was over. Today, she was going to arrive in Amsterdam. Without delay, and amidst the usual confusion of docking, the mother and father and Anastasia arrived in the port of Amsterdam and were soon escorted to a limousine that was waiting.

The Ambassador from Krakow had pre-booked one of the finest hotel suites for their convenience, and after they had

233

robert f. edwards

settled in, he wished them well, and the rest of the day they were on their own. They spent most of the remaining after- noon in their quarters, having servants bring up the familiar cuisine of their homeland, while they discussed the arrange- ments that had to be made. The Count was overjoyed at being able to read the local news from the current editions of news- papers. "Ah, what a delight, " he would mutter, as the two women continually prepared for the event of the year. It was nice to be back in Europe. It would even be better once they crossed over the border into Poland.

Bright and early the next day, they were on the train as it rumbled and clanked across the railroad tracks and the smoke bellowed into the air. Finally, they were nearing their homeland; there was a feeling of happiness. The only one that showed any impatience was Anastasia. For her, it would never be complete until Horus-Salah was sitting beside her, like the Count was sitting beside her mother. She missed him in so many different ways, everything about him. It was going to be a long, long year, and she vowed to herself that she would never let him go again. She loved him deeply, and was looking forward to the new role of being his wife, and the mother of his children, the person who would share his destiny.

She looked out the window, but the scenery was only a backdrop to all her wishes. The train continued the clickety- clack across the ties that bound her toward the homeland. It was late afternoon before the train arrived at Krakow and the chauffer in the families' Düsseldorf limo was waiting at the platform. It was so nice to see a familiar face from so long ago and to be greeted by such a formal European chauffer. The whole family was delighted with the return to their homeland. Even the small things seemed to make such a difference, like being able to speak fluently in her native tongue, and hearing people reply in the same. 'Yes, there is no place quite like home', Anastasia thought. She was not the homesick type, nor did this bring any rush of emotions to the forefront, it was just nice to be home.

River of Life

The fifty kilometer distance to the estate was an enjoyable ride through the countryside, passing through the small hamlets that dotted the landscape. Ah yes, it was home, so different to the flat bareness they had left. The trees, even the trees were so different from the palm trees along the Nile. It was something that all three had forgotten, how much they have missed, even this small part of their lives. As the limousine d weaved its way through the countryside, there was little conversation, just admiration for what they were seeing.

But, in the blink of an eye, the great estate appeared, their home. As the Düsseldorf rolled up the long driveway, they could see already that their arrival had been announced and all the staff was waiting anxiously to great them. What a remarkable homecoming. The Countess tilted her head gently to the Count and said in a very soft voice," I had absolutely no idea we had such a large contingency of servants, it is quite a group when they are all together, isn't it".

He turned and smiled at her, while Anastasia said, "I can't see Nan yet."

The Düsseldorf then pulled to a stop, and the chauffer opened the door to assist the Countess, and then Anastasia. The Count stepped forward to greet his staff, some now of a second generation that served the needs and the requests of this family. There stood Nan, and Anastasia ran to her, like she had in her childhood and put her arms around her and kissed her profusely. After the exuberant homecoming , the trio proceeded to their quarters that had been vacant for so long.

It seemed to feel they had stepped out of the rooms only momentarily. There were all the finest details they cherished so much, each in their own way. From the large crystal ash tray, and the great silver combs and brushes that the Count used to comb his hair, to the fresh flowers that sat on the table in the Countess' suite, and yes, even the dear old rag doll on Anastasia's bed. It was a wonderful homecoming. It was as perfect as one could imagine. Yes, it was good to be back all the same, and to be so very happy.

robert f. edwards

The next day, after having a refreshing night's sleep in her own bed, Anastasia was up and full of energy. She called to her servant and told her she would be having breakfast in her suite, and then asked her to bring the very finest of writing paper. She needed to write her most beloved a letter. The servant returned with a continental breakfast and the finest stationery in the house. After tea and breakfast Anastasia sat at her desk.

August 31/1939

My Dearest One and Only Beloved,
We return to our home yesterday afternoon. All is well, and the servants and staff have maintained all of our things and the property in our absence.
I miss you terribly and haven't stopped counting the days until you come, and take me forever to be your wife and partner for life. However, I must tell you, it was nice to see my old things and sleep in my own bed. I almost forgot what it was like to have all the things that one has gathered in a lifetime around them. I couldn't help looking at some of my old dolls on the shelves. It is going to be the real thing with you, playing dolls with our own real live dolls in the very near future. Oh, my dearest one, I have been back only one day and already it is too long to wait. I know it is silly of me, after all, we have been through this waiting for each other, but I miss you so very much.
Tomorrow, I will start on the long list of things that must be done before the magical day that you come, and that I return with you to our new home in Luxor. The next few weeks should prove to me if I can still get my friends to do what we have planned for the wedding. I will let you know who is naughty and who is nice.
My father is to go to Warsaw later this week. More of the same, with government and all the things men worry about. He said something about that madman, Hitler, and Germany causing

River of Life

trouble. Boys and men always want to fight over something. I guess it must be a man's thing.

The fall is in the air and it is so much colder, more than I want to admit to, from the weather in Egypt. I miss you so very much, and all that I have shared with you these last months. If we were not all grown up and only just a few months from when we will back together forever, I would ask you to come and run away with me. Sounds unlike me doesn't it? It is just that I feel only part of me, when I am not with you, in these last few weeks. I just can't think of anything but being back with you, my dearest Horus, my love.

I will write once a week, to keep you updated with all that is happening, and how I am making out with the wedding plans. It does look good, even when I write on paper about the wedding. In fact, ever time I think of that day, my whole body gets a warm rush, and I am sure my face tells all present what is on my mind. With this, I will say my good bye and start to work on the plans so your dreams come true on time, my beloved. Until next week and my next update, I will take my leave.

All my love now and forever

Yours, Anastasia

OXOX

With that, she got up and gave the envelope to the servant, then added, "Make sure this gets to the post office today."

"I will go now, if you wish mistress," was the acknowledgement from the servant.

"That will be fine, you are excused." was the answer given back from Anastasia. The servant left with this new assignment and Anastasia started to get ready for the things that had to be done for the days ahead.

Within a few days, the routine of their daily life was falling back into place, except there was a peculiar air that the family could not quite put to rest. Though everything was similar, it was different. There was a tension and uncertainty in the air. It wasn't until one afternoon at tea time in the solarium that the Countess mentioned it to Nan. Nan hesitated for a moment," it's probably", and then she paused, "it is without any doubt, that troublesome little man that is stirring up those Huns again. Europe is rather edgy, I might say, about the way that funny little man that looks like Charlie Chaplin, is behaving."

Anastasia interceded, "You are referring to no other, and I gather, than Adolph Hitler, the Chancellor of Germany."

"Yes, yes, and of course, he has that other obnoxious little friend called Mussolini," Nan added to complete her analysis.

"Well, what is so bad? What are they doing that is so wrong?" the Countess asked, puzzled with the direction of this conversation.

Nan looked at her, "Oh, the usual thing, you know, another war that is what they are heading for, that is what this attitude is." The other two women just looked at each other and gasped.

Little did they know that at this same moment, the Count was receiving in his private study an official from the government. He was delivering a sealed top secret document. As the messenger waited in the outer drawing room, the Count opened the sealed document. It was brief: *We request your presence at once at the Capital. War is eminent. Arrive as soon as possible;* signed by the head of government.

He took a long powerful draw on his cigar, the glow from the inner part of the ash accelerated. He tapped the cigar vigorously, and then touched the corner of the document to the tip of the cigar, and it ignited into flames. He casually walked over and dropped it into the fireplace. All that remained was ash of its message.

Calmly, as if he had received a greeting, or an invitation to attend a banquet, he rang the bell. He informed the messenger that he received the message, thanked him for his promptness, confirmed that he would meet the request of the message and dismissed him. He quietly advised his secretary to prepare to leave at once for Warsaw and to make all the

River of Life

necessary arrangements... Next, he rang for his private valet, "Pack for a journey for a fortnight," he quickly added, "to Warsaw."

He left his study and proceeded to the solarium were he sat and joined the others for tea. The conversation drifted back into the arrangements of the marriage, and all that had to be done make it a perfect event. He smiled tentatively, before the butler came into the room and informed him that his requests had been met, and were ready to be activated. He paused for a moment, and looked at Nan. Then, he realized that she was as much family as any blood relative, and quietly said, "This is for your ears alone to hear. I leave for Warsaw at this very moment. It is urgent; our government is in great need of my participation. Guard yourselves, and our dwelling. I shall be gone at least a fortnight."

They all stood as the Count pushed his chair away and made preparations to leave the table. Almost as an afterthought, the Countess asked, "Is there anything we can do in your absence?"

He replied, looking very solemn, "Be prepared for any event that might arise."

There was a somber, almost morbid feeling left in the room. The conversation shifted from the wedding, to bewilderment with no answers. It wasn't until a few days after, that the warning from the Count became a reality.

robert f. edwards

CHAPTER 17

Horus-Salah got out of bed and looked out the window at the street below. The harbor came into view, and his mind went back to last night as he watched his beloved disappear on the sea, with the ship that carried her back to Poland. His heart was mixed with loss and sadness, but also with wanting to get back to Luxor, and have everything in order at their new house. His servant informed him that the train back to Cairo would leave later that afternoon, and that all was in order. Horus-Salah thanked him and added, "What time do we get into Cairo?" The servant replied that it would be sometime in the morning of the next day.

With that update, Horus-Salah was left to his thoughts once again. His mind became more positive when he started to think of the all things that had to been done before he too, left for Poland next year. Oh! Next year, his mind played with the thought. It was such a long time to be away from his love, his only dream in life. Later that day came the first move, back on the train to Cairo, and another night on the move. The compartment was the same as before on the train, and like the boat that carried his beloved; the train to him seemed to be going backward.

But, this time he didn't have his beloved to share it with. As he sat looking out the window, his hand searched for his security, the watch. With an excuse to see what time it was, he brought the treasure out of his pocket. Looking at the casing, and then the small hand moving ever onward, the ticking gave him an inner glow. He just couldn't help himself. He turned it over, and opened the other side. There she was his life, his love, and her picture. His eyes fixed themselves, now locked in place with the picture of his beloved, and he felt as if he could talk to her and she could hear him. The other side

River of Life

kept ticking to let him know that the world was still moving on, and the train for that matter.

The next morning, the train arrived in Cairo and the same cars and servants were waiting outside to greet him. In many ways, things were just the same, but he was alone. After the usual updates from both sides, he would be leaving for Luxor next week. He couldn't wait to get back to his old home, and the new one that soon would be finished for him and his future wife. Oh yes, his wife, it sounded beautiful, even in his mind.

The next days were much the same, with people coming and going. So it went throughout the remainder of the week, and into the first days of the next. By mid-week, Horus-Salah and his personal servants were on their way back to Luxor. On the return to his home in Luxor, all was going well. He was amazed at what had already been done on the wing that was going to be Anastasia's and his new home. It was as if the workers wanted to see the finished results as much as he did. The days moved forward and so did the work, all was going well.

To add to Horus-Salah's happiness, he received a letter from Anastasia. She was still on the ship when she wrote it, and after reading it for the seventh time, he put it back in the envelope and then in his jacket. He felt warm all over, having even a letter of hers beside him.

The days that followed were much the same, as Horus-Salah made his was up to their secret place. Once up at the tomb, he checked out everything. It had, and probably would, always be the same. For this tomb had been built thousands of years ago. For the present, only he and his beloved knew that it existed. He sat in the entrance as he had done throughout his boyhood, and found a pleasure like nowhere else. Most of the afternoon was gone before he made his way back to the mansion.

It was well into the following week that Anastasia's second letter came. She told him that she was back in Poland. After reading through this letter many times, now both of her

robert f. edwards

letters rested in his private desk. He was feeling happy to know all was well with Anastasia, and that she would have everything ready at her end, for the day of magic and their ever-lasting happiness. So, it was back to work for all of them at Luxor. Horus-Salah looked at the calendar and thought to himself, 'September is almost over, one less month without my beautiful Anastasia, one less month to be alone.'

It wasn't until the fourth day of October that a message came from Cairo to return as soon as possible. The message was from his father. Horus-Salah's blood ran cold and his face turned as white as the robe he was wearing. Something of importance was happening for his father to summons him back to Cairo. He asked questions of the messenger, but he knew the answers before he asked them. To each of his questions, the same reply, "I don't know, Master," until he give the messenger permission to leave.

At once, his private servants were packing his travel cases. The next morning Horus-Salah left for Cairo. By the following morning, Horus-Salah made his was down the long hall, towards his father's study. All these years, it was the same for him as he went towards the office of his father. The same feelings were with him as they had been as a child. As he got close to the great door, his heart beat faster, and his hands were wet. The few times in his life that he had walked through these doors were moments in his life that he would never forget. He prayed to Allah that now, it would be different this time. His hands took the great knob on the door and turned it after he heard the word 'enter'.

Slowly, he pulled the great door open and walked through. His father sat behind the desk as always, and everything was the same as Horus-Salah remembered. In due time, his father looked up and the dark searching eyes looked into Horus-Salah's eyes. "There is news from Europe," the voice said slowly. Horus-Salah said nothing, but continued looking into the darkness of his father's eyes.

His father then went on, "The Nazi Germans have moved into Poland." As the words came out, and Horus-Salah's mind

River of Life

heard them, his face turned red and his eyes broke away and found the floor. He sat as if someone out there, in the mist of life was calling him to join the trip to hell.

Once more, the voice said, "I have arranged for the British Office to provide you with details, as much is available." Horus-Salah looked again into those dark eyes, but they said nothing, nor did his father's voice. The older man's face told him the worst was yet to be told. His father's hand said it all, the meeting was over.

Horus-Salah stood up, with shaky legs and left the room. Back in the hall, it took all his strength to return to his quarters. His servant, after finding out what happened at his meeting, helped him into a chair, for Horus-Salah was in shock.

Sometime after, a British officer came to his quarters. The servant announced him and Horus-Salah received him in his study where the officer sat down. Horus-Salah by this time had a list of questions but the answers to most of them were the same from the officer. "We, at this time do not have that information".

By the end of the meeting, Horus-Salah could only come to the conclusion that Poland has been invaded by both the Germans and the Russians. Horus-Salah wished to get to Poland as fast as possible, but the officer said that was impossible at this time. No one knew what was happening. Horus-Salah replied," The Germans do."

With that, the army officer said, "But, we are not on their side." The officer implied that Britain and Egypt were on the same side. The meeting was going nowhere, as far as Horus-Salah was concerned, so he gave the officer his leave.

The days that followed got worse and so did the news, little as it was, coming from so far away. With all his family's connection throughout the world, the information was still unattainable. As he listened to opinions, or his country's view, Horus-Salah realized that no-one knew any more than he did. The British were the best informed, only because of the large military base that they had built up over the years in Cairo. For purposes of world involvement, Egypt was part of the Brit-

243

robert f. edwards

ish Empire. After the Suez Canal was taken over by the British investors, the British government saw fit to have a military base in Egypt. This was of course, to protect the canal from being closed, and thus the shipping lanes and the supplies from other parts of the empire.

As more and more British troops moved in, less and less German military officers and dignitaries were seen at the get-togethers and evening events. The days dragged through to weeks, as Horus-Salah kept trying to find answers to his questions that no-one had the answer to, about Poland. Even the few Germans that he asked what was happening were tight-lipped, or didn't know. The mystery of what was going on in Europe, and more importantly in Poland, continued on until the last weeks of November.

At one of the evening events, a German officer mentioned that they had moved out of the Baltic Republics of Estonia, Latvia and Lithuania; in agreement with the fourth Partition of Poland from Russia.

To Horus-Salah, this meant very little, and he still needed to know about Anastasia and her family. The next days he went back to his quest in try to get to Poland, or at least to Europe. However, the same excuses and delays where well in place. He was in need of the right papers for traveling, and the passage on board a ship. On and on it went, day after day.

By now the British were in charge of all movements in the main ports of Egypt. His spirits became lower with each day's unmerciful progress. On one of these days, sitting with his mother, she agreed with him that he wasn't getting anywhere, here in Cairo. That it would be best if he return to Luxor, and carry on preparations for the wedding and the remodeling for his wife-to-be. She made him feel better by adding, " so the Germans are now in Poland, weren't the Russians there before?" She added, "If we get any news of what has happened, I will send it by special messenger to you in Luxor, my son."

He thanked his mother for helping him through these times. He also knew that his mother would be able to get information from his father better than anyone else. The next

244

River of Life

day, he made plans to return to Luxor and see how the workers were doing.

By the first week in December, Horus-Salah returned to his beloved Luxor, but this time it was with mixed feelings and a heavy heart. He was relieved to see the work that had been done, considering all that was happening in the rest of the world. After a few days, he was able to get back into the ways of living in Luxor, and his true and only home. The servants knew some of the events happening in Poland, but kept the focus on the wedding. To them, it was next year and the completion of the home of their masters new bride was uppermost in theirs mind. This helped Horus-Salah mentally get through the weeks that moved into months.

Since his boyhood and definitely since his return to Luxor, he had made the pilgrimage to the sepulcher and tomb of the unknown mummy cat. There he would pay homage and respect to the past, both his and the occupant of the tomb. This was no exception today, as he made his way on the wandering paths that were elevated high above the ridges overlooking the Valley of the Kings and the Valley of the Queens.

He wandered leisurely in his galabya, up and down these treacherous trails that had endured time itself, working his way back to his beloved home at Luxor. Upon entering the more populated area and then proceeding towards the estate itself, he was neither at peace with himself nor in despair. Just another day in the month of December, that by now had managed to find its way to mid-month. The days had worked their way to weeks, and the weeks now to months.

His dear mother had kept her word by sending her private messengers with highly classified information about what was going on in Cairo and what was far more important, to the world; what was going on in Europe. His beloved Anastasia's country had collapsed within less than three weeks and was now occupied by the Germans. Germany had already made pacts with the Russians and was looking at Finland to be an annexed to their ever-growing demands of world supremacy.

robert f. edwards

As he wandered down the hill and entered into the court-
yards of the estate, his most senior and loyal servant came
running up to him with the customary greetings exchanged by
each. The servant then said, "I have been searching everywhere, Master. There is a messenger that awaits your presence from Cairo." With that news, Horus-Salah thanked the
servant and proceeded to the designated spot in the estate
that the servant from Cairo was waiting.

Expecting the usual high-ranking servant of his mother,
he was taken by surprise when he saw a senior servant of his
father's. Once again, the greetings were passed in the traditional way and after that, the servant completed his priority
mission. He handed him a sealed envelope. At once, Horus-
Salah knew it was his father's. The cotton papyrus paper of
his father's special stationery, to say nothing of the prominent
seal that held the contents, spoke only of one person that
lived – his father. The servant quickly bowed and made his
exit.

Horus-Salah was shaken and moved by the element of
surprise. His hands were shaking and if anyone had been present, they would have seen the pallor on his face as the blood
drained away with anticipation and fear. He quickly removed
himself from the common area and retreated back into his
own quarters. Once in his own library, with shaking hands he
opened the envelope. True to the tradition of his father, it was
direct and without emotion: 'Return to Cairo at once you are
needed,' and with the seal of who sent it.

With that, he rang for his servant to return and summoned the father's head servant. Once the three of them were
in the room together, Horus-Salah issued one simple command, "When and how do I return to Cairo?"

The answer came forthwith from the senior male servant
of his father's, "As soon as possible, by the ship that waits for
your return."

Horus-Salah glanced at his loyal servant and said, "Prepare, I leave within the hour." Both servants dutifully bowed
and left Horus-Salah to his thoughts and his preparation

River of Life

mentally for the journey. Within less than an hour, the small motorcade took Horus-Salah and the two servants to the shoreline. To Horus-Salah's amazement, it was one of his own father's private high-speed vessels that were waiting. Without the usual fanfare and farewells, he was whisked aboard and they cast off before Ra had found the setting of darkness. As the high-speed metal hull sliced through the waters like a hot knife through butter, the small flotillas bounced like corks in the wake.

Horus-Salah stood on the bow of the boat, looking at the shorelines of the river that gave life and meaning to his people from the beginning of time. The small villages dotted their existence as the ship steadily, at full speed tore its way through this artery of life, leaving only the wake behind it. As dusk was preceded by darkness and a moonless night gave only the stars for guidance, Horus-Salah remained standing at the bow looking at the shore line.

He watched as the small fires that were cooking the evening meals and giving light to their inhabitants, gave off a glow like large fireflies that danced along the darkness of the canal of light. Horus-Salah's mind faded to another time, when he had traveled with his beloved, down this mighty river, this vein of life itself that had looked after his people and brought such great happiness. He recalled at that moment, he and Anastasia were being treated as the next in-line of the ruling class of this remarkable land. His heart filled with joy and he savored, like a starving man, the thoughts that swelled and pleased him in those great moments of pleasure.

It was with these thoughts that he was gently interrupted by his servant, reflecting the words, "Master, it is long past the time to retire". Horus-Salah, always obedient to the demands of his station in life, acknowledged and went to the cabin below. Sleep was impossible, now despair had replaced the pleasant moments that had danced through his mind. He recaptured all the small details of each letter that his mother had sent to him, and was in despair as the night tossed and turned the hours away.

By morning, Horus-Salah had looked like he had swum the distance the ship had made, but no one, not even his servant made comment. He went through the rituals of the day as somebody that had been possessed and was in mind and soul at some other place and time. However, the repeat of another night was endured before he would reach Cairo. By the following day, as the clock acknowledged midday, the ship had docked in Cairo. As preordained, the small escort of vehicles was waiting at the dock to receive him and the servants. As the motorcade worked its way through Cairo, Horus-Salah, full of apprehension and dismay, looked at the ancient city with a jaundiced eye.

It definitely wasn't his city, even though it belonged to his land. The congestion, the multitude of different lifestyles flashed before him, blazing to make way through the traffic that impeded their advance to the mansion of his father and of his family, of his heritage. There was a short distance in time before they arrived at the huge gates which opened before them into the long winding pavement of the estate. As he got out, the head servants of his father's house greeted him and welcomed him in the fashions that were accustomed to the period. He acknowledged and returned their greetings.

The one that brought tears to his eyes was his nanny, which broke all protocol of the line and reached out with open arms to hold him. She whispered, "Your mother is waiting in the garden," and with that, he freed himself from the embrace and went swiftly in that direction. Both his mother and sister were sitting in the garden, waiting for his arrival and both greeted him in the customs and fashion that they were used to.

His mother had that long sorrowful look that he had only seen a few times in his life. He asked in a gentle manner, "What has brought me back here to Cairo, other than my father's wishes?"

River of Life

She smiled her all-knowing smile and said, "He will explain everything as is required. As for me, I welcome you back into my presence."

He looked at his sister and said, "Is your enlightenment as vague as the womb from which I came?"

And with a broad smile, she said, "No, my brother dear. I welcome you back with all that is within me."

The small talk continued until his father's servant made his presence known, with more of a summons than a request. Horus-Salah excused himself, and with the servant three steps behind him, he followed the path to the great doors that led to the chamber of his father's domain. Horus-Salah stepped aside as they became adjacent to the door and the servant knocked, and then inside there was a clap. The door opened marginally and the servant retreated to make way for Horus-Salah.

Horus-Salah walked through the door as he had done so many times in his short life and saw his father sitting behind the massive desk. It was like looking at history itself. Though there was chaos and confusion among the mortals, this man, and this mortal had all the ingredients of the leaders of the past of this great nation, for his cold relentless eyes stared at his son. And the son once more quaked in the presence of his father. The hand motioned as it had done so many times before, to be seated; and once again, the obedience was immediate.

His father had seemed to be ageless, for he had not changed since the first days that he had entered into this sanctuary and domain that was his father's. Then, almost as if the room spoke rather than the individual, his father said, "Your presence is needed to secure our allies and our associates throughout Africa. You will assure one and all that our trade routes will not be disrupted nor our relationships be dismantled by this new pestilence of the European front."

There was a long pause and Horus-Salah looked not at the desk, and definitely not at the man, but what stood as a vision before him. Those cold black piercing eyes of his father penetrated his very existence and conjured up everything that he was holding within. He had that eerie feeling of being stripped naked, far below even the surface of the soul. Horus-Salah always had a feeling of awe of this man that knew more than he would in a thousand lifetimes.

Horus-Salah again heard the voice, "You shall prepare yourself with five of our best and then you will leave; first, to cover the North African front. And upon returning, I will advise you further of going to Zanzibar and other important strongholds of our domain."

Again, without blinking, Horus-Salah stared at what lay before him. There seemed to be a silence that permeated the entire room and then, as if all the strength that had been mustered inside him, he said, "It has been said; I shall obey and it will be done." The hand, as usual, waved and the meeting had ended.

After leaving his father's presence, as usual Horus-Salah was exhausted. Drained and stripped mentally, his physical body found its way back into the corridors that would lead him to the chambers of his own quarters. His servant was waiting, as usual, and had fresh clothes waiting and the bath drawn. Horus-Salah was like a man that had been hypnotized and had not quite left the trance. He sat like a mummy being prepared for its next move through destiny and retreated after to the bed, where he slept the sleep of the restless.

River of Life

CHAPTER 18

The days that followed were in preparation of so many events. For the Christian sector of Cairo and the ever-growing numbers of British both at the ports and in the garrisons, were preparing for the celebration of Christmas. But for Horus-Salah, it was the preparation of what his father's commands had wished.

As the New Year approached and there was frolicking and celebration, leaving one decade behind and entering the new, Horus-Salah could not help but reflect back in a moment of regret for his generation. Though he and his family were wealthy beyond comprehension of most that existed in these presence times, let alone in this country, they expanded their horizons ever onward. He could not help but share the poverty and the dismantlement that had plagued the world of the common man with depressions and disparity. Most in his generation would grow up never knowing the affluence or enjoyment of the future. And now, in Europe, they were embarking on bloodletting of the youth that had found no peace in the past. To him, there was nothing to celebrate; the beginning of treachery and uncertainty in this new decade. As January 1, 1940 rang loud and clear throughout the world, there were already people that had felt ironclad advancements of the winds of war. It was well into the second week of this new decade before Horus-Salah with his two male servants, accompanied by one of his father's servants along with ten of the most capable commando-trained warriors, found their way not by a motorcade, but by a very discreet movement to the railroad station. It would take them first to Alexandria and then work their way slowly through the back roads to Libya.

By the end of the month, this small band had reached their first destination. They joined the first of many treks in months and even the years that would follow, on the camel-trade routes that had crossed the great Sahara from the time that Man wanted to trade with each other in this vast openness. The camel caravans looked like the desert itself, unyielding and determined to remain as they had from one generation to another through the centuries of time. Though their faces were different and their camp was new, their mission was always the same – to bear goods and trade, whether it be slaves of the past, salt of the present, or information of the future, these were the trade routes that lined the history of the region.

This small band of non-conformists were neither welcomed nor rejected, but they would submit to the rules of the desert in the caravan that carried their lives through the endless sands. They traveled mostly by night under the guidance of the stars; and when the moon rose high, it was like dancing through sands of time on moonbeams. When the skies lacked the presence of the moon's existence, the stars became more vivid and were able to be read with the accuracy of a map that never changed.

For Horus-Salah, it was an adventure that he neither welcomed nor found distasteful. After a short time in the desert with these men that knew no other way to exist, he found falling into place was both enjoyable and relieved him of the burdens of his mind and the sorrows of his heart. As they traveled endlessly at night and rested in Berber tents during the day from the piercing sun above, he grew to find peace and tranquility that only the deserts of the earth can give Mankind.

He enjoyed the moments of drinking sweet tea with the Turkish heads. Here in the greatest of deserts was the culture of the past and the present, in the serving of the sweet tea. The first glass served is bitter for the meaning of life, followed by the second cup that is the sweetness of love, and than the last glass that is neutral like death. As he finished the last glass of tea he look into its emptiness and had a feeling it was his life also that he was looking at.

River of Life

He welcomed the camaraderie of the evening meals as the bread was prepared in its own oven of sand and served with the common bowl that presented the meal of the evening. As they huddled in groups of six to eight in their desert robes, the hands dipped the bread into the gruel of whatever was available or brought as provisions. Like all expeditions on trade routes, the first weeks were fulfilling with the supplies that had been brought and prepared; dates, and even meats to supplement the hardship of the heat and the endless dunes of the Great Sea Sands.

But as the weeks wore on, and the provisions dwindled, they looked longingly towards the next oasis. Like a miracle, out of a vision of a man's dream, sprung the life-giving nectar – water; and with it, the foliage that surrounded it that gave shade and quenched the thirst of both man and beast. They would linger there almost reluctantly giving up this paradise that surrounded the endless barren sands, the pyramids of the desert.

As the weeks moved into months, one village after another in this remarkable landscape surfaced. Horus-Salah conversed with the leaders that had known his plans since the recording of their existence, and was reassured that his father and the domain remained constant. They had heard of the horrors of the Italian Occupation in Libya since 1911 and their annexing of the northern parts of Tunis in Libya to the reclaiming of a Roman Empire that had crumbled a thousand years before. They heard of the unmercifulness of the Italian penetration, never-ending by going south, demanding, purging and reclaiming what it said was rightfully Italian soil.

They had no ideas of grandeur that co-existence between Arabs or the Ottoman Empire with the Italian agenda could be arrived. It was expelling or annihilating the inhabitants to reclaim it for Italian use and resettlement. However, now, with Mussolini well entrenched in his fascist behavior, this cruel European reinvasion of the Punic Wars had been reunited and the tribes welcomed once again the security of the reas

robert f. edwards

" ... they looked longingly towards the next oasis."

Original photograph Robert F. Edwards
Egypt November, 1999

River of Life

surance of his father's house and his ancestors' continuous involvement.

It remained from one camel caravan to another in this quest of reassuring their supply lines, their trade lines, and their associations that had long existed before records with the people of the south; and they knew that without any hesitation, that the word would spread north, even to the borders of the Mediterranean that all was the same in the house of his father. The leader and ruler of the caravan and the tribes welcomed the new caliph of the house that his father ruled and that someday he would rule. It was almost a form of an advanced coronation that Horus-Salah never realized at the time; and as one day must yield to another, distance must yield with progress.

So it came to pass that this band that represented all of the history of the clan and the heritage that went before him reached Morocco and finally the shores of the Atlantic. He had accomplished what his father has demanded – the unification and reassurance of all the trade in their house, and the ruler of tribes were satisfied. Men four times his age bowed and swore allegiance once again to their common brother in trade and to the house that made it possible.

He wandered for a small period of weeks along the shorelines enjoying the warmth of the beaches and the coolness of the evenings. The houses that sheltered his needs were in the custom of his past, in his own country. It was here that Horus-Salah and time had found the year's midway point. It was also here that Horus-Salah had joined in civilization and the communications of the global community.

He was not only entertained in the presence and manner that he had grown up in, but was informed of what was transpiring in the world around him. He learned that the Finnish forces had held back an army of fifty to sixty times its population, but had finally found the inevitable defeat. He also was brought up to date; that Chamberlain was no longer Prime Minister of Britain, and a man called Sir Winston Churchill of the Labor Party took office. Germany, in its blood lust, had continued its thirst to conquer and invade, adding Poland and Belgium to its continual movement of world domination.

But the latest news was even more devastating to Europe than to Horus-Salah, which had already suffered the most crucial of all blows that Poland had fallen to the mighty axis of Nazism. It was the world that had found Dieppe surrounded. The British and the French mighty armies were entrapped. Rumors had trickled in that the British Army had evacuated to its stronghold, the Island of Great Britain. The news came rumbling in as Moroccans, fully entrenched with the French Occupation, did not understand how the mightiest army of the world had collapsed within weeks, days, and the Maginot Line that was impregnable had been pierced like a balloon that had been overfilled by zealous optimism, a mere pinprick had deflated the security of Europe.

As this news entered more dimensions of Horus-Salah's mind, he could see the red flow of the German agenda spreading like blood on the trails of advancement through Europe. Now that France had fallen, what would become of Morocco, Algiers? Ah, yes. For a moment of flashing back to that room, the room that knew all that contained the knowledge of a man that saw all, his father. Oh yes, his father knew; as he gasped, he knows what lies ahead. He sees what others have yet to do. And with his troubled mind and his awe of his father's knowledge, he retreated once more into the chambers that were designated to him and retreated from the others around. It was only his servant that was allowed for the next three or four days to attend to his needs. He was almost incapacitated by despair.

As his gentle soul and his nature recovered in the sanctuary of his quarters, his soul, his mind and his body gained the strength that was required for the future. His mind now realized that the pestilence of these demented minds of the Europeans were now moving this plague towards the shore-

River of Life

lines of the Continent that his ancestors had in existed since the recording of Man. He was now going to know firsthand what the enemy was and what their intentions were. Before he could leave Morocco, the vizier government of the day was in place and their new commander-in-general was sent to Morocco.

He had been gone almost six months and reported nothing back to his father's domain or presence. This was all part of the plan or accepted rules that had been preordained. His father would not accept defeat. He would not accept failure. And above all, he would not expect anything less than success. So, to advance information that might get into the wrong hands was both unnecessary and foolish, at the best. However, Horus-Salah could not help but feel that he should inform his father that he had reached his furthest outpost in the North African alliance.

And with this, he summoned two of the most aggressive and highly skilled men that accompanied his small band. He gave them one word – "Atlantic". His father would know by the one word that he had arrived and crossed through the first phase by reaching the Atlantic. Without any further instructions, they were to return with that message. If they were captured, tortured, or bribed, which was impossible, the best friend or foe could get was "Atlantic". It would only be one man in the world that would know the meaning and the results; that would be his father.

In weeks that lie ahead, he started preparing the journey that would take him back through this now more treacherous part of the world than it been for many, many centuries. He would join the camel caravans under the escort of the 'Blue Men' down around Marrakech in the southern parts of Morocco, then work his way across Algiers, once again through the endless Sea Sands. The 'Blue Men' had never been conquered by anyone, including the French, whose garrisons had sprinkled themselves through Algiers and occupied most of Morocco. However, these men swore only allegiance to Allah and the caliph that rode in front of them. Once his small able

robert f. edwards

*" He would join the camel caravans under the escort of the
'Blue Men'..."*

Original photograph   Robert F. Edwards
Libya   November, 1999

258

River of Life

band joined with the Berbers and the tribesmen, they started again their endless trek across the sands that welcomed their re-entry.

For Horus-Salah, the mystery of the unknown was no longer present. Only the beauty and the breath taking peace of tranquility of the endless Sea Sands that made their presence known as the caravan worked its way through the mighty dunes of the endless sea. During the day, the tents would be pitched and the camels would be hobbled. They would sit in the shade that they themselves had provided, drinking now the mint tea of the Moroccans with the frothy Turkish heads and smoking the sweet tobaccos with water pipes. Most of them would sit in silence, gazing out in the endless sands that lay in every direction from their small habitats of existence. Horus-Salah was fascinated and spellbound as always, as the breezes of the endless winds removed any of the presence of existence and continually topped the mighty dunes with sharp points of sand.

As the days made way and added to the weeks moving across this perilous land, Horus-Salah found a peace within his soul that these men of the deserts shared. It was the nights that he would climb high on to the sand dunes and welcomes the sunsets that were both magnificent and breathtaking. But above all, when one would turn their back as Ra finally receded to the darkness of the night, the direction in which Ra would return to share the skies with were filled with pinks and mauves. The many color mixes of the sky submitting to the night of darkness made Horus-Salah keep turning his head from east to west, to see the ever changing skies that lay before him.

In their quest to gather more information that might be pertinent to the movements and the demise of this vastness from the enemy, they traveled a different route through the Great Sea Sands. Once again they entered into the lands of the Libyans; the Italians had stepped up their demands for conquering and annihilation of these proud neighbours.

robert f. edwards

It was in one of the villages that changed the outlook of war to Horus-Salah. They had entered this village two days before, and other than a few of the old men and a small gathering of children around the tents, it was just the women that remained. They were received by the elders with the politeness of the desert and once they expressed their needs, these were granted with all that the village could offer. The caravan rested and prepared for its next journey on the endless roads of time.

One night, the elders of the village returned and this time, they had brought with them the prizes of their victory over the Italians, better known as prisoners. There weren't many of them, probably a dozen or so. For Horus-Salah and his small group, there was no need to be involved. It was not for them to either make comment on, nor to be witness to what was taking place. It was just circumstances.

After the normal greetings, Horus-Salah was invited to the tent of the elder, and was enjoying all that was available to him. He sat leisurely on pillows and enjoyed the smell of the sweet tobacco through the water pipes, and nibbled aimlessly on dates when the rhythmic music outside the tents ceased. There was stillness, and then screams. Screams of someone in agony.

Startled, he sat directly up. The elder smiled and said, "It is not for you to be alarmed. It is for those that are waiting to receive that the alarm has been sent."

Horus-Salah asked, "Please enlighten me, for my wisdom is small and I am young and yet to learn the ways of life."

The elder inhaled a large amount of the aroma of the tobacco and exhaled it, and said, "You have witnessed our enemy in our camp. We are now treating them to the entrance of eternity." He paused for a moment and then said, "There are no better prepared to administer vengeance upon the sons that they have lost than the women that have given the seeds of their life to the soil by the destruction of these infidels. So let their blood taste the soil that the sons of the mothers have lost."

River of Life

Horus-Salah continually heard the screams, some louder than others but all in unison and said, "And what is inevitable is understood, but the procedure is vague." The caliph looked once more directly into the eyes of Horus-Salah and he said, "A knife cuts both ways. It is our turn to remove the flesh of those that oppose us. Our wives, our mothers and our daughters know how to keep life from entering eternity and agony to excel to its end. They are removing the skin of our adversaries." Horus-Salah's eyes opened wide as though he had received the first slash of the knife and the caliph looked once more and said, "And what better part to start than on the manhood of Man?" And with that, a gurgling scream pierced the air and the caliph added, "Ah, yes, our Italian officers died poorly. They're such cowards when it comes to the life of man."

Throughout the night, with no sleep for Horus-Salah, the screams continued. However, by dawn, the dozen plus were unrecognizable and the dogs had already started to enjoy their first meal of the day.

Horus-Salah and his companions were among the first to thank the caliph as the caravan started to prepare for its journey to its next destination. They had only been a matter of two days and three nights out, when the gentle winds that had dusted the sand dunes into perfection changed; and became the storms of the Sea Sands, when the sand blurred the vision of Ra and the midday became darkness.

The small, able band of adventurers gathered and hobbled the camels quickly and secured the tents. The storm was amongst them and as it was, so it shall be. There is nothing known like the storms that cover these Great Sea Sands of the desert, the Sahara; and though it roared and screamed for days, the small group made their presence known by uncovering themselves at different intervals. They had not expected or prepared for these natural phenomena.

Finally, as it lifted, they reexamined the caravan. To the camel leader's dismay, yelling and cursing his assistances, the water pouches had been lost or destroyed. The caravan

261

had less than one day's water supply. After assessing this disaster, they recognized that they must set out, regardless of the weather conditions, to the nearest oasis. By all recollection, it should be no more than two days, three at the most, before they could replenish their water supplies. There are many things that can be done living in this hostile climate of Man, but the lack of water isn't one of them.

The ships of the deserts were once again loaded, now only with what was essential so their burdens were lighter, to consume less water in their natural holding tanks. The camel leader broke the trail leading his ships of the desert towards the oasis, and the life-giving water. The first day went smoothly, though still a haze of sand burnt the eyes and covered the body. Though they were completely covered other than a small opening slit of cloth around the eyes, it became unbearable. They didn't have the privilege now of resting in the day and traveling only at night.

It was essential that they get to the oasis. On the second day, they were not lost, but misguided perhaps, for the sands had not cleared the skies; and though the winds were lighter, the vision at night remained impeded. The first order of the day was to let the lead camels wander, for they could smell water much better than man's guidance and ruling hand. However, by the fifth day, the camel leader ordered the first of the camels to be slaughtered and the natural pouches to be opened to feed the many and let the few perish. Now there was water for the men and the other camels, for this day. What would happen in the days ahead when there were no more ships of the desert to slaughter?

To Horus-Salah, it was all new. He realized the tranquility and peacefulness of this sanctuary of wilderness and isolation also had rules to keep the faint of heart and the fearless of conquest at bay. One need not ever have to bury what was left behind, the great sand dunes took care of anything that got in their way or disturbed their existence.

Some of the men became delirious. The animals trudged forward, foot upon foot in their swaying motions, as the race

River of Life

of heat danced and made the landscapes swim before their blurred eyes. They had lost continuity of time, for one day remained the same as the next, and the nights became endless. The darkness was just shades from day to night. No one would admit that this column was lost; this small insignificant group was being swallowed up in the sea of grains.

To Horus-Salah's and his small group of companions, faith or understanding of the situation was one. They had faith in Allah and believed that destiny would be theirs, regardless of their mortal outcome.

Then, almost as it came, it ceased. One of the young camel herders had spotted a star in the sky. And then, they all returned as the skies opened up to the heavens, and the maps that were so desperately needed. The camel leader at once had his first bearing in over a week. Oh, they were way off from the chosen area of the trades, but with luck within five, maybe six days or seven, they would reach a small oasis where they could replenish the life giving nectar of water, or so they would hope.

Choices were few and options were not acceptable. They trekked once again by the map of the sky. Their visions were thin and their hopes were thinner. However, they had an order about them that ruled survival. As the sun rose and set and the darkness dominated the land maps, they moved forward. They could not sacrifice any more camels, even though the small group now had been reduced to walking beside their beasts of burden. They set the last remaining camels loose, for their thirst was as great as those that owned them, and the direction they took was their hope, as well as those lives that could not smell the nectar of life.

After two days, maybe three, no-one could remember which day it was, the camels found the oasis. As the men and the few remaining camels found what was left of this dried-out oasis, despair became the mood. The caliph looked at what remained of the small oasis and said, "Dig. The camels smell it." And before his words had found the ears of all, many had fallen to their knees and started to dig frantically in the end-

robert f. edwards

less sand beds. What seemed to burn their hands was the salt that permeated the sand. But then, one screamed, "Praise is to Allah! Mohammad, the Prophet has saved us." Yes, his hands had found the dampness that yielded the treasure that they sought. And as they concentrated their efforts taking turns, first the sand was moist; and then, the first evidence of water. The oasis was not dry. It was just buried.

After a week of recuperating and accumulating enough of this God-given gift, they had gained their strength and the few remaining camels were prepared to continue on the journey. As they trudged night after night, they followed the many that had gone before them, the caliph told Horus-Salah, "Welcome to the land of Egypt. The soil is yours." Horus-Salah's heart jumped, and his mind soared, while his soul gave thanks. Before the year came to an end, he would be in the presence of his family once more. Of course, he added with these thoughts, "With the will of Allah."

So it came to pass, that his thoughts were true and his requests were granted; for in February, 1941, Horus-Salah was on his way by train from Alexandria to Cairo to bring living evidence of what he had accomplished. In his mind, what had he accomplished? 'Life! Memories of a life-time in the desert.' To those that he had met and those reports that he would give to his father's secretaries, he had secured the new generation of the house of his ancestors.

Without him knowing it, when he first started on this journey, his father had appointed him as the predecessor to all that the family had accumulated through the centuries. To Horus-Salah, he was nothing more than the obedient son of the ruler of his destiny. He returned to Cairo and was received by his mother and sister, and most importantly, by his father. At the dinner table, his accomplishments were acknowledged by his father. "You have returned, therefore you have succeeded. It was the will of Allah."

By March, most of the immediate information had been translated into the endless archives which were required by his father. Horus-Salah had requested that he return to his

River of Life

beloved Luxor, if nothing more than to see how things had progressed in the completion of the wing that would house his beloved Anastasia and their dynasty of reign. It was granted without debate or discussion, and his absence could be of his choice when he felt it appropriate or the preparations were made.

For the rest of the world, the continual demise of civilization and the new world order of the thousand year reign of Nazism poured down endlessly on more than one front. The Russians now, instead of being an ally of the Germans, were the victims of treachery. Mussolini had offered a cheap victory to his plateau of successes of propaganda by conquering Greece. There had been absolutely nothing that showed signs of slowing down the agenda of the madness of the man that looked like Charlie Chaplin.

Once more, Horus-Salah's small entourage moved back to Luxor. He felt exonerated upon returning to the land of his life, the land of his purpose, and to the place filled with memories of Anastasia. It was like rolling back time itself, both in the world around him; but what was most important, in the mind that had gained so much in the little over a year that had passed before him. After the usual formalities that coexisted with those that he loved and found peace in, he returned to the quest that had always been his, from the first day of discovery.

robert f. edwards

CHAPTER 19

Back in Cairo, his family had completed the six months of mourning for the loss of Horus-Salah. A British Army officer had informed the family that Horus-Salah had been killed in action, along with his crew. His men had witnessed the explosion of the armored vehicle and unanimously said no-one had survived. His family and all that knew him grieved for the loved one they were told was dead, not knowing the truth. Only the German hospital knew the British records were false.

December was an emotional month for the African Corps. Both sides of this horror of war took time out for the Christmas Season. For the African Corps and the British Armies, a moment of peace was experienced over the desert. The African Corp celebrated by decorating unrecognizable Christmas trees with small gifts, and food under it for the special day. Even on the Russian Front, the Germans and the Russians took time off during the festive season with hidden delights from the homeland that had been savored and saved for the celebration. The New Year wandered in with skirmishes along the frontlines, as the German Army continually retreated, trying to save as many divisions as possible.

For Horus-Salah, it was another year and that was all. It neither showed promise nor accomplishment. Time had passed on another calendar that marked another period. However, little did he realize that the events that were taking place without his knowledge were significantly going in favor of his release, and reuniting with a family that assumed it was just another year in the loss of their beloved.

By midyear, the British Army had encircled the German hospital and the prisoners of war, including Horus-Salah, were now left in the hands of the British conquering forces. After checking the small amount of files that were not de-

266

River of Life

stroyed by the Germans, the British realized that Horus-Salah, Colonel of the Egyptian Army, was alive. He was in a German hospital.

The weeks that followed saw Horus-Salah for the first time leave Libya in over a year and he was transported to a British hospital in Alexandria. He had just arrived and had been assigned a bed in the long dormitory, when his dear sister and her friend appeared as nursing nightingales. They all wept profusely. His sister related the agonizing moments of the family when they heard the news that their beloved son had been killed. 'Even King Farouk 1 of Egypt had summoned a special inquiry to try to recover his remains, ' Horus-Salah was told by his sister. There was so much news to share, but on the one subject that Horus-Salah wanted to know, there was none. His sister told him everything, but there was no news about Poland, and not a word about his beloved Anastasia.

In the months ahead, the medical doctors of the British Corps hovered and probed and discussed the miraculous surgery of Herr Surgeon General. They marveled at the skill of the incisions, and concurred that by the extent of Horus-Salah's wounds, kept referring to it as a miracle. Horus-Salah concluded that the miracle was Allah's but the skill was Herr Surgeon General's. He was grateful that the course of life had spared him for another moment in his quest to find his beloved.

As the days moved on, he always had the company of his sister and her friend to share his days. The two women nursed over him as if he was their sole responsibility. He had known the young friend of his sister's for many years, as their families were of similar position in the Cairo community. Like his sister, she had grown into an attractive young woman. Her dedication to him was surprisingly more intense than his sister's devotion. All though he found her attention and kindness rewarding, his yearning and the focus for his beloved never wavered for a second.

267

robert f. edwards

His legs were now strong enough with the support of braces and crutches, just to stagger about like the cripple he was. However, his back had proved stronger than even Herr Surgeon General had predicted and soon he could stand erect on the crutches and the pegs that once were his legs. In time, he was well enough to do what most veterans do, and that is return, broken and dismantled to their former life. Medals were both presented by the Egyptian government and the British General, and much later he would receive the Victoria Cross from the King of England.

It wasn't that many months before the agenda moved forward and Horus-Salah returned to Cairo. Once in the mansion of his family, the routine of life became as it always had been. Until one day, his father summoned him to 'the room', as Horus-Salah thought of it. However, this time, instead of being in his normal Egyptian attire of a galabya, he dressed in his military wardrobe with two canes supporting mangled legs.

He walked the distance down the corridor to the great door. When the male servant opened the door and his father's hands summoned him forward, this time, the crippled hero painfully leaned heavily on his canes as he made his way to the appropriate chair that awaited him. He sat, as he had so many times before, and this time he looked directly into the cold black eyes that penetrated the thoughts of Mankind. But this time, they seemed only a hollow shadow of darkness. His father looked for the longest moment at his son, as though he was reading the chapters that he had missed all these months before. Then a voice from deep within him said, "Allah has been merciful to this house and to your soul. In the name of Allah, let all things be possible."

Horus-Salah replied, "And to his prophet, Mohammad," almost mocking the worn-out phrase of Arabic. The haze that covered his father's eyes vanished completely, and a sharp fierceness prevailed. He said, "Do not take lightly of destiny, for it shall succeed where you failed." Once again, Horus-Salah retreated back into his childhood submissiveness.

River of Life

His father paused for the longest time, before he continued in a voice so faint that it could hardly be heard, "Your time is near. You are my replacement. Allah has been generous to our family by giving you back to us."

Horus-Salah looked puzzled and quietly said, "My understanding is vague?" His father then got up from behind the desk, and walked around as Horus-Salah found his canes to stand. It was one of the few times Horus-Salah had ever remembered standing beside his father. To his amazement, they were both approximately the same height and build, though the galabya always did mask a man's figure.

The senior looked into the eyes once more of the son and said, "My time here has ended, and yours is to begin. Our house will fall into your reign before this year finds its end." Horus-Salah gasped. A flash went through his mind, how sacrilegious. It was almost like Allah saying he wasn't going be around anymore.

Horus-Salah looked back into the eyes and asked, "Father, is it an illness that has no cure?"

The old man's lips neither moved, but the words breathed out, "Cancer has no friends." With that, he turned and almost mystically was sitting behind the desk once more, long before Horus-Salah had managed to stabilize his canes to support his retreat to the chair. Once more, the old man looked hard into the eyes of his son and said, "As the ruler and the law of this clan, my word is your command."

Horus-Salah said, "Your wishes are mine to obey."

The senior continued, "You must wed before I leave, and preferably if it is the will of Allah, she will bear the fruit of this next generation that is being blessed by your return."

All the room could hear was a gasp, and then a rattling that sounded like the caving in of life itself. Of course, it came from Horus-Salah's body. He neither stooped nor flinched, but remained motionless as though he had been turned into stone. His father stared relentlessly at the agony produced by his request.

robert f. edwards

From somewhere deep within, and courage mustered through the conflicts of war and agony and despair, Horus-Salah found a voice that had never been uttered in this room before. It filled his lungs and his mind, and his eyes looked directly into the coldness of the gaze before him. "Your wish is my command, but my ability is limited to a mortal. I have no way of bringing your wishes to fulfillment, for both our pledges to Anastasia are unobtainable. Her whereabouts are unknown."

The old man looked frail and for the first time Horus-Salah actually saw the penetration of illness that had claimed the victory of death over life. The only reply was, "Your faith is Muslim. Mohammad, the Prophet of Islam provides you the answer. Take another, for you are entitled to three." The hand waved; there was nothing to be added.

Horus-Salah moved his broken body up from the chair. His two canes gave him the support to leave the room. He looked at the cold eyes behind the desk as he turned to leave the room, and knew there was nothing he could say, or do, other than obey.

He believed, up until this moment, that all that he had endured, not only was the will of Allah, but the blessing of Allah, that once again he would unite with his beloved. The miraculous intervention of Herr Surgeon General who had put together a mangled body, this must be some reward from Allah. 'How could this possibly be, this irony, this games of the gods being played against me, a mere mortal?'

He made his way back, crippled now in body and spirit, to his quarters. His servant received him with a glance, knowing that a tragedy far greater than he had witnessed before, was now upon his master. He helped his master back into the chair, and begged to assist him. Horus-Salah waved his hand, like his lord and master had done shortly before and uttered the words, "I must have my solitude."

His trusted male servant departed, leaving the broken form of humanity placed in the chair. As the day ended and dusk approached, Horus-Salah sat, not even adjusting his

River of Life

uniform. It was as though a bronze statue of a military officer sat in remembrance of these tragic events that the years of this decade had produced.

Dusk gave way to the night, and still he sat in the darkness. The servant observed through the peephole with surveillance, not to disturb his master unless it was requested, and still Horus-Salah sat. He sat motionless and at times, the servant that observed from a distance and elusive of view, thought that his master had fallen into slumber, at last relieved of his agony through sleep.

This was not the case. As the stars gave illumination to the skies and the small ticking so close to his heart added a false security, the little hands endlessly moving second by second, minute by minute, saw the bewitching hour of twelve and the beginning of a new day, and still Horus-Salah sat. He sat motionless and at times, the servants that had now taken up the watch from afar, feared that something drastic had happened to their master. He neither moved, nor stirred, nor showed any form of life whatsoever, as the hours melted from one day into the next. It was the beginning of the breaking of Ra's demand for the skies once more and still their master had not moved throughout the night. He sat erect, staring into oblivion.

However, for Horus it had not been a vigil of blankness. With an intense concentration of all the powers of his mind, he knew he had to overcome many contentious issues and hurdles. To accept the word of Allah, and his ways, to question his father's rule, these thoughts whirled around him throughout the long night. He examined his mind as one would a library, segregating the books of reference from the books of fantasy, the works of art versus the works of labor.

He had learned a great deal through his short years. Above all, he was a servant to his master and his master's house. This had been from the beginning of time, and would continue until the end of his time. He believed in what he had been taught and taught to believe in what he knew. So he had divided, then subdivided, and redefined until each priority

271

had its own preference in the list of events that must take place. He was an obedient servant in the house of his family. But soon, he would have to be the master that preserved this ancient tradition of his family, which dated back to the pharaohs.

He had divided it into two major categories. His first priority; to find his beloved Anastasia at all costs, and time was not his friend but his enemy. From the very beginning to their last moments, Anastasia had always been his guiding light, his force, his vision, and his purpose of life. She had the answers and she was sure-footed with her decisions. If he was to rule his house with any rewards or acknowledgement from history, it was vital that he must have Anastasia to rule beside him.

It did not matter that he was Moslem, or she was Christian. Or he called Mohammed his spiritual force, Allah; or she called hers God, or the universe above. She must be his equal and his queen in the land of the pharaohs. She must share his life, to aid and assist the family of the past and to preserve its place in the future. He resolved this was his main priority.

His second was more questionable than the first. Until his father's last meeting, he had always assumed that he and Anastasia would spend their lives together. They would share their childhood playground in Luxor, and raise their children as they had done, romping through the gardens, playing with the nannies, and maybe even the secret of the Tomb of the Cat.

But now, now, he would rule. He would be the master of the house and have all the responsibilities that came with it. He had never thought about this until now, and in deep penetration of thought, he asked the question of ' Why?' knowing in his heart that he was not suited. He had never been suited for leadership. It had always been Anastasia that had broken the trail that led him forward. He had always thought that in his fantasy world that someday, his younger sister would marry, and her husband would be the favorite son of his father, and that he would rule. Horus-Salah believed that he

River of Life

and Anastasia would live at Luxor and only periodically be forced back to Cairo to endure the pompous splendor of the domain. But that they would soon return back to continue their childlike life in the land and the place he loved so dearly.

But now, without the soul and body that ruled his heart, he would also be burdened with the responsibility of ruling a house whose history was as long as the Nile. As he sat and played the moves from one to the other in his mind, it gave way to a plan. If nothing more or less, the years at Cambridge, the discipline of the Military, and the horrors of war that focused in the haunted world of reality and perseverance of existence, it was his obligation to his ancestors as well as his father to carry the mantle to the next generation.

He swore to the god of whom he was named, "Horus, almighty Horus, I give this mantle of power to the next generation I produce as soon as their limbs are strong enough to support the weight and their mind is quick enough to make the decisions. I will pass this rule that I have to endure over to one that is qualified which comes from my groin the first moment I can."

Ra had found that the darkness had given way to his command of the sky, and though most still were in slumber, Horus-Salah broke his long stay in solitude, and clapped his hands. Obediently, one of the servants appeared and not even looking at him, Horus-Salah said, "Summons the senior servant of my father at once."

The servant bowed and as his head faced the floor, he muttered in a voice, "It is early, Master."

The reply was, "I asked not for the time." The servant bowed back out through the door and within a span of less than half the hour, both men appeared once more.

The senior servant of his father bowed, not as deep or reverently, but acknowledged Horus-Salah's place and requested, "What do you wish of me?", with the absence of 'Master'.

"I command you to give me audience with my father as quickly as possible. Go and do my bidding." The servant looked puzzled for a moment; for he had never heard the young Horus-Salah speak with such command. Both servants bowed deeper than before, as the two men made their way backwards through the opening of the door.

Horus-Salah clapped once more and by this time, all his male servants had been awakened, ready for his commands. He bathed and put on the traditional galabya and his finest of slippers. He looked like the heir- apparent that he would soon be.

By mid morning, his father's master servant returned and said, "My Master requests your presence now," not with a sneer but with an obvious preference of who he wished to serve. Horus-Salah, still with crutches but in his full Egyptian appearance, followed closely behind the servant through the corridors of the great estate.

As the servant acknowledged his presence at the great door, the door opened and this time, Horus-Salah hobbled forward, up into the desk which commanded the ruler of the family. He looked at his father and for a moment reflected these two thoughts that flashed together: One, this man was ill. He was dying. The other was I must not retreat from my decision of the night.

He stood before his father and the hand waved for him to sit. However this time, it went disobeyed. Horus-Salah stood, leaning his full support on his canes. He stared down into the eyes that penetrated his soul. As he stood and his arms adjusted to the full weight, he heard the faint ticking of his beloved watch by his heart. From his soul came a loud clear tone as his lungs filled with air, then delivered their message.

His eyes never left the relentless glare of his father. He started, "A man's word is all that he has, and this is law. When he breaks his word, there is no law that he has for himself, or others. I ask you to honor your word and your consent to my beloved Anastasia". Horus-Salah continued, asking his father to insure that all the knowledge that he had in his possession be shared equally, from this day forth, as the law of honor. "For your laws are my laws and I will honor your word,

River of Life

if you will honor my request? I have said it, let it be acknowledged."

The old man stared at his son and for the first time in their lives, he looked up by force and the lips never moved, but his voice was clear and loud. "It has been said. Let it be done. We rule equally from this day forth."

And with that, he clapped his hands and his senior servant came into the room. The old man got up and for the first time Horus-Salah saw how feeble his father was. He walked over to his son and stood beside him. The senior servant stood before them and the old man looked into the eyes of his beloved servant and said, "You see two of us. We both rule from this day forth as one. We are equal to all that this house commands. Let the word go forth and let the law prevail. "

The servant was bewildered, but then the hand that had ruled the house for so long passed its familiar wave, and the servant bowed his way out of their presence. The two that had a common blood between them looked once more into each other's eyes and Horus-Salah said, "I am grateful for your acceptance and knowledge of my request. I must now attend, with all the powers of our house, to find my beloved."

In a voice as light as the winds of the day, he heard his father's voice, "Your rule has started. Be wise 'til its end." The hand moved in its familiar pattern, and Horus-Salah pivoted on his canes and hobbled through the door as it opened to receive his exit.

Once back in his own quarters at the other wing of the mansion, he summoned his trusted servant and said, "Send the word out that I want to find my beloved, Anastasia. Start with my command to my father's senior servant. Get me a report this afternoon on the progress to succeed in my request. Let it be said, Let it be done."

His devoted servant bowed graciously, and left by backing out through the doorway. Horus-Salah then summoned his other servants and requested that a bath and fresh linen be put out, after a small rest in the afternoon. He had forgotten when he had taken on nourishment, but the nourishment of the soul was far more rewarding than feasting the body. He allowed his wrecked body to have a short period of rest to repair. At least, he could endure the inconvenience for a matter of hours that his body demanded.

Shortly after four in the afternoon, his trusted servant entered his private quarters asking, "Master, would you be prepared to give further instructions to those that request them at this time?"

Without hesitation, Horus-Salah said, "Bring them forth."

Though he did not sit in the office that he would inherit shortly, he sat regally in his small library. The first to enter was his father's most trusted servant. This time he bowed with the same respect that he had shown Horus-Salah's father for all the years that they had been together. Accompanying him was a group of people, including a high ranking British officer. As the number totaled higher than the seats that would accommodate all, the rank and file took place. The British officer, being superior, took center stage in front of Horus-Salah, while the senior servant stood waiting for direction. Horus-Salah's eyes moved him to sit next to the British officer, and his aide on the other side. The rest standing found their pecking order.

Once the audience was in place, Horus-Salah made his request, simple and plain, "Your time is short and my request is but one. Find Anastasia, Countess of Poland. I have no further instructions, but -Succeed."

The first to address the issue was the Colonel of the British Army by saying, "Hear now, my dear chap". With a flash of anger that only his father had mastered over the years, Horus-Salah stared the British officer down.

His trusted servant said, "You will call him Regent, Sir." The British officer turned to the subordinate beside him with an air of dismay and asked, "Pardon?"

The senior servant said, "If your hearing is impaired, leave the room. You are of no further service to us."

Suddenly, the British officer became part of the team that was organized to fulfill the request. It was his father's senior

River of Life

servant that explained the complexity of what had already transpired in the few hours that he had now become the shadow of his father's reign. He would command all that came in his midst, so they asked to verify the time line that was permitted.

Horus-Salah without hesitation responded, "The moon is full but once a month. You have until then." The servants stood and bowed deeply. The British officer sat, befuddled until Horus-Salah's servant nudged him from a bowed position. They left the room with the British officer confused in the assignment, but all others focused on achieving the results. It was the first command of the new Regent of the family. It would not be the last.

The old man leaned his weary body against the embankment of the narrow path that dominated its presence over the Valley of the Kings. He was well past the halfway mark of his destination. He pulled a blanket around his shoulders and held tightly onto the walking stick that he had acquired. He leaned on it, regressing back in thought to when all that would support his weight were two sticks, as his broken limbs waited to heal, before he could stand erect without the support.

Today, age was the deterrent. His old body, weary and tired as well as being decrepit, hobbled along the paths. Once more, he relied on support of another form than his. As his back leaned against the wall of granite and dirt that embodiment the great land of Egypt, his eyes found the life giving source and the moments of contentment that he experienced throughout his life.

It was dark, only a black line of ink between the other shades of darkness, but there was no mistake to his mind; it was his beloved Nile, the god-giving source for all Egyptians. Every Egyptian that hugged its bank had the Nile flow through their veins. All living things attributed their existence

robert f. edwards

to the water of life. Mother Nature blessed its inhabitants and replenished their food supply, year after year by this stream of life.

He gazed down upon it, fixated in the darkness as if it might have been the first time he saw it. But no, it was as much of his body and mind as those that had captured and held his soul. Tonight was no different, for his commitment and love of this country of his ancestors, of the gods that they loved and paid homage to, for he was one of them, an Egyptian.

His eyes traced the shadows of Luxor and a faint smile drifted across the withered face. He knew the buildings and temples just like one would find on a monopoly board in his mind, even though the darkness held them back in the shadows. There was the odd flicker of light from some being unable to find the peace of the darkness and the rest of the night.

"Not too long", he thought, "not too long", for he felt , like so many years of his life, the small ticking close to his heart, of his beloved. "It is time to move. I must move on. I must complete my journey." And once more he looked up into the heavens and the multitude of stars greeted him as though they waited for his acknowledgement.

He pushed with all his strength away from the embankment, as his body once more addressed the trail ahead. His old hands grasped tightly on the staff of the walking stick. He leaned into it for support, inch by inch, to his destination.

Yes, his destination with Anastasia, his beloved. Tonight, today, tomorrow, when Allah will forgive him and release him of this burden of life, he would be with his beloved once more. He had never slackened or wavered in his conviction. Tonight was no different as he trudged step by step towards his destination, the tomb of the mummy of the cat.

River of Life

CHAPTER 20

 The Huns, the Germans, the Nazis had started World War II. They had launched a major assault against the defenses of Poland. The world would record this moment, but for those that were present and accounted for, there had never been anything like it. The Polish army, though well equipped and prepared, was no match for the new game of war, for the speed, like lighting striking everything it touched. Like the precision of a fine orchestra performing its movements. The war machine surged forward and broke the lines and smashed the resistance of the Polish forces.

It was not days, or weeks, but hours that reports of total devastation had taken place. It was like a flood, that no matter how well prepared or how much resistance it was swept away by the force of the German divisions, even in more remote areas of which the Count's estate was.

By the third day of the assault on Poland, a German staff car rolled up the majestic driveway that led to the foyer of Anastasia's home. It was none other than Herr General Hahn's staff car that pulled up. The doors were quickly opened, and Herr General had got out. By this time, the General's staff greeted him as if they were, and had always been the occupants at the manor. The General quickly demanded that all of the important occupants of the building be assembled.

The Countess and her immediate staff were hastily brought into the parlor. Though it was midday, and both Anastasia and her mother were preparing their duties, all were abruptly interrupted. Though the butler was embarrassed, he still made it known that it was a demand, rather than a request, that she drop everything to meet the Herr General in the parlor.

279

robert f. edwards

When the two women met as they were going down the hallway, they both had a bewildered look. Anastasia asked, "What is going on, Mother?"

The Countess replied, "We will find out very shortly."

With that, they entered the parlor. The German officers, along with their General, quickly clicked their heels and greeted the Countess and her daughter. After small formal greetings were exchanged, the General advised the Countess and Anastasia that he would be taking up quarters with his staff, and that they were now being occupied, by direction of the Father-land and the .

The Countess smiled with all of the elegance of her station, "We would be most happy to accommodate your request, but would you be so kind to advise us as to how many members there are, so my staff could prepare for the accommodations that you wish and in which quarters shall be taken by the rank and file."

The General smiled at her formal aristocratic behaviour, "You do not understand Herr Countess. We will tell *you* where you will be staying. My officers and I will choose the accommodations we want, and you will do what we ask, or we will tell you what you will be doing later. Do you understand?"

Both the Countess and Anastasia were completely taken aback. First of all, they have never been spoken to in such a manner, and secondly, they were bewildered at what was happening. The Countess straightened her shoulders back, and held her head high, and in a firm strong voice demanded, "Are you implying that we are prisoners of war?"

The Herr General looked at both of them, and then smiled, "I was trying to be less direct." With that, the two knew what fate had happened to Poland, and now to their household. Then, like a flash of light their house had been taken over. The General and his chief of staff were escorted from room to room, which they designated amongst themselves. He had chosen personally the Count's suite and had taken over his study. The other rooms were designated to offi-

280

River of Life

cers according to their rank and their importance to Herr General.

Before an hour had found its distance in time, the Countess and Anastasia were reduced down to quarters of the servants. The whole house was in panic but not disarray. The Germans had not only taken over the manor but also the administrating. There were no exceptions, whether it was the butler, to the chauffer, or the head-mistress, to the servants in the kitchen; their duties were specifically advised, and precisely given, as to what was expected of them now, under the new man, Herr General. Dinner would be served at a certain time, the wines would be German whites, the food be would of a certain quality. And on and on it went, the details that were minute but precise, and without flexibility.

That evening, sitting in the dining-room, the atmosphere was absolutely like nothing they had ever felt before. Both Anastasia and the Countess were told to dress formally for dinner, and to be punctual at the dinner hour. The General and his officers sat in their dress uniforms of evening attire. It was a formal dinner, and one that Anastasia and the Countess would never forget, as long as they both lived.

The evening progressed uncomfortably for the two feminine participants. Conversation was stilted, in this mockery of a formal get- together. Discussions of interesting subjects, anything from Vogner to the Arts, continued as the officers induced their prisoners of war into a charade of comfort of the aristocrats. Neither Anastasia nor the Countess could distinguish whether they were sincere, or merely mocking the standard of their society.

Although the general and his officers tried to be the epitome of gentlemen of noble birth, there was no mistaking that they were professional solider. Their careers were represented by the ranks that they held. They were part of the past, and now the present of the war machines of mankind. The evening past without further incident, except for the coldness of disillusionment and disbelief that this was happening to Anastasia and the Countess. They were excused.

robert f. edwards

As the evening drew its shadows on the closure of the night, they found refuge. It was a harsh reality when they returned to the quarters that were now assigned to them by the General's staff. It was the modest room of the governess that Anastasia and her beloved shared. The head mistress of the servants quickly abandoned her quarters for the Countess. The Countess and Anastasia exchanged kisses on the cheek and wished each other an evening of a lasting memory. The days that followed were like a storm that showed no mercy or quarter for those that were present and accounted.

There was a tightening of security around what had become the command post of operations directly under the General's command. Staff cars and military vehicles came and went, bringing new information of the collapse and complete unconditional surrender of Poland. The main rooms that were not designated for pleasure and comfort of the General and his commanding staff, were turned into map rooms and command centres for planning strategic maneuvers.

All the staff had to be accounted for in the morning hours, and again in the retiring hours. The grounds, which had for generations been enjoyed for recreation, were now sealed off by sentries. The entrance was monitored for any form of movement, including the Nazi army itself. Security was tight. Even the staff that had been trained in the ways of obedience had never seen, nor could comprehend such strict discipline.

It was on one of these days, during the raging turbulence of adjustment, that Anastasia and the Countess, accompanied by Nan were granted permission to walk the grounds for an outing. As they strolled along familiar paths that led through the gardens that were still being cared for by the head gardener, they nodded from a distance to what used be their employees, their servants.

Nan was the first one to bring the subject up. "My dearest, my cherished and beloved Anastasia and oh, madam Countess, you are my family, and I am as part of your welfare, as my soul is to my body. We are all in great danger, but I fear

River of Life

that you two are in the greater. With the little bit of information that I have gathered in these past days, I fear our army has been defeated. What is worse, we are under the complete control of the Nazi army, at their very whims and wishes. I pray each night; your safety is my greatest concern."

The Countess nodded in understanding, Anastasia agreed, but asked, "What can be done?"

The older woman of the three turned and said, "I have a plan. My sister is less than sixty kilometers away, as you well know. Though her home and the village are modest, it is out of the way, and has no purpose in the great scheme of conquest. I don't believe the Germans will let it go undisturbed. However, I believe that you can escape into the common denominator, if I may say so?"

"Yes, yes, you may say so, "the Countess said with a smile of a true aristocrat." We are all equal in the eyes of God, you know."

Nan once more smiled. "And some to me are more precious than others."

Anastasia laughed, nervously but still in a firm commitment of being herself. "Well Nan, what is the plan?" she asked in her natural way of getting to the point.

"I will send a message to my sister tonight, telling her to expect two women from a distance family relative, hoping to stay with her and her husband. In turn, she will forward a message telling me when two men will arrive and escort you to their home. We will plan it under the cover of utmost security and only others that I trust, will share."

The Countess looked bewildered at first. Anastasia shrugged her shoulders and asked, "Well, once we get to your sister's place, what are we to do?"

Without any hesitation Nan said," Go into hiding, become scarce, become part of the local landscape, and fear for your lives." The last statement sent a cold shudder down the back of the two other women. Nan was definitely more experienced in the world, in day-to-day living, more than either one was aware. Their trust was in her complete.

'Ah,' Anastasia asked herself, 'where is Horus-Salah when I need him so greatly.' Her mother was also thinking of the Count, and what has happened to him.

River of Life

CHAPTER 21

 The trail towards the Valley of the Kings did not change, only the man that walked along it once more. As Horus-Salah gazed across the blue line of life that separated the shorelines, he saw the great Temple of Karnak, and once again he found peace in his soul. As he made his way down his private trail to the tomb that housed the mummy and the treasures of his mind, all had remained as they were the last time he had entered; to the small candles that he and Anastasia had placed in their childhood.

Once more, he reached into the pocket of his galabya and with the reverence and devotion that one would touch a holy sepulcher; he pulled out his beloved watch and placed it on the tomb of the mummy. He sat at the entrance gazing at the Nile, the water of life of his people and of their existence. He watched the feluccas as their tiny sails, like white doves flew across benevolent blue sky. He found peace. He was at the place where his soul would find its rest in this turbulent land; in this planet that had found a new pestilent of Europe that was spreading its venom and its diabolical agenda throughout the world.

After he did his ritual of checking and digesting the minutest detail of this tomb of sanctuaries and memories, he positioned himself once more near the entrance. But, far enough to one side so the mystical body of Anastasia was sitting beside him, as they had done so many times before. He gazed down into the valley and then across the long strip of blue to Luxor. Though his mind raced back and forth in time from the present to the past, his soul found inner comfort against his great loss. The longing to know what had happened to the shadow that in his mind sat beside him was too great to bear.

He continued looking out of the entrance, with-out seeing. Like so many times before, he made his ritual as Ra

robert f. edwards

" He watched the feluccas as their tiny sails,... "

Original artwork, acrylic   Robert F. Edwards
2006

River of Life

abandoned the skies and the shadows of darkness started to fall over the Valley of the Kings. Like a thousand times or more before, he made his way back to the estate.

Progress on the wing that optimistically he still believed would be his and Anastasia's was nearing completion, and all remained as it had in his childhood. In the evenings, after the formal meal of the day, many times he would retire with his nanny into the private courtyard and listen to the stories of the nanny's events with her beloved children. Sometimes, his nanny would tell stories of past events that involved him and Anastasia that would recapture the moments that he treasured so much. Other times, she would tell stories or events that Anastasia's nanny had told her in confidence of Anastasia's childhood before they had come to Egypt.

As the months vanished and the rituals became traditions, he continued asking questions of Anastasia's past that he knew nothing about. It did not matter whether his dear nanny stretched her imagination or her visions into the dreams that he wished to hear. She soothed his soul and calmed his mind, and let his body grow strong with its youth. She was the only medicine that he required to endure his loneliness, his despair, and his lack of knowledge of his beloved.

The letters from his mother continued to come as they had done before and unfortunately for the world, the small letters told graphically of the world of despair. The world of order had been lost. The world of royalty and monarchs that ruled from one dynasty to another was uprooted. This madman that possessed the winds of change would be nothing more than a commoner in the barren lands that inhabit the world.

The names in the letters continually surfaced as Adolph Hitler, Mussolini, Lenin, Stalin, and the Emperor of Japan. Ah, yes, the Asian contingency had now joined force with the madness of Europe. The world was infested. On the other side of the chessboard of life were the names of Winston Churchill, Roosevelt, de Gaulle, and a handful of others. The demarca-

robert f. edwards

tion line of madness had been erased and the blood lust of the world ran parallel with madness of these newfound diabolical leaders, each one screaming that they were the founders and the way of the future. And if they were, then maybe Mars was the planet known as the Red Planet, but the Earth would change its color too with the blood of life. He continued receiving letters and this coexistence with his past to keep abreast of what was prevailing in the future.

Another calendar year had drifted and the time had now ventured past its beginning of the forties. January 1, 1942 came and the only celebration Horus-Salah held was to the temple of the mummy cat. He had prayed to all the gods of the Old Kingdom, the New Kingdom, and the Christian Kingdom, and the Moslem. For all of them, he believed, was witnessing this plague, this byproduct of the Industrial Revolution, the machines of war that destroyed those that wished to survive for another day.

So, Horus-Salah, in his cocoon away from the diabolical movements of the world, lived out his days, morning till dusk and was fed morsels of information from his mother's couriers. By March, he had received word that the Americans had now entered the war on a full time basis rather than a monetary one, and that Singapore, the British fortress of Asia, had fallen to the Japanese. He wondered how much more the world could bear before the decisions of historians could be made, as he continued with his disturbed tranquility.

It wasn't until a day late in March, like so many others that had gone before them; however this one was going to make a difference in his life. For upon returning from his usual sabbatical to pay homage to his temple sanctuary, he was greeted by his servant as usual, but this time again, the servant said that there was a leading servant from Cairo that wished his presence. As he entered into his study to receive the servant, a pain of anxiety grasped Horus-Salah and déjà vu flashed before his eyes. No, it was not his father's senior servant, but it was definitely from his father's servant ranks. And again, the envelope that marked his father's wishes was

River of Life

presented to him. He dismissed the servant and quickly opened the envelope. As usual, the shortness expressed the demand: "Return to Cairo now." At least, in his flustered state, it wasn't 'at once'; therefore, it could not have been too urgent.

Within the next week, he prepared for departure and proceeded down the Nile as he had done most of is life. His thoughts were neither pleasant nor forlorn. His mind was like a vacuum, void in space, without thought. Once he returned to Cairo and the house that possessed the power of his dynasty, he was greeted. And once again, he was joyous to see his mother and his sister. They made up for the loss of his beloved nanny, who remained in Luxor.

The next day, his father summoned him for an audience. He made his way down the corridors that were familiar and the rituals that took place. The aged figure that sat behind the desk with the eyes that penetrated far inward and beyond, looked directly at him. "The lands of your ancestors are now in danger. You will join our military forces and aid and assist where possible. Do your house proud."

Within the balance of the month, Horus-Salah had received the rank of colonel in the Egyptian Army. He commanded a force that was a challenge to his rank. It was a ragtag assembly of an army under the direct command of the British. His 'Egyptian Army' was nothing more than what the British had mustered under their heavy domain of the Empire. There was Australian Divisions and New Zealand's. It was a collection of a global group gathered under the British feeble hands throughout the world. Never had Horus-Salah felt the need for the stiff upper lip of the defeated, demoralized British than he did now. They were strong and determined, as it may be a matter of moments before the tide that swept their Empire into shambles would go back out and they would command the high seas, and the sun would never set on the Empire again.

By June, Horus-Salah and his Egyptian Army, along with the Australians, were bracing themselves for the first assault

robert f. edwards

of a new German general, Rommel. The British had pinned their hopes on the new tanks of the U.S., but they were quickly dashed. The quick retreat to El Alamein was their first taste of the true German panther tanks devastation and the Germans agenda. Rommel had said that he would be in the Valley of the Nile shortly, and every Egyptian was beginning to feel that it was more than just a German wish. It would be the German reality. The German High Command almost had the agenda complete by having their armies moving through the Middle East, down through Syria and Jordan to meet the advancing African Corp of Rommel coming up through Alexandria to the Suez Canal. Cairo would be the plum that they would pluck from the tree. There would be no stopping them. Once this was accomplished, they could unite not only the vast oil fields of the Middle East along with their newly conquered Ukraine supply lines, but it would open up the Suez Canal to their allies in the Asia Theater. The Master Plan was fast becoming the vision of the victors and the defeated.

At the time neither Horus-Salah nor a good many people throughout the theater knew that by some miraculous justice of life were the skies that the "Luftwaffe" had dominated, whether it is in Britain or in the Mediterranean, were slowly giving up their supremacy. The supply lines of the German African Corp that were the life supports of a modern army were being sunk systematically. It was said that this modern war moved not on its belly, but on petrol. With the heavy loss of the tanker ships, Rommel knew that it would be petrol for his army that would be the winning or losing of this theater.

But for Horus-Salah, it was one day after another in a uniform and a cause that fitted neither well. It was not the war. It was not the battle. It was not even the generals. It was like Montgomery and Rommel were two chess masters playing their strategy out on the greatest chessboard of the war. History would record these great battles that were fought, for it was truly war. It was not the massacres and the diabolical events that had already spread their rumors throughout the world of human citizens taking the toll of carnage. This was

290

River of Life

war of generals, strategy, and maneuverability. If one was not the pawn, one might have admired the ingenious maneuvers and the shifting of the lines.

Unfortunately for Horus-Salah and the Egyptian participants in this theater of war, they were disposable and next in line were the Australians and the other Allies of the Commonwealth. Like the Italians to the Germans, these disposable pawns were a mere sacrifice to test the strength of the opponent, not to penetrate.

The casualties, whether it is on a reconnaissance or an assault, were always high. In these treacherous months, Horus-Salah was always in the frontlines of the great tank and artillery battles of this vast plain. It was on one of these assaults that he was driving in his armored vehicle with his trustee aides and anti-aircraft gun mounted at the back, that his vehicle took direct motor shell. It exploded like a great ball of fire and both the driver and the artillery henchman were dismembered and scattered on the sands as they landed in pieces.

It was only because Horus-Salah was standing on the seat trying to get a bearing on the line of assault that was thrown clear as the mortar hit. However, he did not escape the treachery of this modern day war. The shrapnel had penetrated deep into his back and shattered one of his legs. As he lay there unconscious, the battle around him moved back and forth, and with dust the desert buried many of its horrors.

It was long after the battle ceased and the tanks retreated back along their designated lines that the German patrols went out to assess the carnage. It was one of these patrols that were picking up the wounded and the remains of the dead, whether they are German or others that they came across Horus-Salah's mangled body pouring its life-giving blood into the sands. A medic came over and examined the face down Horus-Salah, only to utter, "Herr, Herr, now." A stretcher carried the unconscious remains of Horus-Salah back to the field hospital.

robert f. edwards

By some miraculous God above, Horus-Salah was still alive, barely but alive. And due to his rank, the Germans received him as a priority of wounded. He was placed on the operating table and a captain and medical crew started to assess the damage of this broken body. Once stripped of its military hardware and rank, Horus-Salah lay naked upon a slab, as almost a cadaver with a shallow movement in his ribcage.

The Herr Captain was starting to perform the surgery but at once, there was a clicking of heels and a salute and a harmonious "Hail, Hitler!" Herr Surgeon Colonel of the medical force had entered into the field hospital to inspect the carnage of the battle of that day. As he walked through with the arrogance of a Persian, he happened to notice a captain standing at attention. After a small discussion of what had transpired, the captain informed him that this was a Colonel of the Egyptian Army that had received severe wounds both to his legs and the more serious one to his back.

The Herr Surgeon Colonel ground his teeth and said, "Herr Captain, ah, Head Field Surgeon no, you are Herr Dum Kopf, the butcher. You have no skill other than the sausage maker's son." With a wave of his hand, he immediately dressed for surgery. It was said, even in Berlin, that Herr General was one of the most brilliant surgeons and professors of surgery in the highest ranks of the universities of Berlin. However, even greatness has a falling out with madness, as unfavourable reports had made their way to Hitler's inner circle. Herr General, despite his great skills, had been delegated to a mere field hospital outside of El Alamein.

He was far too valuable and recognized at this point to be disregarded entirely. To be posted out in a field operation would be enough to signify the fierce displeasure with his lack of devotion. But now, his true love, his love of his profession, his skill as a surgeon and his knowledge as a professor was going to show these butchers of medicine how surgeons performed miracles. He looked up through the mask and said to Herr Captain, "Pay attention to what a scalpel is rather than the butcher's blade."

River of Life

With this, he opened up the back of Horus-Salah. He penetrated through the back skin decisively and with the assistants helping him, he skillfully, with the art that had been given him, started to operate. He removed the shrapnel that was so close to the spinal column. He delicately separated the shattered vertebrae and opened up Horus-Salah's hip and removed a part of the thigh to graft in a bone bridge. After he was finished, he looked up and said, "Your lesson is over for today. Look after him. I will perform your next lesson in more suitable conditions. Have him transported to a proper medical service NOW."

And with that, the bloody garments that bore Horus-Salah's stains were removed and Herr General walked out of the field hospital. There was a silence as the busy bees preserving life continued to work on the carnage of the day's events.

The days that followed were not remembered by Horus-Salah nor even recorded by anyone that he knew. It was just in the German records. This Egyptian officer received surgery on four different occasions. And as the battles of discrimination and territory fluctuated daily by the skills of the field marshals of opposing forces, Horus-Salah drifted in and out of consciousness. His young body and the skills of a German professor breathed back the soul into the torn body of Horus-Salah. He was moved more than once, from the field hospital into more permanent in Libya, where high-ranking German officers were convalescing from their experiences of the theater that they had given their body parts to.

It was on one of these occasions that Herr General Surgeon of the German Army came in to see his work once more. Horus-Salah was not walking, but he was alive and gaining strength. His consciousness had returned weeks before and his strength was gathering momentum continuously. As Herr Surgeon General stood at the end of the bed accompanied by a small orchestra of other surgeons, he had them gather around in silence. Horus-Salah looked up at the Herr Surgeon General and with the greetings of the day, Herr Surgeon Gen-

293

eral said, "I have not come to visit, but to examine my work and skill, and explain to these butchers of the African Corps that there is more to surgery than carving up human flesh."

He went into elaborate detail of the three major operations that he had performed personally on Horus-Salah, and what the results were. The company of surgeons stood as if they were raw recruits in their first indoctrination of a military life. Horus-Salah felt more like a specimen than a human being. When the examination was completed, the Herr Surgeon General said to the rest, "Dismissed."

To Horus-Salah, he smiled and said, "With my skill and your youth, we will have you back together in no time." Clicking his heels, he walked out as quickly as he had entered. As Horus-Salah gained momentum and strength, his body mended under the disciplined efficiency of the Medical Corps, it was not too long before the better part of three months had put Horus-Salah in a wheelchair and his mangled legs were now showing signs that they soon might welcome the support of the rest of his body.

Horus-Salah was gathering a working knowledge of the German language, but was still unable to determine between the High German and the Lower. As he gained recognition and admiration from the orderlies and nursing staff, he had requested anything that was left of his belongings from the moment of impact so many months before. They all seemed to be relatively evasive and on one gloomy day, of course, the SS returned.

In his black uniform and his black attitude, the Gestapo asked more questions and implied that though Herr Surgeon General had put him back together, that the Gestapo had ways of dismantling him with more unpleasantness than what he had experienced in the mere battles of war. Horus-Salah had nothing to add to their conversation or their knowledge other than his rank and his serial number with his position in the Egyptian Army and the Allied Forces.

Many weeks later, Herr Surgeon General returned, but this time with a smaller man beside him bearing the rank of

River of Life

major. He looked out of place in the uniform that he wore just as the Herr Surgeon General looked more in uniform in his surgical gown than in his military tunic. Horus-Salah looked at the two gentlemen bewildered and with a few snaps of command from Herr Surgeon General, they were in isolation.

At last, the one familiar face of Herr Surgeon General smiled and said, "Well, you are a remarkable patient. You not only respond to my skill, but your body responds to its environment. I understand that you want to know where your things are and no one has given you the answers."

Surprised by his knowledge, Horus-Salah replied, "Yah, Herr Surgeon General."

Then, Herr Surgeon General replied, "Is there one particular item that you wish to know where it is or the contents?" Horus-Salah looked deep into this general's eyes, not knowing whether to express his most inward wishes or to remain silent in the entombment of his agony. Although the face was stern and the voice demanding, Herr Surgeon General represented a benevolence that had rarely crossed Horus-Salah path in the last months.

Horus-Salah looked directly into Herr Surgeon General's eyes and said, "I have one item that is on my mind. It is my watch!"

Herr Surgeon General replied, "Yah, I told you," looking at the major that stood timidly beside him. "This is what this man wants." Horus-Salah felt paralyzed in both fear and anticipation of what would be answered next. The Herr Surgeon General said, "There were very little of value left to your wardrobe. However, this watch and your pistol, also a few other artifacts that belong to you were managed to be put aside. However, when I looked at your watch, it was not working. Just like you, it was broken. I want you to know that in this army, the African Corps there are not only soldiers, but skilled citizens of Germany, of the fatherland. This man, this Major, is civilized. He is like me, a fish out of water. We are citizens of the fatherland and he is a skilled goldsmith by his natural desires. His skills are like mine, wasted in this desert

295

robert f. edwards

well. However, upon examining your watch, I brought it to him to examine. We have the skills and the ability to fix these watches as good as any of the Swiss that put the movements together."

Now Horus-Salah froze as though he had seen a reincarnation of something more precious than his life. Maybe, just maybe, even more precious than his soul. His eyes expressed everything that was within him when the small Major produced the watch. Instead of reaching over and giving it to Horus-Salah, who sat in a wheelchair, he handed it to Herr Surgeon General.

With a quick snap, the face of the watch opened up and Herr Surgeon General quickly put it to his ear, and looked at his own wrist-piece and the movements then said, "Yah, you do good work, Herr Major." Then, he looked at Horus-Salah with the questions that one man has for another, and they became as one in thoughts. He closed the face of the watch, and rolled it over with the back held in his palm and said, "Yah, a fine piece of craftsmanship and what's more, a fine picture of Fraulein in its casing. You are an interesting person, Herr Colonel Horus-Salah," placing the watch in Horus-Salah's hands. With a smiled, he added, "Now that you both are back together in one piece, look after yourself for this is a treacherous time we live in." Both German officers clicked their heels and moved away.

Horus-Salah was white. Every drop of blood in his face had drained to accommodate the chambers of his heart that were pounding beyond belief of size and capability. His hands trembled as he held the watch, and tears rolled down his face uncontrollably. He remained in this hypnotic state for longer than he could remember or even comprehend. It was only when one of the nursing orderlies came to help him get back into the bed that made him aware of where he was. He quickly hid the watch under his shallow robes.

As the evening meal was placed before him and the return to a normal state of mind prevailed, he asked the nursing orderly if he could relieve himself, and a bedpan was given.

River of Life

Once allowed some privacy, he cautiously withdrew his treasure in life and examined it. Almost methodically his mind disciplined itself to open the face of the watch and to examine the little hands that had moved through time and now told him that his life was back once more in the sequence to the events. After he gained control both over his hands and his mind, he proceeded to place this precious part of his existence in his left hand, quickly sprung the back over.

Ah, almost like the breath of life itself, Anastasia's small picture was in place. His throat tightened, his lips quivered as though he was trying to stutter out some prayer. He reached inward with gentle fingers and traced over the back of the watch until he found the small spring that popped open the hidden compartment. My God, Allah, most merciful, most gracious of all, it was still there. She was still with him. He was still part of her and she was part of him.

As quickly as the discovery had been made, he closed it, and moved his precious heirloom back into the most secure place he could find. It was almost like an aphrodisiac or a tonic made of some mystical potion. His body soared in spirit and wild with recovery. He could not believe the force that energized within his very spirit, let alone his body which recovered almost miraculously.

It was fast approaching the end of another month and October had seen its best days behind it. Now came November with December following, and then January and another year. Would he be a prisoner of war? Was the Gestapo really as bad as he had been told? Will they discover his jewel of life and demand he give it to them? As the restless nights were filled with doubts and despair, the medication didn't help cloud their presence.

As the days came and moved on, Horus-Salah also moved forward. He was no longer confined to his bed or sitting beside it. He now joined the many other officers that had similar experiences of massive wounds or were recovering, waiting to be reassigned to their regiments. The majority of them were German officers. However, there was a small scattering of Ital-

297

robert f. edwards

ians and a few British that had survived being prisoners of war. He had to comment that he was both surprised and impressed in the way the German African Corps treated with equality their prisoners of war officers. They neither received any worse nor better than the Germans in their equal rank and file.

He was also gaining over these long months, not only the comprehension and understanding of the Germanic language but was actually able to carry on a reasonable conversation without the other one going, "Yah? Nah?" and looking bewildered. As his ability to pronounce and converse in this Nordic language grew, he gained respect from his fellow officers of all armies. Though he kept his distance, both in his thoughts and opinions, he was always welcome to join any group of any army.

Long before the acceptance, the Germans had issued him a military uniform of the British of a similar rank, distinguishing him as an officer. They treated these men as heroes of a campaign that all believed to be theirs and just fully right. He got to know the past of many of the officers, and a line that separated them more than nationality was their previous occupations. Over two-thirds were citizens that had different occupations far from a military one before this horror of conflict came into being. They had, at one time, normal lives in different regions of the hemisphere. The exception amongst themselves was the news elitist breed, the Air Force. Many of the convalescing pilots felt a superiority to their fellow ranking officers, with this new introduction in the armaments of war.

As this hospital was so far removed from the frontlines, they had little access to what the world outside their parameters was experiencing. However, in November, the casualties soared and many of the Italian and German men that had been convalescing were sent back on hospital ships to the fatherland or were reassigned to regiments that had suffered heavy officer losses.

For the prisoners of war that were convalescing, they had come to the point of managing for themselves. Any that were well enough were reassigned to prisoner of war camps. However, Horus-Salah was mustering between; he was neither an ally or well enough to attend a prisoner of war camp. As one of the old guards of the hospital, he witnessed the arrival of many mangled bodies of German soldiers, now outnumbering the enemy.

Horus-Salah had become an enigma in the ward, and was considered a mascot for the prisoners' side, and was allowed the freedom that most German officers were experiencing. Even the S.S. has ceased their visits and inquisitive behavior. However, there were a few stories that seeped from the mangled bodies of German officers of the African Corps. They were being badly attacked. Their frontlines were holding but not advancing. The counter-attacks were being stalemated, their supply lines cut. Their air supremacy of skies was gone, along with the aid from the shipping lanes. One did not have to be born a military man to know that the shifting of the tide had begun. Montgomery's steady army was moving its pieces strategically against the African Corps and Rommel was now playing defense.

Horus-Salah had no way of knowing what the outcome of his existence would be, and lived life on a day-to-day basis. As he waited for his body to find its own healing process and his mind to control his emotions, the battles of the two war lords of the desert fought to the end.

CHAPTER 22

 The events were heating up in Poland and Anastasia and her mother felt they could no longer bear the confinement in their own home. The uninvited German ' guests' were stretching their nerves to the breaking point. It was not until the following day that Nan passed a message on to the Countess. All is set, Sunday after church. So that evening, during another tedious meal with the General, one of the conversations that the Countess brought up for all to consider was faith. In her intricate way of bringing up both faith in oneself, and then delicately moving it to her religion, many of the officers practiced no particular faith, and the others were Protestant or Lutheran.

They were well aware that most of the Polish population was Catholic and so being men of religious backgrounds and upbringing, if nothing else, had an understanding of the Christian faith and those that found comfort in it, in their hours of need. It was the General that gave quarter without realizing the move had given a successful checkmate on the board of life.

The Countess proceeded in explaining the importance of cleansing her thoughts and her misdeeds in the confessional booth, as well as receiving the Holy Sacrament at the Mass. After agreeing, he had the capabilities of understanding such needs, he gave away to what he would later regret, and granted permission for both to go to the confessional and to Mass on Sunday.

Saturday came, and true to his word, the General permitted the Düsseldorf limousine with a captain replacing the chauffer, to go to the Church for confession. They were heavily escorted by military jeeps with a full compliment of guards, to make sure that all went according to the wishes and the re-

River of Life

quest of the Countess, and most importantly, the granting of the General.

The two women quickly entered the church and made their preparation for absolution. However, even the priest had heard their confessions was not aware that on either side of the confessional booth , while one was waiting to confess and the other was waiting for absolution ,they were quickly undoing the screws on the small mesh of the window. It was one of the few confessional stations that had the closure of doors, and as the screws became loose but not taken out totally, the absolution had been given and the preparation had been done.

The next day that followed was Sunday, and it now became a routine, each member that left the mansion had to have a pass, where they were going and when they would return. The Governess, along with the head Mistress, and others of the Mansion requested permission for going to Mass on Sunday. It was only Anastasia and the Countess that would have the escort in and out of the Church; however the plan was in total focus.

The Countess and Anastasia, dressed in their finest outer attire with hats that not only covered their brow, but had small veils, were first escorted into the Düsseldorf limo, and the Captain acknowledged politely their presence. Their reply was mute. As they sat in the backseat, they said nothing, but held hands. The long coats covered with heavy embroidery concealed most of their figures. Their hats covered the better part of their features. They did not sit in their regular places but sat very close to the appointed confessional booth.

The guards and sentries at the doors were both alert and attentive. As the priest and the alter boys celebrated the commencement of the Mass, the congregation rose to respect their presence. The Countess quickly slipped into the confessional booth quarters. Without any hesitation, the governess quickly slipped into the seat where the priest would be in the confessional. With a quick tapping on the door, both doors slid open, and the women looked at each other, no conversa-

301

robert f. edwards

tion was required. Quickly, the screws were taken out and the mesh was removed.

They immediately removed their outer attire, with the exception of their boots; and exchanged outfits. The priests' chamber was the only one that had vision to the outside. Quietly, the governess opened the window to the exterior view of the church. The congregation was still standing. She whispered, "Leave now."

The Countess quickly made her exit and returned to where the governess had been sitting. No one seemed to be the wiser. The exchange had taken place. The governess was now standing beside Anastasia, dressed as a replica of the Countess, only moments ago. As the celebration of the Holy Mass continued and the congregation once more stood up, it was Anastasia's turn to do the exchange. This being completed and the screws quickly tightened back into their proper places holding the mesh in, no one was the wiser that a switch had been done.

As the mass ended, the congregation started to disperse. The German officer with the sentry escorts took their stations outside. As two women in familiar attire left the church, the guards acknowledged them with a nod. They did not notice the change, nor anyone else as far as that goes.

Now Anastasia and the Countess left the Church with the rest of the commoners and shuffled through the crowd. Undetected, only for a minute and then two men came up and said in Polish, "My dearest Countess, would you follow me."

Anastasia and her mother followed without question. Only a few blocks away was a dilapidated old truck. Quickly the two men handed over a bundle, and said, "Please, would you change into these more common clothes of the street, before we commence our travels." They were dressed and spoke as the working class of Poland, in a rough dialect of the region that both Anastasia and the Countess would soon call their new domicile.

Inside the truck, the women stripped down, even to their knickers and replaced them with the coarse fabric of the working class. They felt the material scratching on their skin. The rough detergents were so foreign that even though the clinical smell was apparent of the cleanliness, the sheer harshness persisted. However, once this had been completed in the back of the lorry, they quickly scrambled out to the street in their new appearance. Both men approved with compliments at the transition.

They then introduced themselves. Boris was older, and he was now the husband of the Countess. Hans was just a few years senior to Anastasia and so was appointed to be her husband. Of course the women had no identification, no papers, but the men did. The men warned the Countess and Anastasia to say nothing, to shrug their shoulders, as if they did not understand German, as if they were of a lower class that was used to only speaking the dialect of the area. After leaving the perimeter of the city, their servants clothes were quickly burnt and disposed of, and only ashes of the past morning's attire remained.

A similar technique had been devised by the governess and the head mistress. Once returning to the manor, they quickly disposed of the outer garments in a similar fashion. The clothes and belongings of Anastasia and the Countess as last seen by anyone had disappeared. There had only been a few things that both women cherished too much to give up, and they held them dearly in the most secret parts of both their heart and their belongings.

The day ended without the presence of Anastasia and the Countess at dinner. When the two women did not arrive at the designated time, the General sent the butler and a junior officer to remind them of their tardiness, only to find their rooms unoccupied. No sooner did the junior officer return with the information that their presence was unaccountable, when the general alarm was sent out. How could this be, an escaped prisoner of war under the protection and supervision of the General?

Every metre of the premises and then the grounds were covered. Any piece that did not fit was brought before the

General. Everyone, even the senior officers were questioned and interrogated. Nothing was left to the imagination. No-one took this lightly. For the men, it was much harsher. The swagger stick reminded them that information can be gathered and insubordination would not be tolerated.

However, the two women had literally vanished. Everyone agreed on what they had worn, everyone had borne witness to their coming and going. All those questioned remained adamant, not matter how hard the repercussions were, how it had happened. Even the stable boy, when questioned, acknowledged he saw the Countess and Anastasia get into the Düsseldorf limo. When further questioned he said, "Do you think that the Countess would acknowledge a person like me? Do you think she knows I exist? "

The General was furious by the third day. His foul temper reflected on all that were present and accountable. However, on the fourth day he directed that while he was going to inspect the lines under his command, upon his return, the Countess and Anastasia would be dining once more at his table. He left no exceptions, no options available. His senior officers knew their responsibility to completing this task that this was of the utmost importance to their military careers as well as Herr General.

As the staff car pulled up to the front foyer that morning, the General got into the back and muttered something that no one quite comprehended. He drove off to inspect his divisions. The officers left behind then proceeded to do what had to be done.

With a heavy burden, they contacted the S.S. By late afternoon, a foreboding black limousine had arrived. The black uniforms represented that the final authority had arrived. The door of the car opened and a man of small stature stepped out, complete with leather coat and leather gloves. He did not wait to find an escort as the rest of the S.S. officers. He did not wish to be announced. Instead he waved his hand at one of his officers to have the door of the great mansion opened.

River of Life

Once in the foyer, he yelled "Who is in charge?" An officer stepped forward and introduced himself. "Ya, ya, ya, ver is that woman, that governess?" he muttered. The officer quickly ran up the spiral staircase and demanded the presence of the governess.

Aware of who was on the other side of the door, the governess opened it calmly. "The Fuhrer's representative has come to ask you questions, Governess."

She nodded pleasantly and in full control said, "He must have the Fuhrer's full understanding, to send such a senior calling card." With dignity, she walked passed the officer and made her way down the stairwell.

As she made her way down, she quickly observed the five men standing at the bottom, four in black uniforms of the S.S. and the fifth in his black leather overcoat, horn-rimmed glasses and hat. As they looked up, she looked down and proceeded with all the authority of an aristocrat. As she reached the fifth step at the bottom, she stared directly into their faces and said, "Manners, manners, my dear gentlemen, remove your hats."

Quickly, the military commands that govern all that wear a uniform, snapped to attention, the heels clicked, and the hats came off, and were quickly placed under the arms. It was only the little black figure in his robe of mystery that defied her wishes.

She did not move from the platform where she had chosen to make her stand. "That is better. And now, what brings you to interrupt my duties?"

The four S.S. soldiers stood frozen as if they were mere statues. The smallest figure was forced to look up. He snarled, "Where are the Countess and her daughter?"

The governess drew on all her authority and years of experience. With pride and dignity, she looked down at the man with the horn-rimmed glasses and replied, "I am the Governess. I am employed by the Countess. She has the privilege of knowing *my* where-abouts at all times. I do not have that

305

privilege of her, nor does she share it with me. Anyone would understand this if they had any station."

The frozen statues of the S.S. officers stood even more rigidly. They were aware of the discipline behind the cold glacier blue eyes that stared back through the rimless glasses. "You are not capable of remembering or knowing where your employer is. Maybe a trip to my office will enlighten your memory."

She looked down with all the contempt of a school-marm that had disciplined him in the past. Her thin lips narrowed and she replied, "My memory of all that has gone before me is still vivid. I have no more time to waste," and started to pivot back up the stairwell.

The little man looked up in amazement. Flashes of the past came rushing to his mind. He was once more that small skinny child that the school marm delighted in taking into the cloak room to discipline. 'Manners', she repeated, over and over. 'Manners,' ran through his mind, as though he was screaming and no one heard. Told to remove his trousers, and then his knickers, and touch his toes while the cane danced its rhythmic beat on those naughty little cheeks.

He stared at that rigid figure of authority, filled with hate for all that she represented. He struggled to regain his composure, and said in a guttural Low German," I vill be back when your memory pleases what I want to hear. If not, the next meeting will be of my choosing, at my place, Governess."

She did not blink, but returned up the stairs, and the wilted group below realized that she would be of no service. In the days that followed, the S.S. searched and questioned all that were accounted for. Even with their new-found ways of persuasion, they too had little more success than the military officers. When the General returned for a report, the best that the little figure in the black coat could produce was," I am investigating, have patience, Herr General. No reports will leave until I have found the Countess and her daughter in their wayward ways. Heil Hitler," as they both snapped to honour the Fuhrer.

River of Life

Inwardly shaking, the governess knew it was only a matter of time for her. She was aware of the fact that the men had dragged the nanny into her bedroom, and had heard the screams throughout the night.

While the governess was being interrogated, the old nanny felt that this may be her only opportunity. She knew her strength was ebbing quickly. Strapped to the bed, her fingers slipped from one bead of the rosary to the other, from one Hail Mary to the next. In her other hand, held the razor. Without warning or hesitation, the first wrist felt a large slash and then a warm flow of blood. She switched hands, never missing the repeating of the Hail Mary and addressed the other hand in the same manner. Now grasping the Rosary, she repeated the prayers as the life- giving fluid poured continuously on the bedding and soaked deeper into the mattress. As the nanny prayed for forgiveness, the weakness and dizziness started to be felt, as the warmth of life left her body.

When she did not appear the next day at a respectable hour, a maid was sent. After the screams of confusion, and the investigation by the military personnel, the little black coat appeared. Those cold glacier eyes blazed with pure hatred. This old woman had outfoxed him on. He now knew that she was the secret. He realized that she held the key to the knowledge he wanted, and she had destroyed it.

He returned to the Count's library, where the General was going over more preparations and said, "Herr General, there has been a small set- back, but time will produce the results. Continue with your job, I will continue with mine." The General nodded, knowing full well what this meant. He was already aware that the officer who had blundered by not bringing back the Countess and Anastasia had been sent to the Front. There was no mercy in the Fuhrer's never- ending quest for victory.

robert f. edwards

"As the nanny prayed for forgiveness, ... "

Original artwork, oil   Phyllis Verdine Humphries
                          1939

308

River of Life

CHAPTER 23

 Back in Cairo, his family had completed the six months of mourning for the loss of Horus-Salah. A British Army officer had informed the family that Horus-Salah had been killed in action, along with his crew. His men had witnessed the explosion of the armored vehicle and unanimously said no-one had survived. His family and all that knew him grieved for the loved one they were told was dead, not knowing the truth. Only the German hospital knew the British records were false.

December was an emotional month for the African Corps. Both sides of this horror of war took time out for the Christmas Season. For the African Corps and the British Armies, a moment of peace was experienced over the desert. The African Corp celebrated by decorating unrecognizable Christmas trees with small gifts, and food under it for the special day. Even on the Russian Front, the Germans and the Russians took time off during the festive season with hidden delights from the homeland that had been savored and saved for the celebration. The New Year wandered in with skirmishes along the frontlines, as the German Army continually retreated, trying to save as many divisions as possible.

For Horus-Salah, it was another year and that was all. It neither showed promise nor accomplishment. Time had passed on another calendar that marked another period. However, little did he realize that the events that were taking place without his knowledge were significantly going in favor of his release, and reuniting with a family that assumed it was just another year in the loss of their beloved.

By midyear, the British Army had encircled the German hospital and the prisoners of war, including Horus-Salah, were now left in the hands of the British conquering forces. After checking the small amount of files that were not destroyed by the Germans, the British realized that Horus-Salah, Colonel of the Egyptian Army, was alive. He was in a German hospital.

The weeks that followed saw Horus-Salah for the first time leave Libya in over a year and he was transported to a British hospital in Alexandria. He had just arrived and had been assigned a bed in the long dormitory, when his dear sister and her friend appeared as nursing nightingales. They all wept profusely. His sister related the agonizing moments of the family when they heard the news that their beloved son had been killed. 'Even King Farouk 1 of Egypt had summoned a special inquiry to try to recover his remains, ' Horus-Salah was told by his sister. There was so much news to share, but on the one subject that Horus-Salah wanted to know, there was none. His sister told him everything, but there was no news about Poland, and not a word about his beloved Anastasia.

In the months ahead, the medical doctors of the British Corps hovered and probed and discussed the miraculous surgery of Herr Surgeon General. They marveled at the skill of the incisions, and concurred that by the extent of Horus-Salah's wounds, kept referring to it as a miracle. Horus-Salah concluded that the miracle was Allah's but the skill was Herr Surgeon General's. He was grateful that the course of life had spared him for another moment in his quest to find his beloved.

As the days moved on, he always had the company of his sister and her friend to share his days. The two women nursed over him as if he was their sole responsibility. He had known the young friend of his sister's for many years, as their families were of similar position in the Cairo community. Like his sister, she had grown into an attractive young woman. Her dedication to him was surprisingly more intense than his sister's devotion. All though he found her attention and kindness rewarding, his yearning and the focus for his beloved never wavered for a second.

River of Life

His legs were now strong enough with the support of braces and crutches, just to stagger about like the cripple he was. However, his back had proved stronger than even Herr Surgeon General had predicted and soon he could stand erect on the crutches and the pegs that once were his legs. In time, he was well enough to do what most veterans do, and that is return, broken and dismantled to their former life. Medals were both presented by the Egyptian government and the British General, and much later he would receive the Victoria Cross from the King of England.

It wasn't that many months before the agenda moved forward and Horus-Salah returned to Cairo. Once in the mansion of his family, the routine of life became as it always had been. Until one day, his father summoned him to 'the room', as Horus-Salah thought of it. However, this time, instead of being in his normal Egyptian attire of a galabya, he dressed in his military wardrobe with two canes supporting mangled legs.

He walked the distance down the corridor to the great door. When the male servant opened the door and his father's hands summoned him forward, this time, the crippled hero painfully leaned heavily on his canes as he made his way to the appropriate chair that awaited him. He sat, as he had so many times before, and this time he looked directly into the cold black eyes that penetrated the thoughts of Mankind. But this time, they seemed only a hollow shadow of darkness. His father looked for the longest moment at his son, as though he was reading the chapters that he had missed all these months before. Then a voice from deep within him said, "Allah has been merciful to this house and to your soul. In the name of Allah, let all things be possible."

Horus-Salah replied, "And to his prophet, Mohammad," almost mocking the worn-out phrase of Arabic. The haze that covered his father's eyes vanished completely, and a sharp fierceness prevailed. He said, "Do not take lightly of destiny, for it shall succeed where you failed." Once again, Horus-Salah retreated back into his childhood submissiveness.

robert f. edwards

His father paused for the longest time, before he continued in a voice so faint that it could hardly be heard, "Your time is near. You are my replacement. Allah has been generous to our family by giving you back to us."

Horus-Salah looked puzzled and quietly said, "My understanding is vague?" His father then got up from behind the desk, and walked around as Horus-Salah found his canes to stand. It was one of the few times Horus-Salah had ever remembered standing beside his father. To his amazement, they were both approximately the same height and build, though the galabya always did mask a man's figure.

The senior looked into the eyes once more of the son and said, "My time here has ended, and yours is to begin. Our house will fall into your reign before this year finds its end." Horus-Salah gasped. A flash went through his mind, how sacrilegious. It was almost like Allah saying he wasn't going be around anymore.

Horus-Salah looked back into the eyes and asked, "Father, is it an illness that has no cure?"

The old man's lips neither moved, but the words breathed out, "Cancer has no friends." With that, he turned and almost mystically was sitting behind the desk once more, long before Horus-Salah had managed to stabilize his canes to support his retreat to the chair. Once more, the old man looked hard into the eyes of his son and said, "As the ruler and the law of this clan, my word is your command."

Horus-Salah said, "Your wishes are mine to obey."

The senior continued, "You must wed before I leave, and preferably if it is the will of Allah, she will bear the fruit of this next generation that is being blessed by your return."

All the room could hear was a gasp, and then a rattling that sounded like the caving in of life itself. Of course, it came from Horus-Salah's body. He neither stooped nor flinched, but remained motionless as though he had been turned into stone. His father stared relentlessly at the agony produced by his request.

River of Life

From somewhere deep within, and courage mustered through the conflicts of war and agony and despair, Horus-Salah found a voice that had never been uttered in this room before. It filled his lungs and his mind, and his eyes looked directly into the coldness of the gaze before him. "Your wish is my command, but my ability is limited to a mortal. I have no way of bringing your wishes to fulfillment, for both our pledges to Anastasia are unobtainable. Her whereabouts are unknown."

The old man looked frail and for the first time Horus-Salah actually saw the penetration of illness that had claimed the victory of death over life. The only reply was, "Your faith is Muslim. Mohammad, the Prophet of Islam provides you the answer. Take another, for you are entitled to three." The hand waved; there was nothing to be added.

Horus-Salah moved his broken body up from the chair. His two canes gave him the support to leave the room. He looked at the cold eyes behind the desk as he turned to leave the room, and knew there was nothing he could say, or do, other than obey.

He believed, up until this moment, that all that he had endured, not only was the will of Allah, but the blessing of Allah, that once again he would unite with his beloved. The miraculous intervention of Herr Surgeon General who had put together a mangled body, this must be some reward from Allah. 'How could this possibly be, this irony, this games of the gods being played against me, a mere mortal?'

He made his way back, crippled now in body and spirit, to his quarters. His servant received him with a glance, knowing that a tragedy far greater than he had witnessed before, was now upon his master. He helped his master back into the chair, and begged to assist him. Horus-Salah waved his hand, like his lord and master had done shortly before and uttered the words, "I must have my solitude."

His trusted male servant departed, leaving the broken form of humanity placed in the chair. As the day ended and dusk approached, Horus-Salah sat, not even adjusting his

313

robert f. edwards

uniform. It was as though a bronze statue of a military officer sat in remembrance of these tragic events that the years of this decade had produced.

Dusk gave way to the night, and still he sat in the darkness. The servant observed through the peephole with surveillance, not to disturb his master unless it was requested, and still Horus-Salah sat. He sat motionless and at times, the servant that observed from a distance and elusive of view, thought that his master had fallen into slumber, at last relieved of his agony through sleep.

This was not the case. As the stars gave illumination to the skies and the small ticking so close to his heart added a false security, the little hands endlessly moving second by second, minute by minute, saw the bewitching hour of twelve and the beginning of a new day, and still Horus-Salah sat. He sat motionless and at times, the servants that had now taken up the watch from afar, feared that something drastic had happened to their master. He neither moved, nor stirred, nor showed any form of life whatsoever, as the hours melted from one day into the next. It was the beginning of the breaking of Ra's demand for the skies once more and still their master had not moved throughout the night. He sat erect, staring into oblivion.

However, for Horus it had not been a vigil of blankness. With an intense concentration of all the powers of his mind, he knew he had to overcome many contentious issues and hurdles. To accept the word of Allah, and his ways, to question his father's rule, these thoughts whirled around him throughout the long night. He examined his mind as one would a library, segregating the books of reference from the books of fantasy, the works of art versus the works of labor.

He had learned a great deal through his short years. Above all, he was a servant to his master and his master's house. This had been from the beginning of time, and would continue until the end of his time. He believed in what he had been taught and taught to believe in what he knew. So he had divided, then subdivided, and redefined until each priority

River of Life

had its own preference in the list of events that must take place. He was an obedient servant in the house of his family. But soon, he would have to be the master that preserved this ancient tradition of his family, which dated back to the pharaohs.

He had divided it into two major categories. His first priority; to find his beloved Anastasia at all costs, and time was not his friend but his enemy. From the very beginning to their last moments, Anastasia had always been his guiding light, his force, his vision, and his purpose of life. She had the answers and she was sure-footed with her decisions. If he was to rule his house with any rewards or acknowledgement from history, it was vital that he must have Anastasia to rule beside him.

It did not matter that he was Moslem, or she was Christian. Or he called Mohammed his spiritual force, Allah; or she called hers God, or the universe above. She must be his equal and his queen in the land of the pharaohs. She must share his life, to aid and assist the family of the past and to preserve its place in the future. He resolved this was his main priority.

His second was more questionable than the first. Until his father's last meeting, he had always assumed that he and Anastasia would spend their lives together. They would share their childhood playground in Luxor, and raise their children as they had done, romping through the gardens, playing with the nannies, and maybe even the secret of the Tomb of the Cat.

But now, now, he would rule. He would be the master of the house and have all the responsibilities that came with it. He had never thought about this until now, and in deep penetration of thought, he asked the question of ' Why?' knowing in his heart that he was not suited. He had never been suited for leadership. It had always been Anastasia that had broken the trail that led him forward. He had always thought that in his fantasy world that someday, his younger sister would marry, and her husband would be the favorite son of his father, and that he would rule. Horus-Salah believed that he

robert f. edwards

and Anastasia would live at Luxor and only periodically be forced back to Cairo to endure the pompous splendor of the domain. But that they would soon return back to continue their childlike life in the land and the place he loved so dearly.

But now, without the soul and body that ruled his heart, he would also be burdened with the responsibility of ruling a house whose history was as long as the Nile. As he sat and played the moves from one to the other in his mind, it gave way to a plan. If nothing more or less, the years at Cambridge, the discipline of the Military, and the horrors of war that focused in the haunted world of reality and perseverance of existence, it was his obligation to his ancestors as well as his father to carry the mantle to the next generation.

He swore to the god of whom he was named, "Horus, almighty Horus, I give this mantle of power to the next generation I produce as soon as their limbs are strong enough to support the weight and their mind is quick enough to make the decisions. I will pass this rule that I have to endure over to one that is qualified which comes from my groin the first moment I can."

Ra had found that the darkness had given way to his command of the sky, and though most still were in slumber, Horus-Salah broke his long stay in solitude, and clapped his hands. Obediently, one of the servants appeared and not even looking at him, Horus-Salah said, "Summons the senior servant of my father at once."

The servant bowed and as his head faced the floor, he muttered in a voice, "It is early, Master."

The reply was, "I asked not for the time." The servant bowed back out through the door and within a span of less than half the hour, both men appeared once more.

The senior servant of his father bowed, not as deep or reverently, but acknowledged Horus-Salah's place and requested, "What do you wish of me?", with the absence of 'Master'.

"I command you to give me audience with my father as quickly as possible. Go and do my bidding." The servant

316

River of Life

looked puzzled for a moment; for he had never heard the young Horus-Salah speak with such command. Both servants bowed deeper than before, as the two men made their way backwards through the opening of the door.

Horus-Salah clapped once more and by this time, all his male servants had been awakened, ready for his commands. He bathed and put on the traditional galabya and his finest of slippers. He looked like the heir- apparent that he would soon be.

By mid morning, his father's master servant returned and said, "My Master requests your presence now," not with a sneer but with an obvious preference of who he wished to serve. Horus-Salah, still with crutches but in his full Egyptian appearance, followed closely behind the servant through the corridors of the great estate.

As the servant acknowledged his presence at the great door, the door opened and this time, Horus-Salah hobbled forward, up into the desk which commanded the ruler of the family. He looked at his father and for a moment reflected these two thoughts that flashed together: One, this man was ill. He was dying. The other was I must not retreat from my decision of the night.

He stood before his father and the hand waved for him to sit. However this time, it went un-obeyed. Horus-Salah stood, leaning his full support on his canes. He stared down into the eyes that penetrated his soul. As he stood and his arms adjusted to the full weight, he heard the faint ticking of his beloved watch by his heart. From his soul came a loud clear tone as his lungs filled with air, then delivered their message.

His eyes never left the relentless glare of his father. He started, "A man's word is all that he has, and this is law. When he breaks his word, there is no law that he has for himself, or others. I ask you to honor your word and your consent to my beloved Anastasia". Horus-Salah continued, asking his father to insure that all the knowledge that he had in his possession be shared equally, from this day forth, as the law of honor. "For your laws are my laws and I will honor your word,

317

if you will honor my request? I have said it, let it be acknowledged."

The old man stared at his son and for the first time in
their lives, he looked up by force and the lips never moved,
but his voice was clear and loud. "It has been said. Let it be
done. We rule equally from this day forth."

And with that, he clapped his hands and his senior servant came into the room. The old man got up and for the first
time Horus-Salah saw how feeble his father was. He walked
over to his son and stood beside him. The senior servant stood
before them and the old man looked into the eyes of his beloved servant and said, "You see two of us. We both rule from
this day forth as one. We are equal to all that this house
commands. Let the word go forth and let the law prevail. "

The servant was bewildered, but then the hand that had
ruled the house for so long passed its familiar wave, and the
servant bowed his way out of their presence. The two that had
a common blood between them looked once more into each
other's eyes and Horus-Salah said, "I am grateful for your acceptance and knowledge of my request. I must now attend,
with all the powers of our house, to find my beloved."

In a voice as light as the winds of the day, he heard his
father's voice, "Your rule has started. Be wise 'til its end." The
hand moved in its familiar pattern, and Horus-Salah pivoted
on his canes and hobbled through the door as it opened to
receive his exit.

Once back in his own quarters at the other wing of the
mansion, he summoned his trusted servant and said, "Send
the word out that I want to find my beloved, Anastasia. Start
with my command to my father's senior servant. Get me a report this afternoon on the progress to succeed in my request.
Let it be said, Let it be done."

His devoted servant bowed graciously, and left by backing
out through the doorway. Horus-Salah then summoned his
other servants and requested that a bath and fresh linen be
put out, after a small rest in the afternoon. He had forgotten
when he had taken on nourishment, but the nourishment of

River of Life

the soul was far more rewarding than feasting the body. He allowed his wrecked body to have a short period of rest to repair. At least, he could endure the inconvenience for a matter of hours that his body demanded.

Shortly after four in the afternoon, his trusted servant entered his private quarters asking, "Master, would you be prepared to give further instructions to those that request them at this time?"

Without hesitation, Horus-Salah said, "Bring them forth."

Though he did not sit in the office that he would inherit shortly, he sat regally in his small library. The first to enter was his father's most trusted servant. This time he bowed with the same respect that he had shown Horus-Salah's father for all the years that they had been together. Accompanying him was a group of people, including a high ranking British officer. As the number totaled higher than the seats that would accommodate all, the rank and file took place. The British officer, being superior, took center stage in front of Horus-Salah, while the senior servant stood waiting for direction. Horus-Salah's eyes moved him to sit next to the British officer, and his aide on the other side. The rest standing found their pecking order.

Once the audience was in place, Horus-Salah made his request, simple and plain, "Your time is short and my request is but one. Find Anastasia, Countess of Poland. I have no further instructions, but -Succeed."

The first to address the issue was the Colonel of the British Army by saying, "Hear now, my dear chap".

With a flash of anger that only his father had mastered over the years, Horus-Salah stared the British officer down. His trusted servant said, "You will call him Regent, Sir."

The British officer turned to the subordinate beside him with an air of dismay and asked, "Pardon?"

The senior servant said, "If your hearing is impaired, leave the room. You are of no further service to us."

Suddenly, the British officer became part of the team that was organized to fulfill the request. It was his father's senior

319

servant that explained the complexity of what had already transpired in the few hours that he had now become the shadow of his father's reign. He would command all that came in his midst, so they asked to verify the time line that was permitted.

Horus-Salah without hesitation responded, "The moon is full but once a month. You have until then." The servants stood and bowed deeply. The British officer sat, befuddled until Horus-Salah's servant nudged him from a bowed position. They left the room with the British officer confused in the assignment, but all others focused on achieving the results. It was the first command of the new Regent of the family. It would not be the last.

The old man leaned his weary body against the embankment of the narrow path that dominated its presence over the Valley of the Kings. He was well past the halfway mark of his destination. He pulled a blanket around his shoulders and held tightly onto the walking stick that he had acquired. He leaned on it, regressing back in thought to when all that would support his weight were two sticks, as his broken limbs waited to heal, before he could stand erect without the support.

Today, age was the deterrent. His old body, weary and tired as well as being decrepit, hobbled along the paths. Once more, he relied on support of another form than his. As his back leaned against the wall of granite and dirt that embodiment the great land of Egypt, his eyes found the life giving source and the moments of contentment that he experienced throughout his life.

It was dark, only a black line of ink between the other shades of darkness, but there was no mistake to his mind; it was his beloved Nile, the god-giving source for all Egyptians. Every Egyptian that hugged its bank had the Nile flow through their veins. All living things attributed their existence

River of Life

to the water of life. Mother Nature blessed its inhabitants and replenished their food supply, year after year by this stream of life.

He gazed down upon it, fixated in the darkness as if it might have been the first time he saw it. But no, it was as much of his body and mind as those that had captured and held his soul. Tonight was no different, for his commitment and love of this country of his ancestors, of the gods that they loved and paid homage to, for he was one of them, an Egyptian.

His eyes traced the shadows of Luxor and a faint smile drifted across the withered face. He knew the buildings and temples just like one would find on a monopoly board in his mind, even though the darkness held them back in the shadows. There was the odd flicker of light from some being unable to find the peace of the darkness and the rest of the night.

'Not too long', he thought, 'not too long', for he felt , like so many years of his life, the small ticking close to his heart, of his beloved. 'It is time to move. I must move on. I must complete my journey.' And once more he looked up into the heavens and the multitude of stars greeted him as though they waited for his acknowledgement.

He pushed with all his strength away from the embankment, as his body once more addressed the trail ahead. His old hands grasped tightly on the staff of the walking stick. He leaned into it for support, inch by inch, to his destination.

Yes, his destination with Anastasia, his beloved. Tonight, today, tomorrow, when Allah will forgive him and release him of this burden of life, he would be with his beloved once more. He had never slackened or wavered in his conviction. Tonight was no different as he trudged step by step towards his destination, the tomb of the mummy of the cat.

robert f. edwards

CHAPTER 24

Europe was falling under the black cloud of the Nazis, and their presence was spreading. Anastasia and the Countess feared their safe haven that they had found refuge in may come under scrutiny soon. The small community in the hills of Poland had accepted them without question, so far, and they had their own documents now. One was a school teacher and the other a librarian from a province with a similar accent. They were distant relatives of the doctor's family that protected them.

Word had gotten back, meager as it was. Nan had died no details. Both women felt a sorrow that was indescribable. For Anastasia, she was the friend, the companion since childhood, Nan. Oh, what a loss. But the losses around them were equally as devastating.

And just as things started to seem to continually tighten with the Nazi army present and the curfews of the dreaded boots on the cobblestones at night, had become a way of life, life got worse. Their protector, Herr Doctor, was part and parcel of the underground. After his daily practice, he would be whisked away to the underground to provide relief to those that were injured and suffering in the resistance of the Nazi's.

The records did not show whether the S.S. intentionally transferred the little black coat, or it was destiny to reunite good with evil. But, evil showed up. A new interrogation office was created in this remote district, headed up by the little black coat. It could be considered a demotion, but regardless, he was there investigate. In no more than two or three days of his presence, large groups of people were brought in for questioning. Some never returned.

It was at one of these questionings that the two women and the doctor's behavior became suspect. Upon a visit to the house, the women were not present, just the children. After a

River of Life

few curt questions, 'where their parents were', and' who the ladies were', the answers were not given properly. The oldest child was asked if he believed in Jesus Christ, and the boy answered," Yes."

Grinning, the officers said, "You will die the same death," and nailed him to the front door of his house. For the girl, they brutally assaulted in every physical way, and then laid her torn and mutilated body at his feet. When the women returned that night, the mother was hysterical. No comfort could be offered, she bordered on sheer madness. After the doctor returned, he gave her a much-needed sedative.

There was absolutely no doubt now, the three were in mortal danger. It would be just a matter of hours before the Gestapo would return and this time they would know what they were looking for. Without hesitation, Anastasia and the Countess, along with the Herr Doctor, made contact with the underground. It was within hours that they were moved through the network of the Resistance.

But the next day, true as everyone would believe, the Gestapo returned. The hysterical mother had been moved to friends in a nearby small village to try and recoup her sanity. All that was left were the neighbours. The old couple bravely acknowledged that their neighbours had left, but they did not know the where-abouts. They too, were brutally killed in their house after questioning.

And so once again, the trail went cold for the little black coat. But he knew that patience would give him his rewards. He always had others to address, question, interrogate and send on their way to the camps of death.

As the months drifted, the Resistance found a small hamlet for the two women to go and become peasants in the fields. Herr Doctor chose to remain in the Resistance, helping where possible. Little did any of them know that the turn of events would worsen. Anastasia and the Countess found their new way of life more than difficult in the field, hoeing all day with the other babushkas. Their appearance, even though being clothed as a commoner, was definitely not a farming woman.

323

robert f. edwards

They neither had the build, nor the stooped broken shoulders of a peasant. No matter how hard they hoed, it looked like they had some awkward stick in their possession. They tried to stay away as much from the others as possible.

As fate would have it, there were spies within spies, informers within informers. The very Jews that the Polish people had protected were not only being annihilated but being unwitting informers. On one particular occasion, a young house-wife that was six months pregnant was brought in to questioning. Nobody really understood why, it could have been her husband's suspected involvement in the Resistance. But as the word spread that she was in interrogation, her neighbours gathered as much jewelry and precious items that they could.

Both Anastasia and the Countess felt it was their moral obligation to contribute. The Countess took one of her rings to donate to the bounty. Anastasia parted with one of her pieces, not thinking of themselves, only of this beautiful woman that had saved their lives. Unfortunately, they had signed her death warrant.

Yes, the S.S. released the woman; broken hand, a broken foot, broken ribs, no teeth, black eyes, but they returned her and her unborn child. After they had started to examine the bounty of the bribes they had received to release such a peasant, the Commandant's eyes feasted on the jewelry, the rest was junk. There were two pieces of elegance, of real worth. 'Ya,' he muttered to himself. This would give him more recognition out of this shit hole, this sheitzen box in the middle of nowhere.

He sent the pieces immediately to the head bureau of investigation. The little black coat received not only the information but the jewelry. His eyes glowed as the fires of hell, as his hands rubbed the cartouche and the ring. 'Ah, patience' he muttered, 'patience', and screamed in his high pitched voice for his aid.

Before two days and nights had seen their end, he was in the village, prowling around like a hyena following the scent of

324

River of Life

a fallen doe. With his trained eye, it took very little for him to recognize women in the field that did not belong there, especially with the help of the Steinbeck woman who said they were foreign to the district.

It was a pleasant day and the sun was shining, it was not very hot, and a gentle breeze blew over rows and rows of vegetables. The two women, like others in their small group, bent their backs and hoed row after row. In a flash, the patrol cars screeched to a halt, doors swung out and the storm troopers swarmed the field yelling," Halt! Halt!"

Everyone froze as if they had become part of their wooden hoe. No one dared to move, now frozen scare-crows in the field. The little black coat demanded each and every one of them to drop their hoes, and hold out their hands. He only had to look briefly at the gnarled, broken, frost-bitten hands from years of hoeing to know they were of a true peasant, and moved quickly on.

And then, he came to the two heads that were bowed deeply, and the babushka pulled well over their foreheads, demanding the same. He looked once, twice and the cold of his eyes danced the dance of death. "Ah, Herr Countess, and her beautiful daughter, we meet at last. I have been waiting a long time, a very long time. Please come with me now. I have a few questions for you."

The two women were hastily shoved into the vehicle and taken to the interrogation room. It took little to identify them, and they offered little or no resistance, for it was futile. After being tied to chairs and beaten severely, to enhance his pleasure, he did not mar their faces; for he wanted to save them for a special occasion. "Well, well, well, you were under house arrest, and you escaped. You are prisoners of war; you are *escaped* prisoners of war. We have better facilities, so we do not have to look for you like we have. Do you understand?" as he punched the different body parts to emphasize each word.

Amidst their moans, he announced, "You have to be put out in prison, for you are prisoners of a war." He hit them severely with a whip. "You shall go to Auschwitz; we have accommodations waiting for you, Herr Countess. And you too, my little princess." He smiled and with that the fate of freedom had been taken away and replaced by going to the death camp of Auschwitz.

The two women now, fading in and out of consciousness, still grasped their fate. They were hauled away physically into containment quarters and thrown mercilessly on the floor of the cell that waited to take them to their fate. They moaned, and faded in and out of semi-consciousness. There was no way of knowing whether it was day or night, for the room had no window and no light. They remained in darkness except for a small penetrating glow that left an eerie effect under the door cell. As they struggled and sat in a somewhat upright position, the Countess moaned, against the severe beating that she had taken earlier. Anastasia crawled with great pain and difficultly to her mother's aid. As the two women held each other in their arms there was little repose or comfort other than knowing that they were both at least still together.

They were awoken the next day by the clanging of the cell door as it opened and the Gestapo uniform appeared, motioning them to stand and prepare to leave. Once more, they were escorted into the interrogation room. As fear and anticipation grew in the hearts of these two women, they waited on the wooden chairs that had been part of the instruments of the previous day's questioning and answering. Just as both women turned to look at each other ,the door opened and an officer in full S.S. uniform escorted by two military police of a junior rank came in. "Ah, Herr Countesses , we have all the documents ready for your new place of dwelling. Please follow me."

The two women staggered to their feet and were escorted into a large holding room that had a mixture of crowded fearful people in it. Quickly they were pushed into the centre, surrounded by a group of people of all descriptions and walks of life. There were still a few aristocratic ladies that were demanding their rights, that their husbands to do something,

River of Life

huddling in their fur coats. While others of a lower class were holding their children tightly into their waists. The older men, regardless of what origin or nationality were pinned against the walls, some with two or three day's growth on their face. There was a stench coming from unwashed clothing and bodies that inhabited it. There was only room to stand. Others that had collapsed were straddled by those that were still standing.

The hours continued with no change in sight. Just when this crowded room of human flesh felt that if could no longer endure anymore and would just become a mass of piled limbs extending from bodies, the doors flung open. There were guards everywhere and the Gestapo officer screamed, "Follow us now!" There was a pouring of liquid flesh out of this tight container down the long corridor as they marched out into the cold air. It was night and the mist had settled over them.

The large standards with lights glowed in an eerie horrifying appearance as the steam from the locomotive poured out a darker more pungent smoke to join its ethereal surroundings. The wagons were cattle cars. The only distinguishing factor that gave them any knowledge of the true cargo were hands that hung out of the small openings, and the moaning and screaming in despair of their containment.

The small group went to the back of the long cattle wagons where there was three empty, waiting for their arrival. They were pushed and shoved relentlessly, as the soldiers used their rifle butts with impatience to push them further into the wagons.

How could all of these people be contained in three small cattle wagons? It they thought the room that they endured the better part of the day had been compressed; it was unimaginable what they were experiencing now. There was little room to move and breathing became difficult. Just when suffocation seemed to become a reality, the train moved and flow of air provided a small measure of relief.

The train started to move its human cargo towards the point of no return. The Countess and Anastasia clung together like Siamese twins. The ride to Hell had begun. There was no way of knowing the time, it was irrelevant. The misery was omni-present. The human cargo rocked as the train sped along its rails, each clinging and holding anyone next to them, to remain in an upright position, or be trampled.

The brakes squealed to the end of the line. The doors were flung open, the eerie lights prevailed once more, as the human cargo expelled from the wagons. The German soldiers were everywhere, pushing and shoving the cargo into lines, separating the men from the women and children. In the wee hours of the morning, a group of officers escorted by the military personnel, walked through the lines barking, "This one there, over there, this line, that line."

The separation continued. The Jews got preferential treatment by being the first to be segregated. The weak and the old were further segregated. And finally the ones that were standing and could be of some benefit, of some further use, were taken into the quarters of the main court yards. The rest were quickly stripped and escorted to the showers before receiving the kiss of death.

Anastasia and the Countess were escorted into quarters in the containment buildings. The night of horror ended as the morning broke, and another day began. They were first given the cleansing treatment, then issued prison clothes, then tattooed, and finally hauled off to the work fields. As the days perpetuated into weeks, the lines remained constant, but the faces changed.

Anastasia and the Countess started to grasp the hell that they had entered into. There was no escape; only through the doors of heaven was there any hope of leaving this place of death. The rules became simplified; that if you were standing for role call in the morning, you may live for another day. If you collapsed, then you were taken to the showers and the crematorium. The furnaces never stopped burning the remains that had gone before. For those still remaining, it was a horrifying experience. It was a nightmare that one could never wake up, if you were the victim.

River of Life

*" Anastasia and the Countess were escorted into quarters
in the containment buildings."*

Copy of original photograph
Displayed in Auschwitz

robert f. edwards

Both Anastasia and the Countess staggered with their thoughts, the fear that they might be separated. But, by some benevolent act from above, Anastasia and her mother shared a cell with two other women. It was on one of these morning inspections, that the Commandant himself felt it was his duty to inspect the proper discipline that was given, in his review of the prisoners. As he walked by with his swagger stick, poking and stopping periodically at the victims, he came in eye contact with Anastasia and the Countess.

He looked directly at them and stopped in front of the Countess and said, "You are an aristocratic Polish person, ya?"

The Countess nodded. "Oh yes, and you must be her son."

He turned to the officer beside him," Take them to the main quarters now," he said, and then moved on with the inspection.

The two women were horrified. They grasped each others hands, but their own strength drained the blood that was in them. They followed the officer to the large administrative building. What seemed more than one life time in their minds was really less than an hour in reality. Then, the Commandant summonsed them into his office. "Ya, I have your reports here, we have done you an injustice ya? You are with the Jews, you should be with us, we are your neighbours, we are your friends, and we will move you to better quarters." The women were paralyzed.

"Do not look at the floor, look at me," the Commandant snapped." I have the voice, you have the ears to listen, and the eyes to see, now look at me. Now!" They both stared into the eyes of the Commandant; they were those same cold blue eyes of the demented mind of the S.S. Gestapo that interrogated them before entering into this hell hole. There was a

River of Life

cruelty in his face that said it all, the description of his occupation.

"We vill discuss your future tonight, over dinner. You will be taken to the better quarters and provided with garments that are suitable for a proper dinner in a proper fashion. Ya?" The two women nodded. Their voices had escaped them.

As they were escorted out of his office, they were then taken through the administrative building, to the residential quarters of the Commandant and the other officers. They were shown two rooms that in other circumstances would have been considered as adequate dwellings for their station in life, which had disappeared so many years ago. Evening attire that had been gathered from other poor victims was laid out for them. They were allowed to communicate with each other; there was a new found freedom that they hadn't experienced in weeks. Their hopes and their illusions started to create a new vision.

That evening they were accompanied at the dinner table by the Commandant, and six of his fellow officers. The food was exquisite, compared to the years of poverty that they endured and the small gruel that left the masses alive before they entered the final solution. Anastasia and the Countess were continually addressed as guests and treated in the station they had been born to. The politeness of gentlemen and the abundance of fresh food was staggering to their imagination.

After the evening meal had been completely enjoyed by the officers and the bewilderment of the two feminine guests, they were dismissed to their quarters. Once again the two women were allowed to converse with each other before retiring for the night; it was then that the new stage of horror took place.

As they entered the rooms assigned to them, there were two S.S. women waiting. This did not surprise or concern them at first, but when they were strapped to the beds in separate rooms, this heralded the beginning of the torture from the demented minds of their host and his officers. They

robert f. edwards

delighted in their perverse fantasies, and unspeakable behaviour against the two helpless women. This continued for weeks, until both the Countess and Anastasia no longer felt the pain, agony and disgrace of being mere human flesh to be played with and tormented by the minds of the insane.

It was not too long before this diabolical exercise took the toll of what was left of their physical well being. Like toys in an endless supply shop the Commandant and his officers soon tired of these play-things. One morning, after their bodies had been short of being mutilated, they were returned back to the quarters that they first experienced.

It could have been a week, or a month, time had ceased to exist. It was only the moment that had any credence. The fall months had now been replaced by the winter, and the coldness was upon the country-side. In this hell hole of modern evilness, the history books would document.

The Countess had succumbed to illness. There was no way that any prisoner wished to display weakness or sickness. There was a block in which people were taken to the infirmary. All knew the practices that were performed there were not humanitarian, but were something out of a horror movie of epic proportions. Physicians and their aides created experiments that Count Frankenstein would have needed instructions.

So the Countess grew worse. Even with Anastasia and the other two women doing their best, by providing extra clothes to keep the Countess warm, or by giving her mother her portion of food. The dreaded moment was approaching fast. With morning inspections, Anastasia's mother was helped to stay in line, but the inevitable happened, the Countess was too weak to get up.

With the help of the other women, Anastasia tried to support her in the line. But fortune was not with them that day. Anastasia held her mother with all her strength around the waist. The officer said, "Move away from each other. Now!"

With that, her mother collapsed face down on the cobblestones, at his feet. He stood over the Countess and said," Get

332

River of Life

up now! Now!" The Countess struggled with feeble motions to rise, only to feel the strong hands of the soldiers pulling her away to the end.

Anastasia screamed. The officer turned and said, "Your turn is later, do you understand? Ya?" The other two women grasped Anastasia, and pulled her back in line. This was the last time Anastasia saw her mother.

The life-line that had kept Anastasia alive had been snatched from her. Her face had shrunk to a pale transparent skin that covered a skeleton. Her eyes were sunken in hollow madness, a mind in torture. Her body had withered to tightly stretched skin, barely covering a bone structure. Her once firm breasts were nothing more limp flesh upon a flat rib cage. She wasted away like the rest of the victims of the Third Reich.

The only comfort in this madness and insanity was a small cartouche, that by some miracle that she had been able to hide from the insatiable searching of those who controlled the camp. Her little remaining strength in both body and soul, started to diminish rapidly. She feared she may not survive long enough for Horus-Salah to find her and rescue her. In all the years in this demented hell that Poland had suffered, she never lost hope that Horus-Salah would be her knight, her liberator.

It had always been her saving grace that she would be able to overcome whatever lay before her, as long as she believed that Horus-Salah would come and get her. But both the weakness and frailty of her body, and the never-ending punishment of her mind, she realized that for the possibility was there. She may not be able to hang on for that moment of liberty.

The days were as endless repetition. Her body told her that the end was near. So in the coldness of the night she reached into the hidden place that she kept the treasure of her dreams, the key of her existence, the Cartouche. She held it tightly to generate as much warmth as she could. Once the gold metal was as warm as it would get, she broke it into as many little pieces as she could and swallowed them.

If this was to be the end, and she knew it was, no criminal would ever get possession of it. It would burn in the furnace, along with her wasted body, and all her dreams. As she managed to swallow the last fragment, she propped herself up against the cold bricks of the cell, and thought of Horus-Salah, and their childhood. Her mind was no longer with her body.

They were running and chasing each other along the ridge, far above the tombs of the Pharaohs, and the Valley of the Kings. They were working their way down through their secret path, to the Tomb of the Cat. At last, they were sitting at the entrance, watching the flow of the Nile, the River of Life, as it lazily moved its way past Luxor. It was the face of Horus-Salah that her mind closed with.

River of Life

CHAPTER 25

The old figure moved slowly but methodically along the ridge, above the Valley of the Kings. Horus-Salah stopped once more, and leaned against the great walls of nature. He feasted his eyes below on the glow from the small fires burning their way to embers. The great Nile showed small silhouettes against the guiding light of the stars for ships making their last voyages to and from the shorelines. The great temple of Karnak was still lit by its artificial means of lights to attract the never-ending wealth of tourists that provided vast incomes of the region now. Other buildings that had not yet submitted to the darkness still burnt their lights in the windows that gave shadows of eeriness to its vision.

He breathed heavily, for his age was upon him, remembering the journey of his youth, as he and his beloved Anastasia ran these same trails in the past. As his memory ran forward in those past corridors of his mind, it was all that was left of youth. The old body took comfort in the warmth of the rocks that braced him and gave him rest for the bones that no longer supported the strength.

Once more his eyes gazed upon the great temple. There was a longing to return to the old ways, the ancient face of Egypt. The ways of his ancestors that communicated with the gods themselves. His mind fluttered with the gentle breezes that blew across the Nile. He looked away from the temple and down at his feet. The path, this dark line, the dark ridge, that was going to carry him with all his will and strength to the tomb that he wished to see once more. His mind ran like pages through a book, trying to find where it had left off, and then, almost like a magical finger his mind stopped on the page.

robert f. edwards

Yes, that meeting with his father. When his father's last command was to marry. When he was told by his father, the frail figure with the strength of the eyes that burns into his soul that he would soon sit in the chair that governed their clan, their destiny. It was his duty, not only to his father, but to their ancestors, and to the future and legacy that would go beyond both of them, to marry and provide the offspring to follow in the tradition, and the will of Allah, and the clan.

When he asked about his beautiful Anastasia, his only true love in life; his father curtly reminded him of the Islamic law, that he be provided with three wives and the first must be fulfilled before his passing. His father commanded by a wish that was irrefutable.

In less than two months, he began the courting of a beautiful young nurse that had once sat patiently by his side, tending to his injuries from the years in the war. She was his choice and his first request. He remembered like it was a moment, just a few seconds ago. He once more entered into the great room that controlled the power of the clan and sat opposite his father at his desk, that he seemed endlessly occupied at. He had the same fears and the same hesitation, as he remembered the first time that he was summonsed as a boy to these chambers.

With the same reluctance, he sat before his father; it was now, as it was then, that his father looked up ,almost reluctantly at him and in a low voice asked," What brings you to my presence?"

With the strength that he had prepared himself for, he answered," My dearest father, I have a request for the woman that you seek, that I shall call my wife, and the mother of my children." His father's gaze neither changed nor altered his facial expressions.

His voice came deep as if it were more of a moan from within." And what is her name?"

Horus-Salah responded with both her given name and her family name. It was to his surprise that the tired face that

336

River of Life

was showing the strains of remaining in this world, gave a smile of relief. Yes, yes he had pleased his father, he had chosen well. His father would make the necessary arrangements to meet with her father and arrange the marriage. Without any further conversation the hand that spoke louder and firmer than the voice waived him away.

The days found their place and the weeks made no notice on the calendars. The moon proved its position across the sky in its lunar participation on the events. The courtship was shorter than usual in traditional forms and the families understood the urgency due to the deterioration of his father's health. The families were of equal financial rank and heritage. The announcement was immediately accepted by both families and satisfied the demand's of his father and his heritage,

Horus-Salah welcomed the relationship that he would enter into. Though it was not the love that he shared with Anastasia, there was a respect and admiration for her dedication to his needs and her benevolent nature that she presented in all those months that he convalesced in the hospital. Another blessing in this relationship was she was not a stranger to him like so many other betrothals of families. The children had no say and did not even know each other until they were introduced by their fathers.

He had had the pleasure of spending many hours in her presence, in her caring. He had an understanding of her nature. And for her, he was as equal a gift that her father could give her in her station. By the standards both of her families and the faith, it would be more than an acceptable marriage. As the courtship continued under the vigilant eyes of the chaperones, the preparation of the day of marriage was progressing. The guest's lists were constantly being reviewed as the multitude of guests continually grew with requests from different family members on each side. Cairo was abuzz with the preparations of such a wedding to take place. In some ways, it was more the families that participated in the ceremony than the marriage that was to take place.

337

robert f. edwards

Sabrina became the bride and then the wife of Horus-Salah. The age was a matter of two to three years difference, depending on which calendar one wished to examine. The ceremony that bound them together under Islamic law was surrounded by dignitaries that witnessed the vows. Even King Farouk and his wife, and many that were in his favour at that moment attended. To say nothing of the British Ambassador, the General, and Field Marshals that were still protecting their interest in Egypt. Yes, it was a national event of international recognition.

Afterwards the couple returned to the great house in Cairo, and found a suitable wing to settle down in. The social order continued in what was expected from them in those years. As his father's moments of life continued to dwindle from earth, Horus-Salah was brought in to more of the immediate and intricate details of the family's business and what his obligations would be.

Before the tragedies of the war years, he had traveled great distances and met many of the business associates that would now be his representatives in the vast empire of his family. The great wealth that they possessed covered trade routes through the vast continent of Africa and the spanning much of the Mediterranean. There were even small interests of trade relations in different parts of Europe. It was a vast interwoven network that needed constant attention. There was never a moment that the great ruler of the house was not well informed of the status of their business.

As Horus-Salah continued to learn the intricate parts of his family's business, he was pleasantly reminded of how many of the acquaintances and members of this vast empire that he had already met through expeditions to their operations, and to their homes. It was a network of friendship, of families from eons of time that had perpetuated through all forms of change. From transitions of Rulers and governments, of invaders and interruptions, of natural catastrophes and man-made demises. They had woven an intricate part of consistency of this family, of this dynasty, of this legacy.

338

River of Life

During the years that Horus-Salah became more conversant in the intricate secrets and hidden transactions and the ways in which his father had governed this vast network, his admiration for his father grew with respect. While his knowledge was constantly gaining supremacy on the one side, his father's ailing health continued to whither. It was on one these days that once again, Horus-Salah was summonsed to the great office.

The frail figure seemed to have shrunk against the grandeur of his surroundings. Horus-Salah walked in and sat down in the chair that he had sat at before. He had an air of confidence this time, more than ever before. Not because the sharp dark eyes that had looked at him had any less baring of his soul, but it was his knowledge of what lie ahead that gave him the confidence to look back into those burning coals that relentlessly looked into his soul.

Horus-Salah sat patiently, and the voice crackled and gasped as though it was clinging to something that it no longer deserved. The lips moved and with a mist of air, the sound came to Horus-Salah's ears, "Give me an heir, now!"

Horus-Salah looked back without hesitation. "Your wish is my command, oh Father. But, to be granted, it is Allah's, not mine."

The voice once more quivered with the words that it wanted to possess. Then, out of the silence, "Let it be said..." the rasping breath paused. However, Horus-Salah came to the rescue, " Let it be done, oh Father, oh Ruler, oh my leader of my life and the clan." Horus-Salah bowed his head and left the great office and the presence of the frail ruler he would soon replace.

In the nights that followed, Sabrina and Horus-Salah renewed their marriage commitments with a more vigorous lovemaking to fulfill the request of a dying lord. The days proceeded and the nights were filled with passion. The weeks found their way on the calendar and to Sabrina's delight; she informed her husband that she had missed her monthly womanhood. She shared this information with her mother

339

and his mother. But the secret was kept well hidden, not to raise false hopes to their ailing ruler.

His father weathered the days, some better than others. He continued to withdraw from more and more of his daily duties, now placed onto Horus-Salah's shoulders. It was not until the second month of Sabrina's pregnancy, and the confirmation of the doctors that she was expecting a child, that the family brought the news to their dying leader. He smiled with deep satisfaction at their success, and continued on his never-ending path to another world.

The months moved forward, and Sabrina's stomach grew and her breasts became fuller. It seemed the few times that their ailing leader shared a meal with the family, that the sight of her motherhood was the only thing that appeased the pain, and abated the agony of the enemy that was taking him away from them. His body became frailer and more mummified. The skin became a pigment of yellow, and the gaunt look of leaving gave an odor of the presence of the enemy that grew within him.

By the seventh month in Sabrina's pregnancy, the ruler no longer left his chambers. The doctors and nurses in attendance were continuously by his side, to aide in any comfort that would ease the agony of a war that he was losing. It was like a spider holding onto the silk web it had woven that kept him from going to the other side. He clung to the life of this world, not for his own purpose but to see the heir of the new life. Each day his withering form sank deeper away. His life no longer interested him, only the presence of Sabrina and the condition of her pregnancy.

All knew that Horus-Salah's father was in race against time, that he may be able to win, but it would be the last he would participate in. Then midway in her seventh month, he slipped to the other side, unnoticed by those that surrounded him. One night, he ceased to take his last breath. He slipped like a shadow in the darkness. He was gone forever.

The family draped itself in the traditional mourning. All immediate duties were postponed as the funeral proceeded.

River of Life

The sorrow, the loss, and to Horus-Salah, the full burden of responsibility weighed like a stone that anchored any progress .The days that followed were filled with dignitaries honoring the memory of this great man, as they expressed their condolences.

Once the days of wearing the mourning garments had passed, Sabrina was close to the moments of a new life, a new presence, a new gift from Allah. The ninth month found its ways on the calendar and her swollen body was ripe for the moment they had all been waiting for. And like the passing of his father, the moment arrived and though expected, was not witness at first. The mere discomfort of a young mother was like another day. But no, it was like no other day that she had ever experienced, for it was a day that she was to give life. And the wee cry, the following early morning gave evidence the new family member had arrived.

A beautiful baby girl was the next generation of the great families that flowed through her blood. There was a great joyous moment in the immediate family which was followed by the acknowledgement of Cairo itself. It was almost like a coronation, that this great little person had found its way into this world and this dynasty.

As the days do, and time prevails, the years moved quickly when events unravel but have no significant bearing. It wasn't until his first-born, his precious daughter, was almost three that his beloved wife noticed she was with child again. To everyone's great joy, he was again blessed, this time with a son, an heir to continue the family legacy.

By this time, Horus-Salah felt comfortable, as much as anyone who never really wanted to rule could feel comfortable. He felt capable, at least in performing his duties to rule and have his wishes fulfilled. He sat comfortably in the large room now behind the desk.

His quest for Anastasia never ceased, nor had Sabrina been led by illusions that this would diminish as his years of commitment to her and his family would prevail.

robert f. edwards

Things had changed, the world had changed. Of course the wars in Europe and Asia had ceased. The new catch phrases were 'the cold wars' between Russia and what Churchill named as the 'Iron Curtain' and 'the Free World'. Britain tried to grasp and continue its glorious moments of being the rulers of the high seas and 'the empire that the sun never sat on'. But in reality, the setting sun had sank well below their horizons and left Britain with its horrific debts, primarily owed to it previous colleague, the United States of America. Through the burdens, once a proud empire to symbolism was left with few remaining moments.

The Prime Minister Sir Anthony Eden tried to show the pomp and splendor and grandeur of his predecessor, Sir Winston Churchill, a moment of glory in Britain's defiance against evil, only to botch the one accomplishment that he would be recorded for, the Suez Canal. Under Anwar al-Sadat, the canal ceased to occupy the flow of cargo to Europe and to Britain. The long routes that the brave navigators of past history had used were the only option now, to circle the Cape and bring their wares to the ports of Europe.

In another great moment in history, Horus-Salah and his family were witness to the creation of the Aswan dam. The world watched, along with the archaeologists, the creation and monumental task of saving the great contribution of Ramses and the temples that were under his dynasty and reign as a Pharaoh, before the great flooding of the hydro-electric dams. The falling out from Britain had long been present and the expulsion of the last link of the Pharaohs, of King Farouk was in exile.

The squandering and the incompetence, the puppet-like performance of the monarchs of the past had ceased. First to a pro-democratic position, and then an alliance with the Russians, and a flavour of ruling of communism. It was like the changing of the guards. The rulers were different, the costumes were different, but the object was the same, to possess and rule the great dynasties, the great past of the Nile.

River of Life

The Russians were an odd lot, cruder and with little or no etiquette, compared to the overseers of the British, but still with the determination of being right and demanding change of those that surrounded their directive. To Horus-Salah, all these men were foreigners, guests in the house of the Great Pharaohs of the past, the Great River of the Nile and all things associated with the sands of Egypt.

However, it mattered little, for his obsession in finding Anastasia would not cease, nor would it ever, until they were either united or his breath would give way to eternal rest. Like he had in the past, until the British were expelled, he had used every possible means at his disposal to investigate all avenues to find his beloved Anastasia. At least, with the Russians once more occupying Poland, the communication level allowed him a new opportunity for success of finding the quest that never left his heart.

He found more than one way to entice relationships with the tightly restricted embassies and delegations from Russia. Even as his people mingled and infiltrated into the dark secrets of the KGB inner circle to gather information, they always came back with the discouraging news that nothing was available.

He had been blessed with a young son, and together with his daughter, they grew by leaps and bounds in a society that would once be theirs. They often visited the wing of the home that he had spent so many enjoyable years in Luxor. On many occasions, he too traveled by train to his estate, where the family would enjoy the cool months. When not commuting back and forth, the couriers that would bring him daily reports of what was required of his duties. It would be these moments that he would become more withdrawn, with the isolation and the same aloofness that had possessed his father.

On other days, he would be absent as he secretly wandered his way through the path that Anastasia and he had danced to their merriment to the hidden secret tune. It would be like no other moments in his life, when under the cloak of

robert f. edwards

darkness and isolation, he would make his way down to the secret path that only Anastasia and he knew of, toward the Tomb of the Cat. Many times he would be literally shaking in anticipation, that some other mortal had discovered the sanctuary, this holy place of their souls. Their great commitment to each other, the great love.

In other moments, he would sit in the entrance and gaze out, with eyes that did not focus other than at the skies. Without consciously being aware of the action, his right hand would caress the treasured watch, the gift that clung to the existence of his true love. He would run his fingers gently over the intricate carvings and craftsmanship and without daring to look, would touch the small spring and feel the movements of time ticking away with its arms continually marking the moments in their presence.

Other times, he would turn to it over to the back, and would run his hands smoothly over the side, not daring to open it, teasing his mind with never-ending demands and refusals to pop the spring, to feel what was inside, to gaze what was inside. Then pain, the longing, the agony of not knowing where his love was, would jolt him and his fingers would quickly contract the watch back into its pouch, its hiding place, from all other eyes, including his.

After these moments he would come out of a trance, and transfix himself once more on the shrine, the Tomb of the Cat. As was his custom, he would bring food and other gifts associated with the presence of the honouring the dead. He would also bring extra candles in case one day he would wish to lie there and sleep through the night. These were somber moments, these were moments of regression, and these were moments of determination. They were endless in his quest to find Anastasia.

Many times, he would find himself in total despair and the melancholic moods that prevailed for days, and even weeks. These depressions were disturbing to his wife and his immediate family. There was not one that did not know what he was going through. There was always a feeling of relief in

River of Life

his family when he informed them that he must return to Cairo. For once in Cairo, though his obsession never fluctuated; there were other things to distract his attention with.

The years moved like the earth around Ra, the Sun God of Egypt. These times of watching his children grow up, and enjoy the fruits of his labour, gave him great pleasure and satisfaction. His beautiful and dedicated wife never ceased to amaze him, with her understanding and devotion. In many ways he grew to love her in the imagery he hoped to share with another.

But all is not at peace in the world, or in the life that he endured on this planet. For as his children were blessed with good health and grew like a harvest each year, his wonderful nanny, his companion in so many moments in despair, had been struck down by a careless driver in Cairo. She died shortly after the injuries she received. It affected Horus-Salah much greater than the family expected. For some say that even after the period of mourning he never quite recovered from the sorrow he had felt. Though he wore the loss well, the scars of such a tragedy marked the aging process of his face.

No sooner had this tragedy had drained the youth from his body, then his dearest beloved mother suffered her first stroke and was showing the poor health that would continue for the balance of the few years she had left. Her great love and devotion to her grandchildren aided and assisted her to stay with them as long as possible. But as her health deteriorated the strokes became more frequent. Until, one claimed its victory.

So now as his children entered into the school years of their lives, he was alone, with a quest that was not yet fulfilled. Many around him, including his associates and his advisors, felt that his success in all fields, was the mirror of the reflection of his father's disciplinarian ways and that sooner or later Horus-Salah would adopt these ways to perpetuate the family's destiny with his children.

However, as the years drifted like the great sea sands under heavy winds, though the appearance changed, the man's

345

inner being remained the same. He was and would be, as long as the air filled his lungs, a subject of the commands that would prevail to do his duty, first above all else. To seek his quest were secondary. His own personal dreams and wishes were far below on the scales of priority.

It seemed like the twinkling of a moment and before he could realize that the years were slipping away like droplets of time, his children entered their high school years. They were good students as well as good children, and though they spent a limited amount of time in his presence, for he, like his father, became more and more recluse with all that was around him, it was like the sponge found moisture but never enough to satisfy.

The few times through these years that the children would remember his great contribution to their happiness was at special occasions, like their birthdays, national holidays and religious events. The closest period was the Ramadan, and the family shared their fasting and their companionship together. It was during one of these years, that his beloved and devoted wife first felt a small swelling. She was amused at first to think that in her middle age, she might be giving him his final gift, another child. Her periods became erratic and the swelling became as well, erratic. Then, like the practical person she was, she felt that this change was nothing more than age that claimed her fertility, and she was entering into the menopause of her life.

But sad to say, long before she distinguished what menopause was, the evil cancer of the uterus had grown too large. The false pregnancy was the kiss of evil, the kiss of cancer. The years that followed, were both agonizing and filled with sorrow. Their delicate mother, his devoted wife, was slowly but continuously being claimed to enter the other world. It was shortly after Ramadan that evil victory had been achieved by the cancer. She passed into the other world.

The children by now were in their mid-teens and the loss was devastating to their well being. Like their parents they had nannies, but unlike their parents the nannies had not

River of Life

fulfilled the great love and participation their mother had provided. They seemed to drift in directions that ended with no meaning. Though Horus-Salah spent more time with his children he was ill prepared to fulfill both their needs and wants. For the children, it was a period of their lives that they had never experienced such great loss before and bewilderment.

For Horus-Salah, it was a loss that he could not comprehend or accept, for she, his beloved wife, had always been at his side. From the days of his convalescing in the war, to the days of the vows that they had taken together, she was the one person that understood his quest and his endless need to find Anastasia.

The wealth of success seemed to be like the horn of plenty; the less he irritated it the more it prospered. Under his guidance of supervision it prospered like the vast wealth that most empires dream of. For all physical wants and materialistic gains there were no limits to what he could contribute to. His children had everything that most could only imagine. Whether it was the best schools, best tutors or the best of everything that was available in the global community. For him life remained still modest, with little or not changes other than his continual quest to gain access to his lost love.

And then, all things that are constant, all things that remain the same eventually change. And as the world spins on its axis and continually joins the larger bodies of the universe, the change came. Throughout the years, Horus-Salah had tried in every possible means and every financial way to gain to access to the archives of Poland. He even explored channels of espionage that would have made any country proud, but still nothing prevailed. It was impregnable, unattainable, and all lanes led to dark disappointment.

However, the change arrived as sudden and unexpected as a storm that one does not see coming. Or the breaking of a dawn on a beautiful day, it was unpredictable. The Kremlin appointed a man that would change the views of Russia and the Soviet Union. His name was Mikhail Gorbachev. To Horus-Salah, it meant little more than a crumbling empire

347

robert f. edwards

changing its guards, to keep the mythical views of outdated dogmas in place. His sources had long concluded the demise and the total collapse of the shadows of deception that the communists had prevailed on its endless curtain of the Soviet Union.

So when this young man replaced the aging of his equals, Horus-Salah added little more than a mere comment of the position Mikhail Gorbachev held. It was long after the solidarity movement in Poland had gained momentum in the labour camps and the left wing had gained the popular vote and support of the movement, that a change caught Horus-Salah's attention.

Word came through from his advisors, ' There is unrest. There is an uprising. There is a coalition in Poland. They are trying to throw off the shackles of the Russian's once more, to give them freedom of a nation that they have long deserved.' For Horus-Salah, anything that had to do with Poland, grabbed his attention and focus. As if there was anything else that could possibly be of importance in his existence.

He continued observing even the slightest movement that transpired, and was unraveling at a horrific speed in the global community. Words that he had never heard a Russian speak or use, such as Glasnost, and Perestroika, were now on most broadcast systems as well as the newspapers. Would it be possible, he thought, in the far reaching moments of his mind, that he and he alone could go to Poland and find his beloved Anastasia? Had the curtains finally rotted, and were falling to the ground that had kept him from his beloved, his love, his true purpose and meaning of existence? He quivered as the thoughts danced through his mind.

All around him knew of his obsession, but no one had ever witnessed the revival of his commitment, and his unyielding determination to succeed. Though it was many years now, it mattered little, for nothing mattered as far as he concerned. He was no more than just the boy who had been separated from his life-time friend. His vitality rose to levels that many had never seen before. Everyone around him was energized, as he gave commands to seek out what could be done. Yes, yes this was definitely one of the moments, when all around him, including his children, looked in wonderment. It was the beginning of his quest, not the end.

So, as the walls and iron curtain resistance of the Kremlin gradually came tumbling down, whether it was the Berlin wall, or the freedom fought for in the shipyards of Poland, the movement was being felt and planned in Egypt.

robert f. edwards

CHAPTER 26

 The old man's eyes blurred for a moment, as he regained his presence on the narrow path that led from the Tomb of the Cat. He had rested long enough. His mind was capturing everything of the past, and had forgotten the present. The winds further chilled the night and the stars were bright in a cloudless sky. Even the temple of Karnak had given up its imitation lights of electricity. Only the shadows of the pillars remained as the stars dominated and illuminated the skies. It gave an eerie rippling effect on the waters, a graveyard that nothing floated in it. The shore-lines were darkened by the slumber of those that claimed it as their home.

Once more he looked up, high into the skies, to marvel at the clarity the night was providing. It was illuminated like only stars and the moon can, when one is alone in its presence. The long years that he had walked these paths, his feet moved in unison as though they needed no guidance from above. He was making good time through the small passage he knew only too well. Ah yes, he would be there in an hour, maybe less.

His old body shuffled along the dusty trail that led to the destination he sought. His breathing became more laboured with each step. Fatigue hit hard into his stamina. He would not yield until he achieved at least the spot of his hidden marker, which would give him the direction that only he and Anastasia had ever known. His weary body continued to support the demands of his mind, as he dragged one foot in front of the other. Fatigue hit hard into his determination.

He was less than five hundred..., 'ah' he moaned, more like seven hundred metres away. His mind promised his weary body that it would yield, it would give quarter, it would submit to a moment of rest, before he would descend down

River of Life

the path to the Tomb of the Cat. With an almost superhuman power, the body co-operated, and submitted to the abuse that his mind demanded. The aging, withering body responded to his mind once more, as he commanded all the living organs within to obey.

He finally reached the passage that he sought. His lungs gasped as if all the oxygen in the air had been deprived. His body had a cold sweat that had dampened himself. His hands shook, and trembled, and his knees weakened which gave little support left for his quest.

He sat on the ledge, a few hundred meters from the path that he and Anastasia had traveled. They alone had managed to slither down to the existing wider path. He propped himself against the wall of nature, to give himself some form of relief, and his tired body welcomed the mind's compassion. His breathing became more irregular but remained sustainable. The cold perspiration had dampened his galabya, as he leaned against the stones of history.

Horus-Salah once more gazed up at the stars above, some twinkled, and some danced endlessly through their existence. For a moment, he was not sure, he almost lost consciousness, or he had drifted from one world to the next. But his mind was definitely not in the present. It had given this tired, frail, decrepit body its rests. Though not eternal, at least some rest. His mind drifted far, far above into the universe, into the stars, into the skies that his tired eyes gazed onto.

At that moment he passed into another time, another period. Ah, if anyone had been near, they would have heard a sigh, that was like a moan deep down inside of hell. For, he was back now, in the time he remembered only like yesterday. It was the time that the Iron Curtain, the curtain that held the mysteries of his beloved Anastasia fell, and he entered.

All the years that the powerful Soviet Union continued its expansion across the global community, Horus-Salah relent-

robert f. edwards

lessly searched through that vast network, trying to penetrate through their security systems, trying to integrate into their networks, and solve the quest, the dire need, to know where his Anastasia was, without success. The impregnable walls of the Kremlin did not weaken or show anyway of entering if one was not invited.

Throughout these years, Horus-Salah kept a continuing dialogue with the Count. The Count, along with many others, had fled Poland before the occupation. Through Horus-Salah's vast networks, he was able to locate and reunite with the Count. He had invited the Count more than once, to stay with him and his family. However, the Count, like himself, isolated his sorrow and his commitments to the small community that he now lived in, in one of the suburbs in the greater London area.

Of course, his vast holdings in Poland were nothing more than memories, as was his loving wife and his beautiful daughter Anastasia, still missing and untraceable. He had gained some recognition as a resistance participant, and a compadre of the allied front, but after the war, he faded quietly and discreetly into the shadows. He was a very old man and at this juncture in history, in ailing health.

With the new avenues of information, Horus-Salah took full advantage of the moment of opportunity. He made exhaustive inquiries into what it would take for an Egyptian to get permission to go to Poland. The British assisted him with their tracks in acknowledgement for his participation in their active campaign against the axis of Nazism. He pulled out all markers of gone-by-years, and asked for the final favours of his quest, and that was to seek out, and find his beloved Anastasia, personally with his own delegation.

After endless official procrastination, finally the achievement of his request was within his grasp. Without further delay, he selected his most valuable people to accompany him with his final quest, his final achievement of finding Anastasia. This main group set up its base of operation in London. After endless visits to the aging Count, he grasped a deeper

352

River of Life

understanding to the horrific years of the occupation of Nazism. The distance between the channel, and the distance between Egypt and Poland, was not only geographic, but culturally interwoven by the British. The Count had anxiously shared what little information he could gather from behind the curtain of the communist block. It was of little value to Horus-Salah, for his vast network had penetrated even further than the Count's closest remaining allies.

The day finally arrived. Horus-Salah stepped foot once more on Polish soil. At first glance, in Warsaw, other than the modernization that had taken place globally; the building structures, streets and plazas looked unscathed by the decades of absence of his eyes. He was surprised at the attacks that reflected back on his memories. After spending the time required to fully satisfy his knowledge with his network of delegates, they released information that contained the most devastating thought, 'that Anastasia and her mother had probably entered into a concentration camp.'

The mere thought that his beloved Anastasia had succumbed to such a diabolical end, froze a portion of his mind into rejection. Actively, he demanded his delegation to work endlessly, day and night, to seek out the smallest fragment of intelligence. They were advised that there might be more records, obscure as they may be, in the archives of Krakow or in Auschwitz itself. The mere thoughts of these words echoing into his ears brought more than a moment of anxiety, of sheer horror, of what knowledge would lie ahead.

The delegation moved first to Krakow, and visited the estate and the landholdings of the Count's previous wealth. After questioning every individual personally that was associated with the household of the Count, the story unraveled of what happened during those horrible moments of the past. When the beloved nanny had sacrificed her life, rather than give information to the Nazis on the whereabouts of Anastasia and the Countess. And then trail went cold.

Horus-Salah could not believe that there wasn't someone, somewhere, in all of Poland that would have known where

robert f. edwards

Anastasia and the Countess had finally escaped to. His new optimism of hope soared to heights that few around him had ever seen. He became energized as they had never seen him before. The quest seemed insurmountable, but the demands that Horus-Salah put on them superseded it. There had to be a way. There had to be a way.

The greatest minds of his delegation spent endless nights searching through the enigma. Then, like all puzzles, a piece was found, a fragment that at first looked like it could not possibly have fitted. It was the Gestapo itself. The link of information led to the General, and his army, before the demise of his military career, when Anastasia and the Countess disappeared. Investigations into his war crimes against humanity provided further links into finding Anastasia and the Countess. After weeks of endless searching through libraries of information, there it was, in bold records. The Countess and Anastasia had been sentenced to Auschwitz.

The exuberance and enthusiasm of Horus-Salah took a crash into despair. Aghast at the knowledge that was presented to him, the knowledge of the truth that lay ahead. The distance was within kilometers of the residence he occupied in Krakow. Yet, he froze like a statue, not able to go forward. He became irritable, and unreasonable, that they search other avenues. He rejected the truth, as in total denial. It only seemed months ago that he was preparing himself for the worst of what might be the truth. And now, that the truth presented itself, he was unable to cope with it.

He kept repeating," Go out and find me more, Go out and find where she is." As the penetration of searches became more intense, the evidence became undisputed. The days of which Anastasia and the Countess were recorded in Auschwitz and the evidence of undisputable truth. Horus-Salah was more than in depression, more than in denial. After weeks of gathering information, all avenues pointed to the irrefutable fact that their final residence was Auschwitz. Horus-Salah got up one morning and had the group assembled." I will go to Auschwitz myself. Make the arrangements."

River of Life

" I will go to Auschwitz myself."

Original photograph Robert F. Edwards
Auschwitz   May, 1998

he told them. Within days, his small group made the pilgrimage to Auschwitz. As they went through the gates, they looked at the stark buildings that once had been the military base of the Polish Army. But now, only living mausoleums to millions that had perished in theses rooms. They walked the cobbled streets through the narrow buildings; saw the diabolical, experimental buildings of the 'Herr Doctors' that recorded their inhumane acts against life itself. They walked through the cells that housed the victims.

Horus-Salah cringed within his soul. Then they entered the room of honor of the dead. Before them were vast stock piles of luggage that were destined to the points of a journey that had never been taken, the insurmountable heaps of artificial limbs, and clothing that had been accumulated. In their minds, they saw the dark faces of children, of women, the skeleton forms of men.

As they moved through these memorials, they all paused at the side of a bed. On it was a display of what looked like steel wool. Horus-Salah almost turned away to the next exhibit, before asking, "What is this?"

The attendant provided, "This is the hair of some of the deceased, after they were put to sleep with the cyanide gas."

"Ah," Horus-Salah gasped, as he took a stronger examination of the mass of hair, right before his eyes. As his eyes swept from one panel to the next, he focused, as he was trying to push himself through,' There, there... oh Allah... no." There was a braided lock of golden hair.

"Anastasia," he screamed. His eyes rolled back and his body fell backwards. Before his aides could break his fall, he lay motionless. Immediately, a medical aide was called and they rushed him to a hospital in Krakow.

He was breathing but barely, his pulse was erratic and irregular. Upon arrival, the doctors examined him and had no answers, only that he was alive, and in critical condition. They gave him the best medical attention that was possible, and tried to stabilize his condition, before his aides were allowed to transfer him by helicopter, to Warsaw and then by private

River of Life

plane to the hospital to London. The doctors in London confirmed exactly what the doctors in Krakow had feared, that Horus-Salah was in a coma.

They had no way of knowing if that was the extent, or something else. The best they could do was try to stabilize his life support systems by artificial means. For the family, money was no object and had some of the greatest doctors available brought in, to help the life that was at stake. The days found their ways through the darkness of the nights; the weeks vanished into the months. His body became more and more fragile, but eventually the artificial breathing was replaced by natural.

But still, the darkness of the coma persisted. Many of the doctors advised that it was possible, in this deep coma, that he may never come out of it, and if he did, he may be braindead. His daughter and son stayed devotedly by his side and they both took on the responsibility of locating the families of the vast network.

For the better part of six months, Horus-Salah had been laying in a coma in the London hospital. With all the facilities of not only the hospital, but the medical profession throughout the world at his disposal, he remained in a deep coma.

Almost to the day, six months later, the attendants surrounding his bed in their endless vigilance, saw in total amazement his eyes flutter, his fingers move. Immediately the physicians that were on constant duty were summonsed. It was a marked improvement, short of being astounding. There was an air of optimism that had not been experienced since he had entered the hospital in his critical condition. The days that followed were a whirlwind of events.

His daughter had been in attendance, and immediately his son was flown in, to be at his side. As miracles do happen throughout the history of man, there was no exception here. By the time his son arrived, Horus-Salah was not only out of the coma, but was able to make small words. The weeks that followed were nothing less than remarkable.

robert f. edwards

Horus-Salah was recovering. Each day his strength regained its presence in the frail skeleton that had been dormant for so long. The nourishment that had been administrated by tubes was now being enjoyed and swallowed by the living Horus-Salah that was once more able to communicate. Within the month, he was sitting up and preparing to make his long journey back to Egypt.

Fading in and out of those long periods, either resting with his eyes closed, or just looking out endlessly into space still worried the medical profession on the stability of his recovery. It was another month before he was well enough to return to Egypt, under the watchful eyes of the medical profession in his homeland. Eventually, he started to speak more fluently of the long absence, and asked questions of what had transpired during this period. Once he felt that he was fully aware of all that had happened in his absence, he started to rest more comfortably in his own mansion and surroundings in Cairo.

Some think that is was his grandchild that was the first to let him recapture the moments prior to the long sleep, some say it was his homeland, that had been the surroundings of his ancestors ,and all of his duties that he had put first, above all other pleasures and happiness of his life, some say it was when he sat in the great study, the great office that controlled the vast holdings of his family, that he rekindled his duty to those that had gone before him, and those that were present and to the future of those yet to come.

No one had the answers to Horus-Salah's continual strength and recovery. One year to that fatal moment had passed, and yet in the hours of slumber, one could hear him screaming out the name of Anastasia. One could hear the anguish and torture that the heart and the soul concealed in the mask of his face. He never fully recovered the duties and the position as the leader of his family.

In a quasi form of leadership, he continued in the years ahead with a tribune, always at the head with his two children being the counterbalances of his indecisiveness. It re-

358

River of Life

flected in the vast holdings, as some dwindled, and others ceased to exist. Though it rarely affected their prominent position in society, it was an undermining, and the beginning of the end. There were no answers to this enigma that was presented to the future.

In all respects, his daughter was far more capable of making the decisions, with the correct vision of where the company and the family should find its new destinies in an ever-changing world. But, by the customs and the laws of his heritage, after he ceased, his son would be the supreme decision-maker of the family. Though the son was loyal and had many characteristics of Horus-Salah, he lacked the most important one, of duty.

Horus-Salah had sacrificed his life and now it was dwindling fast into the twilight years. Duty above all else, his son did not feel the moral obligation, the sacred vow. And as the years faded from one and another, Horus-Salah became more distracted and disorientated. Though he sat reluctantly many times, studying the decisions that were his alone to make, his mind wandered to distance times and other places.

It always returned to the moments of happiness and joy that Anastasia and he had spent in the growing years, racing up and down the mighty paths over the great Valley of the Kings. Somehow, peace relieved such a tormented soul in his magnitude of loss. He would remember the moments of pleasure as they entered the Tomb of the Cat. In many cases when the period of Ramadan took place, one would find that Horus-Salah had returned to his roots.

He would go back to Luxor. He did not dare go near the great palace of his father. Many years ago, it had been taken over by the state, and even as another guest of the state, he could not bear to walk in the halls or the wing that was specially built for him and Anastasia. Instead, he took a very modest abode near the streets that were busy and congested in Luxor itself. As befitting his station, he lived with more luxuries than his neighbours, and behind that hidden door was his sanctuary.

robert f. edwards

His age became more obvious, and his daily duties were becoming impaired by the deterioration of both his physical and mental capabilities. He retired for greater lengths of time in his sanctuary in Luxor.

Ah, he gasped, wheezing, expelling the last little bit of energy he brought himself slowly back to the present. The stars were still dancing in the heavens, and some gently twinkled in the distance, to assure him that the night was still with him. The mere distance now to the tomb was small, and he knew that his tired limbs could make the final journey to the entrance. Though in agonizing pain, he managed to hobble those last few hundred metres.

And there it was. The hidden Tomb of the Cat. He pulled out a torch and quickly flashed it inside a small opening. Ah, yes, it had never changed, it would never change. It was his, and Anastasia's and the Cat. By now, it was 80 years and the opening had shrunk to be less accommodating to his size, and as he knelt on all fours he pushed himself through the opening.

It was like a moment, like no other. It was like the beginning, yet the past, it was like the present, and yet the future. The torched danced its artificial lights on the wall, and then on the tomb itself and the small candles, the remnants of what were all of the past. The beginning, the moments and the shared times with his great love of Anastasia. His mind fluttered like the wings of a butterfly, endlessly dancing against the light, the moment.

Time had stopped, as he kneeled in a crouched position, staring endlessly at the Cat. He placed the torch gently in the position that gave the maximum amount of illumination. He once more lit the candles that had been stored over the years. And then with shaking, trembling hands his lifted the sarcophagus. He let out a small moan, and then held his breath. The mummified cat was still intact.

River of Life

"And there it was. The hidden Tomb of the Cat. "

Original photograph   Robert F. Edwards
Egypt   November, 1999

robert f. edwards

With old trembling hands, he reached in and felt the aging bounds of mummification. He silently said a prayer to Ra; he silently repeated the ancient passages of the high priest of Ra. And then, as he had done so many times before, he put the lid back on. He staggered; his body had consumed all the strength that had been reserved. His knees felt week, his arms hung loosely at his side, and his bent form continually stared upon the tomb.

· He needed air, fresh air and like some form of mummification himself, he turned to the small entrance. As he gained the presence of its opening, he knelt and looked out onto the · sky. It was peaceful. There was just the first glimmer of the receding of darkness. Further stars retreated from their hiding, and returned into their vastness. Slowly he sat in a position of comfort, and continually looked out at the wonderment of the sky.

Subconsciously, he once more reached into his galabya. He felt the most treasured belonging of all that he possessed. The watch of so long ago, given by the one he loved so dearly. His hand wandered and touched it, as if it was the most gentle and fragile thing. And with all the composure he had left in his mind and his body, he took the watch out. His both hands covered it, as if they too were the tomb that protected such a precious jewel of existence.

He dare not look down, as the tears had started, the rivers that ran the length of his face, and droplets as if blood itself had stained his galabya. He opened the face, and once more his fingers gently touched the dials, the perfect time, the little ticking sounds, the movements danced the seconds away. It was at this moment he dared to reach into the back, and felt gently and patiently for the spring that held the contents of his heart.

There it was, his forefinger pushed strongly but determinedly, with all the strength that he owned. There was a release, a moment of freedom as the back sprang open. Inside, he knew was the beautiful face of his Anastasia. But ah, ah it

River of Life

was the contents, her hair, yes, and a golden lock from the head of his beloved Anastasia.

A moment of reflection. His trembling hands held tightly, for fear of losing the moment that expressed his great joy. He once more touched his Anastasia. He felt the joy of fulfillment, as he gazed continuously into the stars that faded rapidly.

The great sun, the great god Ra broke the darkness for another day. But Horus-Salah never saw Ra. He had joined Anastasia in the other world, at last. They were together.

When his aides came to check on his well being, they found that his lodging had not been slept in, and they were immediately concerned. They contacted their superiors, and after a brief discussion, realized that no one had seen Horus-Salah after he had retired that night. They made discreet inquiries throughout Luxor. Finally they discovered a lonely boatman that had taken Horus-Salah across the Nile.

Without hesitation, without causing undue alarm, they searched the perimeters of the river, and yet no one had seen this old elderly man. Panic set in. By nightfall, the head overseer had the disturbing task of contacting the family, that Horus-Salah was missing, and to advise further instructions.

At the end of the next day, both his son and his daughter had assembled a huge delegation of their staff. The servants that were responsible for Horus-Salah's well-being were immediately put under surveillance in their quarters and questioned relentlessly. By the next day, there was still no word on their father. The wrath of the children started to be felt by all the staff and subordinates.

The search for Horus-Salah continued endlessly, yet no results. By the seventh day, his children were prepared to bring in the authorities. One of the senior servants recalled hearing tales from the past, gossip that had been whispered about, a legend of a secret tomb.

robert f. edwards

If true, then somewhere in this region, and if they found the tomb, they would probably find Horus-Salah. Scouring with relentless perseverance by every member of the staff, combing the trails meticulously, everyone available had descended on the region of the Valley of the Kings. More by accident than method, a junior servant found a small cavity and the upright position of Horus-Salah, still looking out into the sky.

THE END

River of Life

Author's Profile

Robert F. Edwards is presently living in Vancouver, Canada with his wife, daughter and grandson. He is a world traveler and has been on every continent. He enjoys sailing trekking, and mountain climbing. He does fencing with all three weapons, twice a week. He also writes books, travel journals, and fictional short stories, as well as poetry. He has now ventured off into painting in the mediums of acrylic and watercolour. His paintings reflect pictures and places that he has traveled throughout the global community. Many of the paintings are photographed into the books of fiction and non-fiction.

Author's Credo
The difficult is done at once. The impossible takes a little longer.
If a job is worth doing, it is worth doing right.
Don't abuse your friendships, and you will always have friends.

Author's Thoughts
On the Art of Writing
The written work is a thought to be given,
To share a dream, a moment of thought,
And a wish to share it with one and all.
It is not to be understood and enjoyed by all,
Nor is it to bring the author and reader together,
Nay, it is not to get to know each other,
But to share a moment of each other's time.